Love In The Time Of Covid

Pauline Crame

First published in the UK by Pick Lock Publishing
ISBN 978-1-0683379-2-5
Copyright © 2025 by Pauline Crame

Cover design and typesetting by Wayne Kelly for WKW Productions

*To my dear friend Adam Jurewicz for suggesting I write this
and everyone whose life was changed, for good or ill,
by the Covid lockdowns.*

JANUARY 2020

New Year

"Here we go. Happy New Year," Kirsten raised her wine glass. Big Ben striking and the fireworks flashing were in the background, on the television.

"Happy New Year," Daniel replied. "It's going to be an interesting one, I think."

Nabil woke from his dream with a start, but the image stayed with him. He kept his eyes closed, behind which the glare of the sun was blinding, and the terror in Abida's face was all too visible. His ears continued to ring with gunshots. Then, as the cheers reached them, he was reminded these bangs were from the fireworks for the New Year celebration. Flashes of light met his eyes as he opened them. Church bells ringing reminded him that this was a Christian country and that he was safe.

He turned on the light and threw the duvet back; it and his sheet were damp. His T-shirt stuck to his body; his pants were so wet he feared he'd urinated in them. In the bathroom he showered, grateful for once that the water was tepid. He changed his clothes, the sheet and duvet cover, poured himself a large glass of water and returned to bed.

It wasn't the revellers who kept him awake, in fact, he was glad of their company, but fear of returning to the place in his memory where dreams always took him. As the grey dawn crept through the brown curtains, sleep finally found him.

The guests from the party on the other side of the street were in the garden now, singing Auld Lang Syne.

"Hold on a second," Emerson said to his online friend.

He went to the window and looked out; his mother was easy to spot because she stood directly under the security light. *Just as I suspected,* Emerson thought, spotting the man beside her, who was equally illumined. Emerson's stomach and throat constricted. He clenched his teeth in response and returned to his laptop and his gaming companion.

"Sorry about that, needed a pee. Oh, yeah, Happy New Year, by the way."

They were still playing when Emerson heard his mother return. It was two-thirty, she wasn't alone; they were laughing. *Fucking great. Just what I need.* He turned up the volume on his headphones and downed a can of beer.

It was almost four when he said goodnight to his friend. He turned off the computer and tuned in to music on his phone instead, not wishing to hear any evidence of his mother's companion. Just before settling down for the night, he drafted a Happy New Year text to his grandparents, ready to send in the morning.

Mandeep was in bed, reading. Dev popped his head around the door.

"You coming for the count down?"

"Guess I'd better."

"Book good?"

"Too good for fireworks and Big Ben to be honest."

But she feigned enthusiasm as it was the first year the girls had been allowed to wait up. They sat in a line on the sofa, children sandwiched between their parents, one looking bemused and the other as if really she couldn't wait for her bed. They had a group hug on the chimes. The fireworks were extravagant and lasted for a long time.

"It's a scandal really," Dev said to his wife when the children had gone to bed. "All that money on fireworks and just down the road there are people sleeping on the streets."

"And I doubt there'll be any more reason for celebrating this year than any other," Mandeep replied, with a sigh. "Still, it's nice not having to work tomorrow. Speaking of which, I'd best go to bed, or I won't feel the benefit." She kissed Dev on the forehead.

❦

The midnight chimes woke her. The book and the blanket were on the floor, her glasses had drifted to the end of her nose. Margaret roused herself, sitting up straight to prevent sleep reclaiming her. On the final chime she held her glass up to the photograph on the mantelpiece. "Here's to another year," she said out loud, then took a gulp of gin. "Wonder if I'll make it to the end."

She sat for a few more minutes thinking back – to last week and her stay with Lily and, especially to that conversation. *When it reaches the stage where your children behave like they're your parents you know you're getting old,* she thought.

She thought back to the summer and the day she met Daniel. The memory brought warmth to her heart and a smile to her face. Then she thought back to last New Year, which she'd spent in exactly the same way as this one, falling asleep waiting for the midnight chimes. *Maybe I should just admit I'm getting too old for staying up late,* she thought, *but no, that really will be the beginning of the end.*

Finally, she thought back many years, back to the midnight dancing in John's arms. "You were such a good dancer," she said to his photograph. "Well, best go to bed."

Margaret folded the blanket, put her glass in the kitchen, checked both doors were locked and climbed the stairs to the bathroom where she cleaned her teeth, washed and moisturised her face and brushed her hair, before getting into bed.

She woke at seven-thirty and lay for a moment, listening. It was quiet, but not silent. It wasn't only the sounds of the physical world that broke the silence, but also those from her memory. Seasonal sounds: the crunch of snow beneath feet, percussive rain on windows and umbrellas, bird song mixed with children's laughter. So many seasons had passed to bring her here. Margaret took a deep breath; she was acutely aware of each of them, it was as if breath and consciousness had become one.

Hard to imagine she was still alive for the start of another year. Harder still to imagine that before much longer she'd be gone.

"Right," she said to herself out loud, "enough of this, get up. Good morning two thousand and twenty, I wonder what you have planned for me."

From habit, as much as anything else, Mandeep checked the yearly horoscope, it read:

This will be a challenging year.

The December twenty-nineteen solstice was connected to a south node solar eclipse in the Capricorn stellium, this indicates a top-down enforcement of rules. In March, Mars will be conjunct with Saturn and Pluto – indicating, big governmental and political shifts, economic upheaval and advancements in technology or thought.

On June twenty-eighth Mars crosses the world axis into Aries and stays for six months, instead of the usual six weeks. It exits on January sixth, two thousand and twenty-one, travelling back and forth across Aries. It is thirty-two years since Mars was last retrograde in Aries and it will be forty-seven before it happens again.

In August twenty-twenty, and again in December, Mars will make repeated squares to Jupiter, Saturn and Pluto in

Capricorn – indicating it has come back around to resolve what was started in March.

This is the warrior, pioneering energy, intensifying the life force, the libido, and physicality. The shadow side is ego and refusal to consider others in pursuit of your goals. In the collective the one per cent are going to be repeatedly challenged by the rage of the ninety-nine per cent, caused by frustration, financial losses and hardship, mixed with demands for social equality.

Growth and evolution will come from how well you trans-form strong will into skilful will through psychosynthesis. We all need to become Sacred Actioneers.

'*That doesn't sound great,*' she thought, turning the computer off in response and immediately forgetting about it.

Chinese New Year

Kirsten carried her coffee to the bathroom, then to the bedroom. By the time she was dressed and back in the living room she'd drunk it all. There wasn't time for another, neither was there time for breakfast, so she grabbed a cereal bar and an apple. She put on her coat, hat and scarf before turning off the television; hesitating only a second over the images of people in hazmat suits, looking like they were going into space. Then they were gone, immediately replaced by the more familiar image of the suited BBC presenter, talking about the upcoming Brexit. Kirsten had voted to stay in the European Union, but the transition out had gone on so long she barely cared that in six days they would be leaving. As she walked the fifteen minutes to work, she reflected on this; despairing at how easily she had come to this position of apathy.

"Good morning," Mandeep greeted her with a smile. "You look frozen, grab yourself a coffee while you still have the chance."

Kirsten checked her watch, "It's ten to."

"Better hurry up, then. Will you go on checkout six, please, take second break. Okay?"

Kirsten passed on the coffee, feeling too rushed.

"Morning," she greeted Emerson with a smile.

"Morning, glad you didn't qualify it with a good."

"Why? Isn't it?"

"No. Not since December twelfth."

She laughed. "You not over that yet?"

"I'll never be over it. That was our last chance. I promise you, things're gonna get tough from now on."

Kirsten sighed, hoping he was wrong, but believing he was right. The conversation was interrupted by a customer.

"You're early this morning." When he didn't appear to understand she pointed at her watch and said, "Early."

Now he smiled and nodded. "Yes, early. Is finished." Nabil pointed at the milk.

"Ah you need more milk. And you can't have coffee without biscuits." Kirsten smiled and nodded at the packet of bourbons.

Nabil always went to this lady's till if he could, because she was the friendliest.

"People will soon see their mistake, I'm sure of that," Emerson continued at the first opportunity.

Kirsten, not being sure whether he was referring to Brexit or the Labour loss, answered with a non-committal nod of her head.

✢

The stove was always Daniel's first priority; get the room warm and the kettle boiled. He turned the radio on, tuning it to Four from Six. Despite his contempt for it, he still liked to hear what the BBC had to say; currently it was all about the impending Brexit.

Just as he was about to turn it off the presenter said, "The Chinese authorities are warning travellers of fears of a major outbreak of a novel virus, as they head to join their families for the New Year celebrations."

I wonder why they want us to know that, Daniel asked himself. Over breakfast he flicked through a couple of online articles and checked the gold markets. Time to get started. He had three log deliveries to attend to, and bread supplies to deliver to the shop. The windscreen on the van was frosted over, so he started the engine and left it running as he opened the door to the chicken coop.

"Morning ladies, I'm hoping to see a plentiful supply when I come home, please."

The logs were already loaded into the van. He put the basket of bread on the back seat. By this time the windscreen had almost defrosted so only required a superficial scrape.

Soon the van was bouncing down Mrs. Paget's uneven drive. She was looking out of the window as he arrived. He jumped down from the driver's seat.

"Morning," he said, as he took the bag of logs from the back and carried them into her kitchen.

"Chilly today," Margaret said.

"Yep, still mild for the time of year, though." He checked the thermometer on the wall, felt the radiator. "No wonder you're complaining about the cold. I think this should be getting hotter, d'you have a key to bleed it?"

"Somewhere."

"Look it out for tomorrow and I'll sort it for you."

"I'm alright, don't you worry about me."

"It's not you I'm worried about, it's me. If you get ill who's going to make my cup of tea?"

Margaret laughed. Daniel sat down at the teak table where tea and biscuits were already waiting. Margaret sat across from him, smoking a roll up.

"Only a few more days to B Day," she said. "I wonder how long before we notice the effects. Economic, I mean, the social divisions are already clear."

"Shame that. Pity people aren't a bit more informed; they might put the blame where it's deserved, then. Tell you the truth, I was in two minds, might've voted for it if we'd had a friendlier government. There's plenty of reason to, the EU being as it is."

"Oh! You might not be too shocked to hear that I did, then?"

"Not shocked. Interested."

"Well, you said it yourself, it's not that our own government is any less corrupt. My kids weren't impressed with me, not one of them."

"Sorry to hear that. It'll be interesting to see where this goes. These are interesting times."

"That's an old Chinese curse, you know? May you live in interesting times."

"I know. We'll see how it pans out. Could be a bumpy road for a while."

"Thing is, we all live with the illusion of security, but really there's no such thing," Margaret replied.

"Wise words," Daniel said, getting up from the table to empty the log bag into the wicker basket, after which, he riddled the fire and took the ash drawer outside to empty it. The door caught as he opened it, and again on the way back in. He returned the ash drawer to the fire, then went back to the door and examined it more closely.

"It's just a bit warped from all the rain," Margaret said.

"A bit more than a bit, Mrs. P. I'll come and replace it as soon as the weather improves."

"Ah, you're a good lad."

"I'm hardly a lad."

"Well, you are to me."

"Right Mrs. P, much as I'd love to stay here and chat all morning, I'm going to have to love you and leave you."

"Ah, promises, promises," Margaret laughed.

Daniel did too. "D'you need bread?"

"I'm alright for a couple of days."

"See you tomorrow, then."

❧

"How's your mother-in-law?" Kirsten asked her manager as she sat down to join her for coffee break.

"The same," Mandeep replied. "Thanks for asking."

"She's done better than you expected, hasn't she?"

"Much. She was diagnosed nearly five years ago. We'll be going to visit in the Easter holiday, review it then, Dev might stay on a bit, depending on how she is."

"I guess that'll be easier and cheaper than keep coming and going."

"Exactly. I'll miss him, though, if it does come to that, it'll be the first time we've been apart since being married."

"Gosh."

"Anyway, I've got to go. Anastaja needs a bit of support; she's worrying herself half to death about what happens after Friday."

"Is she? Poor thing. She applied for settled status, I presume?"

"Hasn't heard from them, that's what she's worried about."

"I'm sure you'll do a good job of reassuring her."

"Hope so."

Kirsten returned to find a long queue at the tills. *People must be stock piling for Brexit,* she thought.

During lunch break she telephoned Rosie.

"How's the little man?" she asked her daughter.

"Much better today and don't I know it."

"Playing up, is he? That's good, he must be well and truly over it, then. How about Sally? Good, perhaps she escaped it. Anything going around that you know of?"

"It's not like when were kids, Mum, for one there's vaccinations for everything now. For another, if you take them to the doctor, they just say it's a virus, never a named illness anymore. Not that you would bother with the doctor these days, more trouble than it's worth."

"Wouldn't know, can't remember the last time I went. Anyway, glad Ryan's better. I'm looking forward to seeing you."

January 31st

"Girls, come and talk to Grandma," Dev called to his daughters, and passed the phone to the youngest, as she was the first to arrive in the room.

"How is she?" Mandeep asked Dev, as he came into the kitchen.

"The same."

Mandeep rubbed her husband's shoulder. "That's good."

"She's certainly a fighter." He took hold of his wife's hand and kissed it. "Just hope I get enough notice when it does come to it."

"I'm sure you will. Anyway, we have to go, can you hurry the girls up please? You got everything?" she asked, opening the front door. "Got your inhalers, Indrani?" Mandeep checked her own bag to make sure she had hers. "See you," she called out to Dev, as she shut the front door and opened the car doors.

The radio came on with the engine. That it was Brexit day was the headline that hit her; as if she needed to be reminded. *So, we finally got here* she thought. *Let's hope, whatever happens next, that people will at least start to be civil to each other again and some kind of trust can be rebuilt.* Her thoughts were barely interrupted by the news broadcaster as she said,

"The chief medical officer has announced that two people in the UK, from the same family, have tested positive for coronavirus."

Mandeep paid no heed to it, her concentration was on reversing out of the drive, and the day that lay ahead.

&s

A big change was coming, Emerson was sure of it; he could feel it in every bone of his body. He turned from YouTube to the news, although the headlines were hardly a surprise. *One good thing about Brexit,* he thought, *at least people finally give a fuck.*

"I never thought I'd see that in England," Mandeep had remarked to him once, not so long ago, in response to the jeering crowds in Parliament Square that filled the television screen in the break room. To which he'd replied, "'bout time. People need to wake up and smell the coffee."

And Mandeep had replied, "That's fine for the coffee drinkers, but what about those who like tea?"

He'd thought her rather witty, actually, not something she was noted for. He phoned Kirsten, now, knowing she'd be about to leave home to cover his shift.

"Thanks again for this, Kirst," he said. "I know you don't really like working lates."

"Well, I couldn't bear the thought of you missing out."

"Don't suppose it'll be very exciting, but…you know, it's like New Year's Eve, you don't want to miss it just in case."

"It'll probably be a lot like that, in every sense: Big Ben, fireworks and resolutions that don't get kept."

Emerson laughed heartily at this.

"Anyway, I'd better go, or I'll be late for your shift. Enjoy."

"I won't."

Now Kirsten laughed. "I know everything in the world is as it should be when I hear you say that."

Emerson returned to YouTube. Although it was too late to change anything, nevertheless he liked to keep reminding himself of all the evidence. Everyone knew about the three hundred and fifty million to the NHS promise, but no one he'd spoken to seemed to know that the date of the referendum had been deliberately scheduled to coincide with Glastonbury Festival.

"Why's that even relevant?" a Pro Brexit acquaintance had asked.

"Why's it relevant? You kidding me? To keep the younger votes out, obviously. Don't tell me you haven't heard about the involvement of Facebook and fake news, either?"

"Strikes me that you're only interested 'cos the vote didn't go your way."

Emerson had flung his hands in the air at that, and walked away. *No point in arguing with someone who's got a rigid mindset.*

His phone pinged, indicating a text message. '*What're you up to? Fancy a game?*' it read. It was from his online friend, Alex.

Emerson checked his watch, one-thirty, his mother would be home in less than an hour. '*Give me forty minutes,*' he replied, then went downstairs to make himself a sandwich.

There was bacon in the fridge, but the only bread was in the freezer. He took two slices from it and put them in the microwave. He got the frying pan from the drawer in the cooker, put two dessertspoons of vegetable oil in the pan and turned it on to heat while he fetched four slices of bacon from the fridge. He buttered the bread while the bacon cooked, feeling harassed by the oil spitting as he turned it over. When it was cooked, he topped it with tomato sauce and, as he sat down to eat, turned the television on. The news was just coming to a close with the summing up of the day's headlines. Brexit dominated, no surprise, but then there was the announcement from the Chief Medical Officer. *What's this about? Loading the next lot of bullets, already.* He turned the television off, ran his plate under the cold water tap and made himself a coffee with three sugars.

Better have a shower, or mother will be nagging me, he thought. He put the coffee cup in his room, took clean underwear and socks from his drawer and went to the bathroom. He tied his hair back, because he didn't have time to wash it. He was back in his room and ready for gaming before his coffee was cold.

The library was Nabil's place of sanctuary. Here he could be with people without the need to engage with them. Today, as usual, he chose a seat in the corner, where he could sit with his back to the wall and face the door. He took off his outdoor clothes, pulled his notebook and pen from his bag and started to write.

For weeks he'd been struggling with where to begin. Initially, he'd thought his first memory from the war, but then he couldn't identify when that was. There was no one incident, not one defining moment, rather a gradual invasion that robbed them of normal life.

So, begin with a scene of that normal life, he thought. He wrote, ripped out the page, wrote again, ripped out the page again and again and again; until finally admitting his normal life scene was too far from his memory to describe accurately.

Then he tried with his father's disappearance. But that was in the middle and the middle didn't seem like the best place to start. The same was true of his mother's death, from an illness unspecified, a fever that grew big, from which she seemed to recover before big became bigger and stole her life.

He could write from the end. But there was more than one of those. Then suddenly he decided on where to begin, without conscious thought it came to him and now that it had arrived, he was sure the story could be told.

'This was the morning Abida decided she'd cried enough tears. She told me this over breakfast. "It's just you and me now, Nabil, we're going to take good care of each other."'

On his way back from the cash and carry, Daniel called in on Mrs. Paget, she hadn't seemed quite herself in the morning.

"Well how nice to see you twice in one day, to what do I owe this pleasure?" she asked.

"Just passing. Been to buy flour and thought I'd just check the measurements for that door while I'm passing."

"It's good of you to pretend you're checking it and not checking up on me."

"Checking up on you? Been doing something you shouldn't?"

"If only. Anyway, I'm fine now, it was just lack of sleep as I told you."

"Anything in particular stopping you sleeping? Something on your mind?"

"Same thing as on everyone's mind, I should think, Brexit, but mostly just age. I definitely don't sleep like I used to."

"You blame everything on getting old."

"Only 'cos it is to blame. You'll find out; wait and see."

"If I'm like you at the same age, I'll be more than happy. In fact, I'll be more than happy to get to your age, with all the things there are out there to get us."

"I see we have two cases of coronavirus in the UK."

"Yeah, so I gather. Wonder why they want us to know that? Right! See you next week. Got my number if you need anything before then."

When he got home the hens had already put themselves to bed. He checked for eggs before locking them in. There were only two. "Don't like the cold do you ladies? Roll on spring."

The sun and warmth of spring were motivating for Daniel. During the winter he tended to do only what was absolutely necessary. There were some outstanding jobs that needed doing to the cottage as soon as his energy levels and the weather made it possible. *The next dry day I'll clear the gutters,* he thought. The window and door frames needed painting, too. *Should really decorate the spare room. And there's the door for Mrs. P.* As he thought this, Daniel made a mental note to check what wood he had when he was next in his workshop. The cabinet for Hannah Lightfoot was almost done, he'd start on the table and chairs for the next customer soon and fit the door in around that. He'd have to be careful not to take on too much work in the next few weeks or else he wouldn't get those jobs of his own done.

Daniel hoicked the sack of flour onto his shoulder from the back of the van, then emptied it into the plastic bin in the kitchen. He topped the stove up with coal and logs and put the kettle on. He opened the fridge to review the contents. Not a lot; a pepper, a courgette, and some chicken pieces. There were two onions in the vegetable basket, and he had a jar of curry sauce. *That'll do, a chicken curry,* he thought. He checked the cupboard again. *Damn, no rice.* He turned the television on while he decided what to do. "Ah, I know," he said out loud to himself. Then, taking his mobile phone from his pocket, he telephoned the takeaway and ordered pilau rice and naan bread to be collected at eight.

While the curry was infusing Daniel checked the trends charts, feeling some satisfaction in the fact that he'd seen the crash coming well in advance and taken necessary action; feeling none at the financial chaos he was certain lay ahead for many.

When he left the library, the sky was changing, from grey day to grey dusk. As Nabil walked up the street, he kept close to the shop doorways, attracted by the light. He stopped and browsed a few windows, looking at shoes he could never afford, and holiday advertisements he couldn't read, then his attention was drawn to the many television screens with their differing pictures. One in particular drew him in, it was the image of people in hazmat suits. The hair on the back of his neck prickled in response. *What's this? What's happening?* he thought. *Is this here? In the UK?*

He turned and ran, splashing through puddles and almost colliding with someone. "Sorry, I sorry," he said, when the man shouted at him.

The front door lock stuck. Nabil's hands were clumsy. He pulled the door and turned the key at the same time, but still it didn't open. He tried again, this time wiggling it; finally the door opened. On the other side of it he slipped out of his shoes and tiptoed up the stairs, through the door to his room. On the other side he pushed his back into it and stood panting for breath.

FEBRUARY

The knocking was getting louder and more insistent, finally Emerson could ignore it no longer.

"What? Yeah, I'm getting up in a minute." He shouted out to his mother. "What's it matter? I'm still in plenty of time for work."

A few minutes later he dragged himself from bed; the empty cans rolled off it with the pulling back of the duvet. He opened the curtains a crack, and then fully, realising there wasn't much light to let in. The laptop was still on, reminding him that the game had finished so late he'd closed the lid and his eyes at almost the same time.

From downstairs came the sound of the vacuum cleaner. From next door, children's voices blended with the muffled sound of television. He looked out of the window into the street below, where the neighbours from opposite were unloading shopping. A typical Saturday morning. The post-Brexit world looked no different so far.

Emerson picked up his phone and dialled his grandparents' number.

"Morning," he said, when his grandmother answered. "Okay if I nip in on my way to work?"

"Of course, you know you're always welcome."

"See you soon, then."

"Sorry I'm late," Kirsten said to Rosie.

"Hello you two." She picked up each child, one at a time, and gave them a kiss.

"Have you ordered yet? Oh, you didn't need to wait for me, but thanks. I'll have the usual. I had shopping to do, I worked yesterday if you remember. And then I had several people to catch up with by phone. Fran's not long lost her dad, so couldn't exactly hurry her. Anyway, I'm here now."

After lunch they went to the park. Pushing swings and turning roundabouts was something Kirsten had never enjoyed, but it didn't seem as arduous when it was for her grandchildren, as it had when it was for her daughter's amusement.

The children were now running around, chasing pigeons as well as each other.

"I've got something to tell you, Mum." Rosie said.

Kirsten felt the weight of the words and guessed, "Another baby?"

"No. I don't think you'll like it."

"You're not splitting up with Andy?"

"No, don't be daft. We're moving. It's quite a big move."

"Oh." It felt like being hit by a big wave.

"Devon, we're going to Devon."

"Oh, that is a long way." Now the wave poured over her.

"We'll be back from time to time and you're always welcome there, of course. Andy got offered a promotion and, well – we've always fancied the coast. So much better for the kids."

Tears stung Kirsten's eyes. "Is it definite? Is the house up…?"

"Sold, the house is sold."

"What? You didn't tell me…"

"I was going to, it was all so quick, first person who came to look at it."

"But you don't have anywhere yet?"

"We'll rent for a while if necessary. We've seen one that's a possibility. We've an appointment to go and view it next week. Was going to ask if you'd come and stay with the kids – we can ask Andy's mum…"

"No," Kirsten said, quickly. "I want to have them. Sounds like I'd better make the most of them."

"Don't be like that, Mum. It's not as if it's another country."

"I didn't realise I was being like anything. It's just a shock, that's all."

"Kids're coming back, they don't know, so shush."

"And that was it," Kirsten told Daniel later. "I don't think I've taken it in yet, actually."

"Oh," Daniel replied.

"I don't know what I'm most upset about, the fact they're going or the fact they left it until this stage to tell me."

"Oh," said Daniel.

"It makes me feel so uncared for."

"Oh."

"Especially since it seems Andy's parents have known for a couple of weeks."

"Oh."

"Is that all you can say? Oh."

"I guess it was a bit of a bombshell."

"That's an understatement."

"You'll be able to visit, though?"

"It's not about being able to visit or not. It's not about how near or far it is. It's about not being told. Don't you get that?"

"Yes."

"Well, good, and…?"

"And?"

"See, you don't get it." Daniel's hazel eyes were full of confusion, he wrung his hands then separated the waves of his hair with his fingers.

"I'm hurt, I want reassurance," Kirsten said.

"Oh, I thought I had reassured you."

"You could offer me a cuddle. Why d'I always have to ask?"

"Oh," he sighed, then pulled Kirsten into an embrace. She cried. He pulled away slightly, but then realised his mistake and tightened his hold whilst rubbing her back. Then, easing himself away, said, "I'll put the kettle on."

They always had eggs for breakfast. Kirsten had boasted to most of her friends about eggs fresh from Daniel's chickens being accompanied by his home baked bread. This morning's hangover made them less palatable.

"I was stupid to drink so much."

"Drowning your sorrows," Daniel reassured.

"Didn't work, feel worse. Always feel sad with a hangover. Do you?"

"Not sure."

Course you're not, Kirsten thought, as she put the plates in to soak. "I might have to go and visit Greg; need to talk to him about the move."

"Probably get more of a response from him than me."

Suddenly Kirsten was overwhelmed by love, she kissed Daniel's face and stroked it.

"Tickly," he said and pulled away.

"You are who you are, and I love you for it," Kirsten said. "You probably think I'm crazy talking to a dead man. It's just my habit. From before I had you to tell."

He didn't answer, but got up and started on the dishes.

"Oh, sorry, I was just about to do that." Kirsten picked up the tea towel and dried. "Sometimes I talk things over with you in your absence."

"Bet you can hardly tell the difference," Daniel laughed.

"You're wrong there. The feedback from the imaginary you is far superior to what I actually get." Kirsten laughed too.

Daniel picked the kettle up and waved it at Kirsten.

"Coffee," she said, "black, and then I'll go."

Less than an hour later she was squatting at Greg's graveside.

"I don't even know why it bothers me so much." Kirsten spoke out loud because she was the only living person there. "I want her to live her life how she wants to, of course. I think it would be easier if you were still here. Oh, I know I have Daniel now, and it is a lot easier since he's been in my life, but not the same, not yet anyway. Yes, you're right," she said, as if she was actually being conversed with. "I will be fine. Everything is as it should be."

That had been one of Greg's sayings. He said it even when it clearly wasn't true; he'd said it when he knew he was dying.

Kirsten was getting cold, she pushed up to standing and dusted herself down. She stood for a while, with her hands clasped in front of her, then turned and walked away.

We were in the maths class. The teacher was walking up and down between the desks, he kept slapping his palm with the cane he carried; I suppose he was reminding us of who was in charge. Fear knotted my stomach. I'm not very good at maths. I think I might have prayed, asking for help.

Suddenly there was a whirring noise, everyone looked up; we all held our breath. Everything seemed to stop for a second. Then came the loudest bang I've ever heard. Then silence.

Silence! I felt like my mind and body had been separated and wondered if I was dead; but then, I noticed the dust in my nose, inhibiting my breathing; the gritty taste drying my mouth; the ringing in my ears. I moved; first my arms, then my legs then I pulled myself to sitting. I could only see one whole person, everything else was limbs or torsos, protruding from the rubble.

There was crying, no, wailing. I stayed quiet, expecting a reprimand for disorderly behaviour. I begged for it. None came.

Nabil put his pen down. He felt extraordinarily tired all of a sudden and had to fight the urge to lay his head on the desk. Instead, he rested it in his hands and closed his eyes, but behind them was the scene he'd just been writing. The feared teacher lying, mouth and eyes wide open, still and silent.

Nabil shook with the memory; he put his notebook and pen in his bag and his outdoor clothes on. But, not feeling ready to leave, he sat and watched the other people for a while. Several of them were becoming familiar to him.

He reviewed the room. There were now two free computers, so he went and sat at one of them. Before he logged on for his free thirty minutes, he took a second notebook from his bag. He put on the headphones that were provided and tuned into YouTube on the computer. He couldn't repeat the words out loud, but he could write them down and practise recognising how they looked, then later, at home, he'd tune in again on his phone and continue with the English lesson. When his time had run out Nabil checked for an appropriate place to sit for a while longer, but none of the spaces that were left would allow him the opportunity to sit facing the door, so instead he headed home.

The pizzas were in the oven, the children were in the bath; Kirsten felt in control. She flew the rubber duck around the bathroom and splashed it into the water with a quacking accompaniment. The children responded with gutsy laughs. Kirsten's duck landed with little grace, but she'd noticed that neither did the real thing, often she'd been amused watching them land, looking as if they were panicking.

"Five minutes and you'll have to get out," she told the children. She would need to check the dinner soon. When it was time, she lifted Sally from the bath, explaining, "You're the eldest so you get the special privilege of coming out first. You can show Ryan how good you are at drying yourself and getting your pyjamas on."

Bath time ended without tears.

Half an hour later they were curled up together on the sofa taking it in turns to read to each other. Sally stumbled over only two words; Ryan invented a story from the pictures. Kirsten revelled in their company.

"One more, please, pretty please," Sally begged with her hands in prayer.

"In your beds then, and I'll read you one more each."

The nine o'clock news had only just started when Rosie and Andy returned home.

"Well?" Kirsten asked.

"I liked it, Andy wasn't so sure."

"No! I liked it too, but it's the only one we've seen. I guess I'm just a bit more cautious. Kids been okay?"

"Of course."

None of them were taking much notice of the television, but as she gathered up her belongings Kirsten's attention was drawn to the screen. The scene, a quarantined ship and an online interview with a British passenger, disgruntled at being held on board.

Fleetingly Kirsten wondered how she would feel in that situation, but there was little time for more as Andy was urging her towards the door and her lift home.

Mandeep visited the farm shop on her way home. She had called in there once, having forgotten eggs, and ended up buying not only them, but also bread, both of which were so nice she never again bought either from anywhere else.

When she reached home the girls were watching television and Dev was in his office. She knocked on the door. "I'm home. You busy?"

"Quite. You okay with cooking this evening?"

"Of course." She kissed him and left, closing the door.

The lentils had been soaking all day – before rinsing them Mandeep washed her hands, then topped the pan up again with water and put it on the stove.

"You two got homework?" she asked, going into the living room and picking up the plate and cups they'd used for their snacks.

"I was going to take them in a minute," Manjit said, "then go and do my homework."

"It's okay. How was school?"

"Good."

"And you, Indrani? Oh, just a minute."

Mandeep hurried into the kitchen, where she turned down the heat on the cooker and skimmed the froth that had formed. In the process she spilt a little, she tutted as she wiped it up.

"Sorry Indrani. How was school?"

"It was okay. Can I do my homework after dinner, please?"

"I don't mind when you do it as long as you do."

Mandeep chopped the vegetables and mixed the spices, rinsed the rice and put it in the rice cooker. While she was doing this, she thought about what Indrani had said, *Okay,* or rather the way she had said it. *I'll speak to her later, make sure everything really is okay.*

When the meal was at a stage where it could be left, she went upstairs and checked the bedrooms; the beds were made, school uniforms hung up, dirty clothes put in the washing basket, so she felt satisfied.

Manjit was sitting at the dining table with her books open.

"How much more to do?" her mother asked.

"I can finish it later if dinner is ready." She closed the books and set them aside, took the anti-bacterial spray and cleaned the table and the place mats before setting out the cutlery.

The evening meal was one of Mandeep's favourite times of day because the whole family were together. And it was always the point at which Dev stopped working, no matter how much was still outstanding.

This evening, in common with most, they chatted about their day. Dev was so good at the individual attention he paid them all. Mandeep sat back and watched him talking with their daughters, feeling so much love for them all and so grateful for her family.

The dishwasher was on, the surfaces and floor had been cleaned, Mandeep was looking forward to Coronation Street, but first she needed to chat with Indrani.

"Everything is fine, Mum, really," she said.

"You would tell me if it wasn't, wouldn't you? Promise?"

"Promise."

"They're making a lot of this coronavirus, don't you think?" Margaret asked of Daniel.

"To be honest, Mrs. P, I haven't given it much thought. I guess it wouldn't be much fun being quarantined in a harbour when you thought you'd be enjoying a cruise. And probably a bit scary to think some of your fellow passengers have died."

"We've got a few cases. The Health Secretary has apparently granted public health officials the power to quarantine people against their will."

"You worried?"

"I'm outraged. One little cough or sneeze and you could be arrested."

Daniel laughed, but then, becoming serious, said, "They do seem to be making a lot of it. Makes you wonder what they're up to."

"No good, as always, I should think."

"Won't argue with that one. You agree with them on Brexit, though."

"I agree with Brexit, not with them. I have no idea why Johnson wanted out. In fact, my suspicion is he doesn't, only said it to get where he is. I wonder if they ever come up with a deal that suits and if it does, what it'll look like. My reasons for wanting out is the undemocratic nature of the EU. I voted against going in, for coming out, and apart from that I've only voted in national elections twice in the last thirty-eight years, once was last year."

"Thirty-eight years. Michael Foot?"

"Only two chances in all those years and we blew them both."

"Won't argue with that one either, Mrs. P. Anyway, better go, see you tomorrow."

Daniel spent the next few hours at the wood, but the constant drizzle hindered the log cutting, so it wasn't complete when it was time for him to leave.

There were roadworks with three-way traffic lights on the way to the farm shop. Daniel was going to be late. They turned from amber to green, but there were several vehicles in front of him and they were red again before he got through. Mrs. Paget's words kept his mind busy. It was the busyness of hers that kept her sharp, he felt sure. If only his own mother had been like that.

Finally, on the other side of the traffic lights he resisted the urge to put his foot down, despite the advancing time and the driver in the car behind urging him to do so. One of the perks of being self-employed was having no boss to answer to. Even so, he didn't like to be late, or keep Dianne waiting, it was nearly closing time for her.

She was peering out of the window as he pulled up; that she was keen to lock-up and leave was more than clear.

"Sorry," Daniel said, "roadworks."

Bread was the first and last chore of every day. In the mornings he dropped off the required number of loaves at Dianne's farm shop, late afternoon he picked up his basket and the order for the next day; as soon as he got home he started the next day's batch. He could count the days of his life away with the bread routine. It was the most constant part of his life. Management of the wood varied with the time of year and the number of casual workers. People's requests for furniture varied too, but every day there was someone who wanted bread. It would hardly make him a fortune, but it was secure. For Daniel, bread was like a loyal friend.

Today he was home early and soon preparing his dinner. He Daniel likedliked it when his meal required the use of the oven, because it didn't waste the heat that was necessary for the proving of the bread. Today he was having a casserole and baked potato. While he waited for it to cook, and the bread to rise, he turned on his tablet to study the day's trends in the market.

☙

Emerson was in the break room, watching the news. The smell of smoke clung to him. Kirsten felt conscious that the noise of the kettle was interfering with the television, but she needed a coffee. She sat down to drink it and took her phone from her bag. There was a message from Rosie:

'What time you home? I'm coming around for a chat'. Um, that sounded ominous. *'Should be there by three,'* she replied, wanting to allow herself time to grab a few bits of shopping first.

"You know that came from a lab, don't you?" Emerson said, meaning the coronavirus and taking it for granted that Kirsten would know to what he was referring.

"I heard it came from bats, not that I've been taking too much notice."

"Nope, man made."

"And somehow it got out?"

"Somehow, or on purpose, depending on how you see it."

Kirsten recalled his having a similar opinion on the Salisbury poisoning; Porton Down was the lab in question on which he lay blame that time.

"Who and why?" she asked.

"China as a bio-weapon against America. America as a bio-weapon against China. Who knows? But if it gets out of hand it could become a wild card. Viruses don't respect boundaries."

Kirsten sipped at her coffee and re-read her text, as she continued her conversation with Emerson. "Looks pretty under control from the little I've seen."

"In China, sure, everything's under control in China, even – or I should say *especially* – the people. Least that's what they tell us. Could just be propaganda. Either way, we don't want controls on us like that." He waved his cup at the screen which showed people in hazmat suits restraining those who weren't.

"Well, only a few cases here."

"So far."

It'll be news on the move, Kirsten thought, paying attention to the more immediate concern of what her daughter's plans were. "Well, let's not panic yet. We've had enough to deal with this year so far with Brexit and the assassination of Soleimani."

"Italy have suspended flights to China, and they only have a few cases."

"You're really taking an interest in this, aren't you?"

"I like to keep up with what's going on. I figure there has to be something after Brexit. They don't want us to notice what's really going on."

"The infamous *they* again. *They* have nothing to worry about with us Brits, we complain to each other, but we get on with it anyway."

"We came close with Brexit."

"True."

"Right! I've got five minutes for another quick drag before I go back. See you."

The smell of the first quick drag, lingered even after he'd gone. Kirsten took a deodorant aerosol from her bag and sprayed it liberally.

"Kettle's just boiled, I wasn't sure exactly when to expect you," Kirsten told her daughter.

"I'll have a quick one, but can't stop. I just wanted you to know we've arranged the move for March thirtieth."

"That soon?"

"Our buyers are cash. They want to move quickly. There's a baby due in July. Andy's job starts at the beginning of April."

"I see."

"It's not that far you know, Mum, you could easily come every couple of weeks. You could get a railcard. Or, if Daniel's happy to drive, you can both come."

"Thanks. So, are you taking the house you saw?"

"We're going for a second look. Probably have to rent for a while."

"Won't that be a hassle? What about the cost? You could always stay with me."

"I know that – and thanks. Andy's parents said the same, but…, it'll cost almost as much for him to stay away on his own. It'll cut into our savings, of course, but we'll be okay for a while. Don't want to rush into anything."

"I get that, but…not just the extra cost, two moves. What a hassle."

"Well, yes, but…"

You want me to have the kids for the second look?"

"Andy's parents really want them, sorry."

"No, it's fine. I'm sure they want to make the most of the time left too." But the truth was that she did feel disappointed.

"Thanks, Mum."

They hugged.

It was signing day and, for the second time only, Nabil was going alone. The knowledge of this kept him from sleeping until four-fifty in the morning, and he woke again a little after seven.

There was no point in staying in bed, so he got up, showered and dressed, then got back into bed to keep warm. His eyes were hot from lack of sleep, his body ached and his mind floated; from inside it his thoughts were formless, and echoed as if his head were hollow. There wasn't time to return to sleep, but in any case nausea prevented it from coming. It prevented him from eating too. To fill the time Nabil watched YouTube videos. Currently his viewing was dominated by images and information on the new virus. The images scared him, but not knowing how the disease was progressing scared him more.

After the television scenes, Nabil had spoken with Abdul, who'd said, "There's only a few cases here, try not to worry."

It was time to leave, Nabil checked for the third time that he had his ID card and the instructions from Abdul on buses, which, unable to offer his actual support this time, Abdul had written down for him. He left the house, pulling his scarf around his nose and mouth and his hat over his ears. It wasn't the cold that made him put up his hood, but the desire to make his way unnoticed.

He walked quickly, his breath was the most visible thing about him. At the bus station he hesitated. He thought he remembered from which stand to catch the bus, but the crowds and the artificial light spaced him out. *I must concentrate,* he told himself, as he reviewed the information on the paper in his hand.

I thought it was here. He stood underneath the information board and looked around. *I was sure it was here.* He went back to the door and retraced his steps, stopped under the board, checked his information again, then walked up to each stand that was close, but none of them bore the number he was looking for.

A young woman approached, she looked at him, then stepped back, seemingly afraid. Being conscious of his appearance Nabil pushed the hood from his head and the scarf from his face. He wrapped his arms around himself and rubbed them, wanting to cry.

"You okay? You need help?"

Nabil jumped at the sound of the voice, but the owner was smiling and looked interested in him.

Nabil held out the piece of paper. The man took it from him.

"Ah, this way." He kept the paper and walked away slowly, beckoning to Nabil, who followed. It was then he realised his mistake. Just inside the other door was another notice board, and to the left of it; stand twelve.

"There you go," the man gave him back the paper. "I'll wait with you until the bus comes."

Nabil didn't understand what was being said to him. "Thank you," he said, anyway.

He expected the man to leave, but instead he stood close and kept speaking. Nabil shifted his body and his gaze often, he wanted to cry, but he kept smiling and nodding.

"Here's your bus," the man gestured, and Nabil responded with a nod.

"Thank you," he said again.

"You know where you're going? Need any more help?"

Nabil moved towards the bus, wishing the man would just go away.

"You need the right money, they don't give change."

There were two people in front of Nabil, he wanted to push them out of the way. He hoped this man wouldn't sit next to him on the bus.

When he reached the driver, he handed him the money and said his destination.

"Ah, good," his helper said. "Bye then."

But Nabil didn't hear any of this, he had rushed to the upper deck and a seat near the back of the bus, because, although he was grateful for the help, he couldn't bear the thought of being forced into more of this person's company. As the bus pulled out of the station, he was relieved to see him walking away.

Nabil kept checking the time on his phone. He knew it was about twenty minutes until he had to get off and had memorised the sign on the pub that came just before the stop. When he saw it, he rang the bell and descended the stairs, thanking the driver as he got off.

The immigration reporting centre was easy to recognise; a stand-alone, red-brick building that rang of officialdom. Today the queue was short and the Arabic interpreter available. Nabil took his ticket and sat down to await his turn.

Hunger gnawed at him, making him feel nauseous, but then his attention was diverted by something going on. There was shouting and crying, the man was obviously objecting as he was being taken from the room by two immigration officials.

Nabil froze, he put his hand to his stomach, as if to halt the rise of the nausea; sweat teased his brow, his spine tingled. He'd heard about this, how some people went for signing and never returned. The rumour was that they were taken to a detention centre before being deported. He was so distracted that he almost missed his number on the screen.

Thankfully, it was straightforward for him. With the help of the interpreter, he confirmed there had been no changes to his circumstances. The next signing date was written on a card for him in Arabic and English; March twelfth, at one.

It was Nabil's intention to buy a snack for the journey home, but the bus was coming, and he had to run to catch it.

When he did reach home his hunger was raw. He went straight to the fridge and the left-over chicken he expected to be there. But it wasn't. Now anger competed with hunger in his gut. He suspected all three of his housemates of theft; but couldn't challenge a single one.

A visit to the supermarket was now required before he could eat. *From now on I'll keep all my food in my room,* he decided, feeling aggrieved and disappointed at the necessity of it.

"I'll sort that door out when it finally stops raining," Daniel told Margaret. He'd come to bring her extra logs, eggs, and a loaf.

"At least we haven't got it as bad as those poor people." Margaret was commenting on the homes that were devastated by floods. "We seem to see scenes like this every year now. Floods here, fires in Australia, it makes you wonder what's going on."

"Mother Nature getting her own back."

"Shame she can't be more discerning and get her own back on those who deserve it."

"Who would that be Mrs. P?"

"The insurance companies who didn't pay out the last time this happened for starters. Then the banksters and politicians who stole money from the rest of us through austerity."

Daniel laughed. "How'd she do that? Put something nasty in caviar?"

"That'd do it," now Margaret laughed.

"I had no idea you were such a rebel."

"In my youth."

Margaret's eyes took on a misty look of nostalgia. Daniel waited, expecting more.

"Right, time I wasn't here," he said when it became obvious no more was coming.

Kirsten was leaving, Emerson arriving.

"What's it doing out there?"

"I'll give you three guesses."

Kirsten sighed, "Well, at least there won't be a drought."

"Don't you believe it, come July and two weeks without rain and we'll be being told we're in danger of one. We can't enjoy anything these days without it being linked to a health risk or climate change," Emerson continued.

Kirsten sighed, heavy from the rain and Emerson's prognosis. "Does feel like that sometimes. I know it's important, but it would be nice to enjoy the sun without fear of global warming or skin cancer." She put on her coat, wrapped her scarf around her head and face and took her umbrella from her bag.

"I'm not sure on this climate change stuff myself."

"No?" Kirsten wasn't really surprised to hear him express this opinion.

"No. Jury's out as far as I'm concerned. Could be just another way to control us. Keep us all living in fear and guilt. Not to mention keeping the developing world from doing just that."

"It's an argument I've heard. There's certainly no shortage of fear around." Kirsten had one glove on and was putting on the other.

"Yeah, well fear is the best means of control. Scare people enough and they'll not only police themselves, but their friends and neighbours too."

"There's truth in that."

Although all the evidence indicated that climate change was man made, Kirsten had found the arguments to the contrary quite compelling. So, it might be a debate worth having with Emerson one day, but now, he had to work, and she had to go home.

Darkness. That was the predominant sensation. The sky was dark, the room was dark, Nabil's mood was dark. Low cloud emptied heavy rain; it poured relentlessly down the window and seeped in through the crack in the wall. The wind tormented him, sounding like lost souls wailing. Feeling claustrophobic he turned on the light, but the illumination from the bare bulb was stark and created a sense of an interrogation room, so he turned it off again.

He needed to go shopping so grabbed his coat and boots, opened the door of his bedsit and stuck his head out. There was no one on the landing. He snuck along, back to the wall, reaching the top of the stairs as if by osmosis. Once there he stopped and listened – silence. His descent was almost a run; he put his boots on as fast as was possible, with a part of his consciousness tuned to the rest of the house for advance warning of anyone's approach.

On the doorstep he stood for a few seconds, breathing deeply, as he prepared himself for the ten-minute walk. The rain pounding him was almost painful, like shrapnel ricocheting off him. The wind seemed to broadcast warnings that he was prevented from hearing. At least there were fewer people on the streets and from those few he could hide his face behind the hood.

At the supermarket he picked up a basket and shopped for a few essentials, adding up the price as he went along, as he only had half of his allowance left and three days before the next payment. He reached seventeen pounds with the purchase of the coffee, so he put it back, needing at least five pounds to get him through the remaining three days; there were still some tea bags at home. When he'd finished, he walked up and down the aisles looking for the nice, red-haired lady, but she wasn't there. Sometimes, when his confidence wasn't too low, he'd go to another till, but today he headed for the self-service.

The rain seemed heavier when he left the shop. It ran off his hood and dripped onto his nose. It seeped into his shoes and his bones. Even the key to his accommodation was impeded by the weather, Nabil was struggling with it when the door was opened from the other side. His housemate was as startled as him, he moved his gaze from Nabil to the outside, then back again, curling up his nose in a look of disgust.

"So wet," he said in Tigrinya.

Nabil nodded, guessing his meaning, and wondering if this was the man who had eaten his chicken.

Both went to their rooms.

Nabil hung his coat on the bathroom door, then he changed his jeans and socks, hanging the wet ones on the radiator. As he did so, he put his hand on it, just above cool, as usual.

Before going to the kitchen Nabil once again opened the door of his room to check the landing was empty. He took the necessary items from his room and in the kitchen cooked toast and eggs and made himself a cup of tea. He hunted for sugar, hoping that one of his housemates would have left some there, but it seemed they too were in the habit of keeping their food to themselves.

He ate quickly. When he'd washed up, he poured himself a cup of hot water to take to his room. Once there he turned on YouTube on his phone, took up his notebook and pen and, getting into bed for warmth, tuned into the English lesson.

Netflix until midnight and a couple of gin and tonics on Friday and Saturday evenings ensured Margaret's rising late at the weekend. Today, Sunday, it was almost ten o'clock. She'd better hurry because Alison would be phoning at eleven.

As usual, her daughter's phone call was exactly on time.

"Hello, Mum."

"Hi, all okay?"

"Yep, we're fine. You?

"Fine too. What you been up to?"

Margaret's children took it in turns to phone on Sundays. She heard three different versions of the same story from each of them. Work was fine, the children were fine, nothing much to report. She'd been hearing the same for as long as she could remember. Just occasionally something changed. A grandchild's school play performance, an exam, someone was a bit under the weather, but, thankfully, mostly it was 'everything is fine'.

Once a month her children took it in turns to visit for the day, so she saw each of them four times a year, and then all of them over Christmas. Next weekend it was Alison's turn.

"Anything in particular you'd like me to get for dinner?" she asked her now, on the phone. "I'll do a roast then. Chicken be okay for you?"

"I'm happy with the vege option, Mum."

"Well, if you're sure. Look forward to seeing you. Bye for now."

Not long after she and Daniel had met, Margaret had felt it necessary to explain: "It's me who moved away, John and I came up here when Alison, the youngest, went to university."

Now they wanted her to go back. They were unanimous in it according to Lily. *But I could never leave John,* Margaret told herself, but told her children, "I've got my friends and clubs and stuff up here, I'm too old to start all over again."

After lunch she donned her coat, hat, and gloves, ready for the visit to John's grave.

Sometimes, times like these when the rain was relentless, Margaret regretted having given up the car, but it was only occasionally, and the walk wasn't so far. She'd left it until now, wishing to avoid the church goers. Without them the graveyard was so peaceful, besides, she couldn't talk to him if there were others to hear.

The umbrella barely offered any protection against the rain, and wellington boots weren't the best for walking in. Normally it was a lovely walk along the bridleway, too far from the road for it to be a nuisance, although the occasional car could be heard. On a fine day, birdsong accompanied the trip. Today neither bird nor car were audible, only the thrash of rain on her umbrella.

There were no flowers, John hadn't been a fan. It was his excuse for so rarely buying them for her. "Soon as they're picked, they're dying," he'd said. "Why'd I want to give you something dead?"

Margaret remembered that now and chuckled. "I find myself thinking more and more about dead people," she told John. "'spose it's 'cos I got as many family and friends among them as the living."

She told him the news from the week and that next time she'd come on Saturday because of Alison's visit. Margaret never brought her children here, she would have done if they'd asked, but they never had.

❧

"D'you think I should leave him?" Kirsten's friend sounded calmer now; Kirsten had put her on speaker phone while she got ready.

"D'you think you should?"

"I'm asking your advice."

"Only you can decide."

"But what's your opinion?"

"It was a really shitty thing to do." This was as close to offering an opinion as Kirsten was comfortable with.

"And not the first."

"Might not be the last."

"Probably not. He'll never change, will he?"

"People can, and do, but they have to have the motivation."

"Fat chance when I keep letting him off. So…I reckon I should leave; no, fuck it, tell him to leave."

Kirsten checked her watch, she really needed to get ready.

"I don't think anyone would blame you."

"So, you do agree?"

"Just saying," she sighed, "it has to be your decision, but, well, the last few times we've spoken…"

"Yeah. Exactly!"

"I'm really sorry but I've got to be at the centre in half an hour.

"It's okay, shouldn't have kept you so long. Can I phone later if I need to?"

"Course you can."

Kirsten ended the call and put two pieces of bread in the toaster. As she did so she put on her coat and hat, and her shoes ready by the door, and grabbed a herbal tea bag to take with her. The toast popped up; she buttered it, took a bite, put her shoes on, took another bite, checked her bag for her keys and purse, took another bite then, taking the rest of the toast with her, headed off to her voluntary job.

Voices came from the room next door, one belonged to the occupant, one to the person on the other end of the phone. The first was almost shouting, the second only just audible. Nabil couldn't understand their language, but the fact of the call disturbed him, because it meant his housemate had someone left to speak to.

There were ten minutes more before he needed to leave for the meeting with his support worker. He exited YouTube, put his coat on, picked up his shoes and sat on the bed, back straight, feet on the floor, holding his shoes as he watched the minutes pass digitally on his phone.

Five to the hour exactly he left the house. The timing was planned precisely, he didn't like to be late, but neither did he want to arrive ahead of Abdul. He understood that going out was good for him, and knew that's why it had been planned this way; however, it would have been preferable to meet in his room, as they always had before.

As he approached the clock tower Nabil could see that Abdul was already waiting. They greeted each other with hello and a handshake.

"So, how are you?" Abdul asked.

"I am fine."

"I thought we could go for a coffee at the community café."

"Okay." Despite saying this, Nabil's stomach was gripped by fear; he wondered, but didn't ask, if there would be many other people there.

"I've been wanting to introduce you to this place for a while, Nabil. You can get a meal and a drink for one pound there; it's open every day from ten until two. Also, on a Thursday you can buy a bag of groceries for five pounds."

Nabil nodded. He paid no attention to where they were going, just tagged along. It was a fifteen-minute walk.

Abdul pushed the door open and held it for Nabil to go in ahead of him. There was a small group of people sitting at a table, they turned to look at him as he came in. Nabil's stomach clenched at the sight of them, he turned around and headed towards the door, but Abdul stopped him.

"Hey, come on, you'll be fine. I'll sit with you. I'll introduce you, they're all really friendly, and Mahdi speaks Arabic."

Nabil remained standing by the door. He reviewed the faces that were turned towards him. Their ages, gender and ethnicity varied, but he noticed that despite this, they all looked similar, lost, like him. Now he reviewed the room; along the back wall was a counter with a serving hatch. A tall man in a brightly coloured jacket was spooning sugar into his cup, the woman on the other side was leaning on her forearms engaging with him. As the man walked away the woman stood up, her eyes met Nabil's and she smiled and waved. It was the red-haired lady from the supermarket.

He lowered his gaze as she approached, but smiled a half-smile.

"Hi, about time we had a proper introduction, I'm Kirsten," She offered her hand. "What's your name?"

Nabil thought he understood, but he didn't want to make a mistake, although he did accept the extended hand.

Then she pointed to herself, as she said, "Kirsten. What is your name?"

Now he was sure, "Nabil."

"Nice name." Kirsten put two thumbs up. "Welcome."

"You two know each other?" Abdul asked.

"Nabil comes into the supermarket I work in."

Abdul translated and Nabil smiled and nodded.

"That's a good start, someone you know," Abdul said to Nabil, and then translated for Kirsten.

"I'm only here on Thursdays, though."

Abdul didn't translate this time, he didn't want to put Nabil off attending.

"Come and meet Mahdi," he said, guiding Nabil in the right direction. He indicated where Nabil should sit, introduced him to the whole group, then said, "I'll be back," patted Nabil on the shoulder and walked away.

The group welcomed Nabil, who sat amongst them without uttering a word. Without actual or emotional involvement, he watched them play cards, draughts, and chess, for what felt like an eternity.

At the end of the session Abdul returned and asked, "How was it? Going to come again?"

Nabil shrugged.

"Tuesday, then. We'll meet by the clock like today, same time."

Nabil nodded, but his stomach churned at the thought.

They reached the place where they would part company.

"See you Tuesday, then," Abdul said.

Nabil was cold, and the grey sky turned his mood the same colour, but he didn't want to go back to his room. Instead, he went to the library and was happy to see that his favourite spot was free. For a moment he just sat. Recovering from the contact with so much noise and unfamiliar expectations, he took his notepad and pen from his bag and wrote:

> *Abida's voice was loud, it drowned out the ringing in my ears. She was screaming and shouting my name. I couldn't call out because the dust was in my mouth, drying it, but I raised my hand to her. She ran towards me, wrapped her arms around me and cried, 'Are you hurt? Can you move?'*
>
> *I didn't know.*
>
> *I could see dust and rubble shifting as the other boys struggled to free themselves. And then the room was full of people who'd come from outside; they were on their hands and knees, tearing at the rubble.*

Nabil wrote, until no more words would come.

As the taxi pulled away it drove through a puddle; Margaret stepped away from the spray, too late. Her eyes strained against the fading light and her hand kept slipping as she tried to get her key in the lock. "Stupid old woman," she said to herself.

She took her phone from her bag and turned the torch on, now getting the key in the lock was easy, but the door required a hard shove to open it.

Before taking her coat off she checked it. There were two dark patches where the muddy water had splashed her. Margaret tutted. She turned on the light and the heating, shivering in response to the cool room. She filled the kettle and put it on, then rolled herself a cigarette. "Ah." She inhaled deeply. "I was dying for that."

From her bag she took the copy of 'To The Lighthouse', which was the latest reading group book, she turned to the page identified by a book marker. *I get what Alex was saying, but it's not floating my boat. Is it worth hours without a fag? Two more weeks of it yet. I'm looking forward to Great Gatsby, though.*

She made herself a tea, put on her jumper, and turned up the thermostat.

She moved to the armchair, put the blanket over her knees and turned her tablet on, intending to browse on Twitter. The headline caught her eye: 'Quarantined Brits Return to UK.' So, instead she tuned into Sky News to catch the full story.

It was marginal, but noticeable, a change in the light this morning. Spring was in the air. Mandeep finished the run with cool-down stretches on the porch, then she took a puff on her inhaler. Spring would improve her asthma too.

She crept into the house at six-fifty. Although there were only ten more minutes until she woke the household, she needed that time undisturbed for her prayers. At their conclusion she stood for several seconds with her head bowed, making the transition back from internal world to external. Then she filled the kettle, switched it on and went to rouse the family.

Coming back into the kitchen after her shower she was greeted by the televisual images of people dressed in hazmat suits; the sound was turned down so that instead of the presenter's commentary she heard the crunching and slurping of breakfasts being eaten.

"This China again?" she asked, turning the volume back up.

"Think it's Italy," Dev replied.

"The UK now has sixteen confirmed cases," the presenter said, "and there's one confirmed case in Ireland."

"The numbers are growing," Mandeep said, keeping her voice calm for the sake of her daughters.

"Don't think we need to worry about sixteen cases, and no one's died yet." Dev replied.

"You two finished? Need to go and do your teeth then and get your stuff together." When they had left the room Mandeep said, "Why d'you think they're reporting it, then? Considering there are so few cases."

Dev shrugged. "Probably because it's new."

"You don't think we need to worry?"

"What over sixteen cases?"

"There were fewer than that in China when they shut down."

"That's China. Don't worry, we'll be okay." Dev rubbed his wife's upper arm.

✥

"I've seen several people wearing masks this morning," Kirsten said to the centre manager. "I suppose it's because of the coronavirus thing. It disturbed me a bit."

"Yes, it's unsettling. There's been some discussion about how we proceed here if things get worse."

"I meant the masks, not the virus. Discussions? Who with?

"The council."

"Really? To what end?"

"None yet, just what ifs. If and when it becomes more, we'll let all our volunteers know."

"I haven't been taking too much notice until now."

"Me neither."

Kirsten was putting out the cups and filling the urn as she spoke. She checked her watch against the clock on the wall, both said the same time for a change.

"D'you need any help?" she asked the chef through the serving hatch.

"Could wash the bakers." He inclined his head towards the potato store.

"How many?" She walked through into the kitchen.

"Twenty should do it."

"Anything else?" she asked, when the task was completed.

"Nah, we're fine thanks."

"I'd better get back to my post, then."

A few minutes later Kirsten scanned the room to see who was there. *How conformist we all are,* she thought, observing how the service users were in their usual corners, and their usual groups.

She sighed, seeing Nabil on the periphery of one. *Still at least they're trying to include him; it's bound to take time.*

He looked in her direction, so she smiled and waved, he gave a half-hearted wave back. *He looks so scared, I wonder what his story is?*

☞

Thursdays were Emerson's baked potato day. He always worked a late shift Thursdays so got one on his way between visiting his grandparents and work. There were several benches on which he could sit after purchasing and, if it was raining, a closed down shop doorway to stand in. There was no rain today.

There was, however, a substantial queue. As he approached, Emerson checked the time on his phone. He wanted to check out the gaming shop, too, before work, so thought he might do that first, but then, he reasoned, the queue might be just as long so may as well wait.

A man and woman came up behind him, the woman sighed. "It's going to take ages."

"Don't you want to wait?" her companion asked.

"Might as well, got nothing in at home. Just saying that's all."

The queue inched forward.

"What you looking at?" the woman enquired.

"Sam sent me a post. Some people are apparently saying there's a link between 5G and this coronavirus stuff."

Emerson's interest was grabbed, now he paid full attention to the conversation.

"What's 5G?" the woman asked.

"Where you been? High speed internet. Haven't you heard all the talk on the news about the involvement of the Chinese company, Huawei?"

"Yeah, just didn't take much notice. What's it got to do with coronavirus?"

"Some people think the symptoms of coronavirus aren't a virus at all, but the radiation effects of 5G. You've heard of coronavirus, I take it?"

"There's no need for sarcasm."

Emerson turned around, "Sorry couldn't help overhearing. Some people think the virus and 5G are both part of the Big State." He addressed himself to the man.

"Yeah, I heard that too."

"Which means?" the woman asked.

"They're both designed to control us," Emerson answered.

"Don't get that," the woman answered. "Why'd they want to control us? And who are *they*, exactly?"

Emerson's stomach clenched and he fought the urge to question the woman's intelligence. "To steal our time and money, so they get more. The virus most likely came from a lab in China, did you know that?" He was now third in the queue.

"Heard it came from bats. Seems to me they got control anyway," the woman replied. "We all gotta work, haven't we? And purchase."

Emerson sighed, but he had to concede that she had a point. "True, but…" now he was at the front of the queue.

"Hi Emerson, usual?" the baked potato seller asked.

"Yeah, please." He turned back to the woman. "People who crave power and control just want more and more of it, there's never enough." He turned his attention back to the stall holder. "Thanks, mate. Yep, see you next week."

Emerson waited on the bench that was closest to the stall, hoping the couple would join him, but they didn't.

Daniel checked the order a second time, nine loaves and twenty-four rolls, "At this rate I'll have to buy another oven," he said to the shop manager, Dianne.

"Word's got out about how good it is."

He nodded his thanks.

The queue at the temporary traffic lights was long. Daniel tapped the steering wheel, as he waited for movement, then sighed and tutted as the lights turned red with him still stuck behind a line of cars. He turned the radio on, a rap song greeted his ears, so he turned to Four where he was greeted by the voice of a newly repatriated quarantine passenger from the Diamond Princess talking about his ordeal. He listened for a while, turned it back to Two, then off as the traffic began to move.

He sighed as the lights turned red once again.

The windscreen was steaming up, so he opened the window. He was hit by the sound of idling engines, the smell of exhausts, and the damp feel of fog. Finally through the lights, he drove just above the speed limit; fast enough that no other driver was justified in complaining, but not fast enough to warrant a fine.

Once home he drank coffee and listened to the television news while he got the dough ready for the first proving. He was looking through the contents of the cupboards and fridge, deciding what to have for dinner, when Kirsten rang.

"That's good, isn't it?" she said when he told her about the bread order.

"Well, yes, but it's pretty hectic getting it ready. Good job I went to the cash and carry recently; if I run out of flour, I'll be letting people down."

"Well, the best way is to buy well in advance, before you're anywhere near needing the next lot."

"I guess. Better get on with it, anyway. Have a good evening."

Kirsten felt she'd been dismissed. Her rational head understood that this was just Daniel being who he was, and he didn't much like talking on the phone. Her heart told her something else, and she had to resist the urge to phone him back and instead trust to the fact that it was all okay between them.

MARCH

"Mum's sounding rough this morning," Dev told Mandeep. "She didn't want to speak to the girls."
"Oh dear."
Mandeep reached out to touch him, but Dev pulled away.
"You're worried?"
"Been worried for the past five years, but yes…"
"Maybe just a bad day."
"Maybe."

The homeless man was sheltering in the shop doorway. He spoke to Nabil as he passed; it was obvious from the gesture he wanted money. Nabil put his hand in the pocket of his jeans and counted the coins without removing them, then, turning his back, took some from his pocket and counted again, to make sure. He turned back to the man and handed him a fifty pence piece. Their hands touched in the process. Nabil flinched, unused to physical contact.

The man in the doorway grabbed at him and shouted, "I ain't got nothing catching."

Nabil broke into a sweat, his knees shook, and his heart raced. He moved away at a pace that was quick, but not a run, because he didn't want to draw attention to himself.

He'd been going to the library, instead he went home and, in the relative safety of his room, broke down and cried.

$$\sim$$

"It's good of you to spend your day off doing this, Mum. I'm sure they're things you'd rather be doing," Rosie said.

"Not really, it's help you pack, or clean my own place," Kirsten replied.

Rosie slid down from the breakfast bar stool and put the kettle on. She went into the living room to check that Ryan was still watching the film she'd put on for him then returned to the kitchen and made two cups of coffee. She yawned as she pulled herself back onto the stool.

"I don't know where to start."

"Well, if it were me, I'd start upstairs and work down. And do one room at a time."

"Okay, come on then."

$$\sim$$

Margaret decided to walk into town. She'd not long had an online shop delivered, but, apart from fancying the walk, she needed a few small items. The weather made the bus a tempting option, but once she got going, Margaret enjoyed the walk. She kept to the side streets as much as possible, as the traffic noise harassed her. In fifty minutes she'd reached her destination. She filled her basket quickly; supermarket shopping wasn't her favourite activity.

"Still raining?" the young man on the check-out asked of Margaret.

"Drizzling."

"Feels like it'll be raining forever, doesn't it? Find everything you want?"

"No actually, I couldn't find any Quorn sausages."

"Ah, they're popular. I'll get someone to check for you." Emerson rang the bell, and his colleague was sent to look for them. A few minutes later he arrived, sausages in hand.

"I never thought to look for fresh ones. Thank you, young man."

"You vegetarian then?" Emerson asked.

"Yes."

"Don't know how you manage it. I like my meat too much."

"That's okay. It's like anything. It's a choice."

The rain was heavy again when Margaret left the shop. She tutted at the sight of it. The bus stop was right outside so she checked the timetable, half- an-hour to the next one. *I'll go for a coffee and see what the weather is doing then,* she thought.

"Can you spare any change, ma'am?"

Homeless people broke her heart, especially the young ones and this one looked hardly more than a boy.

"I'm sure I can, one minute."

She took her purse from her bag to check her change.

"You alright, love?" It took a while for Margaret to realise it was her the woman was addressing. "You don't have to give him anything, you know."

"I beg your pardon."

"These people annoy me, sitting there begging. We've got a social security system in this country."

"Not without an address we ain't," the homeless man interjected.

"He's right, and I am perfectly able to decide for myself what I do with my money, thank you. And I'd rather you didn't call me love."

"Oh! Sorry, I thought…I didn't mean to offend."

"Well, you have, you've offended me, and you've offended this young man and I think you should apologise."

"What? Sorry."

"I mean to him, not me."

The woman looked aghast and walked away. Several people at the bus stop were watching, one in obvious amusement.

"Shame people don't realise where their disapproval should really be aimed." The words were intended as catharsis rather than for anyone's ears. "Here." Margaret passed the young man a five-pound note and started to walk away.

"No," he said and offered it back.

"Keep it, please." As she crossed the road, she could hear him calling after her, "Thank you, thank you so much."

The rain continued so she caught the bus. It was standing room only. She was still cross about the woman at the bus stop when she got home.

Why am I so cross? she asked herself. *She made assumptions about me based on my age, that's why. Ah! I shouldn't be so grouchy, she probably thought she was protecting me. And I probably feel so strongly against being protected because of my age.*

She made herself a cup of tea.

She made assumptions about him, though. We've had years of anti-discrimination and what's changed?

She turned the television on, only to be greeted by pictures of people in protective clothing; it sent a chill up her spine.

The next time she saw Daniel, Margaret told him about the encounter.

Daniel laughed. "I'll bet that surprised her."

"She probably has me down as a grumpy old bat, which I guess I am. What d'you think about this virus now?"

"Not sure, Mrs. P, keeping an open mind. It pays to be cautious, but…I'll reserve judgement for now." He offered Margaret an elbow bump. Seeing the confusion it caused, he asked, "You not familiar with this?"

"Should I be?"

"It's the new way of greeting people, in place of handshakes, supposed to help limit the spread."

Margaret sighed and rolled her eyes. "Whose suggestion?"

"I think it started in America. Yeah, a surgeon, General Adams, I think."

"Might have known it had come from there. I think we'd be a whole lot better off if we stopped following everything America does. Never mind Brexit, what about USxit?"

Daniel laughed again, "Oh, Mrs. P."

"And what a contradiction, a surgeon and a general, either save life or take it, you can't do both."

Daniel laughed louder. "You've made my day, Mrs. P."

Several times throughout the day he chuckled, remembering the conversation.

*

"Well?" Mandeep asked.

Dev shook his head.

Mandeep approached him with care. "What you going to do?"

"Don't know yet."

With a stomach full of butterflies, she swallowed and sighed. "Can it wait six weeks?"

"Maybe not."

"Just think how you'd feel if you left it too late."

"Oh don't." Dev pulled her into an embrace. "I know we only see each other once a year, but if I didn't see her one last time, it would . . .it doesn't bear thinking about."

"So, go now." Mandeep sighed. "I just keeping thinking if it were me – I couldn't – I wouldn't – it's not that I won't miss you, but…"

"I know. You're a good wife and a good human being."

"I'm just thinking, if it were me…"

Now Dev sighed. "I'll wait a few more days, see how it goes."

*

"This coronavirus is starting to dominate the news," Margaret complained.

"Yeah, apparently someone has died now."

"She *was* in her seventies."

"Still, sad, though." Daniel drank the dregs of his tea and got up ready to leave.

"Course, but my point is – when you get past seventy it all feels like a bit of a bonus; well, it did for me. God only promised three score years and ten."

"Never heard you mention Him before, Mrs. P."

"I'm not that God-fearing, just saying. Infants die; that *is* sad. Especially when it's because of human behaviour. I'm not bothered about dying – haven't been since John went."

Daniel paused in doing the buttons up on his jacket, he looked down at his feet

"No, I don't mind the thought of being dead," Margaret continued, "either there's nothing, in which case there's nothing to fear, or it's a better place than this. Even Hell couldn't be worse than this is sometimes, and I don't think I've been bad enough to deserve that." She laughed. "Should've tried harder."

Daniel laughed too.

"I wouldn't like to die alone, though, that's the only thing. I'm not afraid of being there, it's the getting there."

Daniel tapped his mouth with the edge of his thumb, keeping his gaze on the floor.

"Oh, I'm making you feel uncomfortable, Daniel, I'm sorry."

Now he relaxed, "Nothing to be sorry for. Anyway, I'm sure your children will be here when the time comes, and I'm equally sure that's ages away."

"Won't be ages. Even if I'm destined to make it to a hundred that's only another sixteen years, it'll pass in the blink of an eye. As for my kids being here, well they'll only be able to if we have sufficient warning. Ideally, I'd like a bit of warning, not too much, don't want to linger, but don't want it to be too sudden either, don't want the last emotion I feel to be fear. My John used to say, 'Wake-up, find yourself dead, the shock's enough to kill you'." She laughed, but didn't sound amused.

Daniel's laugh was awkward.

"Well, he didn't die suddenly," Margaret continued. "Far from it, poor man. Mind you I guess the more you suffer the greater the relief." She sighed.

Daniel's attention was on one of his buttons, which he did up and undid repeatedly. He waited to be sure Mrs. Paget had finished, then said, "Right, I guess I'd better get going."

"You'll not be wanting to come back if I keep talking like this." Margaret replied. "Death's an uncomfortable subject."

Daniel nodded.

"Thing is you think about it more when you get older." *He looks like he's standing to attention,* Margaret thought. "There I go again, sorry. It's just…John and I were together most of our lives. Well, most of his. You been with your lady friend long, Daniel?"

"A while. Don't know how long she'll put up with me, though."

"Can't imagine you're hard to put up with. You've been a godsend to me."

"I'm not very good at the relationship stuff."

"No?"

"Women like to share their feelings; well, she does anyway, men like to keep them to themselves; well, this man does."

"Ah."

"Right, Mrs. P., I really do have to go now."

"Of course, I shouldn't have kept you so long."

Alone, Margaret wondered about Daniel's parents, he'd never mentioned them. He didn't look very old, early fifties at the most she'd say, so chances were his parents were still around. Perhaps not though, maybe all that talk of death had raised some uncomfortable memories for him.

❦

Mahdi watched Nabil approaching. His shoulders were pushed up so tight into his ears he'd lost his neck, his head was bowed, his walk a fast shuffle. Mahdi saw himself from a few years earlier. When they were within touching distance Mahdi offered his hand. Nabil hesitated, took it, shook it once, then let go. Mahdi patted him on the back, taking no offence at the recoil away from his touch.

The first few minutes of the walk they spent in silence, neither paying much attention to their surroundings. For Mahdi they were familiar enough to be taken for granted; for Nabil, familiar enough to prevent him from getting lost, yet unfamiliar enough to keep him ill at ease.

Eventually Mahdi said, "Abdul used to be my support worker."

"Oh."

"He's a good man."

"Yes."

"He helped me a lot."

"Yes."

The door to the community centre was still closed. A group of people were outside, Mahdi approached them and went around shaking hands. Nabil recognised them all; he nodded a greeting.

The English class attendees piled out as they piled in. Nabil let everyone else go in before him. As the group, which included Mahdi, clamoured their way into the room they looked homogenous to Nabil, like one animal with multiple limbs. He crept in, to find Mahdi had left the group and was waiting for him. Together they approached the corner of the room where some of the students from the English class had already claimed their spot.

Kirsten came out from behind the counter and meandered her way around the room greeting people.

"Good morning, Nabil," she said.

"Good morning, ma'am." He lowered his gaze. It didn't feel the same as in the supermarket, where conversation was necessarily brief; here informality was fraught with many dangers.

Kirsten, sensing his discomfort, moved away quicker than she had intended. Back behind the counter she started serving the teas and coffees. One of the clients, Marie, was particularly chatty this morning and leant on the counter as she did so, "What made you wanna work here, anyway?" she asked Kirsten.

"Good question. I think the fact that it's community-based and not aimed at any particular group."

"What d'you mean?"

"Well, it's difficult to decide which group to offer support to – learning disabilities, mental health, refugees, single parents. All of those come here. And I like the biscuits." Kirsten helped herself to a bourbon and offered one to Marie, who took it and laughed, finally appreciating the light-heartedness of Kirsten's words.

After lunch Kirsten helped with the dishes and clearing up, then moseyed around chatting to people.

"Won't be long until we can sit out there," she said to one service user who was going outside the back door for a smoke.

"We need to tidy it up a bit."

"Not exactly been the weather for gardening."

Kirsten stepped outside too. She remembered how the garden used to look when she'd brought Rosie here for Brownies, compared with how it looked now. Then it had been a typical institutional garden, grass, hedges, and benches, but since the users of the community centre had taken it over it had completely changed. There were two large vegetable patches, the produce from which the centre either sold, or used in their meals. In the flower beds the Azalea and Mountain Fire were already beginning to bloom; Kirsten thought the mild winter must be the cause. She looked forward to the Foxgloves doing the same, as they were her favourite. There were still two wooden benches for those who, like Alana, wanted somewhere to sit all winter, but as soon as it was warm enough the Parisian café-style tables and chairs would be brought out too.

She went back inside and continued moseying around. She reached Mahdi and Nabil's group. They were playing cards, Nabil too, so she didn't interrupt, but instead she went to the kitchen to help with filling the vegetable boxes.

Nabil's hand won him second place. Mahdi patted him on the shoulder. "Well played."

He turned to the group, "I think we're going to have to watch this one," he said in English because it was the common language. Then he translated for Nabil, who responded with a shy smile.

As Mahdi and Nabil were leaving the centre, Mahdi asked, "You ready for that English class now?"

"It's here?"

"Yeah, Tuesday and Thursday, before the café opens."

"Maybe."

"Fatima, the one who played cards with us. She'll be there." Nabil nodded.

"I could come first time, if you like."

"Thank you."

❧

Daniel was catching-up on market trends when Kirsten phoned.

"Good day?" she asked.

"Uh huh." Daniel scrolled down the screen.

"Many bread orders?"

"Twelve, and two dozen rolls."
"They cooked?"
No answer.
"Daniel?"
"Uh! Sorry, yeah, all done."
"So, Flybe have gone bust then?"
"Yeah."
"I thought you'd be interested in that."
"I am."
"Well, you don't sound it. You sound distracted."
"Sorry, I am a bit; my mind is still on what I was reading."
"Not only your mind, your eyes as well."
He laughed. "Only a bit. The equity markets in the States are down eight-per-cent."
"That's bad, right?"
"Yeah! And that's despite the Federal Reserve dropping interest by fifty basis points."
"Fascinating!"
"It's being described here as economic terror. The economic nine eleven."
"You can tell me about it when I see you. Meantime can I tell you about my day?"
"Course you can."
"Put the tablet down then. Please."

There was someone in the room. Margaret was lying on her side with her back towards them. There was the smell of frying; it made her feel hungry. There was a voice somewhere in the distance. She lay for a second, taking in the information as she tried to process all of the sensations. The presence in the room was watchful, it felt comforting, it was her mother. As Margaret understood this and started to turn towards her, the impression fell away and she realised it was a memory, and remembered where she really was; and now she felt a little afraid. She pushed her spine into the mattress leaving no space for ghosts to creep up it. But in reality, it wasn't the ghosts of the dead she feared, it was those of her mind. Never before had she slipped in time, but one time slip could easily slide into another, and another, until identity was lost.

"Stupid old fool," she said out loud to herself, as she sat up and then climbed out of bed. "It's Saturday March seventh, two thousand and twenty. See, you're okay, not lost it yet." *Just as long as I keep my body and mind active, I'll be okay.*

There was reassurance in her morning routine. Shower, breakfast, then a walk. While she ate her breakfast she listened to the news. *What is going on with this coronavirus? So, we got an epidemic coming. Not the first one. Hardly sounds like bubonic plague. What about all the other things going on in the world?*

She turned the radio off, but the silence was deafening, so she put the television on, only to be greeted by scenes from Italy that looked like something from a science fiction film.

"Health officials in Italy are considering a proposal to put the Lombardy District into complete lockdown, in order to try to contain the spread of the novel coronavirus." The presenter was saying.

A shudder of fear tingled her spine for the second time that day.

She put on her coat and shoes, grabbed her bag, and put a cloth carrier inside it. She left via the back door, which led down the garden path to a small wooden gate. At the gate she turned and looked back up towards the house. It gave her such a feeling of warmth and delight that she knew she could never give it up. *Nope, sorry kids,* she said to her children in her mind, *if you're that worried about me, you'll have to come here.*

One good thing about the winter, in Margaret's opinion, was that the garden didn't need tending, but now spring was just around the corner and she would need, at the very least, to mow the grass. *I'll have to get a gardener one of these days,* but she thought that every spring and never had yet. Somehow it felt like giving in, owning up to her age, so she kept on doing it herself.

She liked to go out the back way for two reasons: the first, it led directly onto the playing field, across which she often took her walk. And the second, she didn't need to acknowledge either of her neighbours. Not that there was anything wrong with her neighbours, it was just that she didn't always feel sociable, and today was one of those days.

Margaret meandered her way across the field and through the children's play area, where a boy was swinging, and a girl was climbing the frame.

They look too young to be here alone. Margaret was concerned enough to pause in her walk and was just about to ask them if they were all right, when a Labrador came bounding up to her, so enthusiastically it almost knocked her over.

"I'm so sorry," the owner said, grabbing hold of it and putting it on a lead.

"Oh, it's okay, I like dogs." Margaret patted it on the head, feeling relieved when she realised this was the mother of the children.

And what would you have done if they were alone? Reported it? I don't know. There's a fine line between being helpful and being interfering. And she recalled the incident with the homeless man, remembering how unasked-for help felt to her.

She ambled on to the shop, but didn't go in, deciding there was nothing she needed immediately, and she'd probably go to the supermarket sometime in the week. She walked back along the road, because she didn't like to return the same way she had come. Cars passed frequently. The noise and fumes harassed her, and the steadiness of the traffic made crossing the road difficult.

"This," she said out loud, "is the reason I don't use my bike anymore." Although there was too, the fear that she was no longer fit enough.

On her way back into the house she came through the front door; her bicycle was in the hallway and, as she squeezed past it, Margaret felt nostalgic, remembering the picnics with John, and this fuelled her urge to get back on it. *I think I will, when it brightens up a bit, on a Sunday, when it's quieter.* She ran her hand along the frame. *It might need the tyres inflating, I'll ask Daniel.*

The walk had refreshed and enlivened her. Margaret made herself a cup of tea and sat down to write her shopping list. She started with a list of meals for each day, then checked for the absence of any ingredient and added it to her list.

Um, probably too much to carry on the bus, she thought, when the task had been completed. *I'll do it online. I can always go into town just for the sake of getting out.*

Margaret prided herself on the fact that, despite her age and living alone, she continued to cook herself a proper meal every day.

She got her tablet out to begin the shop; once again she was greeted by images of people in full-body protective clothing. Margaret sighed. It was gradually becoming a topic of conversation at her reading group; some other health worry to add to all the others the members had. Another point of pride for her was that she didn't talk about her health.

Once someone starts on that it's down-hill all the way, but it would be a lie to tell herself she had no concerns about the virus. *I wish whatever it is would just go away. If wishes were horses…*

Noises, both internal and external, kept Nabil awake: automobiles and human traffic from outside, snoring and moaning from next door, the radiator clicking, an occasional unexplained bump, his own heartbeat, the ringing in his ears that had been in them so long he couldn't remember where it started. A cacophony of memories.

As the light began to break, he checked the time on his phone, six thirty-four. *Saturday,* he thought. He pulled the duvet over his head and finally fell asleep.

He was startled out of it by the ringing of his phone, his heartbeat was fast, and his mind confused as he stretched out and reached for it. "Hello."

"Hi, it's Mahdi, come for a walk."

"When? I'm not ready."

"Get ready. I'll meet you by the clock in half an hour."

"One minute." He sat up, shook his head, rubbed his hair and face, checked the time, it was almost midday. "Forty minutes, please."

In exactly that amount of time Nabil was at the clock.

"My friend is waiting over there in his car. I thought we might drive out into the countryside," Mahdi said.

"Okay," Nabil nodded. His only experience of the English countryside was from behind the windows of the vehicle that had brought him from the detention centre to here.

Mahdi's friend wasn't an Arabic speaker. Nabil sat in the back of the car. The men in the front spoke in English. Mahdi translated one or two conversations, but after a few minutes seemed to forget Nabil was there. Once more he observed the countryside from behind glass. The roads became smaller and a little quieter, trees and hedges took the place of buildings and there were open spaces where you could see across the fields. So many shades of green.

The car pulled into a layby, next to a wood, into which they now stepped.

What Emerson liked best about his weekends off was that he could take the bike out for a long ride. Today he was especially pleased about this because it got him out of the way of the thing he liked least about his weekends off, being forced into the company of his mother and her boyfriend. They were sitting at the table, eating, when he came through.

"You're a sleepyhead today," his mother commented.

"What of it, it's my day off?"

"Hey, no need to speak to your mother like that."

Emerson grunted.

"He's right you know. I'm only saying."

"Well sorry, then."

"Accepted. Going out?"

"Yep."

"To see Nan and Pops?"

"Yeah, then on my bike."

"Anywhere nice?"

"Don't know yet. See where I end up."

"You be careful, mind. Take your phone. Just in case."

"Hum!"

It had always been his intention.

Emerson took the bike from the shed and inflated the tyres and oiled the chain because this was to be his first long ride since October. Before he left, he went to the shop opposite his house and bought himself a chocolate bar, a packet of cheese biscuits, a sausage roll, and an energy drink. He ate the chocolate straight away and put the rest in his backpack.

On his bike it only took twenty minutes to reach his grand-parents' house. He took it around the back, so that he didn't have to bother locking it up, opened the door and called out, "Only me."

His grandfather was in the kitchen washing up. "Hello there, mate."

"Hi." Emerson hugged his grandfather, went into the lounge, bent over, and kissed his grandmother on both cheeks.

"I was wondering where you'd got to," she said. "Brian, get Emerson that sandwich, would you?" she called to her husband.

"It's okay Nan, a plate'll do, I've got some snacks." Emerson took off his backpack.

"You'll eat them later, won't you? Well then."

"Coffee?" Brian asked, putting a cheese and ham sandwich down in front of his grandson.

"Thanks, Pops, yeah that'd be good."

Brian was back with the coffee in no time.

"How's your mum?"

"Okay, she sends her love."

"Still seeing that chap?"

"Yes."

"And you're still feeling the same about him, by the sound of it."

Emerson grunted. Brian chuckled.

"Boys and their mums," his grandmother said.

If it had come from anyone else's mouth, he would have had a good few words to say about it.

After about half- an-hour Emerson left. Often, he stayed and watched some sport on the television, in which he had little interest, but he liked to share in his grandfather's likes, or play a card game with his nan. But today he wanted to go for a cycle.

On his phone he selected the language app, secured the mobile in his inside pocket, and plugged in his earphones. Then he mounted the bike and headed out of town. The traffic made concentration on the language course difficult, but it wasn't long before he was on the country lanes, where it was relatively quiet, and it improved. Then he reached the wood. There were a couple of cars in the carpark; he hoped there wouldn't be too many walkers to get in the way.

There was still lots of water on the track. Some were puddles, through which he could ride, others were more difficult to negotiate without dismounting. He enjoyed the challenge of staying on the bike as it bumped its way through; he even enjoyed the spray of water in his face.

In just a couple of weeks from now, Emerson knew, the trees would leaf. *Oak before ash, there will only be splash, ash before oak there will surely be a soak,* Emerson remembered his grandfather telling him. *I hope the oak is first this year, we've had enough rain.*

He knew too that the buzzards would be starting to nest at about the same time. He knew this from observation. And it had been confirmed by the man who worked the wood, with whom he chatted whenever he was around, and from whom he'd learnt that the birds made three nests and watched to determine which was the safest before laying the eggs.

I wonder if I'll bump into him today.

There was a clearing where he always stopped for food and a drink, as long as it wasn't raining. He propped his bike against a tree, then perched himself on a fallen log. Although he wasn't very hungry, he decided to eat his sausage roll, and as he did so, Emerson paid proper attention to the language course. He had read somewhere that listening to information while exercising aided learning. So, whenever he cycled, and often when he walked, Emerson tuned into the course; and every time he stopped to revise, he was able to recall enough to convince himself of the truth of this.

Confident of his solitude, he responded out loud to the question concerning the weather, "Tenki ga idesu."

There were voices and the sound of sticks snapping underfoot, and three men came into the clearing – two walking side by side, a third behind. At the sight of Emerson, the third man stopped, suddenly, as if he were being confronted by the enemy he thought he was escaping.

"Afternoon." Emerson stuck the thumb of his right hand up to accompany the words.

"Good afternoon," one man replied in accented English.

"Good afternoon," came from the second.

The third man nodded.

Emerson recognised him from the shop. He looked for clues of the same in the young man, but there wasn't even a flicker to suggest Emerson was familiar to him.

They passed through the clearing without further comment, speaking in a combination of English and what Emerson guessed to be Arabic.

He got back on his bike and continued to cycle through the wood. He drew figures of eight around trees, jumped over fallen branches, slid up and down muddy slopes, all the time making his way towards the road on the opposite side to the way he came in. When he was ready for the return journey he plugged back into his phone, this time tuning to the music, which he put on shuffle.

The journey home was longer, and the road a little busier, but he didn't mind either, what mattered most was how free he felt on his bike.

Dusk was falling as he reached home. His mother and her boyfriend were sitting in exactly the same place as when he left, this time, in place of coffee, was a bottle of lager each.

"Hi, Emerson," his mother greeted, "we're getting a take-away a bit later, you wanna choose somethin'?" She slid a menu across the table to him.

"Thanks. I'll have the usual."

"You sure? You don't fancy being a little adventurous? Okay, so long as you're sure."

"You not going out then?" Emerson asked.

"Maybe much later, but there's a film on the telly looks quite good."

Emerson took a can of coke from the fridge and went to his room. He sent a text to Alex arranging a game for later, after the takeaway. He logged on to the internet and then Facebook.

Looks like interest in the 5G theory has started to take off. There were several posts on the subject. Emerson clicked a link and was taken to a page created by the Stop5G group. He noted, with interest, a couple of famous names.

He opened another tab and typed in: '5G and coronavirus, the science', where he was met by nothing but allegations of its falsehood.

Later he explained to Alex, as they were setting up for the game, "Could be it's not true, but it's a plausible theory and I'd like to work out for myself whether it is or not. Doesn't seem to be anything except reports that it's false, which doesn't reassure me 'cos they would say that, wouldn't they? I'll try a different browser next time."

"So, you were going to tell me about the equity market crash," Kirsten reminded Daniel while they waited for the dinner to cook.

"You're a glutton for punishment, you could've got out of that."

"Not once you've had a drink."

"I've told you really."

"Okay, so what does it mean, exactly?"

"What I predicted has come to pass."

"In the news they're talking about the economic problems being caused by coronavirus."

"Course; but let's not forget September seventeenth. You remember that?"

"Repo market spike?"

"So you do pay attention."

"Excuse me, pots and kettles come to mind here."

Daniel laughed.

"So, where *does* the coronavirus fit in?"

Daniel sighed. "I'm not sure yet. I study market trends. I wasn't expecting a virus. Need to be cautious and watch for a while. Coincidence? Maybe. But let's just say, the timing is rather convenient."

A couple of days later Mandeep addressed her assembled team. "I have to attend a meeting this evening with the Area Manager."

"I don't suppose I need to ask what about?" Emerson said.

"I don't suppose you do. Apparently, the World Health Organisation have now declared it a pandemic."

"Yes, I heard that."

"So, I guess we're bound to have to make some changes. Anything you think I should tell them?"

"People are panic buying. But you know that." Kirsten said.

Mandeep nodded. She was about to move on when Kirsten asked, "Can I have a word please?"

They went into Mandeep's office.

"I was just wondering how things are for you at home?"

The question felt like a door closing in Mandeep's face, she'd expected something work related. Her shock showed.

"Sorry," Kirsten said, "looks like it's a sore subject. I just thought you don't seem quite yourself."

"No. Thanks for asking. Just wasn't expecting it. Dev's mum, you mean? She's not good, really not, actually. He's going to have to go out there."

"Ah, that'll be hard for you."

"Yes. But necessary. And it's only a few weeks until we all go on holiday."

"He going to stay until then?"

"Makes sense."

"Uh huh!" Kirsten nodded.

"Thanks, Kirsten." Mandeep sighed. "Well, I'd better get on."

"Yeah, me too. Mandeep, I know it's not much help, but if you need a shoulder, I'm here."

"It's a big help. Thank you."

"All booked," Dev told his wife, sighing and getting up from the computer. "I'll WhatsApp Bal, tell him when to expect me." He sighed again, pulled Mandeep into a hug, and kissed the top of her head.

She felt lonely already. "Okay, well I'm off to bed."

"You'll be still awake when I come up? Won't be long."

Mandeep kissed her husband deeply and smiled at him. "Don't keep me waiting, then."

She had a quick freshen up shower, brushed her teeth and dabbed a little perfume behind each ear. She climbed into bed, keeping the main light on so as not to get sleepy, she set the alarm, noticing that it had already gone ten so she wouldn't get her eight hours now. Then she lay back on the pillow and waited for her husband. Ten minutes later she felt bored, so picked up her book from the bedside table.

The next thing Mandeep knew was the alarm going off. She rolled over in response to it and cuddled into Dev's back, he responded with a grunt. Momentarily she felt annoyance, with Dev that he'd taken so long to come to bed that she'd fallen asleep; then she felt disappointment with herself for having done so. Neither emotion lasted long.

She crept out of the bed and then the room, used the toilet, brushed her teeth, and donned her track suit. In the living room she did her warm-up stretches, then she put on her trainers, grabbed her head torch, and set off for her run.

An hour later she was home again, she'd showered, prayed, and woken the rest of the household by seven-thirty.

The television was on when Nabil entered the lounge, but there was no one around. He felt annoyed. *It must have been on all night,* he thought.

On the screen were images of people in hazmat suits, the scene was becoming ever more familiar. Nabil felt sick at the sight; too sick to eat breakfast.

It was his signing day. As he headed for the bus station, he felt so tired. His eyes were hot, his body heavy and his brain foggy. He no longer knew any other feeling than this and fear in his heart.

As he boarded the bus Nabil remembered the last time, then there had been no doubt in his mind that the most awful thing would be deportation, as it would surely result in his death, but now this new threat seemed to be everywhere. His only longing was for peace, in whatever form it took.

As soon as she arrived at the centre Kirsten was called to the manager's office. All of the staff were there, the atmosphere was grave; if she'd been a paid employee Kirsten would have expected news of her redundancy.

"It'll probably come as no surprise that this virus situation is getting serious." The manager spoke with authority. "We're going to have to make the clients aware of what's expected. I've had some leaflets printed, think I've covered all the languages, but if someone wants to check… thanks, Ben. There could well be questions, best just to refer them to the governmental advice about social distancing, hand washing, using their cards instead of cash. Offer plenty of reassurance, which of course I know you will. And I'll keep you posted – there is the possibility we'll have to close. Yes." He was responding to a question from the cook. "But that's not the advice at the moment."

"They seem to be taking it pretty seriously in Italy and Ireland," Suzanne said.

"Yeah, they're sufficiently worried as to close the country down, but not our PM," Ben said.

"It'll cause economic chaos," Suzanne said.

"It's already doing that," Ben continued.

"The economic issues were already there." The words were leaving Kirsten's mouth without her consent, making her heart pound.

There was silence for a few seconds, before the manager came back to the conversation.

"Let's not get political, eh. Our job is to ensure we keep the clients safe. So, I'll put the leaflets out, could you all please encourage them to read them and maybe just check that they're okay when they have. Great, thanks everybody."

He went through to the other room and put the leaflets on the table.

Kirsten moved to set up the tea and coffee. She watched the clients coming in, several of them wearing masks. As Marie arrived and picked up a leaflet Kirsten thought, *I wonder if she'll understand.* She left her post to go and see.

Marie was studying the leaflet. As Kirsten approached, she looked up. Her face wore a suggestion of pain, her nose was wrinkled, and her eyes squinted.

"You okay, Marie?"

"How far is two metres?" she asked.

"About this far." Kirsten moved back the appropriate few steps.

"I can't hold Barry's hand?"

"Well, it's okay for people who live in the same house to touch."

"Well, he don't." Her bottom lip was stuck out.

"Is he your boyfriend? It'll be hard for you, won't it?"

"You wouldn't want to give him the virus, would you?" Ben interjected.

"Ben!"

"Well, she wouldn't."

"How do I know if I've got it?" Marie said, sounding alarmed.

"There's a list of the symptoms." Kirsten turned the leaflet over to show her and was relieved to see there were some pictures included to assist with understanding.

"If I get it, will I die?"

"Not very likely."

"But I could?"

"Yes," Ben said. "That's why you have to follow the advice and keep your distance from people.

"Try not to worry, Marie, it's not very likely to kill you," Kirsten said, her ears pounding under the weight of her rage.

Marie continued to study the leaflet.

"How many times should I wash my hands?"

"Like you normally would, after using the toilet, before eating, if you sneeze or anything."

"My support worker said after I been shopping."

"Okay, it's best to follow her advice."

"What about when I get home from here?"

"If it makes you feel better."

"Course you should," Ben interrupted.

"I'm scared, I want it to go away."

Ben picked up a leaflet and waved it in the air. "Following the advice in here will help it go away. It's important."

"Try not to be afraid, Marie," Kirsten said.

"I'm going to wash my hands now." She almost ran from the room.

"Can I have a word?" Ben asked Kirsten.

"Sure."

"Outside," he ordered.

Ben's attitude left Kirsten feeling like a naughty school-girl, despite the seniority of her years. In the same manner she followed him across the room; as she did so she noticed who was reading the leaflets, so that she could check they were okay later.

"You undermined me in front of Marie," Ben accused, once they were in the garden.

His words shocked her. "Really? I'm so sorry, I was just trying to reassure Marie."

"She needs clear information."

"I know. I thought we were giving her that."

"Mixed messages. Leaflet and me saying you should be scared, you saying not."

"What good will it do for her to be scared?"

"Make her cautious about her behaviour."

"It's possible to be alert without being afraid."

"You told her she won't die and said it'd be okay for her to hold her boyfriend's hand."

"I told her she is unlikely to die and empathised with her not holding his hand."

"We really do need to take this thing seriously, people are dying."

The anger that had been boiling inside Kirsten suddenly reduced to a simmer, with the realisation of how Ben felt. "You're really scared, aren't you?"

He hesitated, looking like he'd moved out of the way just in time to stop a blow to the head. "Aren't you?"

"Cautious, rather than scared."

Ben folded his arms across his chest and chewed the side of his mouth. "Well, just be careful your blasé attitude doesn't put the clients at risk." He turned and walked back into the building.

Kirsten's face was hot. There was a brick in her throat. She went to the toilet, shut herself in a cubicle and quietly cried.

When she felt sufficiently composed, she gave her face a splash with water, took several deep breaths and returned to the tea and coffee counter.

"You okay?" the cook asked, coming out with a tray of scones.

She nodded.

"That's not what your face says."

Kirsten put on a smile as some clients came to the counter, Abdul amongst them.

"No Nabil today," Kirsten observed.

"It's his signing day."

"Ah, he doesn't have leave to stay? I thought he was part of the Syrian group."

"Nah, he made his own way here."

"All by himself?"

"Yep."

"Gosh. He's so young."

"Some are younger."

"I know."

Every time she thought about this Kirsten felt sad, angry, and ashamed; that the world should be such that anyone, leave alone children, needed to walk across continents and cross oceans in rubber boats, just to be safe.

On the way home she called into the shop, needing a few top-up items.

She was shocked by the empty spaces on the shelves. No tinned tomatoes, no muesli, no toilet rolls.

At the till another shock. "Afternoon, Madam," Emerson said, playfully. "Please wait and unpack on that side of the marked area and then load up from this side, once this lady has left."

"What's going on?" she asked as she went through.

"Please stand that side of the line, Madam," Emerson repeated. He looked around and seeing there was no one about said, "What the fuck, eh? Orders from on high. Management, I mean, not God." He chuckled, "We have to maintain 'social distancing'," he clawed the air, "to keep us and our customers 'safe'."

"I understand the reasoning but…"

"This is just the start, you wait and see."

Kirsten wanted to cry again.

"They've locked down in Italy and I think Ireland is about to," Emerson continued.

"This is getting scary."

"I'm not scared."

"I mean the reaction to it, rather than the virus. Makes me wonder what's going on and where this is going."

"I wonder that."

"I'm glad to see someone taking this seriously," said the man who had just come up to the unpacking line. He was wearing rubber gloves and had a scarf around his mouth and nose. "I hope we follow the example of Italy soon, before this gets out of hand."

Emerson and Kirsten exchanged glances, "I'm glad the measures make you feel safer," Kirsten said to the customer.

Emerson grunted, then said to Kirsten as she walked away, "We'll catch-up when we're both in next."

Kirsten stuck her thumb in the air in acknowledgment. She exited into the street where she stood for a moment feeling as if she had been catapulted into a drama without being given the script. Looking around she observed all the faces, some wearing masks, others wearing worried looks. Those without masks were unsmiling, those with them showed the clue to their feelings in their blank eyes.

&

The bus looked packed, so Margaret waved it away in favour of walking. *Should've done this in the first place. , I've made myself late, now.* She tutted. She needed to be at the Church Hall for the reading group in twenty-five minutes.

The scenic route was also the quickest. Through the park and then the cemetery, the latter of which was so well kept it was the more pleasant of the two. It was also a route that was almost devoid of people. The park would be busier later in the year, but today Margaret passed no more than ten individuals, and in the cemetery, she saw only two, both of whom were tending graves.

It wouldn't be so bad to cycle here, she thought. *At least if I fall off and die, they won't have far to carry me.* She chuckled to herself. *I'd like to shake that reading group up a bit, bloody old bores; arriving on my bike should do it. I can just hear them, 'Oh, take care on that bike, love.' Yes, I've reached an age where everyone wants me to take care and thinks it's okay to call me love.*

The last part of the journey was along the road. Although it was no more than ten minutes on foot, by the time Margaret reached the church hall she felt flustered, due to the traffic. *If only it weren't for that last bit.*

Len the lecturer, and Betty, were the only people in the room; both were wearing masks.

"Hi, Margaret, good to see you. Looks like it might be just the three of us today. I think they're worried about this coronavirus. Unless they're just put off by this cold weather," Len said.

Or the bloody book, Margaret thought.

"Not wearing a mask, I see," Len continued.

Full marks for observation. "Never occurred to me."

"I bought some in case." Len offered her the box with a smile.

"I'm okay, thank you."

The smile dropped from Len's face. He hesitated, still holding the box out to Margaret. She was deciding how to respond should he insist, which for a moment looked as if it would be the case, but then he put it down and picked up the book.

"Right, let's crack on then."

After the meeting she decided to go into town, pick up a few provisions and get the bus home, even though it would likely be packed. Outside the supermarket was the usual young homeless man, she smiled to herself with amusement, remembering the last encounter. This time she gave him two pounds.

"Thank you, Ma'am," he said.

"You're welcome," she replied.

Inside the supermarket her mood soon changed. Big spaces on the shelves were reminiscent of post-wartime Britain. Although it was distant, she remembered being sent to the village shop with a list and coming home with only a few of the requested items. Her mother's disappointment had felt like a personal failure on her part.

There was another surprise at the tills, yellow and black markers on the floor made her think of a marked-out crime scene.

"Whose idea was this?" she asked.

"It's aimed at protecting staff and customers," Emerson replied.

"What poppycock."

"You don't like it?"

"It's the implications I don't like. Herding us around like sheep."

"Well, I approve," the lady behind her said, "it makes me feel safer. I'm surprised you don't. People like you are supposed to be more vulnerable."

"People like me?" she almost snapped.

"Sorry I didn't mean to insult you. Sorry." The lady raised her hands submissively.

"You and the Government both. I'm old, not stupid, and still able to make my own choices."

"Of course, I'm sorry."

"Doesn't mean they'll be good ones," the customer who was packing his bag on the other side of the till piped up.

Margaret's blood ran hot. "Good or bad, it'll be mine. The day may dawn when I can no longer make decisions for myself; all the more reason to continue doing so for now."

"That attitude will likely put you in hospital and strain our poor NHS."

"Put strain on it? I can assure you that hospital is the last place I'll be going if I get ill."

Margaret's face was so hot she was sure it must be shiny. The blood pounded in her head and ears. How dare he speak to her like that?

Emerson watched as she almost threw her shopping into the bag. This lady was fun. "Did you find everything you wanted?" he asked. Feeling nervous about how the next question would be received, he rolled it out almost as an aside. "D'you need any help with your packing?"

"I'm fine, thank you, and no, there are no tinned tomatoes and no toilet rolls."

"I know, sorry, it's a bit random what we're running out of."

"I don't get why toilet rolls," the lady she'd first spoken to said. "You can't eat them."

"No," Margaret agreed, "but people seem to be shitting themselves over this virus."

Emerson supressed a laugh, but it wasn't easy.

Margaret enjoyed the look of shock on the other customers' faces. She hoicked the bag onto her back, as she said thank you and goodbye.

As predicted, the bus was packed, but her heavy bag made it necessary to board. Most of the passengers were teenagers returning from school. Margaret delighted in them, it was their enthusiasm and lust for life in which she revelled. It gave her hope, their collective energy felt irrepressible, she smiled at the thought and at the memory of her own youth. Then at the irony. *How stupid. Keeping me apart from everyone in the supermarket and then I'm cramming in here.*

Her reverie was interrupted. "'Scuse me lady, you wanna seat?" It was a boy of about fourteen; the group he had been sitting with were doing a poor job of hiding giggles behind their hands and shoving each other. Margaret glared at them.

"That's very kind of you, young man, but I'm fine thank you."

Margaret thought he looked somewhat relieved.

As the bus neared her stop it was difficult to reach the bell, she only just rang it in time and almost lost her balance. The driver looked disgruntled, she gave him a cheery farewell, then descended the steps as elegantly as she was able, given that her legs did feel a little stiff from standing.

Stupid old has-been, she told herself. But, when her legs loosened up and it only took her five minutes to walk from the stop to home, *you're not totally decrepit yet.*

Life was turning into a battle for Margaret. Fighting to stay fit, well, and most of all, motivated.

❧

Mandeep was greeted by the smell of spices cooking; it was warming. She shook the rain from her coat as she hung it up and made her way to the kitchen. The dahl was simmering nicely, but there was no sign of Dev.

"I'm home," she called up the stairs and then made her way into the living room where the television was on, without an audience. Mandeep turned it off.

"Hi," Dev was behind her now. "Dinner's almost ready. Hungry? Cold? Girls are helping me pack."

The mention of packing brought tears to Mandeep's eyes; she fought them back, not wanting Dev to feel guilty.

"You won't miss this," she inclined her head towards the window, where the rain continued to pound down.

"But I will miss you." Dev stroked her face, then, seeing that it provoked tears, pulled her into an embrace. "I'll WhatsApp every day, and it won't be long until you all come to join me."

"I hope not."

Dev offered a quizzical look.

"We've put in social distancing measures at work. People are panic buying stuff. I think a lockdown is expected."

Dev nodded, it had occurred to him, too. "Shall I cancel the flight?"

"You can't do that. We've discussed it. How you'd feel. Your family. Your mother. It's got to be about her."

He hugged her and kissed her forehead.

"I'll go and get the girls, you dish up," he said.

Dev had one foot on the stairs. "Let's have an early night." He stepped down, pulled his wife close, kissed her deeply then, as he pulled away, smiled wryly and said, "We've got an early start, after all."

♨

Friday thirteenth, Mandeep thought, as she was leaving the airport, holding onto the hands of the child either side of her and holding back the tears. *I hope it's not an omen.*

Both girls slept on the way home. Mandeep woke them at the school gates. Afterwards she went to the local shop, avoiding the supermarket so that she didn't have to face any of her colleagues.

Home. The silence seemed foreboding. She went into the kitchen to unpack the shopping and make herself some coffee. The fridge hummed. *Has it always been that loud?* she wondered. The kettle coming to the boil was deafening, the spoon clattered in the cup as she stirred in milk. Mandeep turned on the radio to be greeted by new virus death statistics from the Continent. She turned it over to a music channel, just in time for the news to start and the same statistics to be quoted. Nausea was rising and tears were threatening, they exploded in a torrent with the prediction that Spain would soon lockdown.

What if Dev can't get home? She asked herself between the sobs. *What if one of the girls gets the virus? Indrani, with her asthma? Or me – who'll look after the girls if anything happens to me?*

She slumped in a chair and allowed the tears to flow freely. On the radio, tunes too cheerful and superficial for the circumstances soon annoyed her. She silenced it, fetched her laptop and turned it on, she'd catch up with her emails, then phone her parents and remind them about tomorrow.

On the screen, as she logged on to the internet, were images of people dressed in hazmat suits, and again the news of a likely lockdown in Spain. She moved her eyes around the screen in search of something, anything, else. In a column down the side a horoscope provider advertised. Although Mandeep did subscribe to the view of astrology being an ancient science, she didn't believe in the popular daily readings as part of this. However, sometimes she checked them anyway, especially if she needed solace.

Today it read:

'You may not feel like being sociable today. With a major focus on an emotional zone, this is a time to think deeply. You may find you are drawn to spend time quietly contemplating key issues which might prove helpful. No-one can be the life and soul of the party all the time, so try to be gentle with yourself.'

And it seemed portentous. Life and soul of the party she might never be, but the rest rang true.

Her text alert sounded, making her jump. The scrape of the chair on the wooden floor, as she pushed it back, grated on her nerves. The phone was on the work surface next to the kettle, she picked it up and stared at it as if it were to blame for the message she'd been expecting:

Just about to board. Be in touch on landing. Dx

Safe journey, she texted back.

Then she stood with the phone in her hand for a moment, feeling as if putting it down would separate her from her husband even more. Another quiet and subdued cry followed before she could bring herself to check her emails. There were none of any significance, so she phoned her parents.

"Hi, Dad, still okay for picking the girls up tomorrow?"

"Yeeees," he said hesitantly. "Dev's gone then?"

"We dropped him off at seven-thirty. He's just boarded. Sent a text."

"O…kay."

"You don't sound sure."

"Oh, you know, just this virus stuff, but we'll do it. They are our grandchildren, after all."

When she put the phone down Mandeep just wanted to run to the school, bring her children home and lock them and herself in the house until Dev came home.

❧

"The lockdown in Ireland is a worry, don't know what'll happen if we follow suit." Rosie paused for a sip of tea. "Pass me some more newspaper please."

Kirsten did as requested. As she wrapped the crockery, she recalled doing the opposite on the day she'd brought it from her mother's house to here, wondering whether it would be to Rosie's taste, and whether she'd appreciate the gift.

As if to echo Kirsten's thoughts Rosie said, "At least we don't have Nan to worry about."

"True. Funny to think of being grateful that someone's dead. She would never have coped with this."

"It must be terrifying for those vulnerable groups. Whereas for me it's more annoying than anything else. Interfering with my plans."

Mother and daughter both laughed.

"You never liked your plans being thwarted, not even when you were little," Kirsten said. "But this is quite a big plan to be spoiled."

"Looks like Spain are about to lock down. I can't see us being the only country not to."

"I thought the plan for us was to go for maximizing immunity by not locking down."

"People aren't happy about that, though I think the PM will give in to the pressure eventually."

"D'you think he should?"

"Don't know. From my own selfish point of view, no, but…I'm really not sure."

"I don't get it."

"Don't get what?"

"These lockdowns. It seems disproportionate to the risk."

"Thousands have died in Italy."

"I know."

"And the death toll is still rising."

"True. It's just…if it's really true that it's only killing the *vulnerable* groups…and there's never been a lock down for flu, or TB."

. "This is new, though, we don't know what we're up against. Anyway, it isn't okay for anyone to be dying."

"I never said it was, I just don't understand why fit and healthy people are being quarantined instead of only the sick and vulnerable." She sighed. "Daniel thinks – Oh, I don't know." The fist in her belly clenched tighter. "There's one thing of which I am sure, though. Whatever the truth is, we're not likely to be told it."

"D'you think it's worse than they're saying?" Rosie looked up from her task; the look reminded Kirsten of her childhood requests for reassurance.

"Possibly. Although something else could be going on."

"Like?"

"That I don't know. I just have this feeling…" Kirsten sighed, an image passed through her mind, of hospital corridors blocked by beds. "I guess we'll find out soon enough."

"That's what I'm worried about."

Kirsten squeezed Rosie's shoulders. "We'll be fine, I'm sure of it."

All crockery, apart from the necessary four of each, was packed. Kirsten assembled another couple of boxes then went into the lounge and opened the cupboards and drawers to check what she was up against before starting in there; she was now very bored by the task.

Rosie wasn't far behind her, "You can go if you like; you've already done loads."

"It's a big task on your own, I'm happy to help. Might as well do a bit more and wait to see the kids." She checked her watch. "Four o'clock they're back, yeah? Well, it's twenty to now."

Rosie's mobile rang. "Hello, yes, speaking." She took it to the kitchen.

Kirsten opened a drawer and was greeted by paperwork. She closed it again, for reasons of privacy. Two similar drawers opened in her memory, the first was housed in Greg's writing bureau: the second belonged to her deceased mother. In the first, no surprises, but many prompts to her tears. In the second, a pile of letters from the father she believed had never been in touch.

The discovery had left her feelingShe'd felt like an alien life form had taken over her body. It tore at her vital organs and constricted her throat. She had no idea if her father was alive or dead, but either way it had been difficult to morn a father who had never cared. The realisation that he'd been kept from her changed all of that, and made it intolerable to grieve for a mother who had lied.

The feeling of alienation returned with intensity now, as she considered the possibility that a lockdown would keep her from those whom she loved. It coincided with Rosie's return to the room. Her face was screwed into a frown.

Kirsten swallowed her memories away. "What's up?"

"That was the Estate Agent, the buyer wants to move the sale forward in anticipation of a lockdown."

"Forward? By how much?"

"Just a few days, the Thursday or Friday of the week before. We can probably get ready by then. Just hope the owners of the rental will be okay with that."

"Any reason why they wouldn't?"

"A lockdown. Somehow it seems more real now that some-one…" she clawed the air with her forefingers "…'official', has said it. I'm scared the move won't happen."

"If it comes to the worst, it'll surely only be a delay?"

Rosie shrugged. "Don't know. The new job starts on the sixth, don't forget."

Kirsten hugged her and said, "Worrying times. Strange times."

Strange indeed, Kirsten thought as she strolled homeward. *It just doesn't make any sense to me. Something feels really wrong.*

Today's worries and yesterday's disappointments became jumbled in her mind. *Truth should be sacred. Sometimes it's hard to handle, but lies just create insecurity. Rarely is the truth worse than the one created by the imagination.*

She'd imagined so many reasons why her father failed to acknowledge her existence: he didn't care, he lived in another country, his current wife wouldn't allow him to; he was dead.

There was a very distant memory, so distant she wondered if it were real, of a man at the door. Raised voices, some kind of struggle, a door slamming; her mother in tears as she held her close.

Once, at least, maybe more, she'd asked, "What was my dad like? Why doesn't he come to see me?" And her mother had replied, "He's a man who likes his freedom, he didn't want any children." But that didn't necessarily mean he'd ignore one who'd arrived, did it?

Sometimes she was envious of her friends' dads, when she saw the love they had to offer. And sometimes she was glad she didn't have one, when she saw the fear a father could provoke. Always her own father was the scapegoat for her anger. And she didn't even know his name.

'I've got to stop this; I need to focus on something else,' she said out loud to herself.

She took her phone from her bag and rang her friend, keeping the conversation light and without mention of any virus, although her friend kept trying to bring it in. As she crossed the final street before reaching home Kirsten passed two people wearing face masks.

Later she spoke with Daniel. "Rosie's move is happening a few days early. It seems the people are afraid of a lockdown."

"I think it likely."

"Oh!" That wasn't the response she'd hoped for. "Everything feels so out of control."

"Yep."

"Do you still think this is all about the economic crash?"

"Not sure. Wasn't expecting a virus. Need to wait and see." There was a long pause, "What time you coming tomorrow?"

"Usual, I guess." Kirsten was still reeling; she'd hoped for more from Daniel. "Do you want me to cook something?"

"No, I'll think of something. See you then. Have a good evening."

How could she follow that instruction when she felt like everything was falling away from her?

Margaret was waiting for her monthly visit, this time it was Joe who was coming. He was the only one of her children born late and it had carried on since then. Margaret knew to add at least an hour to his expected time of arrival, so, lost in thought and the drone of the lawn mower engine, she jumped in response to his:

"Why ever didn't you leave that for me to do?"

"Hello, darling. I was killing the time until you arrived." She checked her watch. "You're only ten minutes late."

He laughed. "The girls would've killed me if I was late today."

"What's so special about today?" She looked from him to the lawn mower, as if expecting some exchange between them. "I can't really leave this half done, but… Oh, hello, Lorraine, what a lovely surprise,"

Margaret hugged Joe, who flinched slightly in response, and went to do the same to her daughter-in-law, but was greeted by raised palms. "We shouldn't."

Irritation flushed through Margaret. "How are you? How are the girls? Good? And that baby, how's she doing?"

"She's gorgeous, of course."

"How does it feel being a grandma?"

"How does it feel being a great-grandma?" Lorraine replied.

"Glad I made it far enough." Margaret noticed the look that passed between her son and his wife. "I'll make us coffee before I finish the lawn. I thought I had plenty of time, you see," she laughed.

"I'll finish it off." Joe was removing his jacket as he spoke.

"Oh, thank you, I'll put the kettle on, then."

Lorraine followed Margaret into the house. She took her coat off and scanned the room, before hanging her coat on the back of a dining chair and then sitting down.

"I'll do a few more spuds and veg." Margaret said. "Shame Joe didn't mention you were coming. It's very nice to see you, of course."

"Only decided this morning. Thought we might take you out for lunch, actually. While it's still an option, if you're comfortable with being in a crowded place. We can keep our distance. Unless you're self-isolating?"

Margaret sighed. "I'm not and I'm perfectly comfortable with it, and thank you." Margaret put the cup in front of Lorraine, along with the sugar bowl. "I remembered you prefer tea, wasn't sure about the sugar, though."

"No, thanks. Joe said you wouldn't be. People your age are being advised to. You're at the most at risk of dying from this damned thing."

"People my age are at risk of dying full-stop."

Lorraine put her hands in the air, before resting her elbows on the table and putting her head in her hands. Joe came in, pushing hard against the sticky door, "Should've told me about this, I'd've brought my tools."

"Daniel's going to fix it."

"Daniel?"

"A friend of mine. Not that kind of friend," Margaret was amused by the look on her son's face.

"I should hope not."

Why might that be? Because I'm your mother? Or because you think I'm too old?

"He's about your age. Makes bread for the farm shop, where I get my eggs and veg. Last winter he started bringing them to me because of the bad weather."

"And he does odd jobs?"

"Well, this'll be the first."

"How much does he charge?"

"We haven't discussed it."

S'pose now he thinks he's after my money. An image of Daniel, with a swag bag over his shoulder and a balaclava covering his face, popped into Margaret's head, which amused her.

"What're you smiling at?" Joe asked.

"Your disapproval."

"Um. Just trying to take care of you."

"Thank you, but I'm not in need of that quite yet." She handed him his coffee.

"Well, I'm not so sure, after what you just said." Lorraine turned to Joe. "She isn't intending to self-isolate."

"Told you." Joe offered his mother a bemused look and shook his head. Lorraine and Joe exchanged glances again.

"You might ask me why instead of assuming I've lost it, or I'm too blasé, or whatever else it is you're assuming."

"Okay, then, why?"

"I thrive on the activities I do. I enjoy meaningful conversation with people; without them I might lose it. I'm old and going to die soon anyway."

"I, for one, would rather delay that as long as possible."

"It's not that I don't understand, Joe, I do, but I think it should be my choice. I'm not going to do as I'm told because someone else thinks they know better than I do what's good for me. Especially a bunch of politicians."

"It's not just about you, though. The NHS won't be able to cope with too many sick people."

"I've said it before, I'll say again, that is not my responsibility. I paid into it all my working life. It would be able to cope if it was the NHS of the nineteen fifties and sixties; it's been eroded by the same people who now claim to want to protect it."

Joe sighed. "Yeah, you're probably right, but…"

"There you go again with your buts."

"Which you have listened to."

"Okay, go on then."

He sighed. "Come and stay with us. You'd have company and stimulating conversation that way," he laughed. "Well, you'd have company at least. And you wouldn't have to take unnecessary risks."

"Thank you, but I'd rather stay here." She patted Joe's hand.

 "Knew you'd say that."

"It's a very generous offer, please don't think I don't appreciate it, but an old horse likes its own stable."

"I'll worry about you every day."

"Please don't try to blackmail me."

"Blackmail? I'm just saying I care about you."

"I know you do. Since you do, please respect my wishes."

"What if you get ill?"

"I'll phone you."

"What if you can't?"

"I'll recover or I'll die."

"Mum, this isn't helping me."

"Look, every day I could get too ill to phone you; fall over; have a stroke, a heart attack."

"Stop!" Joe had his hands on his ears. Lorraine rubbed his back.

"I think you *are* being selfish, Margaret," she said. "I'm not scared to tell you that."

"I am, you're right, but so are you. You want me where you can see me, so you feel better. I appreciate your concern, but I want to stay here. I'm sure Daniel and his lady friend will keep an eye on me, anyway."

"Who is this Daniel?"

"I told you who he is. Come on, let's not quarrel. Shall I put the dinner on, or are we going out?"

"I said we'd take you out."

Joe took hold of his mother by the arm, grabbed her coat, shepherded her towards the door and then the car.

Over pub lunch Margaret said, "I'll phone one of you every day. If I don't phone, you have my permission to be concerned."

"But what'll we do?"

"I'll give you Daniel's number. Have to check with him first, of course."

"Is it a good idea to have regular visits from someone who's out in the community?"

"He works in a wood," the words were followed by a heavy sigh and the shake of her head. "Anyway, I'll be going into the community to my groups and to do my shopping."

"I wouldn't count on the former, there'll possibly be a ban on group meetings soon."

"Anybody'd think it was bubonic plague."

"People are dying, Mum."

"In the sixties there were multiple thousands of deaths from Hong Kong flu, did you know that? No? Well, there were. Some reports say thirty-thousand, some say eighty. World-wide, there were between one and four million, and as far as I recall life went on pretty much as normal. And the Spanish flu killed nearly two-hundred and thirty thousand in the UK, did you know that?"

"Well, this one could do the same for all we know. However many, or indeed, few, deaths there are, I don't want you to be one of them."

Later, alone again, Margaret sat thinking. *I should have been a bit softer on him,* she thought, remembering his fat baby face; then the skinny adolescent, who was always in trouble for something, and always had wonderful excuses, which were perfectly good reasons in Margaret's eyes.

In no time he became a young man, oval face and eyes, an energy that was infectious. It seemed overnight he'd reached middle-age, face and figure becoming round, as father became grandfather.

So many years. Passed by so fast. What was the point of it all? Knowledge gained and lessons learned, only to go with you to the grave. *What is the point of me?* She wondered; had wondered, ever since John died.

It's probably impossible for Joe to understand, but I have to stay near to John. Now she cried. "Stupid old woman," she said out loud to herself.

Usually, the middle of the shift was the worst part as far as Emerson was concerned. It would be reasonable to assume it was the start, but he didn't mind this, because, feeling fresh meant he could engage in conversation, maybe even some banter, with the customers. After a few hours however, conversation was becoming repetitive, the breaks were all behind him and the clock seemed to slow down.

That was the usual pattern, but of late things had changed and conversation was always repetitive. Coronavirus dominated even more than Brexit had. He didn't mind when there was someone with a different approach, like the old lady the other day for example, she was funny, but there weren't many like her. Mostly people complained about the missing items, expressed contempt for the panic buying, whilst doing the same themselves and, if there was any comment on governance, espoused the view that a strong approach was needed.

Sometimes he had to admit being glad his favoured party weren't in charge under the circumstances, and several times lately he'd wondered how they would have been dealing with the situation. *Don't suppose they'd have dared to do anything different,* he thought, without knowing what he expected the 'different' to be.

Apart from Kirsten, there wasn't even anyone on the staff with whom he could have a candid debate on the subject. Yes, everyone, it seemed, was towing the party line on this one. Mandeep in particular seemed stressed to the max. She wasn't often what you'd call witty, but now it seemed she'd had a sense of humour bypass. He could understand that she was in a difficult situation, she had to been seen to be doing the right thing by her staff and customers, but… *That's what being a manager is about I guess and one reason why I could never be one, but blimey, is she short with us these days.*

In all his reveries concerning the virus it never once occurred to Emerson to consider his interpretation of the situation could be wrong. There was never any doubt in his mind that the accepted view was erroneous.

The two possible correct explanations carried equal weight as far as he was concerned. It was his intention to investigate further. There were people coming out in favour of the 5G argument, some even of celebrity status. Not that that was anything to go by; allowing it on YouTube could be a decoy, celebs had been used in that way before. *All those sources are tools of the state,* he thought, *no such thing as unbiased information. That's why I have to look at it all, think about it, compare and contrast and make up my own mind.*

His musings were interrupted by a customer.

"Still no toilet rolls," she complained. "I've come in every day this week."

"Sorry about that. Did you find everything else you wanted?"

"Bet you lot don't go without nothin'."

"There's a genuine scarcity, sorry."

"Hum." She put her items on the conveyer belt and took up her place on the opposite side of the social distancing tape.

"I'm sorry, I can only let you have two of those bottles of wine," Emerson said.

"Shame you don't ration the toilet rolls," the customer replied, surrendering one of the bottles of wine without complaint.

We would if we had any to ration. "Yes, the shortage is annoying, isn't it?" he said.

"Whole thing is a bloody nightmare. 'Bout time the PM did something decisive. It's not like we didn't know it was coming. World Health warned us, China warned us. I heard there was even a simulation to prepare…"

Emerson's attention was grabbed now. His heart was thumping, the words he wanted to utter were demanding release. *It wasn't just to prepare; it was a dress rehearsal for those who planned this whole thing,* he thought, but said, "You can watch it on YouTube, Event Two Thousand and One, it's called."

"It's been months since it was first reported, they could be halfway to a vaccine now if they'd got their finger out." The customer was now on the other social distancing line packing up her shopping.

If the stories about the virus being engineered are true, they've probably had it since the start. "Yes."

"At the very least they could make sure there was enough PPE to go around. I foresee this getting out of hand. Government's a bloody disgrace."

"No argument with you there."

"So, we're getting a briefing from our glorious leader this evening."

"Seems so."

"I can hardly wait. More war propaganda."

Daniel laughed. "It is a bit like that."

"The question is why, Daniel?"

"Not sure, Mrs. P."

"Divide and rule, yet again. The war on drugs made enemies of the poor; the war on terror of foreigners; this'll make enemies of our neighbours."

"That's a grim idea. You still not worried about the virus?"

"Wouldn't be true to say not at all, but not much."

"Only I was wondering, should I stay away; in light of current advice."

"No, please – unless you…"

"No. I'm just concerned for you."

"Thank you. Don't be." She repeated her discussion with Joe from the day before.

Daniel nodded. "I get all that, but I also get why he'd want you to be with them."

"Yes, I do feel bad for him. By the way, is it okay to give him your phone number? You know, just in case. And I'll give you his."

"Sure."

As she approached the house Kirsten heard shouting. She baulked at the sound of it and the door in her memory, which was always open a crack, took her back to her own experience of motherhood. There were plenty of incidents to choose from; in the one that sprang immediately to mind she was running up the stairs in pursuit of Rosie, who'd called her the worst mother ever. Although she knew she wasn't that, she still felt regret for every angry interaction that had taken place between her and Rosie. Now, she knocked on the door loudly before entering.

"Hi, it's me," she called out.

"Nanny." Ryan ran into her and grabbed her around the knees. Kirsten picked him up, squeezed him and kissed him on the forehead.

He squealed, wrapping his arms around her neck and snuggling into her. Their entry into the living room, still entangled in each other, lent them the look of a mythical creature.

Both Sally and Rosie were in tears, easy access to them wasn't only impaired by Ryan, but also by boxes piled high.

"Oh dear," Kirsten said. "Looks like I've come at a bad time."

"No one asked you to come," Rosie snapped.

Instantly tears leapt to the back of Kirsten's eyes, yet she understood and could hardly criticise. "I can go if you want, but I came to offer help and it looks like it might be needed."

Kirsten put Ryan down and climbed over the boxes to reach the sofa, where daughter and granddaughter both sat. She stood for a moment, then, sitting at the opposite end, still wearing her jacket, she said, "I can cook, pack, or whatever else you'd like, including leave."

"No point in packing." Rosie burst into tears.

"Oh, no. What's happened?" Kirsten slid along the sofa to get closer and wrapped her arms around her daughter, wishing it didn't feel so awkward. "What is it, what's wrong?"

"People renting the house in Devon have pulled out," Rosie spluttered out between sobs.

"Oh no! Why?"

"Why d'you think? Corona-bloody-virus, that's why."

"Aw, Mum, you said a swear," Sally chastised.

Despite everything, both women laughed.

"Sorry," Rosie said. Then, to her mother, "I don't know what to do now. What makes it worse is, because we're the ones causing the delay, we'll have to pay any expenses the buyer accrues."

"That's harsh, it's not your fault."

"Doesn't matter, that's how it works." Rosie fought back tears. "Andy finishes this week. If he can't start that job I don't know what we'll do."

"It's not going to help with that, but you can all stay with me." There wasn't a second's hesitation in the offer.

"It could be ages."

"I know."

"What about social distancing?"

"What about it?"

"Andy's parents don't want us going there anymore."

"Well, I don't mind one bit."

"D'you really think we can all live under that small roof?"

"It won't be easy, but what's the alternative?"

"Where we gonna put all this stuff?" Rosie swept her hand around the room and started to cry again.

"We'll think of something. Buyers are still on?"

"At the moment, but if there is a lockdown…"

"Let's not worry about that yet. One step at a time. You come to my house and we'll sort something out about storage."

Kirsten was thinking of the room in Daniel's workshop but didn't say so.

"It'll cost a bomb."

"You don't need to worry about that."

"You can't pay it, Mum."

"Let me decide what I can or cannot do, please. Now, what's the most useful way to employ myself here?" Kirsten stood up and removed her jacket. "I need to leave just before five."

"*Um,*" Emerson thought, '*well this list of symptoms doesn't have much similarity to coronavirus symptoms, except for extreme and prolonged fatigue.*' He checked through the information from the 5G and health site again. '*No mention of respiratory symptoms, but still, it's not good, I didn't realise it'd be like sitting in a micro-wave.*' He checked the time in the corner of the screen, almost time for the speech, so he switched his television on.

A few minutes later the briefing was in full flow.

"Information based on scrupulously best scientific advice! Since when have your lot been interested in scruples?" he shout-ed at the screen. "Save lives? Don't make me fucking laugh!"

"Emerson! Emerson!" The second shout was louder and more insistent.

"Yeah? What? I'm watching something important."

"Keep your voice down, will you? And cut the language out."

"Yeah, whatever," he said under his breath, then, "Okay, sorry," out loud.

Kirsten tapped on the door and crept in quietly, Daniel was sitting in front of the television, as expected. She pecked him on the forehead and sat down next to him.

"Tea?" he asked.

"After this."

"I'm only paying minimal attention." But he didn't take his eyes from the screen. Kirsten sat down beside him, leaving her coat on.

When it was finished Kirsten went to the kitchen and put the kettle on. After it was made, she brought the two cups of tea back and sat down again.

"That bit about people dying indirectly as a result of not being able to get treatment for other conditions is tantamount to saying the lockdowns will kill people."

Daniel sighed, "Yeah, and 'negative effects of the measures we take'." He turned to look directly at Kirsten for the first time since she'd arrived. "God know where this'll end up."

"I want to ask you something, Daniel."

He sat bolt upright and started looking around the room.

"Don't get all defensive, it's nothing to do with our…" Kirsten hesitated, looking for the right word. "Nothing personal about you and me."

Daniel sighed and his shoulders relaxed down. "What then? What is it?"

"There's a problem with Rosie's house sale."

"Aw."

"The buyers are still in, but the house Rosie and Andy were renting has fallen through. I said they can stay with me, but they need somewhere to store the furniture."

"My workshop? Yeah, sure, just need a couple of days to move stuff around."

"Naturally. Thank you so much. We'll pay of course."

"I shouldn't worry too much. I'll fetch some things in the van a bit at a time."

"Oh, it'll be such a relief for her. Thank you." She grabbed hold of Daniel to hug him and planted a kiss on his mouth.

He recoiled, then, realising his mistake, put both arms around her and returned the hug, but turned his body slightly away from her. He patted her on the back.

❧

Daniel got up half an hour early so that he could clear some of the shed. He'd agreed with Kirsten to go straight from work and fetch some boxes. *I hope it's dry enough in here,* he thought. *The last thing they need is damp ruining their furniture. Still, the weather will soon be improving and we won't need to worry for a while.*

He almost forgot the time in his busyness, so was late arriving at Margaret's house.

"What d'you make of the Johnson speech?" she asked him.

He sighed. "Not sure. If he plans on keeping the economy growing, we can't follow the rest of Europe into a lockdown, and yet there were hints that we're headed that way."

"Yes, I thought that. When he said there'd be some deaths as a result of the measures they put in place, I thought, it seems like choosing who the victims will be. At least if we leave it to the virus, it's God's decision. All that talk about keeping us safe made me feel like vomiting."

Daniel laughed, he should be used to her by now, but she never ceased to amuse him. "I guess we can rely on you not to follow the advice and stay home."

"You can be as sure of that as that they'll cock up the country."

He laughed again. "You never let me down Mrs P. I'm coming to do that door at the weekend. I've made another, thought it best."

"Oh, you're too good to me."

"Best get on then." Daniel stood up, rubbing his hands together. "See you tomorrow."

As Kirsten reached the end of the chapter, she checked the time. Too late to start the next. She was eating her pasta bake as she read. She closed the book and put it down on the table in front of the pile of those waiting to be read. How she had often wondered, could anyone think they'd be bored without a job when there were so many books to read?

Really, she liked to snack at lunchtimes and have her main meal in the evening, but this wasn't possible when she didn't finish work until ten. She washed the dishes and took from the fridge her bottle of water and the sandwich she'd prepared earlier. Opening the door to check the weather she sighed – *still no sign of spring.*

The walk to the supermarket allowed transition from home to work mode, it was a necessary process as far as Kirsten was concerned. *I'd never get it together to work from home,* she thought. *Far too many distractions, far too many more interesting things to occupy my mind. I'd have to have a really interesting job, or a lot more discipline, if I was going to do that.* Her musings were interrupted by a woman approaching her, pushing a double buggy and clinging tightly to a third child by his wrist. Kirsten smiled at them, and stepped into the road to allow access.

"Thanks," the woman said, but her expression remained blank.

Kirsten felt inclined to offer an explanation about lack of passing space being the reason and not fear of catching the virus. It felt rude to her, somehow, to think of a fellow human as a potential disease source. With this thought she noticed how many people were hopping on and off pavements and standing aside to let others pass.

Inside the supermarket it was the same, people waiting at the bottom of aisles allowing others to take items before them.

Just outside the break room Kirsten met Mandeep, who looked distracted.

"Hi," Kirsten said, "how are things with your mother-in-law?"

"What? Sorry?"

"Things not good? With Dev's mum?"

"She's still alive, if that's what you mean. We're taking each day as it comes. You know he's out there?"

"I didn't; no wonder you look so stressed."

"He could get stuck there." Mandeep blurted the words out in a way that suggested this thought had been dominating her mind for some time, her eyes were watery.

"I suppose he'll come back as soon as she...it's...as soon as he can?"

"Yes, but the way things are now... I, I know it sounds awful, I wouldn't say this to many people, but I wish she would... I wish it would hurry up and happen."

Now Mandeep bit her lip to stop the flow of tears. Kirsten's inclination was to hug her; instead she patted her shoulder.

"It's not awful. I felt like that with Greg..."

"You did?"

"Yes, when it was inevitable, and his suffering was continuous. It's best for everyone."

"I'm so scared he won't be able to get home."

"D'you want a hug?"

"Yes, but better not, it's not recommended at the moment," Mandeep said, with a half-hearted laugh, putting her hands up and stepping back slightly in emphasis.

The words arrested Kirsten just in time, who had already made the move towards Mandeep. It felt like a terrible day indeed when she couldn't comfort a friend with a hug.

Nabil closed the notebook and shut down YouTube on his phone, that was enough English for one day. He pushed aside the duvet and climbed from the bed, then stood with his ear pressed to the bedroom door. Silence. Still, he only opened it a crack, enough to check the landing was really empty and to listen for sounds from downstairs. When he was sure there was no one else around he took his bread, cheese and spread, crept down the stairs and into the kitchen.

The mess that greeted him sent him into a rage. *How is any-one to stay safe from illness in this filth?* He washed down the work top, took a plate from the cupboard and a knife from the drawer, tutting at the grease and bits of food inside the latter. He boiled the kettle as he washed the plate and knife in soapy water, then tipped the boiling water over them both, he looked around for something clean enough to dry them, but finding nothing, took them, and the food, to his room. Once there he dried them with a T-shirt from his drawer, then prepared the sandwich, which he accompanied with a glass of water. He decided to buy his own utensils and cleaning products to keep in his room. It would be safer that way, in every respect.

He remembered home. Water spilling on the floor as his mother cleaned in preparation for the meal, then, on her hands and knees scrubbing the floor. The scent of fresh air in the crisp bedding came to mind as he climbed into bed and pulled his own, musty smelling, around his shoulders. His heart became heavy. *Just keep your mind busy,* he told himself.

After eating, Nabil donned his coat, hat, and gloves, put his notebook and pen in the bag and headed out of the house.

The atmosphere in the street put him on alert. It took him home in his thoughts once more. Something was wrong, the air had changed, indifference replaced by watchfulness. People in masks were making just enough eye contact to ensure the stranger kept out of the way. They were stepping off pavements, and into doorways, stopping in their tracks to allow others to pass.

Nabil hurried to his destination. The only place that still offered him sanctuary. The library doors were closed, and the lights were off.

*

When she heard the announcement, Mandeep's stomach sank. *This virus must be worse than they're telling us. How am I going to work with the girls at home?* And yet, home was where she wanted them.

Mandeep looked towards her daughters, both of whom were sitting at the dining table doing their homework. The responsibility for protecting them was hers alone. It was a burden too big to bear. Her inclination was to run to Dev. Without that possibility, the only option left, was prayer. She'd offer God any bargain asked for, just as long as they stayed safe.

Manjit looked up from her work. "What the matter?" she asked her mother.

"The schools are being closed. I'll have to see if you can go to Grandma and Granddad's, otherwise I can't go to work."

"We'll be okay on our own."

"No, not all day."

"Some people at school are really scared," Indrani said.

"Are you?" her mother asked, trying to keep the fear from her own voice.

"A bit."

It sounded as if she felt no right to be afraid. At once Mandeep lost her own fear.

"They keep on saying that mostly it's older people who are already ill who are at risk."

"So why are they closing the schools?" Manjit asked.

"Isn't asthma an underlying health condition?" Indrani asked.

Oh, my word, she has been worrying. "You're young." Mandeep offered reassurance that she didn't fully believe in, in as light a tone as she could muster. "And your asthma isn't that bad."

She sat down beside her daughter and rubbed her back. "You'll be fine, try not to be scared."

Indrani cried, "I wish it would just go away, and I wish Dad was here."

Me too. "He'll be back soon."

As soon as she was sure they couldn't be overheard by the children Mandeep called her parents. Her father answered.

"The schools are closing from Friday."

"Yes."

"Will it be okay to leave the girls with you when I'm at work?"

"We're supposed to be self-isolating. An hour or so after school is one thing, but all day, I'm not so sure."

Tears stung the back of Mandeep's eyes. "What'll I do? They're too young to leave alone all day."

"If it's money we can help."

"Thank you, I appreciate that, but longer term...I can't afford to lose my job."

"When's Dev back?"

"Not sure."

"He shouldn't have gone – not under the circumstances."

Well, he did, Mandeep thought, feeling angry with him and protective of him at the same time. "There wasn't really much choice."

"Under normal circumstances I'd agree, but...I'll speak with your mother and call you back."

"Thanks. If you can just help me get through the next week."

"You think Dev'll be back then? I think India will shut its borders any day now."

The words, and especially the tone, sent a shock wave through Mandeep, her stomach clenched, and her ears rang, she felt rage boiling inside her, as if the whole notion of a lockdown was only possible because her father had voiced it.

As soon as the call ended, she was on the phone to Dev.

"I'll have to think about coming home, let's get through this week and take it from there," he said.

Now Mandeep's rage was transferred to him, *that might be too long,* she thought, but she didn't say anything.

There were voices in the room. Nabil's heart was racing and sweat soaked his skin. *Turn on the light. Make them go away.* But he couldn't reach the switch without sitting up and fear gripped him; he knew it would seize his spine if he didn't keep it pushed against the mattress. Someone was so close they were almost on top of him, he could hear their rasping breath, so close it restricted his own. "No, no, no," he cried out loud, jumping up and hitting the switch, illuminating the room.

No one. Only me. For a second his breath continued to pound in his ears, sounding as if it belonged to someone else. He slowed it, then pulled the duvet up to his chin and his knees to his chest. He curled into a hug and cried.

He lay down again, keeping the light on and the duvet over his head. He lay on his left side, then on his right, both left him feeling exposed, so he lay on his back. Now it became impossible to block the light from his eyes, unless he pulled the duvet over his face, but that felt like suffocating.

The lack of a lampshade made the light interrogation-room stark, but darkness brought the risk of ghosts. Nabil stretched inside his cocoon and pulled his phone into it to check the time. Two-ten, so much of the night remained.

Time in front of him was endless and empty. Time behind him was like a film on a loop.

The alarm ringing at seven was a relief; Kirsten had spent a restless night, waking every hour since one. Finally, it wasn't too early to get up. She did so without enthusiasm. Thursday was normally her favourite day, but that was because she usually had volunteering at the centre to look forward to. She checked the message on her phone again:

Due to the coronavirus the centre is closing for the foreseeable future, therefore we don't need you to come in tomorrow. Someone will phone you soon with a full explanation.

When she first looked at it, it had read like an apocalyptic forecast. Now she felt sad more than afraid. She had so many questions, not least amongst them, *what will all those vulnerable clients do?*

She headed for the kitchen and put the kettle on for tea. Making tea brought her thoughts back to the clients. *Marie and those like her will be okay. She has her support workers, and they're always going off somewhere doing stuff; that is, unless they send us into total lockdown and stop us moving around at all.* At this thought Kirsten felt her stomach lurch and her heart stop for a second. *Suppose I can't get to see Daniel?*

She was reminded of the scene in Nineteen-Eighty-Four; such empathy she felt for Winston, as he stood back to back with his lover. Worse than the betrayal was the knowledge he must face what lay ahead alone. Anything was bearable when shared, little was bearable when not. *I wonder how much he would mind?* She asked herself. *How long it would take him to miss me? Would he miss me at all?*

It was a while since she'd asked the question directly. The last time she had, he'd said:

'*I'll be seeing you again next weekend.*'

'But if you weren't?'

'That's daft, I will be.'

'Will you miss me until then?'

'I don't really miss people.'

'*But I'm not people, am I?*'

He'd laughed, but not replied.

Although she knew by now it was not about her, but Daniel's inability to show strong feelings, sometimes it left her feeling bereft just the same. *Yes, I wonder, would he miss me?*

The thought of separation brought Mandeep to mind, *It's so much worse for her. They've never been apart before, poor things.*

She took a sip of her tea. *I'm pathetic. Worrying about whether I'll be able to see Daniel for a while, I've learned to live without Greg for ever, haven't I?* She sighed. *Imagine how it is for all those poor people who are kept away from their families; people whose children live somewhere on the other side of the world. Refugees who might never see their families again, don't even know if they're still alive.*

The thought was terrifying, it felt like standing on the edge of a cliff.

It brought Nabil to mind. *He was just starting to integrate a little. I hope someone phones to explain today. I need to know what's going on.'*

She showered and ate breakfast whilst listening to the news on the radio. Coronavirus was the only news, it seemed, and every bit of it inched towards the outcome she most dreaded. Illness, even death, were as nothing compared to the fear that free movement would be taken away from her.

It was still only eight-fifteen. The whole day stretched ahead. It wasn't that there was nothing to do, indeed many times she'd complained that there wasn't enough time for the things she enjoyed. Now, with Rosie and Andy moving in soon, there was even more to do.

She sent Daniel the usual good morning text, then went upstairs.

I'll move my stuff out of the bedroom today. My clothes can go in the airing cupboard, the kids'll need the wardrobe and chest of drawers in the spare room for their stuff.

She opened the wardrobe and sifted through the clothes hanging there, wondering which clothes to hang and which to put into bags. *I need a seasonal selection,* she thought, not wanting to be either too optimistic about the weather, or too pessimistic about the length of their stay. *Much as I love them it's not going to be easy. As long as I can escape to Daniel's every weekend it should be manageable.* The feeling of uncertainty regarding him crept back; she quickly banished it.

Her phone rang and she ran downstairs, reaching it just in time for it to stop. It was a cold call, not the one she hoped for. *I wonder what their idea of 'soon' is.* Whatever it was, it wasn't soon enough for her.

&

Daniel was thinking about Kirsten as he drove towards the wood. *Shame about the volunteer post though, I know how much she enjoys it.* He did admire how she cared so much about people.

I wonder what the situation with our temporary staff will be, if there's a lckdown. The van bounced its way over the uneven ground and then he brought it to a stop. *I'll certainly be busy if they don't take them on. Could end up with too much to do at this rate. Which reminds me, I best go to the cash and carry on the way home, get some flour.* He breathed out, long and slow, his hair blew up from his forehead. *They're going to do it, I'm sure. Nice excuse for the economic crash. Still, things do look bad in Italy. Best to keep eyes and mind open for now.*

He gathered his tools together and headed deeper into the wood, on foot. *Whatever the truth is, a lockdown can only make it worse. Swap one problem for another, or a host of others.*

Imagining how solitude felt for those who didn't enjoy it, was difficult for Daniel, but Kirsten had said, '*You know how nervous you feel around people sometimes? And how you crave your own company in order to stay sane? Well, for me it's exactly the opposite of that. If I'm alone too long, I feel I'll lose my mind.*'

He wondered how she would react to a lockdown, in that case. He wondered, too, how strictly it would be imposed. If the television coverage were anything to go by, and it might well be a propaganda exercise, he knew, but if true, the Spanish police were patrolling the streets. It was difficult to imagine anything of that scale in England, but if that happened, then the three miles between them may as well be thirty.

There was a text message and a missed call, Nabil discovered upon his return from the shower.

The missed call was from Abdul. The text message from the Home Office. At the site of it, Nabil's knees turned to jelly. Could be about his hearing. He couldn't wait to see Abdul and ask him to translate. Without credit on his phone, he was unable to return the call, but in a couple of hours they were due to meet at the centre.

Nabil poured cereal into the bowl he now kept in his room, took the lid off the milk, and sniffed it before pouring. After eating, he took the bowl to the kitchen along with his cup, and made himself coffee, and washed and dried his bowl and spoon.

Back in his room he was annoyed to find he'd missed a second call from Abdul. *Why's he keep calling?* He thought, feeling anxious because it seemed whatever it was couldn't wait until their meeting. He sighed, because without credit he couldn't even make a prank call.

And, without credit there was no internet either, so no YouTube while he waited for the time to pass. It hardly mattered, he didn't have enough concentration anyway after the night he'd had. He avoided getting into bed, because sleep was bound to claim him when he needed to stay awake; it was only when he desired it that it refused to come.

This time the phone was in his hand when Abdul called. It was with news about the centre's closure. Nabil felt sick and hot in response to the news; everyone had assured him there was nothing to fear from this virus.

"You said there was nothing to worry about." Nabil's tone was almost accusatory.

"There's been no cases recorded in this area."

"So, why they close?"

"Following Government advice," Abdul told him. "Sorry, I think you were starting to enjoy it."

"Um." Enjoy it? He didn't enjoy anything, but it was something to do. "I have a text from Home Office."

"You can forward it to me."

"I don't have credit. Can you come here?"

"No, sorry. I'm not supposed to do that."

"Meet by the clock?"

"We could do, but not today. When you get credit send me the text and I'll phone you."

Nabil got up and paced the room.

"I don't have money until next week." he said.

"I think if it was urgent, they would have phoned."

But I want to know, Nabil thought, feeling like a little boy. "Can we meet tomorrow?"

"Maybe. I'll let you know."

"The library is closed."

"I know. I'm sorry." Abdul hung up

One, two, three, four, five, six, Nabil counted as he paced, then turned around, as he reached the wall.

One, two, three, four, five, six, seven, Nabil had shortened his paces. A door banged at the end of the landing; Nabil jumped.

Outside the traffic noise built to a crescendo, then died away, leaving a brief silence before it started again.

A box on the floor served as Nabil's pantry, the bath as his fridge. He checked the contents of both and decided there was enough of everything except milk, until his next payment. He could spend ten pounds on credit.

The local shop was hardly more than two hundred metres away. He could run there and back in no time. Nabil picked up his boots and sat on the edge of the bed with them in his hand. He put them down. He picked them up. His throat felt dry and constricted. He put them down, licked his dry lips; picked them up, put them on. *Come on, just two minutes,* he encouraged himself.

He stood up, opened the door a crack and looked out onto an empty landing. Leaving the door of his room unlocked for speed he hurried down the stairs.

On the front doorstep stood a man. Nabil's whole body jerked, then froze and a cry escaped him, sounding to his ears as if it belonged to another person. It took a while to a second or two before it registered who it was.

"Hey, sorry, didn't mean to scare you." Abdul put his hands up as if submitting to something.

"I'm going to the shop for credit." Nabil's body was working independently of him, it kept moving forward despite Abdul being in his path.

"Whoa!" Abdul said.

Nabil stopped.

"You'll want this if you're getting credit." Abdul handed him a twenty-pound note.

Nabil stared at it as if it held some terrifying secret.

"I felt bad for you," Abdul explained. "Go get your credit and then I'll take a look at that text."

"Thank you, thank you." Nabil put his hands in prayer and bowed his head. He ran to the shop.

"Credit please," he said, presenting his phone and the money.

The man behind the counter was wearing latex gloves and a mask. "Put them down there."

Nabil hesitated, unsure of the instruction.

"Put them down there." The salesman raised his voice and pointed towards the counter.

Nabil put the money and the phone in the spot that was indicated. The salesman nodded his head, picked them both up and delivered the phone and the payment card back to the same spot.

"Thank you," Nabil bowed his head.

Back on the doorstep he said to Abdul, "I can pay you back on Monday."

"It's a gift."

"No, I…"

"Please," Abdul took both of Nabil's hands in his. "Please."

"Thank you." Nabil bowed his head again.

"Welcome. Now, show me the text."

Nabil handed over his phone.

"Ah, it says signing is suspended. You don't need to go to the reporting centre until further notice."

"Oh." This wasn't what Nabil had hoped for. He felt like he'd woken up on an empty stomach to find there was nothing for breakfast.

❧

Although she'd been expecting it, and thought herself prepared, nevertheless, this step towards the total lockdown came as a shock. A cold shiver ran the length of Mandeep's spine. The announcement that all pubs, clubs, and restaurants were being ordered to close sounded like a declaration of an alien invasion. Dev was going to have to come home now.

"I think we'll be in full lockdown within a few days," Mandeep told her husband, later.

"Yes, I agree, I'm coming home."

The relief was like reaching shallow waters after being stuck in the tide, "I want you home of course, but…"

"No buts, there's nothing more I can do for Mum. The family will have to understand."

"But you're the eldest."

"I said no buts, I'm coming home just as soon as I can."

At bedtime Mandeep cuddled into the pillow that usually supported Dev's head, feeling more relaxed than since he left.

"Hello." Kirsten could only tell how to press 'accept' on the phone because it was green. She could see neither the word nor the name of the caller without her glasses. Tears had made their removal necessary; tears that flowed in response to the briefing.

"Hi, Mum, it's me. You okay? You sound like you've been crying."

"Just a bit upset. Lockdown seems inevitable now. Are you calling about tomorrow?"

"Yes, but also to say buyers are trying to push it forward even more."

"Hardly surprising under the circumstances. Forward to when?"

"As soon as we can manage it. I said Wednesday, we have moved it forward already after all."

"Indeed."

"I get why they're worried. I'm so scared of losing the sale so close. When will you be ready for us?"

"Pretty much am, but are you ready?"

"Looks like we'll bloody well have to be."

"Should be okay," Daniel said, from his end of the phone. "We'll start tomorrow and do a bit each day."

"What if they put an end to free movement next week?"

"We'll cross that bridge when we come to it. Outhouses are ready."

"Oh, thanks, Daniel."

"I'll pick you up at nine. Have a good evening."

"You too. Love you."

"Bye, then. Bye."

Kirsten held the phone in her hand for a while looking at it, as if she were expecting him to call back. "Love you too," she said, but, much as she wanted to hear it, she didn't want any lies.

Margaret stood staring at the television, somehow she'd never really believed it would come to this, despite all the signs. She beat the eggs so vigorously that her arm ached.

The onion was just turning to a light brown. "Overcooked, thanks to those bastards." She poured the egg on top and watched it slowly form before sprinkling the cheese all over. She put the salad on her plate whilst waiting for the omelette to finish off under the grill.

On the television there was no escape, even the channels that didn't feature it directly had coronavirus messages running the length of the screen. *Can't even relax while I eat my supper.* She turned the television off and the radio on, feeling pleased and surprised that the Archers was transmitting as normal. *No virus in Ambridge, thank God for small mercies.*

Usually, Margaret left the washing up until the morning, but this evening there were emotions that produced restlessness. She not only did the dishes, she swept and washed the floor too, then sat back down in her chair and picked up her book. *Might as well start this, anyway.*

Before she opened it Margaret sat a while and reflected on the situation with the book club. This week she'd been the only person to arrive to hear the announcement that they would be moving onto Zoom. *Much as I love to hate them, I will miss them. It won't be the same online.* She turned the book over and read the reviews on the back, even though she knew the story, having read it years before. *I've been looking forward to this one.*

The phone rang, making her jump. It was Joe.

"I'm still hoping to change your mind, Mum. After this weekend it'll be too late."

"I know, I haven't, don't worry I'll be fine."

But would she? Living alone was fine when she knew there were options for seeing other people. The threat of immobility or dementia were enemies she kept at bay with her activities, fear of them moved a little closer now. It was as if she had only just noticed the pawn gradually creep across the chessboard until it was almost at the other side. And the virus? A seed of fear planted itself at the base of her spine, as she considered the possibility that she would fall victim to it. She turned the television back on, suddenly hungry for news on how it was advancing.

"We should go into the removals business," Daniel said with some pride, as he stacked the final kitchen chair into his van.

"You've done well," Kirsten said.

"Yes, we have," he agreed. "So, we'll pick up what's left as soon as it's ready. That'll just leave the cooker."

"The man's coming to dismantle it on Wednesday, can't do it before." Andy said. "If he shows – I have my doubts."

Daniel shrugged. "I know someone who will, if he doesn't."

"Great. Cheers mate." Andy offered his hand, hesitantly, wondering if he should elbow bump instead. Daniel accepted it.

"I'm off tomorrow," Kirsten said. "We'll get the rest ready then and do the last bit of cleaning."

"I wouldn't worry too much on that," Andy said, "after the way they rushed us."

Daniel and Andy drove off. Kirsten, Rosie and the children stood surveying the almost empty house. The upstairs echoed in response to their footfalls, only one wardrobe and a chest of drawers remained.

Rosie sighed deeply. "It all has an unreality about it."

"Moving always feels a bit like that."

"Thanks so much for letting us stay. I hope we won't be there too long."

"You can stay as long as needed."

Rosie sighed again. "I can just imagine having to move it all back in."

"Oh don't. Come on then, let's go and get the dinner on. I expect you two are hungry," she said to the children.

Sharing the meal preparation was nice. It felt close and homely.

"I hope the kids'll be okay in the same bed," Kirsten said. "Mind you, if it turns out to be a problem, or goes on for some time, we could always put their singles in and store that one."

"I'm more worried about you on the floor on that mattress."

"Don't be, I'll be fine. Well, I reckon we can leave this now. Let's have a cuppa while we wait for everyone else to arrive. Good job I've got a big kitchen table. Should've got some crackers, it's like Christmas."

On the third circuit of the park Nabil started to feel warm enough to remove his jacket. He sat down on one of the benches, to prolong his time outside. He watched.

A metre or so from his feet two pigeons strode around, their heads bobbing, and chests stuck out like men spoiling for a fight. They looked intent on the task, scratting for food, Nabil presumed, but they were alert enough to flee their human companions when they came too close.

There were fewer people here than usual. A woman with a pushchair came by, the two children sitting one behind the other, one sleeping, the other crying. The mother's face was blank, she paid the screaming child no heed.

A young man circled on a skateboard, talking to an invisible companion, earphones sparing him from madman status. An elderly couple walked hand in hand, heads down, stopping every few metres and looking around.

Images of his people kept creeping into Nabil's mind, but he banished them. Memories were sacred and all he had left of the past, he didn't want to share them with these strangers.

The clock struck two. Without knowing why Nabil checked the time on his phone. Then he checked the contacts, as if in so doing their numbers would increase.

I'll go back in an hour, he thought. *Might as well be bored here as in my room.* Whoever would have guessed that boredom would become his worst enemy?

Less than an hour to go to the end of the shift. Emerson felt exhausted. They weren't even as busy as this in the lead up to Christmas. He watched two customers fighting over the last pack of toilet rolls. And another piling tinned tomatoes into her trolley. He shook his head, wondering what hope there was, come the apocalypse.

A customer arrived at his till and began unloading. He wore a face mask and rubber gloves and was almost throwing his shopping onto the conveyer belt.

"Just want to get out of here," he explained. "Can't say I ever much enjoyed shopping, but now..."

"Did you find everything you want?" It was an automatic, well-practised response.

"Course not, no tomatoes, no bloody toilet rolls again, but I'm not behaving like that, not in a million," he tossed his head back towards the aisles. "If I was the manager, I'd ration them."

Emerson didn't comment.

"Those of us supposed to be self-isolating have to keep coming out for the stuff we couldn't get last time."

"Do you need any bags?" Emerson asked.

"What I need is to only have to come in here once a week."

Emerson nodded. "Need any help packing?"

"You haven't even got gloves on."

Emerson took a pair from under the counter and started to put them on.

"No, no, it's all right. I can do it myself."

The man limped off. Emerson was annoyed with the customer for almost provoking him into glove use. He put them back under the counter.

❧

"There are times when I wish I'd got a dishwasher," Kirsten said to Daniel, who was helping her with the washing up.

"I'll do it if you like, only fair, you cooked."

"But I like cooking. Nearly done now, anyway. One good thing is, I'll sleep well. You did bring that mattress, didn't you?"

"No."

Kirsten paused in her task, she checked the tone of her voice as she said, "I did remind you."

"I thought perhaps you could stay at mine. Until they move out, I mean."

She stopped what she was doing again and turned to look at him, feeling like his girlfriend for the first time.

"That's a very generous offer. Thank you, I'd love to, if you're sure."

Daniel lowered his gaze. "Yeah."

Turning her phone back on after evening prayers Mandeep noticed there was a voicemail from Dev, *'Call me please.'*

Her heart leapt and sank at the same time. When they'd spoken earlier he'd said, "I can't see her lasting the day out, but if she does, I'll book the flight anyway. I'll get the first one available."

Mandeep clicked on his name, guessing what the news would be at the time of night it was there. He answered immediately.

"She's gone," Dev said, "just over an hour ago."

Mandeep tried to keep the relief from her voice. "I'm so sorry. How was it? How are you?"

"Okay. I'm okay."

"And your dad?"

"Well as you'd expect. It's been a long time coming, still when it does…"

Mandeep waited for more.

"I'll stay for the funeral now, naturally, since it's only a few days."

The words caused her stomach and throat to constrict. Disappointment blunted her words. "Of course." Fear sharpened her senses.

"It's best to do it all the right way."

"Yes."

"I'll be back by the end of the week."

"Yes." Mandeep felt her voice beginning to break and didn't want Dev to hear it. "I'll go and tell the girls. Speak tomorrow. I hope the rest of your night is okay. Love to everyone. Love you."

As soon as she hung up, the tears flowed, feeling like razors ripping her throat.

"You absolutely stink of cigarettes; it doesn't create a good impression with the customers."

"Sorry." Emerson shoved a mint in his mouth.

"It'll take more than mints to get rid."

"So, what you want me to do, Mand?"

"I don't want you to do anything. I'm just saying." She turned her attention on the next victim. "Sam, how long have you been on your break?"

"I'm just going back now." Sam shot Emerson a conspiratorial glance.

Mandeep went charging off towards the shop floor.

Emerson shrugged his shoulders at Sam then went to relieve Kirsten for her break. He looked around to ensure there were no customers before saying, "What's eating Mandeep? She snapped my head off about smelling of fags."

You do, Kirsten thought, but said, "Don't take it personally, I think she has stuff going on."

"It's not like her, but we've all got *stuff* going on, right now."

"Some more than others, though. See you later."

Kirsten looked in on Mandeep's office before going for her break, but she wasn't there. In the break room the television was on. *I wish people'd turn this off when they leave,* she thought, turning it off herself. She made tea and sat down with it, then turned on her phone. No messages, that was good, everything must be okay then. Daniel was fetching the last of the boxes from the house later, leaving the house empty except for the cooker. In her bag was the book she was currently reading, but she didn't dare start a new chapter because it was too hard to stop when she needed to. *How wonderful it would be to write a novel that someone couldn't put down,'* she thought.

Since her late teens Kirsten had harboured the desire to write. Lack of time and confidence were the two biggest inhibitors. Excuses some would say. Greg's death had brought her the closest. She'd written reams on how she felt and threatened herself with fictionalising it into a novel, but nine more years had passed without her doing so.

She put the book down and switched her phone off, but not before noticing the news headline reminding of the Prime Minister's pending address to the nation. Daniel's suggestion that she stay with him had come as a very pleasant surprise. If there were to be a lockdown at least they would be together.

On the way back to the shop floor she bumped into Mandeep. Her face was like thunder.

"You look really stressed." Kirsten observed. "Home? Work? Both?"

"Both. All these fucking restrictions – now they want us to get people queuing outside."

Kirsten had never heard her manager swear before, and, in fact, would have thought her incapable.

"And the schools closing have really caused me a problem, with Dev still away."

So, that was it. She was still separated from the man she loved and knew the danger of it being prolonged. No one understood better than Kirsten, the pain of separation and the fear of loss.

"Aren't they open for essential workers children?"

"It would be like sending them into the Lion's den. I'm not doing it."

"I get that. Your mother-in-law still hanging on?"

"No, but he is, until after the funeral." Mandeep burst into tears.

"Hey, hey," Kirsten shepherded her along the corridor and into her office, closed the door, put her arms around her and waited for the tears to subside.

By the time they left the office Kirsten had offered her help with childcare.

❧

"Such lengths the BBC go to, to boost their ratings," Daniel joked, putting the two cups of coffee down, then sitting down himself. "Most of the nation will be watching, no doubt, even though we know what's coming."

And, when it was announced, Kirsten felt like she had been dropped into an apocalyptic film. She imagined roadblocks; the police stopping cars, or approaching people in the street asking for ID and sending them away from their destinations; children being wrenched from their mothers' arms. The thought was terrifying. Enforced separation; there was nothing worse. *Poor, poor Mandeep*.

Her musings were interrupted.

"It doesn't make sense to me. If you save one life, you'll sacrifice another. People will feel too scared or too guilty to use the NHS."

For a second Kirsten felt another kind of fear. "You don't think it could be worse than they're saying do you?"

"Possible, but I doubt it. Virus? Maybe. Lockdowns are definitely nothing to do with it, though, judging by what's going on with the market."

That someone else was responsible for deciding what she did, or did not do, that sanctions could be brought against those who did not comply, made Kirsten feel she'd been robbed of her humanity. She recalled a trip to the zoo when Rosie was a child. Greg and his daughter had moved on to the giraffes, but she was stuck with the empty-eyed gorilla who, it seemed to her, had lost even the will to shake the bars of his cage.

"Don't make me fucking laugh."

"Emerson, watch your language in front of your mother."

Like I said, don't make me fucking laugh. He hated this man, who messed his mother around so much, behaving like he cared more about her than Emerson himself did. "She's heard it plenty of times before. Anyway, what *they're* saying is obscene. Protect the NHS, since when did the Tory Party do that?" *And it's obscene having to sit here and watch it with you two, like that.*

Emerson's mother and her boyfriend were cuddled into each other.

"Even so, I'd rather you didn't speak like that in front of your mother while I can hear it."

Fine when you can't then, eh? "Well, knew that was coming," he said, in response to the announcement. "I'm going to my room."

I don't know what this is, but I know what it isn't, and I'm going to find out. Emerson felt a responsibility to be the whistle blower.

Rosie clung onto Andy's hand as if it were an anchor. The tide of emotions pulled hard against it. The noises from upstairs gave the impression of feral children. Someone needed to respond to them soon.

Andy put his arm around his wife, "It's not like we didn't know this was coming."

"I'm so worried about the house. I don't suppose they'll be able to move in now."

"They seem pretty determined. I'll give them a call in a bit."

"If we haven't got that money…"

"I know."

"You should've withdrawn your notice," Rosie said in an accusatory tone.

"Oh, come on." He withdrew his arm from her shoulder.

Rosie sighed, she turned her eyes towards the ceiling in response to the bump that resounded from upstairs.

"I'd better go and see what's going on," she said, standing up. "Hey, I'm sorry, it's just so frustrating knowing your work colleagues are all furloughed and not having to worry."

"Yeah," Andy sighed too. "I'll give the buyers a call." But as he got up to do so his phone rang. "This is them."

There was an even louder crash from the bedroom. Rosie ran up the stairs two at a time. The children were taking it in turns to jump off the bed. *Mum's neighbours'll love us,* she thought.

"Right," she said. "Sorry to spoil your fun, but it's too noisy." It was also too early for Netflix, but she was desperate to know what was being said to Andy. She deployed the laptop, but there was no consensus over what to watch.

"Right, I'm putting Peppa Pig on, if you think it's too baby-ish, Sally, you can come downstairs and watch some CBeebies."

Sally was already glued to Peppa Pig. Rosie hurried back downstairs.

Andy was sitting with his head in his hands.

"Well?" Rosie asked.

Andy sighed. "It depends on the removal company, chances are they will have to cancel. They're not backing out, they're keen to leave the rental."

Rosie propped herself against the door frame, "I'll not be able to relax until they're in."

"Me neither."

"And I think we'll be here for ages."

There were shouts from upstairs again. Rosie sighed. "No school, no garden and we didn't even need to come here." She moved towards the stairs.

"I'll go." Andy said.

The televisual images left Nabil in little doubt of the severity of the message. The Prime Minister he recognised and his grave expression spoke volumes.

He turned it off and went to his room to await the call he knew would come. He didn't have to wait long.

"Nabil, it's Abdul. I have to tell you that now you're only allowed to go out for shopping or for a one-hour walk. The British Government are ordering this, you must be careful to stick to it, or your asylum case might be affected. Understand?"

"Yes," he said, experiencing an involuntary slip in time.

The agent shook him awake, at the same time he put a hand over Nabil's mouth and raised his forefinger to his own lips in warning. Nabil sat up, nodded in response to the silence order and followed him through the dense darkness to the truck.

This was the third attempt. The first time the driver returned too quickly. His shouts were intended to warn the authorities, but Nabil ran too fast for them. The second time the gendarmes found them and sent them to prison, then back to the camp to await deportation. He was lucky to have this chance before the dawning of that day.

The look-out beckoned them on. Nabil held onto the side of the truck and pulled himself up, then scrambled to the back, where two more pairs of watchful eyes looked out from behind the freezers. All three squared themselves against the wall of the truck, hardly daring to breath. It would be many hours before they felt free to do so again.

This was a fruit and vegetable truck, the best kind, Nabil had been told, because the mix of smells confused the tracker dogs. Nevertheless, their snuffles, only inches from him, were as fearsome as a tiger's growl.

The sound of the doors closing and the engine starting, were both terrifying and a relief. Freedom beckoned, but

*the threat of discovery loomed, and every stop of the truck
lent weight to that fear.*

Nabil was sure he could manage a couple of weeks of confinement in his room.

❦

"What time's dinner, Mum?"

Mandeep was transfixed by the television screen. She felt like she was standing on a surfboard drifting out to sea, while her family looked on from the beach. Every instruction from the television took her further away from the shore.

"If this pandemic is bad enough to close the country down, we had better be sure to take the Government's advice," her father had said, earlier that day, thereby withdrawing any further help.

"Mum, Mum." Manjit's voice was louder and more insistent on the second call, bringing her mother back to the room.

"Sorry, what did you say?"

"When's dinner?"

"Same time as always, why?"

"Lauren wants to see me. She's in the park with her dog."

"No. No, you mustn't."

"We'll be outside, we'll keep apart."

"I don't think it's a good idea. Stick with WhatsApp."

"You said we don't need to worry." Manjit's tone was almost accusatory.

"Just do as you're told, will you? Don't you think I've enough on my plate with your father away?"

Manjit fled the room, her bottom lip quivering.

Mandeep returned her attention to the television, but the broadcast was just about over. She switched it off and headed for the kitchen thinking, *they said it's mainly killing the elderly who are already ill, so why are they doing this? So as not to overwhelm the NHS, so they obviously expect a lot of people to get ill. I can't. There's no one to look after the girls.* Without her mind fully on the task of chopping onions, Mandeep almost cut herself. *I feel like they're keeping something from us. What if it's killing more people than they're letting on?* She felt sick and hot. *Please come home, Dev, please.*

Now she cried, the tears rolled into the dinner. Mandeep remembered her grandmother telling her that meals should be cooked with love because the emotions of the cook were passed on through the food.

"This meal'll choke us to death, then," she said out loud, forgetting Indrani was within earshot. The thought of her younger daughter provoked guilt concerning the elder. She paused in her task and went to Manjit's room.

"Sorry," she said, through the closed door because her daughter wouldn't open it. "Please let me in."

There was no response.

"Please Manjit, I want to explain." The door remained closed, held fast by her daughter's hurt, Mandeep knew. But then there was a rustle from behind it and it opened, just a crack. Apologising through it was like reading with a torch.

"I'm stressed by the changes we're having to make at work and worried about Dad not being able to get back. It's not an excuse, I know."

"Doesn't explain why you wouldn't let me meet Lauren."

"You're not supposed to."

"Might've got away with it today, tomorrow will be different."

The words sounded like the judge's hammer landing.

"I said I'm sorry."

"Can I go now, then?"

"I'd rather you didn't." She paused. "I'm just trying to keep you safe."

Manjit closed the door again, decisively, although she didn't slam it.

When the broadcast ended Margaret turned down the sound with the remote and sat staring at the silent screen, feeling like she was trapped in the house by snow with the forecast of worse to come.

Parents who'd lived through a war had taught her never to run low on provisions. Plenty of food in the cupboard, a good supply of books and regular meetings on Zoom should ensure life proceeded fairly normally, but the feeling of isolation couldn't be reasoned away so easily. Being alone and feeling alone, were quite different entities.

She never felt fully alone as long as she was in this house with all of her memories. And yet, neither did she feel connected, not in the way she used to. With John and her children to care for, and her teaching job, Margaret's life had had purpose, but that had long since gone. Every day now was just passing time until the grave. It wasn't that she wanted to die, or that there weren't things that interested her enough to make staying alive attractive, it was just that…

She rolled herself a cigarette and sat at the dining table to smoke it. *Just what? Exactly?* She wondered, now. *It's relationships with people that give our lives meaning*, she decided, taking a big drag on her cigarette. *So many people are going to have that taken away. Yes, that's what it is, that's why I'm so angry. The whole country is going to be thrown into grief. Is there no other way we can deal with this? Must we break the heart of the nation?* She sighed, put the cigarette in the ashtray and her head in her hands.

Yet, even as she thought this, she acknowledged her own fear and, for a fleeting moment, felt grateful that the choice had been taken away.

✿

"You're breaking the law," Margaret joked with Daniel when he arrived.

"Aye. Well, if the police break the door down, they'll have done half the of the replacement job for me." Daniel put the loaf he'd brought on the table.

"At least we won't starve with your bread supplies."

"The orders have really increased. I'm having a job to keep up. Should count my blessings. I've got plenty of work. More than some."

"What are they doing, Daniel? Is there no other way? I've been wondering about that a lot. This furlough scheme is all well and good, but it won't last forever, and the debt'll never be paid off. Our grandchildren, our great-grandchildren'll be paying for this." Margaret thought of her own great-grandchild, who she'd only seen once and wondered how long it would be before the next time.

"Makes me glad I never had any kids," Daniel said, in a tone that said the opposite.

He finished his tea and stood up to leave. "What're you up to today, then?"

"The reading group are meeting on Zoom, whatever that is. Guess I'll join them. Then I'm going out on my bike."

"Good for you."

"I've been meaning to for ages. If I fall off, I probably won't get any medical attention, but that suits me. At least when I breathe my last, the air will be fresher with fewer cars on the roads."

Daniel laughed heartily; he did enjoy the company of this woman. "Well, I sincerely hope it doesn't come to that. Shall I check the tyres for you?" He did so without waiting for a response, then took the pump and inflated them. "That'll make it a bit easier at least. Take care and enjoy. See you tomorrow."

Margaret followed him to the door and watched as he drove away. It felt like it would be the last time, but then everything she did recently felt like it was for the last time.

When Emerson arrived at work the doors were still locked. Finding them so was a shock, this had never happened before. He went up to the nearest window and peered in. There was a light at the back of the shop, but it looked empty. He checked the time on his phone, only fifteen minutes and they were supposed to open. Now he stood with his back to the door looking up and down the road. Someone was approaching from down the street, they were still too far away to be sure, but it could be one of the colleagues he was expecting. Other than the lone figure there was no one, and nothing in the street. It felt like a zombie apocalypse.

What the...? But before the thought was properly formed, Mandeep arrived.

"Sorry," she said. "I had some childcare issues."

Emerson said, "Jesus, man, you look awful."

"Thank you."

"Sorry, I meant, I mean, you look really stressed."

"That's about right."

"Where is everyone, anyway?"

"I've had two phone in sick. Here's Kevin now."

They both greeted him with a nod. And then three more colleagues arrived.

"Am I pleased to see you," Mandeep said. "Right, someone is going to have to stay by the doors, it's one way in and another out and we're limiting the numbers in the shop, so people'll need to queue."

"Fucking ridiculous," Emerson said.

"We have to do our best to keep people safe," Mandeep replied.

"Yeah, well I think this whole thing is…"

"Right now, Emerson, I don't care what you think," Mandeep replied. "I take my orders from above and you have to take them from me."

Well, fuck you!' Emerson thought and grunted an acquiescence.

Mandeep knew she had spoken harshly to Emerson, and she did regret it somewhat, but he was too blasé about the whole affair, and she couldn't allow that. Normally Mandeep found his wacky ideas amusing, but this time was different; there were lives at stake. The Government took it seriously enough to close the country down and Emerson's dismissiveness seemed arrogant and dangerous.

Better not put him on the doors, she thought.

She spent the morning on the shop floor, monitoring what was going on. *I think a daily briefing might help;* she was thinking of herself as much as of the staff. *I'll organise it from tomorrow.* There was a churning in the pit of her stomach and a ticking in her head. *I've got to calm down,* she thought. *I'll give myself a heart attack at this rate.*

She checked her watch before issuing instructions for the first break, and her taking over the till to allow it to happen. She used to enjoy the stints on the till, infrequent as they were, hearing the customers' various stories, but not so today, even with the gloves and mask she didn't really feel safe. *My staff feel like this all the time,* Mandeep reminded herself and she was fully aware that there were some who, given the opportunity, would have elected to stay home. She too wished they could just shut up shop and do that.

Churning became nausea and the tick in her head a thud. *Maybe I'm getting sick,* the thought fuelled her fear. *She felt hot and her limbs ached, I can't get ill, no, no, I can't.* She was distracted by the arrival of a customer at the till, but all the while she served them and made small talk, in the back of her head was the conviction that she was getting ill; it came to the forefront the second she was alone. She longed to hide away like everyone else, and wait for a vaccine.

When she was relieved of till duty, she made her way over to the front door. Hayley looked quite content in her marshalling role and outside it appeared that the customers weren't merely accepting the queue, but that there was an atmosphere of camaraderie. At least there was that to feel grateful for.

Mandeep didn't fancy lunch, what was happening in her stomach put her off completely. Her phone pinged with a text message. It was from Dev, asking her to call. She did so without taking a breath.

"I'm coming home as soon as I can," he promised, "but not sure when that'll be. They're about to close the airport."

Mandeep barely had time to hang up before running to the toilet and being sick.

Waking up alone in Daniel's bed disoriented Kirsten, and it took a second or two to remember where she was. The room was light and still, only her breathing broke the silence. Peace was soon snatched away by the memory of why she was here and the feeling that life would never be the same.

It wasn't like when Greg had died; grief had swamped her then, had kept her body prostrate despite her determination to move. It was terrible, but there was some peace to be had in the finality. This…this was more like waiting with Greg for his diagnosis. Praying for an unexpected outcome; knowing that the likely one promised many unwelcome surprises on the way.

Kirsten climbed from the bed, wondering why she hadn't been disturbed by Daniel's alarm as she picked up his clock to check the time. It was obscured by the lack of contact lenses, but she thought it said eight thirty-five.

Blimey! It's Sunday lie-in time, not Wednesday workday time, she thought. Then she decided she'd better phone Rosie before she did anything else. Rosie's tone was cheerful.

"Well, money's in the bank, so don't care now whether they make it to the house today or not. I know that's selfish."

"Well, that is good news."

"Frankly I don't know what we'd've done without it, with one wage packet left for Andy, but we can't spend too much of it."

"I'll help where I can."

"You've already done plenty, Mum. I'll have to look for something."

In August, having listened to Daniel's opinion on the state of the economy and the likelihood of a major crash, Kirsten had spent the money left her by her mother on seven gold coins. Intending either to sell them back when the price increased, or leave them in her will to her daughter and grandchildren, at this moment she wished the cash was still in her account so that she could give it to them now.

Never before had Kirsten been alone in this house. She made herself porridge for breakfast, feeling like Goldilocks as she ate it. Then she showered and dressed. She was working from two until the close at ten, when Daniel was coming to fetch her. *I'd better buy some provisions.* But then, thinking about what those might be, decided she'd better discuss it with Daniel first.

She turned the radio on, swapped channels, then turned it off because, there was only one topic on the BBC, and the advertisements and middle of the road music on the commercial stations annoyed her.

It wasn't that there was a lack of things to do, it was just that doing them, without Daniel's consent, felt wrong, yet, not doing them felt like she wasn't pulling her weight. "Don't be so bloody daft," she told herself out loud, "it's only been a couple of days."

She fetched her book and curled up on the sofa to read.

&s

The Zoom session was at ten. Margaret was in the waiting room before the host. She felt insecure, had she done everything that was required? Then, when the host let her in, she felt proud – despite a dislike of the virtual world she'd successfully negotiated it.

They talked little about the book. There was only one topic on everyone's mind and tongue these days. Margaret listened to the discussion but joined in hardly at all. They were all so scared, it upset and puzzled her. *People our age are obviously more susceptible to death,* she thought. *If we give into fear, we'll stop living before we get there. Am I being too blasé?* She wondered, thinking it would be humiliating to lie on her death bed with *I told you so* in everyone's minds.

When the session ended Margaret changed her clothes, from dress and blouse to track suit bottoms and sweatshirt, then got out her bicycle. An internal conversation took place in her head as she prepared to mount. One of the voices belonged to Joe and was telling her off for being so reckless, the other was her own and was offering reassurances, by which she wasn't really convinced. She felt hot, her stomach tingled, and her heartbeat was hard enough to make her aware of it. *Right, come on,* she said to herself, as she took a deep breath, mounted the bike, scooted a few turns of the pedals then pushed up onto the saddle, and was away.

She stayed on the pavement as she headed towards the village. Every few spins of the wheel she encountered pedestrians, so had to stop and start many times. Margaret didn't think she'd ever seen the village so busy.

Finally, she found the nerve to cycle on the road, which was devoid of any traffic. As she cycled, she felt proud and regal, shame she saw no one she knew to whom she could offer a wave. She carried on out of the village towards the crossroads intending to turn back before she reached the main road, but it, too, was traffic-free so she cycled up it to the next turning, which would take her on a circular route back home. The entire journey was about two miles. She covered it slowly, but she didn't care. When she reached home Margaret felt like she'd won the Tour De France and she couldn't wait to boast about it.

❧

Kirsten was on her way to work, on foot, so had plenty of time for contemplation. *Think I'll fetch my bike. It'll save a lot of time.*

She stopped in her tracks as she realised people were queuing outside the shop. *What the…?*

She skirted along it, feeling the need to explain her role to those who offered quizzical looks. Near the front of the queue, she spotted a familiar face. "Hello, how are you?" she greeted Nabil, with a smile and an extended hand.

He looked at her with blank eyes and pushed his body backwards. Kirsten lowered her hand. Then Nabil's expression changed to one of recognition and he almost smiled, as he nodded by way of a reply.

"This is a bit of a nightmare." Kirsten held open palms skywards and shrugged her shoulders.

Nabil nodded like a toy dog.

"Well, see you soon, I've got to go." She used her head to point to the entrance and hurried away from him, feeling his discomfort like a heavy bag on her back.

❧

When the letter box clunked with the delivery, Margaret felt surprised; a letter was a rare occurrence these days. She didn't rush to respond, knowing it was likely to be junk mail. *Life insurance offer*, she thought, *or an advertisement for a funeral plan, just what you need to help you live life fully.*

The reality was worse. Her vulnerable status became official with the government advice to stay home. Margaret burst into tears. So copious were they that she had to sit down for fear of falling.

"Stupid old woman," she said out loud to herself between the sobs. "The way you're behaving you're living up to your vulnerable label. For God's sake pull yourself together."

This instruction to herself became easier to follow with the knock on the door as Daniel entered.

Margaret shuffled the letter under the cushion on her armchair and stood up to greet him. The look on his face made his concern clear.

"The news," Margaret offered by way of explanation.
"Ah!"

"I guess you've heard? About the new act, I mean."

Daniel indicated that he had.

"Powers to detain someone they suspect of being infectious. How does someone look infectious?" Now she laughed, and so did Daniel, feeling relieved.

"P'r'aps they haven't told us all of the symptoms, p'r'aps we get purple spots on our faces," he said.

They both laughed.

But when she was alone again Margaret read the letter once more and allowed herself to feel a little afraid. Of the virus; of the isolation; of the fact that she was old and death could come to claim her any day.

It wasn't the same as when she was young. Then the fear of death was annihilating, so great that it seemed just to think of it was all that was needed to invite it. Now it was more like the nervous anticipation that precedes an unwelcome journey, coupled with sadness at what's being left behind. If there was anything beyond; now that was something to fear.

Margaret failed to understand why some felt comfort in this. As far as she was concerned, for there to be nothing meant there was nothing to fear. True there was some consolation in the thought that she and John would be reunited, but she didn't really believe in that. At least not in the sense that they would be two individuals sharing love like they did when alive. However, to be free of constantly missing him offered much relief. At the very least, death would provide her with this.

Yet, what if it was as some believed? A questioner waiting to examine her conscience. What then? She hoped it wasn't like that, she hoped too that it wouldn't hurt too much when it came. Or be so sudden it provoked fear; it would be dreadful if fear were the last emotion she experienced. Hell for Margaret was being in an eternal state of fear; heaven an everlasting state of love. These could exist on earth as well as in heaven. *Thy will be done on earth, as it is in heaven,* she thought. Remembering being a child, kneeling, hands in prayer, beside her bed uttering the words, which had no meaning for her at that time.

'Stop this,' she told herself now. 'You're not going just yet and certainly not today.' With this thought she donned her jacket and got her bicycle out.

Nabil awoke early, from a disturbed night's sleep. It was too early for breakfast, but too late to try to return to sleep. He lay for a while, drifting between states, dreams full of fear beckoned him inwards and downwards; dreadful memories flooded in the instant sleep released him. At seven-ten Nabil gave up the struggle and gave into the demands of daytime.

The shower water was tepid. His clothes were damp and musty smelling. It was still too early for breakfast, but he ate it anyway because there was nothing else to do. He was alone in the kitchen, so he stayed around, grateful for the change of scenery.

He washed up his bowl and made himself coffee, but without sugar it tasted too bitter. He risked going into the lounge and turning on the television, feeling relieved when there were no disturbing images, no one dressed as if they were expecting a chemical attack, only two well-dressed individuals talking out of the screen. One man, one woman, one black, one white; this was in keeping with his expectation of the United Kingdom and re-newed some of his hope. Along the bottom of the screen scrolled words which had no more meaning for him than those coming from the mouths of the presenters, although he understood they were talking about the virus because he recognised one or two words and there was a picture of it on a board behind the presenters. Nabil turned it off again and went back to his room.

He climbed into bed, grateful for the duvet and YouTube channel on his phone. Nabil was keeping account of every min-ute that he spent online, making sure to allot himself some time every day and eking out the minutes to maximize the number of days of internet use.

He decided not to check the Arabic news channel, not wanting to hear anything that would upset him further; instead, he tuned into English lessons. He whispered the responses, not wanting to draw the attention of the other tenants. He wished there was someone on whom to practise, but also was glad that there wasn't, for fear of making mistakes that would show his ignorance. When he'd used all of his allotted minutes, he took out the textbook and practised writing.

'I am a student of English,' he wrote, without being certain that he understood every word. Of the purchasing requests he felt more confident, 'I'd like to buy some bread, please, and 'I'd like a cup of coffee, please.' When he'd copied them from the textbook he closed it, took his notebook and tried to replicate it without looking, feeling frustrated with his imperfect attempts. He kept going until he was satisfied with the result, then he spoke the words, wondering when there would again be the opportunity to make these requests for real.

Checking the time on his phone Nabil decided he would allow himself another coffee and a snack, then go for the hour outside he was allowed. As he prepared to do so he realised he hadn't once thought of Abida. But, now that he had, she wouldn't stay out of his mind. His sandwich was soured by guilt and his coffee tasted of her tears. Behind his eyes was her face, sometimes suffering, sometimes angry, but never with him; never accusing. Nabil owed it to her to do more than just survive, he must grow and thrive.

He got himself ready, then took a deep breath as he stepped into the street.

His first day in this town it had rained, lending the place a sense of claustrophobia, even though there was in fact more space here than in his home city. As he'd traversed the streets, he'd taken comfort in the many similarities, and felt confident of a future when familiarity would bring a sense of safety. But in that same moment he'd also been grateful for the rain; and for being able to hide from people inside his cagoule.

Today, the empty streets intimidated him. The silence rang in his ears, like the seconds after a bomb blast, before the cries begin. He kept his head inside his hood. Every vacant side street, alley, shop doorway felt threatening. There was no one else around.

Each of Nabil's breaths was deliberate, as he hurried down the street towards the park. Outside the supermarket there was a queue. He felt himself drawn towards it, not because of any need to shop, but because he needed other humans. He checked his pockets and counted his change, perhaps he'd buy himself some biscuits on the way back.

There were at least as many people as always in the park. Nabil stood under the clock, watching. Today they behaved differently. The way they shifted around each other, or stood to attention to allow passing, reminded Nabil of prisoners being shepherded around.

On his way home he joined the queue at the supermarket. The yellow and black distance markers frightened him, reminding him of another order to stay back. The memory made him shake and sweat, and then he coughed, re-experiencing the barrel of the gun as it was thrust into his stomach.

He fought with the memory as in the present an androgynous person in front of him turned themselves sideways and shouted, waving their gloved hand in the air in a manner that made the instruction to back off perfectly clear. Angry eyes glared from behind glasses that were framed by a hat and scarf, the person was small, their anger was huge.

Nabil backed away slowly, until he felt the gap was safe enough; he was just about to turn and run when someone spoke to him.

"Hello, how are you?" The woman was holding out her hand to him. Fear had temporarily robbed Nabil of manners and sense, but as recognition dawned and he began to feel calmer, he offered Kirsten his hand and a smile.

The BBC newscaster's voice was lost to Mandeep, her attention was on the figures scrolling the screen. Six more people have died in Scotland, it read, and five more in Wales, bringing the total in each case to twenty-two. She'd missed the overall UK figure. She sat on the edge of the sofa with her thumbs in her mouth. *It's okay,* she told herself, *that's not many people, we'll be okay, odds in our favour. Older people and those with underlying health conditions, remember?* But the reassurances she offered herself didn't create the calm she hoped for and the conversation she'd heard from the staff room returned to her in Emerson's voice.

How come everyone trusts the Government all of a sudden? Even those who previously doubted them.

Well, she wasn't sure that she did. Something big was going on, she was sure of that. Maybe the virus was worse than they said. *Oh God, I hope Dev's back soon.*

"Mum," she was called out of her reverie by Manjit. "It says on the internet that India has closed the airports. All international flights have stopped."

Mandeep's stomach dropped, her heart stopped, her ears rang, she felt like she was about to pass out.

"Is Dad going to be able to get home?"

"How the hell do I know?" As soon as the words left her mouth Mandeep felt guilty. She reached out her hand to her daughter. "Sorry," she said.

Manjit pushed the hand away with her shoulder. "It's not my fault."

"I know. I'm sorry, I'm so worried."

"How d'you think we feel?" Manjit was almost shouting. "Dad's away and you're falling apart."

"What?"

"You're supposed to look after *us,* not the other way around."

"I'm not fall…"

"Oh, doesn't matter." Manjit stormed out of the room.

Mandeep's shame turned to anger. *How dare she speak to me like that? If I'd spoken to my mother like that…* but then the emotions flipped back again, with the acknowledgement that the last thing she wanted was for her daughters to feel as afraid as she did.

Anger rose again: *What was Dev thinking of? He'd done his duty. And why hasn't he phoned?* Then fear: *There must be something wrong.* Mandeep checked the time, even though she knew already it had just gone five. *Still not too late to call him,* she thought, picking up her phone to do so. She selected his number, but didn't click on the dial symbol, fearing that lack of a response would only make the conviction that something was wrong, stronger.

She felt like she was locked in an iron box. It was so unlike Dev not to call her. *He must be dead,* she decided, her stomach cramping so violently in response to the idea that she was sure she'd be sick, so she ran to the bathroom.

Crouching beside the toilet reminded Mandeep of the first weeks of pregnancy. She'd been afraid then, too, afraid that the retching would cause her to miscarry, and afraid of becoming a mother. She didn't feel up to the job; she was too young, too selfish, too much the opposite of everything she should be. It was incredible to think that both her daughters had grown success-fully to the age they were. Much of it was down to their father. To the love and support he offered that kept her feeling strong. If he didn't come back, if he was… The thought made her retch, causing pain to her empty stomach.

You need to feed the girls, get yourself together. Mandeep pulled herself to standing with all the grace of an elderly woman.

The smell of spices greeted her as she opened the kitchen door.

Indrani was chopping vegetables, Manjit cooking the spices. She looked up as her mother came in. "Sorry," she said.

"Me too."

"We need to pull together," Manjit said, sounding so like her father.

"No, I need to pull myself together."

"I wish Dad was here," Indrani said.

"Me too. Typical of Grandma to time her death so incon-veniently." Mandeep's attempt at humour fell flat.

"Why don't you call him? See what's going on," Manjit asked.

"I will, in a bit. I've been waiting for him. He knows our routine, but we don't know what's going on for him."

"You could do it now, we're okay with the cooking."

Really Mandeep knew she must, it was getting near mid-night in India. She took her phone into the sitting room. Her heart beat so hard she worried it would leap out of her chest. His phone rang and rang, every ring reinforced anxiety. She'd heard rumours of curfews being imposed. The authorities were strict there. Images of stick-wielding police beating her husband about the head flickered behind her eyes, she saw him dragged away in handcuffs, then, as the phone call dropped out, pictured him lying in a pool of blood.

Mandeep stared at her phone, wondering whether to redial. The ring tone made her jump, she answered it feeling a mixture of relief and anger.

"What the hell's going on? Why haven't you been in touch?"

"They've locked us down, the airport is closed." Dev's voice echoed, as if it were coming from another world, he sounded distressed.

"I know. We've been worried by you not phoning."

"I'm sorry. I didn't think of that. I was saving my battery. I wanted to wait until I could tell you I'm on my way."

I've been worried to death you selfish bastard, but relief was bigger by far than anger. "Well, you're okay, thank God you're okay. What's happening?"

"They've closed down the embassy. I don't know where else to go. No one seems to know what's going on. I'm so sorry, I should've come back before the funeral."

Well, you didn't. "Too late for should've, just get back as soon as you can, *please.*"

"That's my intention. I'll sort it in the morning, I'm just checking into a hotel. That cost an arm and a leg, no one wants any foreigners here."

"You're not a foreigner."

"It's only my heritage that got me a room. Getting home is going to cost big time."

"I don't care what it costs."

"Me neither, just saying. How're things there?"

I'm as scared as an abandoned child. "It's really difficult with work, my parents aren't keen on having the girls. And I miss you."

"I miss you too. I'm so sorry."

"Please stay in touch, just a text'll do."

"I will, I promise."

It's not as if anyone could have foreseen such circumstances, Mandeep reasoned, when she was off the phone and had taken over the cooking.

Indrani cleared the table after the meal and between them the two girls filled the dishwasher, then went to their rooms.

After prayers Mandeep sat down to do the work rota. It took several attempts; because concentration was difficult, she kept making mistakes. She also wanted to arrange it so that she and Kirsten never had shifts that coincided. If Dev was away much longer, she might have to use some holiday time. *Not much point saving it if we won't be going anywhere.* There was no sadness attached to the thought. There was nowhere she wanted to go; home was the only place that felt anything like safe; she just wanted Dev to be there too.

"It's getting more like a police state every day," Emerson complained to Kirsten as they swapped places at the till.

Should've known better than to ask. She wasn't really in the mood for this.

"We've even got a top judge saying so now," he continued.

"Yes, I heard that too. Something about over-zealous police in Derbyshire."

"And there was that woman fined for refusing to give her name or say where she was travelling."

"Times are strange."

"*They* carry on as always, of course. Some of them even embarking on two-hundred-mile journeys," Emerson said in a tone that almost sounded pleased.

"Yes, I had heard that, too."

"What d'you think about it?"

"Same as you, but don't suppose it'll make any difference. Can't see him getting sacked."

"I reckon he's got something on our glorious leader."

Kirsten laughed. "You could be right."

"I reckon really he's the PM." Emerson was standing on the customer side of the till now. "It's sickening that senior members of the cabinet can go gallivanting across the country while ordinary folk have their neighbours ratting on them for every small step out of line."

"I haven't heard of anything like that, Emerson, have you?"

"Not personally, but…"

"I hope they don't do that to me." Mandeep interrupted, coming up behind Kirsten.

"You've got enough to worry about, don't even think about it."

"Just tell them you had to get your eyes tested," Emerson said, and was pleased when they both did seem at least a bit amused.

"Anything I need to know?" Kirsten asked, accepting the key she was offered.

"The girls can tell you anything if so."

"Any news?"

Mandeep sighed, "He's still trying to get back. He seems to think he might have some luck with the German Embassy."

"Let's hope so." Kirsten rubbed Mandeep's arm. "Can't be much longer. Anything you want me to do while I'm there?"

"You're doing enough as it is."

"It was fun last time. They're lovely girls."

"Thank you." Mandeep turned to Emerson. "You need to use the sanitizer."

"Sorry, but I'm not doing that."

Mandeep felt like her blood was congealing. "I'll get you some gloves, then."

Emerson felt his face harden. "Is that an instruction?"

"It's for the best."

"In whose opinion?"

A customer was approaching, Mandeep swallowed both the words and her annoyance and decided she'd discuss it with him later, right now she had to get back to the risk assessments, which were overdue for completion.

Mostly they were the same. Level of risk, medium to high for those working on the tills. Social distancing, hand sanitizer and gloves brought the risk down. The introduction of the screens, which was due over the weekend, would bring it down lower. There wasn't a category for refusal to comply. Perhaps she should suggest to Head Office that they add one, but then, there might be awkward questions; she didn't want anyone losing their job, least of all Emerson, who worked hard and was popular with the customers.

In her imagination Mandeep visited Emerson in hospital. The ventilator made him barely visible; his weeping mother stamped on the flowers she presented. Then she was in Head Office, the Area Manager asking, *How could you be so irresponsible?*

and, *What kind of manager are you?* The responsibility hunched her shoulders.

I'll have a word with him before he leaves, she thought, picking up the next risk assessment.

Never before had paperwork been so arduous and sitting still so difficult. She stretched her aching back and rolled her shoulders, as she did so, she became aware she was chewing the side of her mouth. Time for a rest, she decided and headed for the break room for a change of scenery.

It smelt of disinfectant, which reassured her. When she'd suggested to the staff that they spray the room after each use, it'd gone down well; much better than she'd expected, in fact. However, despite this, she couldn't resist giving it another spray. Chairs, kettle, work surfaces, all were cleaned before she put the kettle on.

Mandeep paced the room as she drank her coffee. She'd go back in a minute and make the second of her twice daily calls to her parents, before phoning Dev.

Emerson arrived in the room. "Oh, Mandeep glad you're here, do I need to apologise?"

The shock must have shown on her face because Emerson continued with, "I was told I was rude. About the sanitizer and the gloves. Didn't mean to be. Sorry."

Mandeep sighed with relief. "I…it's…I have to keep everyone safe."

"Course. It's just I think this virus stuff is a load of bollocks – whoops, sorry. Don't 'spose you agree, and even if you did…"

"I'd still have to keep you safe. But how can you say that, anyway?"

He lifted the kettle, filled it with water, put it back in its cradle and flipped the switch to 'on'. "They're cooking the figures. It's about control."

Mandeep really couldn't be bothered to argue. *And they, are who, exactly?* She thought, then said, "Surely if *they* were going to lie, *they'd* want us to think there are fewer deaths."

"Depends on their agenda."

"Which is?"

"The Great Reset."

"The what?"

"I can suggest some stuff to look at online if you like."

"No thanks."

"We can only change it if we all wake up and fight."

"Fight what?"

"The reset."

Mandeep looked so stressed it was evident even to Emerson; he decided he'd better back off.

"Well, if you ever want it, I can point you in the direction. I'll wear gloves, that sanitizer is shit. Mask, if you order me to, but I'd sooner not."

"The customers prefer it." She sighed again.

"They're bad for you, breathing in your own germs and carbon dioxide."

"Okay, whatever. I've been wondering how I could get around it on your risk assessment, that's all, but we're getting screens fitted over the weekend anyway."

"You're kidding me?" Emerson threw his hands up.

Back in the office Mandeep called her parents.

"I can hardly believe this is happening," her mother said.

"I know it's scary, but try not to worry, Mum."

"How can I not?"

"Is there anything you need?"

"We will do soon."

"Write me a list, then."

"You can't come in."

"Put it under the plant pot, I'll fetch it on my way home. I'll bring the shopping tomorrow and leave it on the doorstep."

"Okay. What's the news from Dev?"

"He's still in India."

"What's he playing at?"

Mandeep eyes brimmed with tears. "There's no flights."

"You tell me not worry when the whole world is locking down."

Mandeep put the phone down and cried. The call to Dev would have to wait until she had the tears under control.

She went back to the break room, to get some water, but also to cleanse, because she didn't have faith in Emerson having done so.

Her mobile was ringing when she got back to the office. She hurried to answer the call from Dev.

"How're things your end?" he asked.

"Daily deaths increasing. My parents are really stressed. A work colleague's looking after the girls because you're not here. Shall I go on?"

"Okay, okay."

"Sorry, I know you can't help it. Any news?"

"Rumour has it there'll be rescue flights from early next month."

"Rumour? Next month?"

"It's only a couple of days away. You sound really fed up."

"What d'you expect?"

"If I come home via Germany it's gonna cost."

"I thought we'd agreed we don't care about the cost?"

"Eight thousand, don't care?"

"I need you to come home. Please." She bit back the tears that threatened again.

"Okay."

"Thank you."

Yet, as she hung up Mandeep felt numb, she'd believe it when she saw him standing in front of her. She had an overwhelming sense of an omnipotent presence being in control of her fate. If it really was a paternalistic father-like God, he was being too strict.

⌘

"Excuse me, Kirsten, could I ask you a question, please?" Indrani asked.

"Certainly." Then realising what task Indrani was currently involved in, "If it's a maths one, though, don't expect a sensible answer."

"It's nothing to do with schoolwork. I was wondering – how safe is it at the shop?"

This was not at all what Kirsten expected. Questions about safety only had one meaning these days. "You're worried about your Mum?"

"Well, she seems so stressed at the moment. She's had a few arguments with my sister. She keeps cleaning, *everything*."

"Come and sit down." Kirsten patted the sofa next to her. "We have all kinds of measures in place to make sure it's safe. The staff use sanitizer on their hands, they clean the counter after someone's been through, lots of them wear gloves and masks. Shouldn't think many germs survive all of that. And mostly your mum is in her office doing paperwork."

Indrani nodded, but looked miserable.

"The extra responsibility is probably getting to her. And I'll bet she misses your dad."

"The thing is we don't know when he's getting back."

Kirsten thought her heart would break.

"Are you frightened by the virus?"

"A bit. Well, yes."

"That's understandable. But it doesn't seem to be affecting young people."

"That's what Mum says, but she doesn't behave like she thinks that."

"D'you know what? It's confusing and worrying with all the different information, I'll bet she's just being cautious. She loves you both so much, she wants to make sure you stay well." Safe was a word Kirsten was coming to despise.

Indrani shrugged her shoulders and chewed the side of her mouth.

Kirsten continued, "It's 'cos it's new, the virus, I mean. That's why everyone's stressed about it. But we're gaining knowledge all the time. The more we know about it, the better we can deal with it."

"Everything I hear on the telly makes it sound worse than I thought."

"What are you watching?"

"The news."

No wonder you're fucking worried. "BBC?"

"All channels. And a bit online."

Jesus. "Well, the news is about keeping people on their toes, so they're going to emphasise what's bad. Make sure people do what they need to stay safe." *And scare the arse off us in the process.* "Tell you what, would you help me get the meal ready?"

"Okay."

It wasn't difficult. Mandeep had cooked it, all there was left to do was heat it up and boil some rice. While they were doing so, Indrani said, "You going to tell Mum what I said?"

Kirsten stopped what she was doing and turned to her companion. "Don't you want me to?"

"Sort of, but sort of not."

"Why not?"

"She's worried enough."

"How about I mention we had a chat, but tone down how scared you are? I'd kind've like to tell her you're watching the news."

"Okay." It was said without conviction.

"I wouldn't feel right saying nothing, but I'll respect your confidentiality if…"

"No, it's okay. You can tell her."

Anger surged through Kirsten. How could it be good for anyone to see those statistics scroll the screen every day? What was that about, if not ramping up the fear?

When Mandeep arrived home looking exhausted, Kirsten understood Indrani's concerns better.

"Day off tomorrow," she said when Kirsten passed comment on it. "Then, hopefully Dev will be back. Girls been okay?"

"Of course. I have something to tell…"

"I'm so grateful for this, Kirsten."

"We all need to support each other through this."

"It's been such a shock. It doesn't seem real."

"I know," Kirsten rubbed Mandeep's shoulder. "Especially difficult for you on your own."
"I'm scared he'll never be back."

"He will, of course he will."

Mandeep's desperation and urgency were palpable. It reminded Kirsten of the dreadful feeling of lack of control that she'd experienced with the announcement of the lockdowns.

"What did you have to tell me?" Mandeep asked, as if coming back from some far-off place.

"I hardly like to when you're so stressed, but…"

"What? What is it? Are the girls okay?" Mandeep turned her body towards the stairs as she asked this.

"Yes, but…Indrani has got herself a bit worked up about the virus. Not helped by the fact she's watching the news, on telly and online."

Mandeep sighed heavily. "Thank you for telling me. I do keep an eye on what they're watching, this one slipped by me." It was said as if it was taken for granted that Kirsten would blame her for Indrani's viewing.

"You can't watch them all of the time."

A horn hooted outside.

"That'll be Daniel. I'll call you tomorrow." Kirsten rubbed Mandeep's shoulder again. "I hope you sleep well."

As she climbed into the van Kirsten felt such gratitude for Daniel that she took his face in her hands and kissed him on the forehead.

"Thanks," he said.

Kirsten told him about Indrani.

He shook his head and rolled his eyes, "They've started to refer to it as a war, have you noticed?"

"I hadn't actually."

Without any other traffic on the road Kirsten felt vulnerable. It was like starring in a dystopian film. She said as much to Daniel, as the van bounced up the driveway and the lights hit the front of his cottage.

"Better check there's no zombies before I let you in," he said, laughing.

The smell of fresh bread hit Kirsten's nostrils, it displaced fear with a feeling of homeliness.

"God that smells delicious, there's nothing quite like it."

"Can't spare any of the fresh one, but there's some of Saturday's loaf still."

"Better not, I'm not hungry. Just that it smells so good."

"The orders are getting too big for me to manage. I've said regulars only. Feel bad, but can't be helped. You must be tired."

"I am, but I don't know why. I was far less busy than I would have been at work."

On the other side of town, Mandeep was losing her battle to get to sleep. Every time she closed her eyes the story behind them became more distressing. It wasn't only the noise of her thoughts that kept her awake, but a twitching leg that reclaimed her every time she was on the edge of drifting off. She turned on the bed-side light and reached for her book, but today the plot between the pages was less compulsive than the one that went on between her ears. She dropped it on the floor and lay her body back down, ordering it to go to sleep, as if it were a naughty child. But, like a naughty child, it failed to comply with the demand.

Sleep teased her by coming close then running away, finally she climbed from bed and went downstairs, made herself a drink of hot chocolate and sat down at the dining table to drink it. She turned her phone on. The start-up message was deafeningly loud in the silence of the night. There were no new messages, not that she expected any, so she scrolled back through the last few. Every hopeful one was followed by a disappointing one. '*I'm going to the embassy first thing tomorrow. Love you x*' '*Embassy closed, can't believe it. Love you. x*' '*Some tourists told me there's flights to London from Mumbai, I'll check it out. x*' '*Can't find any flights to London. Sorry, I'll phone shortly. x*' '*Europe looks like a possibility. x*' '*I'll call you about 6, UK time.*' '*On my way to airport and then Frankfurt, speak soon.*' What had happened to love you, and x? Mandeep wondered now, and at three-twenty in the morning, their absence seemed portentous.

APRIL

"Hello, still here?" Margaret asked of the homeless man, then, realising her words could be misconstrued, "I thought the government had found you all accommodation."

"Nobody'd wanna stay where they put me." His tone was unequivocal.

"Oh dear, sorry to hear that."

"So many stupid rules, no phone signal, nuffin' to do. Couldn't have people in our rooms, neither. I mean, I know all about coronavirus and social distancing, but this woman asked someone to change her light bulb, which he did, and then they both got chucked out of the lodgings. Don't s'pose you can spare any change?"

Margaret handed him two pounds. "That's terrible. Would you like a sandwich?"

"I tell you what, if it's okay, could I have some paracetamol?"

"You can have both."

"Not hungry, but I am achy."

"You might be later," Margaret's mothering voice echoed back to her.

"Well, thanks then. Chicken or cheese, well anything really."

As she joined the queue for the supermarket Margaret heard the young man coughing. Just for a second a tingle of fear crept up her spine.

The person in front of her was wearing a scarf around their face, gloves on their hands, and sunglasses. It made them genderless and ageless.

The one-way distancing arrows on the supermarket floor irritated Margaret, the half empty shelves made her sad; panic buying indicated fear in people's hearts. It was difficult to shop under these circumstances; although she always came with a list, she liked to browse and take the time to compare and consider. But this was a luxury that could no longer be afforded, it felt ill-mannered when there were people waiting to come down the aisle. She checked her list again and again, finding the items on it elusive because hurrying interfered with concentration. About the whole place there was an atmosphere of tension. Margaret wasn't the only one feeling harassed, that was clear. Naked fear was dressed in guarded politeness.

Margaret stopped short at the sight of the Perspex screens and felt she would cry. For her they symbolised alienation, and instilled the notion that there was real cause for fear.

The very young woman was telling the customer at the tills that she felt safer with its inception and hoped that the customer did too. She said the same to Margaret, as she checked her items through the till; Margaret grunted a non-committal reply.

Outside she handed over the sandwich, paracetamol and a bottle of water to the homeless man. "I hope you feel better soon," she said.

There was a bus already waiting, it was empty; Margaret was the only passenger all the way back to the village.

Mandeep's stomach was churning. Necessary journeys only, who decided what was necessary? She wondered, terrified at the thought of breaking the law. She was no less afraid of the lie. She'd been too scared to say one of the girls or one of her parents was ill, in case God punished the lie by making them contract the virus. So, although the same applied to herself, she'd decided to say she was. The mandatory two weeks of sick leave would be nice at least, spent with Dev after so long an absence. Better hope no one saw them leaving town.

"Come on girls, please," she called up the stairs. Then checked for the third time that her driving licence was in her bag.

She ushered them into the car, feeling like a criminal.

"Why're we going this way?" Manjit asked, as they left town.

"I don't want to pass work."

"Oh, course not." Manjit's tone was almost amused.

When they hit the motorway, Mandeep initially felt relieved, but it didn't last long. There was no other traffic. It felt like they were driving in pursuit of the only other people still alive. Signs flashed: '*Essential journeys only. Stay home, protect the NHS.*'

Most of the journey was spent in silence. Mandeep didn't want the radio on, the music annoyed her, the news scared her, and neither she nor the girls seemed to have anything to talk about. Eventually Mandeep said, when the silence was no longer comfortable, "You two okay there?"

Their replies were hardly more than grunts.

"Oh, there's a car," Indrani said, as if she were a little child who'd been instructed to look out for red vehicles to count. "And another, and now a van, it's busy here."

"Well at least we don't have to worry about getting stuck in traffic."

The phone rang, Mandeep pressed the telephone symbol on her Bluetooth. "I've landed, I'm home." Dev sounded relieved.

"Yippee!!" Indrani shrieked.

"So, where are you?" Dev asked.

"Just coming up to the M4 junction, should be there in about half an hour."

"I'll wait in the pick-up area, save you any hassle with security. Let me know when you're five minutes away."

"Will do." Now, at last, Mandeep felt she could breathe.

On the junction there was a stationary police car. Her stomach dropped at the sight of it. A few minutes later it was behind them, then in front, flashing them into the hard shoulder.

Mandeep's stomach hit the floor; her legs were shaking so much it was difficult to come to a controlled stop. She wound down the window as a very young policeman approached, closely followed by a not-so-young woman.

"Good morning, Madam," the policeman said, as he approached.

Mandeep replied with the same, exchanging 'madam' for 'officer' and becoming aware of the falter in her voice.

"I take it you're aware of the current restrictions?" the officer continued.

"Yes." A dry mouth necessitated few words.

"So, I find myself wondering where you three ladies are going that is essential."

"To fetch my husband; their father, from the airport."

The policewoman approached the car. "Been on holiday, has he?"

"His mother's funeral. He got stuck there."

"And there would be? Ah ha! I take it you can verify this?" The woman turned to her colleague. "Got any details on flights from India?"

He began scrolling through his phone. Mandeep took deep breaths, trying to still her shaking. Indrani and Manjit sat as still and silent as statues.

"Says here," the policeman continued, "that they stopped all flights from India on twenty-fifth of last month, and rescue flights are planned in the next few days."

"He came via Frankfurt." Mandeep knew she sounded pleading and, despite its being the truth, felt like she was lying.

The police officers moved away from the car and had a whispered conversation. When they returned the policeman asked, "Could I see your licence, please, Madam?"

Mandeep grabbed her bag from the floor of the passenger seat and began ferreting through it; in her panic she couldn't find the licence, although she knew it was there, she'd checked; hadn't she? She tipped everything out on the passenger seat and sighed with relief on seeing it.

The police officer seemed to take an inordinate time to check it. Mandeep was sure he could find all he needed by punching her registration details into his phone, she felt like a mouse, being played with by a cat.

Finally, he held the licence out to her and said, "That all seems to be in order. I'd advise agreeing a place at the airport where you can do a quick pick-up, things being as they are."

"Thank you," Mandeep thought the sound of relief in her voice lent the impression of guilt. She was still shaking badly, as she pulled away, taking care to observe the speed limit, despite feeling the need to hurry.

"That was exciting!" Manjit said.

"That's one word for it." Mandeep replied.

For the rest of the journey Mandeep felt like she'd been tranquillised, so, when they reached the airport turn-off, she was numb to any feelings. "Would one of you phone Dad and tell him five minutes, please?"

A few minutes later she pulled into the pick-up layby, got out of the car, threw her arms around Dev and burst into tears.

He held her close and tight. "I'm sorry, so sorry."

"It's been tough. Never mind, you're here now. How was your journey?"

"Uneventful. Yours?"

"I'll tell you on the way home."

"You'll have to drive, I'm too tired," Dev said.

"Fine. Just get in the car, please, and let's go home."

Writing about Abida brought about a kind of resurrection. Although, every day he ached with the loss of her, Abida's ghostly company was worse. It teased him. She looked over his shoulder as he wrote. *'You're flattering me,' she told him. 'Tell the truth, if you want to keep me alive. You have to tell me like I was.'*

'That is how you were for me.'

'Ah, love is blind.'

'Where are you now?' he said out loud.

'Nowhere and everywhere.'

'What's it like?'

'Nothing and everything.'

Her mocking made him angry. He put down the pen and paper to make himself a sandwich. Mostly, writing her story, their story, helped. It was cathartic and passed the time, and, if he wrote enough, one day he could turn it into a book. He'd have it translated into English. It'd sell a million copies. Abida would become a household name.

Before he ate the sandwich Nabil prayed. He was in the middle of eating it when Abdul telephoned.

"Hi, Nabil, you okay?"

"Yes, I am, thanks to God."

"What've you been doing?"

"Learning English. Going for walks."

"Walking is good. We can meet sometimes, now the weather is improving. I'll phone again in a couple of days."

"Thank you."

Yes, the weather was improving. Nabil swapped his heavy coat for a jacket and put the gloves in the pocket, just in case. He was learning about the unpredictable nature of the English weather.

Nice to talk to Abdul, he thought. Sometimes he didn't use his voice for days, so when he did it sounded strange to him.

His route, as always, took him past the supermarket. The queue of people waiting to get in was already starting to seem normal. Sitting in the doorway was a man with a cardboard cup in front of him and a grey-green coat draped over his knees. Nabil wasn't sure if this was the same man he'd seen before. He was about the right age, but his hair looked lighter than Nabil recalled, and his manner seemed defeated, rather than aggressive.

Nabil approached him cautiously, worried that his mood would change. He held up a pound coin for the man to see, then dropped it into the cup.

"Thanks, man. How you doing?"

"I am okay, thank you." It felt good to test out how the words sounded when spoken out loud.

"Fucking good job one of us is, then." The words were followed by a bout of coughing.

The only word Nabil understood was the expletive. He did, however, crave some company and he had the feeling that his poor and broken English would be better received by this person, than by many others.

"I am new to UK," he ventured. "I am learning English."

The man on the floor nodded. "Fair play to ya. Where you from, then?"

Nabil shrugged.

"Your country?" There was another round of coughing, from which Nabil recoiled.

"Syria."

"Oh, you poor fucker, I'll bet you got some tales to tell."

Nabil nodded, although again he only understood one word. He stood for a while, feeling self-conscious, but as if he were glued to the spot. The homeless man interjected now and then with words that were totally alien to Nabil's ears, until finally he said, "Look mate, I feel sorry for you, being as you're from Syria and no doubt had a rough time, but you need to bugger off now; no-one's gonna give me money with you standing there."

All Nabil understood was sorry, Syria, money. But he understood only too well the gesture and the tone, this man was asking him to leave.

"Goodbye." he said, meaning to be polite.

"Hey, no need to be like that, I didn't mean to cause no offence, right?" He grabbed hold of Nabil's arm.

Nabil tensed and his spine tingled, he shook his head and repeated, "Goodbye."

The homeless man let go of his arm, coughing yet again, this time sounding as if he would choke; as it subsided he held out his hand. Nabil understood it was offered in friendship, he accepted it and they shook hands.

Nabil reached the park, which he walked three times around, sitting down every now and then to prolong his time outside, not because he felt tired. On his way back the supermarket queue had lessened. The homeless man gone. Nabil joined the queue, he'd need some bread in a day or two, might as well get it now and hopefully the red-haired lady would be there. Kirsten, wasn't that her name? Yes, he was sure that's what she'd said.

She wasn't there.

Although it was still light outside there was no point in walking around for the sake of it, so he returned to his room. There was nothing to do here, except what he'd been doing all day. Writing the story for Abida, learning English, pacing the room. He wondered for how long this would carry on.

�

The nights were drawing out at last, with it came a growing sense of optimism. Everything would soon be back to normal, Rosie felt sure. There was a knock on her door, she answered it to a neighbour, who took a step back as soon as it opened, then said, "Oh, where's Kirsten?"

"She went to stay with her boyfriend for lockdown. I'm her daughter, Rosie."

"Oh, I came to see if she wanted to join in the clapping for the NHS." The woman giggled nervously. "I live there," she inclined her head to the opposite door. "I hadn't realised you were here. Surprising, really. Anyway, I do think they deserve to be applauded, but you feel a bit of a fool if you're the only one, don't you?"

"Sorry I don't know what you're talking about."

"It were on the news, eight o'clock, there's gonna be a national clap for the NHS."

"Oh yes, I did see that come to think of it. I'll keep you company, if you like."

"We'll have to keep our distance mind."

"Of course."

Rosie grabbed her jacket, told Andy where she was going, then followed her neighbour down the steps. She was surprised to see how many people there were in the street, and there were others at their windows. Someone called a count down and the clapping began. Despite the crowd Rosie did feel a little self-conscious, it was like being informally dressed in a formal setting.

Back inside the flat she said as much to Andy.

"Why'd you do it then?" he asked.

"The neighbour wanted moral support. And the NHS deserves to be recognised, doesn't it?

"I should think they'd prefer a pay rise."

"Well, I can't arrange that, can I? Do we have to watch this?"

Andy was tuned to the twenty-four-hour news channel.

"Don't you think we need to know about it?"

"So we can do what, exactly? It's so depressing, it makes me want to cry."

"Okay, see what you fancy." He tossed her the remote.

As Rosie flicked through several channels, across the bottom of the screen ran a catalogue of the daily death toll. On Film Four there was no such message, but there was a Stay Safe logo in the corner, and the film was one they'd seen more than once before. Rosie threw the remote, it hit the wall, then the floor knocking off the battery storage door.

"What the f…?" Andy shouted as he bent over to pick it up.

"I just want to relax, for fuck's sake. I have spent all day looking after our children, remember? Not a minute's peace, cleaning up after you all. No let up. Shopping in a supermarket where I've been herded around, I don't want to sit here and see how many people have died today."

"I cooked and washed up."

"Don't overdo it, will you?"

"I've got things on my mind."

"Don't I know it?"

"It's a for-real issue, Rosie. How long d'you think they'll hold that job open for me? Even if they do, we can't go on spending the money from the house, there'll be nothing left."

"I'm just as aware of that as you are, but I haven't got time to sit around wallowing in misery all day."

"Wallowing? Wallowing?"

Andy went silent, he lowered his head. One of the children was crying, Rosie started to get up from her chair.

"I'll go," Andy said.

Rosie sat with the silence ringing in her ears, and her words reverberating around her head.

"We scared him, shouting," Andy said when he returned. "Come on, let's not argue, neither of us is to blame for this."

"I know, I'm sorry. I just want to switch off. They're not giving us any respite with those figures."

"We could find a Netflix film."

"I'm not really in the mood now."

"There's loads of books on the shelf that your mum left."
"Can't remember the last time I read a whole book." Rosie went over and checked the bookcase. "I've always meant to read this one," she said, picking up a copy of Rebecca by Daphne du Maurier.

"You going to read, then?"

"I think I will. It's a good habit to reinstate. I'll go in the bedroom so you can watch whatever you want."

"It won't be any more telly, I'm with you on that."

Rosie sat on the arm of the chair and took Andy's hand in hers. "It'll be okay. We'll be okay."
"I hope so."

"I could try to get a job."

"Like where?"

"The supermarket, maybe. Mum said there are two people not going in because they're too scared."

"Worth a try I suppose. I'll be here for the kids."

"I'll speak to Mum tomorrow. Night then."

"You're not going to sleep yet?"

"Probably fall asleep reading, it's been so long."

"Shall I come and keep you awake?" He gave her hand a gentle squeeze.

"Not really in the mood tonight, sorry."

If Mandeep hadn't been off sick, a temporary job for Rosie would have been as good as read, no harm in asking the stand-in manager, Alison, she decided.

Alison was in the process of the waking-up and moving on of Roy. Usually, on her early shift Kirsten bought him a sandwich and a coffee, but she was later than usual today. So, instead she gave him three pounds, waiting for his hacking cough to subside enough to pass it directly to him.

Alison shot her a disapproving look and, as they entered the building together said, "He's probably not genuine you know, all the vagrants have been rounded up. He's probably got a BMW or a Jag in the multi-storey."

Kirsten squirmed at the word 'vagrant' and the term 'round-ed-up'; it conjured up an image of jackboots and rifles. "He's a regular, been on that doorstep every morning as long as I can remember."

"Maybe he slipped through the net, I'll give the police a call."

Kirsten's stomach hit the floor. "P'r'aps we should check with him first what's going on," she ventured to suggest.

"Well, I'm certainly not going to do that." Alison replied, as if Kirsten had suggested she run naked down the street. "You can if you like, but I imagine by the time your shift is done the police will have dealt with it."

No point in 'putting in a word for Rosie' with this one, Kirsten thought. And this thought was reinforced by the sight of the newly-returned Nick.

"Hi, how you doing?" she asked. "Good to see you back."

"I wish I wasn't," he said, donning a face mask and gloves, "but I didn't get much choice."

"No?"

"No. My finances dictate on that. Wish I was on the non-essential payroll of a company offering furlough."

"Oh, sorry. You're really worried by the corona stuff then?"

"Who isn't?"

Kirsten nodded, as if in agreement, "You'll probably be glad of the screens, then?"

"I guess they'll be some help, still rather not be here."

"D'you know about vitamin D?"

"What about it?"

"It boosts the immune system."

"Rather put my faith in a vaccine, but thanks. Heard Mandeep got sick," Nick said, picking-up the sanitizer and heading for the shop floor.

Kirsten followed, "I think she's just being cautious. Thinking of her staff."

"Ump!" came the grunted reply.

Later, leaving work, Emerson asked, Kirsten, "What d'you think of the new Labour leader, then?"

"Too soon to say, but the one I expected, not the one I hoped for. You?"

"Same as. It doesn't help me feel more hopeful for the future."

What would? Kirsten wondered, feeling an outpouring of pity for the lad. "All we can do is our little bit, in our own community. And actually, Emerson, it's always been that way. It's just we forget most of the time until something like this comes along to remind us. In my youth the big fear was nuclear war."

"D'you think there's less reason to fear it now?"

"Probably not. Seems to me we've always had some big threat to live with. Safety's an illusion, but, if we don't live with the illusion of it, how can we live at all?"

They turned the corner where they would be parting company.

"They used to tell us to hide under the table if the atom bomb went off," Kirsten said, as much to herself as Emerson. "What use would that have been?"

"About as much use as a mask is against a virus."

"See you Monday, then. Got any plans for the weekend."

"Nah! Might go for a bike ride if the weather stays fine, gotta go somewhere to avoid my mum's *boyfriend.*" He clawed the air with his forefingers.

"What's wrong with him?"

"He's a jerk."

Kirsten wondered how true that really was. "I'm going to start cycling. Thought I'd walk today though, it helps me clear my head."

"I like to ride out to the woods. It's been busy out there recently, though. Since lockdown everyone seems to be going there."

"Yes, I heard that. My partner," the word still sounded strange, "works the wood."

"Nah! You're kidding me?"

"No. Why?"

"Bit taller'n me? Fifties, dark hair going grey?"

"Yes, Daniel, his name's Daniel."

"Never asked his name, but I chat to him loads. He's a really smart guy."

"Yes, he is." Kirsten felt proud of this recognition.

"Well, fancy, him being your partner."

"I'll make sure to tell him our connection."

"Yeah, do that. You got plans for tonight?"

"Eat copious amounts of food, drink copious amounts of wine; watch a film."

"Sounds good to me. Enjoy. See you next week."

Kirsten's walk took her through the park and along the river. Usually she saw one, maybe two other walkers, today she stopped counting, but it seemed every few yards she was giving way, or they were giving way, everyone overly polite. It moved Kirsten: that people were so considerate of others was pleasing; that they were fearful, distressing. Which of these two options wasn't clear from the person's demeanour: a step back, or a turning away as she approached, could imply either. She wondered, not for the first time, about her own behaviour, wanting neither to offend others, nor to perpetrate fear. She certainly didn't wish to be aggressive and defend a point of view so contrary to that of others, as Emerson was inclined to do. How should she behave to be the best human being she could be? Always a dilemma, but never more so than now.

As she carried on with her walk Kirsten concentrated on her surroundings, rather than her internal state. She was enjoying the signs of the emerging spring. The air was crisp and tasted fresh in her nostrils. She took deep breaths of it, feeling grateful for being able to; that her lungs were healthy enough, and that she was near enough to the country to have fresh air to breathe. Now she became aware of the sweet smell of hawthorn blossom. On top of the bush a female blackbird aired her wings as she sang tup, tup, tup. The earth beneath Kirsten's feet was firm enough for stability, yet yielding enough to leave a print behind. The river ambled along beside her, like a loyal dog walking to heel. She felt herself connected to it and imagined living in the inner city, where there were few such places to walk.

The river walk ended and she was back on the road. It was only five minutes more along it to Daniel's cottage; usually there was a continuous stream of traffic that made it difficult to cross the road safely; today there was not a vehicle in sight. Kirsten ran across anyway, from habit.

"Hello," she called, as she entered the house, still feeling like a visitor.

There was no reply and no sign of Daniel. She removed her shoes and jacket and put the kettle on. The television was on, and the fire had just been lit, so she knew he wasn't far away. The house smelt of wood smoke and yesterday's bread. *I'm so lucky to be in this house with him,* she thought. *Why do I feel so sad all the time?* And then, as if in answer, her eyes were drawn to the television screen and the scrolling death toll across the bottom of it.

She sat down at the table, so that she couldn't see it. Daniel's tablet was on it, she picked it up and saw that he'd paused something. Kirsten clicked on the play arrow and was greeted by an American commentator telling his audience the daily financial tallies that proved the rich had got richer and the poor, poorer. '*Goodbye to the middle class and the bank of mom and dad,*' he said. '*The central banks want to be the buyer and lender of last resort.*' She sighed, paused it again and got up to make the tea.

"There you are," Daniel said, carrying eggs in each hand. He put them down and took two from his pockets.

"I walked home along the river. It was busy."

"Yeah? Everyone wanting to go out, now that we've been told to stay in."

"Seems like it."

"The woods've got busy, too."

"On the subject of the woods, it turns out that you and my work colleague, Emerson, are pals."

"What?" Daniel had been putting the eggs in a box, now he turned to Kirsten and gave her his full attention.

"He told me today that he goes cycling there and has had several conversations with you. Said you're really smart," she giggled. "Easily impressed, obviously."

"He's clearly a discerning chap. I think I know who you mean. Early twenties, long hair, plumpish build."

"Yep."

"Emerson, you say?" Daniel nodded at Kirsten's reply. "I'll have to introduce myself properly next time."

"You could have a chat with him about the current situation, he's a big-time conspiracy theorist. What?"

Daniel's flinch hadn't escaped her notice.

"Don't like that term, it's dismissive."

Now she felt told off. "Sorry. He's on the same page as you with regard to the current situation."

"It's just come to really grate on my nerves. Any narrative that diverges from the established view is a conspiracy, no matter what evidence there is for it. What's wrong with having a contrary view? In a democratic society, we're supposed to be open to opposing views."

"True."

"Not only that. We're supposed to welcome them and debate them so that we can reach a consensus on the truth." He made tea for himself and coffee for Kirsten without checking that was what she wanted. He put them both on the table, then sat down and gave his attention to his tablet.

Kirsten sat down beside him. "I had a look at that while you were out."

"I'm glad I've been watching this stuff for as long as I have, gave me a chance to prepare. I'll just sit back and wait to see what happens for a few months."

"How bad d'you think it'll get?"

"Really bad for some. Great for others. The Bigs getter bigger at the expense of everyone else. Whatever the truth about the virus, the central banks are going to use this to their advantage."

"It's always been that way I suppose. The rich robbing the poor."

"Yep. As George Carlin said 'With a gun you can rob a bank. With a bank you can rob the world'."

"How true. I used to think there was a chance it would change one day; not sure I do any more. I worry for Rosie and Andy. The timing in terms of his job couldn't have been worse."

"I've been thinking about them, actually. If they made the right investment, they could do alright."

"I doubt they'd be up for anything like that. Andy's too cautious."

"In real terms, money in the bank is depreciating."

"I could suggest it, I guess. After all the money isn't going anywhere for a few months."

"It'd need a few years, not months."

"I doubt they can spare it for that long. There'll be another mortgage soon. At least I hope there will."

"Um, yeah!" Daniel made his right hand into a fist, cupped it with his left and tapped his chin with his thumbs, "Worth a thought, though."

There were two pieces of interesting news this morning, as far as Emerson was concerned; both needed further attention, as either could hold the key to what was really going on.

The first, the PM in hospital and his health seemingly deteriorating. If he'd have considered such a thing, Emerson might have imagined the thought could offer some perverse pleasure; either that, or evidence that contradicted his opinion that there was no virus. But neither of these occurred to him , nor did he acknowledge the *If he gets really sick I might have to…* There was a seed of fear forming in his stomach. *That'll be a propaganda exercise.*

The second piece of news. A mobile phone mast had been set on fire. Emerson's earlier research hadn't led him to a connection between 5G and coronavirus, but now he was beginning to have second thoughts. *I mean what's it even for? Faster internet they claim, but I haven't seen one new phone equipped with it.* And that there were significant health risks from it was well documented, someone even said right in front of one it'd be comparable to sitting in a microwave. *It would make gaming faster, but . . . well, gaming is pretty fast already, actually.*

His musings were interrupted by a knock on the door.

"Yeah, what?"

His mother opened the door and stepped cautiously into the room. "I've got a small list here, would you mind?" She held it and a twenty-pound note out to him.

"Yeah, all right. The time on the computer read thirteen-ten, it was almost time to go.

"What're you looking at?"

"Nutin'."

"That 5G's really dangerous you know," his mother told him. "Don't believe what they tell you, it's not for faster internet, well, not only for that. Apart from the fact that there's all kinds of health concerns, people are saying it'll be used to control us, turn off electric cars for example."

"Why'd they wanna do that?"

"Climate concerns, control travel."

"Um, dunno about that."

"And it can be used as a weapon. It was used against the women at Greenham Common."

"Really?" Emerson was genuinely interested in this. "How d'you know that?"

"Just one of the things I've picked up over the years. Anyway, I've got sympathy with those who burned it down. Even if none of that stuff is true, but I'm pretty sure it is, it's a bloody eyesore. Shouldn't you be going?"

Typical! Just when Emerson thought they had found some common ground she had to go and ruin it with a nag. He didn't reply, just turned off his computer in obvious ill humour.

"You haven't even left yourself time for lunch. I'll make you a sarnie."

❧

The new door smelled of undercoat, but there remained a faint scent of wood. Margaret liked the latter, it had a sense of authenticity about it.

Daniel put the brush in a jar of white spirit. "Right Mrs. P, I'll be back by four to put the first coat on, should be dry enough by then, on a day like today."

"I'll cancel my appointments, make sure I'm in."

Daniel gave a light laugh. "You going to be okay with it ajar?"

"Aye, I don't anticipate anyone coming in to rape me or anything. I should be so lucky at my age."

"Mrs. P!"

Margaret giggled. "I didn't realise you were so easily shocked."

"You should be able to close it by lunch time, if you need to go out."

"There's nothing here to steal. All my gold is hidden away, only my children know where."

"You kidding me again? Or do you really have gold some-where?"

"Really."

"Well done on that one."

"Yes, it's real money for when this shit-show goes down. It's my insurance. My dad taught me that."

"Wise man. See you later, then."

Margaret watched Daniel until he reached his van, feeling wistful. It was a strange emotion, not quite reliance, but something close. Like a dog's relationship with its master, perhaps? But no, not as reliant as that; she was more like a cat, perfectly okay alone, but better for his company. If she'd been a dog, or a cat, she might have curled up in her bed and slept now, but wasting time at her age was a sin, she needed to keep busy.

Although, she had often questioned the point of anything before, since lockdown the feeling that she was just biding time until death had grown stronger. It was hard to find meaning in a life that was running out so fast; with all the major events, bar one, in the past, and with no one needing her anymore. *Never mind the virus, loneliness can kill. Thank God for Daniel.*

Her routines and the groups she attended provided some distraction and some tentative reason for carrying on, but she wanted real experiences, not virtual ones.

The thought of Zooming and the literature group led Margaret to the pile of books. There had been a change of direction and a decision to discuss dystopian novels. *No prizes for deciding why,* she thought, picking up Brave New World.

She'd read it before, of course, along with We, and Nineteen Eighty-Four. There were common themes in them all, she decided: censorship, lies, state-generated fear, and synthetic worlds, all designed to disconnect people from each other and nature. "Notice any similarities?" She asked the imaginary group.

It was a bright morning, although not yet warm. The sun, shining through the window, cast a long shadow on the table, making a shadow-twin of Margaret's empty cup. Daniel had washed his up and put it in the drainer. Margaret did the same with hers, but then decided she'd have another drink before doing…? What, what would she do? Reading was an afternoon or evening activity; except when she'd been studying, she'd never read a book, or even a newspaper, in the morning.

As she headed back to the table with her second cup of tea, Margaret broke a beam of light. *I'm like a ghost, walking through things,* she thought. Now she sat and looked at the restored

beam, marvelling at the perfect lines and the myriad dust particles floating inside it. Dust. That was what she, what everyone
returned to, eventually. It seemed the light was holding the
particles, and that they were striving for something. In so many
small ways, it seemed to Margaret, the universe was offering clues
about itself. Dust particles held by light.

Now she looked around the room at all the places the sun
was showing her she needed to work on. Winter-hidden house-
work was illuminated now. Margaret felt shocked that a kitchen
she prided herself on keeping pristine, was, after all, so dirty.
She also felt grateful that she had been shown a way to spend
her morning. She finished her tea and gathered up her cleaning
materials.

✍

"Mrs. P. Whatever are you doing?"

"Oh, my goodness, Daniel, you scared me half to death."

"You scared *me* half to death. What're you doing up there?"

"I've been overcome by a cleaning fit."

"That's all well and good, but you look rather precarious."

Margaret took a careful, backwards step down from the
work surface to the chair; Daniel was holding onto it as she did
so.

"I'd rather you weren't climbing around like that at all, but if
you must, you could at least have used step ladders."

"Oh, I couldn't be bothered to get them out."

"I'd never forgive myself if you'd fallen."

"Why? You didn't send me up there. Anyway, done now."

"Thank God for that. You got any other plans I should
know about? Painting ceilings, or anything?"

"Well, there's an idea. I could make decorating my lockdown project."

"You are joking, aren't you? Please tell me you are."

"Of course I'm joking. I hate decorating."

"I can just imagine what Joe would have to say about this."

Margaret sighed. "Well, he doesn't need to hear about it,
does he? I know you and he are concerned for me, but it does
make me feel like such an old lady. I know I am, before you take
the trouble to remind me, but I don't like to feel like one."

Now Daniel laughed. "Mrs. P, you'll never be that. So, am I getting a cuppa while I do this door, or not?"

❧

The Prime Minister's admission to hospital was worrying. It wasn't that Mandeep was a fan of his, although she liked the opposition no better, but if he could be that ill; with all the privileges he enjoyed, then…

She was glad to be at home. She felt inclined to seal the house up, fill in every crack and keep the windows closed; it was such a struggle to ensure that everyone else in the house followed her rules.

"We'll suffocate if we don't let some air in," Dev said. "Even those who're shielding are allowed to open a window."

And, in response to her suggestion that they shop online, "I'll bet everyone's doing that, and there's no need. I'll go, just me, once a week should do it."

She'd told him, this morning, that she'd woken with a headache.

"I'm not surprised, with all the worrying you've been doing." He gave her temples a rub and fetched her some paracetamol and a glass of water. "Stay here and rest a while, you're supposed to be sick anyway."

"God is paying me back for the lie, he's given me the virus."

"Don't be so daft. You're a good person, you've done nothing to offend God." Dev sat down on the bed and put his arm around Mandeep. "You really went through it while I was away, didn't you?"

His sympathy brought her to tears.

"I'm sorry I was gone so long."

"And you've come back to a wife who's falling apart."

"I'm just glad to be back. There were times I thought…well, doesn't matter now."

It had never occurred to Mandeep that Dev had been afraid he wouldn't get back, too. She took hold of the hand that was resting on the bed.

"How d'you feel about your mum?"

"I don't feel anything. When I was there, I was busy doing what had to be done, then supporting everyone, especially Dad and Gurjit; they took it the hardest. Then I was just concerned with getting back to you and the girls."

"I've been very selfish."

"How so?"

"You need my support and I'm asking for yours."

"We need to take care of each other, these are difficult times."

Mandeep sighed. "I've been – I am, so scared. Especially now, with all these cabinet ministers getting it and the Prime Minister sick enough to go to hospital."

"It's going to be fine." It wasn't that Dev didn't sometimes feel scared himself, but he was trying to keep some perspective on the whole thing, and he needed to be strong for the family.

He patted her hand. Momentarily Mandeep felt annoyed, it seemed patronising, it was okay for him, he was fit, and hardly ever ill.

Now she thought back to the day Indrani's asthma was diagnosed. Mandeep had felt responsible, like she'd done something terribly wrong, failed with her genes or her mothering to protect her daughter. Dev's response had seemed dismissive, he hadn't even wanted her to have the inhalers.

"Why? " Mandeep had asked him.

"They're steroid based. She's so young. Steroids have ill effects on the health, long term."

"But you saw how she was. She couldn't breathe."

"I prefer to try something else first, that's all. Herbal or homeopathic."

Mandeep agreed to give the latter a go, but it slid into the background as the weeks went by; and soon the inhaler and Indrani were so synonymous with each other that their interdependence had become taken for granted. She was brought back to the present by Dev saying, "Well, I'd better get on with some work. You stay here and rest, though."

"I want to look some stuff up." She got up and started gathering the necessary items for taking a shower and getting dressed.

"What stuff?"

"Some things I've seen online."

"You think Facebook is a reliable source of information?"

Mandeep shrugged. "I'm just making sure." Although she didn't believe it, she wanted to check out what was being said about 5G being the cause of the illness, rather than a virus. Not that it was much better if it was true, except that might make it easier to protect everyone. What she really wanted was some reassurance. Something to convince her the danger was less than she feared.

Half- an-hour later she was sitting at the dressing table in front of the laptop. She clicked on the link that was on her Facebook page and read the article to the end. She found nothing to convince her that the claim was true, but had found plenty of cause to consider 5G a health risk. The study looked sound, it said two hundred and forty scientists had peer-reviewed the research. Now she had 5G *and* the virus to worry about. And, alongside the fear, a question, *why isn't anyone official talking about 5G health risks?*

There was another claim on Facebook, that the deaths from the virus were being exaggerated. Mandeep, so wanting to believe this, decided to look at the data for herself. Although she thought it more likely that the Government would under-report them, she couldn't see the advantage of inflating them, unless you were a conspiracy theorist, and she didn't want to go down that crazy road. She clicked onto the Office of National Statistics website, only to be greeted by graphs and figures that confused her more. Dev would be able to translate them, of course, but she didn't want to ask him. By how much, she wasn't sure, but she could see the daily death figures were higher than the previous year. She felt her spirit sink.

I wonder how many people die in a normal day? She typed in the question alongside the thought, and was surprised to find the number in excess of one and a half thousand. In light of that, the daily death toll scrolling the screen didn't seem so scary. Her spirits lifted.

Mandeep clicked off the site and typed in a link she'd been sent the day before. It took her to a female Indian doctor. She felt a rush of relief and excitement as she took in the information. The claim, which was backed up by evidence that appeared to be sound, was that vitamin D was a protector against the virus.

"Dev." She was so excited she wanted to show him the clip. "Dev," she called a second time.

He came rushing in, looking concerned, "What? What's the matter?"

"Look at this, she says vitamin D will protect us against coronavirus."

"God. I thought there was something wrong." He stood watching over Mandeep's shoulder for a few minutes. "Okay, good, we'll get some." He made to move away.

"It looks scientifically sound, doesn't it?"

"Yeah."

"I want to tell everyone."

"You would." He kissed the top of her head. "Right, best get back to it."

"What's the best source of vitamin D?"

"Sunlight. We're in the wrong country. We need supplements." He left the room.

A few minutes later Mandeep had ordered a supply of high strength vitamin D, enough for her immediate family and her parents. She had also sent the link to several people.

Feeling almost elated Mandeep made to turn off the computer, but just before she did, she decided to check her horoscope, feeling sure it would read well. On the site was a headline that caught her eye:

The December Conjunction and The Coronavirus:

On December twenty-sixth, there was an astrologically rare event, in which five planets were in conjunction at the same time as a solar eclipse. In Hindu mythology the absence of the sun during an eclipse is inauspicious. Such an event would lead to natural disasters, political upheavals, and the spread of epidemics.

Reading this Mandeep remembered that the New Year prediction had been worrying, something about economic challenges and social change, she seemed to recall, she'd have to look it up again.

Today's big news was that the Prime Minister had been sent to intensive care. Kirsten felt afraid in response, her certainty that the virus was being propagandised undermined as a consequence – and, if that wasn't true, then…

When they heard the news, earlier that day, she and Daniel had exchanged a glance. It felt as if they shared the same emotion, but it was immediately followed by a shrug from Daniel and him saying, "I'm sure he'll make a full recovery."

Now she checked her watch, feeling surprised at the lateness of the hour. *Work already.* Kirsten knew she should be grateful for her job, and indeed she was, but there were so many more interesting things to do, if only there were time. She made herself a sandwich, keeping half of it for break time. The worst thing about shifts, as far as she was concerned, was the disruption to her meal routine. It was the reason she disliked working afternoons so much. Mandeep knew this and compensated for it as much as she was able, she was good like that, always trying to accommodate everyone. This temporary manager didn't share the same concern for her staff.

Kirsten packed all necessary items into her backpack. There was no room left for her jacket, so she had to wear it, even though it was likely she'd be too warm once she got moving.

The chickens looked up from their scratting and seemed to Kirsten to watch her as she fumbled with locking the door. It was as if they viewed her suspiciously as a new, and not entirely welcome, member of their tribe. Stupid, of course, it was doubtful they had any feelings about her at all. Although it didn't work the other way around, Kirsten was growing increasingly fond of them.

Pushing her bicycle from the shed she tried to recall the last time she'd cycled any distance, especially one that included a big hill.

Hope I'm up to it.

One consequence of the lockdown, the quiet roads, made cycling feel much safer and yet, in a strange way less so; it was like the aftermath of a disaster.

There were, however, two other cyclists on the same route, both of whom were male, lycra-clad and riding with their hands on the dropped handlebars. They both sped past her, the second of whom acknowledged Kirsten with a 'Hi'. She watched them both climb the hill with apparent ease, standing on the pedals and wiggling their backsides.

Kirsten approached the hill with trepidation and wobbled up half of it, gasping for breath, until both legs and lungs were defeated, and she got off for the final part of the ascent, her legs shaking and her heart pounding. When she reached the top there was no sign of either of the other cyclists. She climbed back on and freewheeled much of the remaining mile to the edge of town. She reached the supermarket in plenty of time to lock the bike, recover her composure, and have a cup of tea.

A few minutes later Emerson arrived in the break room, looking annoyed.

"Hi Kirst. You're early."

"Came on my bike, didn't know how long to allow."

"Well done."

"Pah, you wouldn't be saying that if you'd seen me on the hill."

"It's substantial. You'll get better."

"Hope so. It's my intention to keep it up, get fit through this lockdown if nothing else."

"Loads of people thinking that, I reckon. I've never seen so many cyclists and walkers."

"Me neither." She paused before saying, "So, PM is in intensive care."

"You don't believe that d'you?"

"Don't you?"

"No. It's a propaganda exercise. Make us more afraid; win him some Brownie points. I'll worry when I hear he's dead."

The words sounded harsh, but Kirsten had to admit feeling something similar herself. Any anxiety she experienced around his fate, was entirely selfish.

"I have wondered, if I'm honest, but also it has made me a bit more afraid."

"Course, that's what it's meant to do."

Whatever the truth: deadly virus, not so deadly virus, being used by opportunistic agencies, Kirsten just wished the whole thing would go away.

"I'd better get going, I suppose."

"You sound keen," Emerson mocked.

"I'm okay, but truth be told there's plenty I'd rather be doing."

"Not to mention how hard it seems to be to please our new manager. Heard how Mandeep is, by the way?"

"She's okay. Just erring on the side of caution."

"Hum!"

Kirsten wasn't sure how to interpret the 'hum.' She could hardly tell Emerson that Mandeep was actually fine.

"She has all of her staff to protect, don't forget."

"Course.Anyway, wanna fag. Laters?"

Two weeks of the same route around the park was becoming boring, it wasn't only the same scenery, but also the same people, and the same dogs. Nabil was currently sitting on one of the two benches that weren't banned for use by black and yellow tape. He was watching one of those people, with one of those dogs; it was small, brown and tan, podgy and scruffy. There were a variety of canines in this country, Nabil observed many colours and sizes. At home they were mostly a standard size and colour, and all were skinny. It seemed to him that the British variety had been bred for particular owners, their dimensions made to fit individual requirements. This one was now being carried and cooed at.

English people love their dogs more than their children, Nabil thought, observing a woman shouting at a boy of about three or four, who was crying. Nabil had missed whatever it was had provoked the tears. It wasn't that in Syria children were treated especially well, or British ones particularly poorly, it was just that Syrian dogs were servants rather than friends.

An elderly couple approached the bench, hand in hand. Nabil stood up, smiled and nodded, moving away. When he looked back the woman was dusting the bench down. He felt violated by their action, as if they considered him unclean.

He wandered back towards his lodgings, thinking to phone Abdul and ask for suggestions on places to walk. He hesitated outside the supermarket, looking for the man who was usually in the doorway; it was several days since he'd seen him, he still wasn't there.

Inside his room the blackness soon crept back into Nabil's soul. And today there was something else too. Alongside the heartache, there was pain and tiredness in his body. It felt overwhelming, he wanted to give in. Outside, where there were people and it was warm, he hadn't noticed it so much, but here, inside, it was chilly and lonely. It was time for writing Abida's story.

Nabil fetched the appropriate note pad and pen, sat in bed, for warmth, and started to read over his last excerpt.

> *'Thirty-three thousand eight hundred pounds…', the agent told them, '…each.' His supercilious smile, as much as the words, was responsible for my collapse into the seat he offered. I was defeated.*
>
> *Not so Abida.*
>
> *She knew what to do, although she cried over some of the sales, even though we had no more need for the items. Perhaps she'd hoped we would come back some day.*
>
> *'This chair lasted my grandmother a lifetime, it'll do the same for you. You insult me with your offer,' she told the buyer of one such item.*
>
> *It was she, too, who did all the bargaining.*
>
> *Nabil began writing again.*
>
> *We were left with a blanket and mattress each.*
>
> *'It's only two nights,' Abida reassured.*
>
> *We were preparing to sleep. 'Layla has the money,' Abida suddenly said, 'in case you need to know.'*
>
> *As if she knew.*
>
> *I never asked her where the rest of the money came from, but I think I knew, yes, I did, even before that man came to get her back. And rob us.*

Suddenly Nabil felt so exhausted. He couldn't write another word.

He put down the pen, closed the book and lay down, thinking he'd feel better if he just had a nap. Sleep was interrupted by dreams that made no sense, but frightened him. He was back in his hometown playing cards with a group of men. His hand fell to the floor, except for one, the Jack of Spades, which leapt now at his face, laughed mockingly, receded, then returned, over and over. Someone beckoned to him from the other side of a raging fire.

Nabil woke in a sweat, his throat dry, his body chilled and restless. The light was dimming into dusk. He checked the time on his phone and was shocked to find he'd been sleeping for hours. It was with effort that he dragged his heavy body from the bed to fetch some water. He had no appetite for food. Then the coughing started, and each hack of it burned his throat and pounded in his head. In his bedside drawers there were some paracetamol, bought as a precaution some weeks before. Nabil took two, drank a full pint of water then lay down and went back to sleep.

Rosie had many times decried the crowded streets, but empty ones felt threatening. She hurried towards the supermarket.

Before starting shopping, she went to the check-outs, looking for her mother, who was busy and didn't notice, but Rosie had the confirmation she wanted. Shopping was something she normally enjoyed, taking her time to browse for new taste experiences, and bargains on the familiar; but not any longer. How could she peruse and social distance at the same time? To a naturally sociable person, such as herself, this all felt so surreal.

She stuck with the items she knew, shoving them into her trolley like she was taking part in supermarket sweep. There were no tinned tomatoes – with spaghetti bolognese and ratatouille on her meal list this was going to make her life awkward.

Her mother's till was busy, but she wanted to see her so stood in the queue. Third in line, and at a two-metre distance from the nearest person, Rosie was halfway down the aisle. It struck her as stupid that, in keeping her distance from the person in front, she was cramping the space of shoppers.

It was worth the wait to see the look of delight on Kirsten's face.

"Hello, love, great to see you."

"It comes to something when the only way to meet your own mother is like this," Rosie said, with good cheer.

"Any news?"

"Um, let me think, what've I been up to? No, no news."

"Did you find everything you wanted?"

"No tomatoes. Or flour."

"I might be able to help with the latter," Kirsten almost whispered it; she was thinking of Daniel's supply from the wholesaler.

"That would be great."

"I'll let you know later." She was thinking she'd drop it off tomorrow, but didn't want anyone overhearing.

"When did you acquire those?" Rosie nodded her head towards the T-shirt saying: 'We're All In This Together.'

"Oh, don't ask."

Rosie laughed, having some idea how her mother would feel about it.

What did Kirsten feel? There was a sense of togetherness to some extent. She did subscribe to the respect people showed each other with their social distancing, and did acknowledge their fear. And yet, the conviction that there was some other agenda behind it all, made her feel like a double agent. She imagined wartime Britain – most people sure they were doing their bit, and equally sure of their bit being right. The minority who didn't agree were silenced by this, looking furtively around for a glimpse of recognition in the eyes of another to assure them they weren't alone. Both were equally afraid, sometimes of each other as much as the war.

"You serving?" The question was quite curt, and brought tears to the eyes that were watching Rosie walk out of the door, as if they were witnessing her walking away for ever.

"I'm sorry, I was distracted. My daughter." Kirsten pointed at Rosie, who was heading out of the store. "We haven't seen each other for a while."

"Ah, I'm sorry." The customer's tone changed to understanding.

The street opposite Kirsten's house had two convenience stores in it, neither of them had any tinned tomatoes.

"I've got fresh ones," one of the shop keepers suggested. "If you cut an x in the bottom throw into boiling water for about one minute, lift out, put in cold water, colder the better, skins come off easily."

"Okay, thanks, I'll give it a go."

The shopkeeper weighed out the amount she considered correct for two meals. "You'll never want tinned again" she assured Rosie, "except for the convenience. Not seen you before, you new?"

"It's a long story. Staying at my mum's for the lockdown."

"Who's your mum? Ah, really? Why didn't you say that in the first place, I have a supply out here for the regulars." She tottered to the storeroom and then returned with two tins. "Take these as well. In case we're still short next time."

"Oh, thank you."

The shopkeeper buried them at the bottom of Rosie's bag, as if she was hiding them. Rosie felt like a member of the resistance picking up a secret message.

When she got home, she discovered a large bag of flour had been delivered.

"Daniel brought it," Andy explained. "Apparently he gets it wholesale."

She told Andy about the tomatoes and how she'd felt, and they laughed, thinking the flour added weight to it. "I might check with the neighbour later, see if she has everything she needs. Maybe we can do swaps and stuff, if necessary."

"That's a good idea. We need to look out for each other."

"Despite their efforts to prevent that."

"God! You sound like your mother."

"Um! I'm just starting to think – I get that if we stay away from each other, we help stop the spread, but this social isolation – it's just not right, humans need company. She – the neighbour – is on her own with her kid, it's difficult." Rosie sighed. "I heard her shouting at him the other day and wanted to knock and offer some help, but how could I? Not just reluctant in case she feels judged, but now this social distancing lark. They speak about it on the news like a war, but in wartime there was a strong sense of community. Then you get all this 'in it together stuff'," she clawed the air with her forefingers, "at the same time as telling us to stay apart. It creates confusion and division, and I don't like it."

Andy nodded his agreement.

"I'm going to try building a bit of rapport. We can stay six feet apart and still be friendly, and if she needs help, I won't feel patronising offering it."

"What you going to do?"

"Not sure, take the kid to the park maybe, with our two."

"We're not supposed to mix households."

"Who's gonna know? What they gonna do?"

"Any one of the other neighbours. Fine us."

Rosie laughed. "Shame you're not furloughed, then you'd be paying with their money. Look, if members of the cabinet can drive miles in search of family support, then how can they complain about me taking a neighbour's child to the park?"

"They can't, but…"

"Well, I'm going to ask her on Thursday at the next clap, see what she says."

"Fair enough."

Despite his concerns Andy admired that Rosie had spared a thought for her neighbour.

The cycle back to Daniel's house was easier, being mostly downhill, but no quicker because Kirsten was scared of the descent; especially in the dark. She did, however, feel proud of herself when she reached her destination.

Daniel was listening to music and browsing on his tablet; when she entered the room, he turned his attention to her. "Glad you're back. I almost came to get you."

"What stopped you?" Kirsten regretted the curt tone.

"You said you wanted to cycle." Daniel sounded confused.

Kirsten went to him and kissed his forehead. "I would've been annoyed and relieved at the same time. It was a bit scary, but I'll get used to it. I do want to do it," she assured him.

Daniel put the tablet down and the kettle on. "D'you want tea, or you prefer wine?"

"I'll go with the wine, if that's okay. God that bread smells delish."

"You want a slice? Not fresh today, I'm afraid." He cut a slice, put butter on it and offered Marmite, to which Kirsten agreed. "I took some flour to Rosie," he continued.

"Oh, thank you. It's great having our secret supply in one way, but I also feel a bit guilty." She sat down beside him, took a sip of wine, and then said, "What were you watching?"

"Just browsing. Checking some stuff out. There's a lot of anti-lockdown stuff on the net. Plenty of people in the know who agree with me that whatever the truth is about the virus, lockdowns make things worse."

"I must admit the PM getting ill has made me a bit more scared of the virus."

"Oh."

"Aren't you?"

"How's being afraid going to help?"

"It's not, just can't help it. You been sticking with the vitamin regime, by the way?"

"Yep. I've been thinking, I could invest some money for you?"

"What?"

"Two thousand, I thought."

"What?" Kirsten felt like she'd been shaken awake. "How much wine have you had?"

Daniel laughed, "About two sips."

"It's very generous, but I wouldn't feel right about it."

"Why not? I've got the money, you haven't. Think of it as a birthday present."

So, he hadn't forgotten her birthday was coming up. "That's an expensive birthday present – I'm not sure, it doesn't feel right somehow."

"Okay." Daniel looked really hurt. He thought for a minute before suggesting, "How about this then? I invest the money. You have whatever profit it makes and I get the investment back."

"That could work."

"If it makes you feel better. Suppose I spent two thousand on some jewellery, would you refuse to accept it?"

"Well…no…but I probably wouldn't ever wear it, for fear of losing it." Kirsten smiled to herself, this was a definite sign of his investment in the relationship, and Kirsten felt more pleased about that than any amount of money. "I don't know what to say. Except thank you, of course."

"You're not usually stuck for words."

Kirsten laughed. *I could use it to help out Rosie,* she thought.

Good Friday

"I didn't expect to see you today," Margaret said to Daniel.

"Shop needs its bread supply. Anyway, I need my cup of tea. You okay Mrs. P? You look a bit peaky."

"I'm not exactly sure, I feel really cold and tired."

"Like you're coming down with something?"

"Maybe."

"Shall I call…?"

"No, I don't want you to call anyone. I don't even know if I'm ill. Shouldn't have said anything."

"Well, I'm glad you did. I promised Joe, remember." Daniel took a sip of his tea. "Where's my Easter egg, anyway?"

"There weren't any in the shops – no, seriously, there weren't. Fortunately, I sent money to the grandchildren weeks ago, when it looked like this might happen." She put her head in her hands and shut her eyes.

"You're not right are you, Mrs. P?"

"I'm okay, please don't fuss. If I don't feel better soon, I might go for a little lie down."

"Good. And I'll be back later to see how you are."

"Maybe you should stay away in case it's *the* virus, I don't want you or your lady friend to catch it."

"If it is, you'll need an eye keeping." As he was saying this Daniel was considering the options. He was sitting with his elbows resting on the table and his hands to his mouth. He was thinking that if she was ill, he would probably have to keep away from Kirsten anyway, just in case. And Margaret would need looking after. "I think you've been doing too much partying again," he said.

Margaret's laugh sounded weak, reinforcing Daniel's concerns.

"I'm going to the wood for a couple of hours, I'll be back by teatime."

"Okay. Thank you."

As soon as the door closed behind Daniel, Margaret burst into tears, but lack of energy soon stopped them. There was a ringing in her ears and a strange taste in her mouth, both of which made her feel dizzy.

Might be sensible to have a lie down, she thought, as she was washing the cups under the tap.

She poured herself a pint of water and put two biscuits on a plate then climbed the stairs with some effort and lay down on her bed.

❧

Hi, please phone me when you can, D x the message read.

Although Kirsten tried to follow this instruction several times, the call always failed to connect.

He's probably in the wood, she reassured herself, although she couldn't help but feel a little worried because he rarely got in touch without a prior arrangement. She finished her lunch and cleared it away, three more hours of her shift to go. She tried once more; still nothing.

Hi, you don't seem to have a signal, I did try, K x she wrote, and was checking it ready to send when Emerson came into the break room.

"Hi, Kirst," he said, putting on the television before the kettle.

"Hi. How can you bear to watch this?"

Daily death figures scrolled along the bottom of the screen.

"You got to know your enemy. Looks like a bomb or a mine, doesn't it?" Emerson was referring to a picture of the spiky virus, turning like the world beside the statistics.

"S'pose it does a bit, gotta get back to work."

Kirsten was almost out of the door when Emerson said, "You heard about the mobile phone towers being burned down?"

"No. Because people think they're linked to the virus?"

"Exactly."

"I'd be interested to hear your thoughts on that, but not now, I have to go."

"Won't take long. Not sure, didn't think so at first, but now, well, there is some evidence of 5G links to health problems."

"People always say that about new technology though, and they might be right, but we're still here. And thriving."

"Well, some people think the fact that we are thriving is what this is all about. Eugenicists who want to kill us off."

"Again, interesting, but another time. See you." *Global warming, nuclear war, corona bloody virus, and now 5G. It's too much.*

At the end of the shift Kirsten felt so tired. Was it boredom perhaps? She reached her bicycle, feeling a combination of dread and excitement. *At least it's a nice afternoon,* she thought, *it might be quite pleasant. Better try Daniel again.* There was still no answer. That he was somewhere without a phone signal, was the most likely explanation and yet – there was a little knot of anxiety forming in the pit of her stomach. The seed had been planted with Greg's illness and, like a garden weed, it needed very little nurturing to make it grow.

Necessity took Nabil from the house, indeed from his room, for the first time in three days. In that time, he'd eaten little and slept much, but despite this, today he needed to buy food.

The fresh air had a strange effect upon him. He felt light-headed, dreamy-eyed, almost other-worldly, as if he were a voyeur on his own life. He walked towards the supermarket, unaware that it was closing early until he arrived there. He felt anxious; if they didn't let him in, he would have nothing to eat. He joined the small queue. His legs felt as if they didn't fully belong to him, and as if they might decide at any moment they did not, and desert him.

As he struggled to remain standing, he recalled the same sensation, this time from fear, as he waited towards the back, while others pushed their way into the small boat, too small he'd thought at the time. In that instance his legs were taken from underneath him, not by the fear, but by the person behind him, and Nabil's place in the boat was lost. Later, when he heard the news, he was grateful for this, but sad for the person who'd shoved him out of line.

He moved forward slowly in this queue fearing he'd get to the end too late, but he didn't. Inside the supermarket the tense atmosphere made him want to hurry. The social distancing arrows on the floor, and the hesitant body language of the customers, made it clear this wasn't possible. He wondered if he should even be here, if his fever was the illness of which they were warned, and if so, was he putting others at risk? But what choice did he have?

Some of the shelves were almost bare. Nabil felt troubled in response. Although he wasn't deprived of any item, he hadn't expected any of this in the UK. Queuing, shortages, and suspicion of strangers, were not what he'd expected.

He was shepherded out of the opposite door to the one by which he entered. Because of the absence of his homeless friend at the front door, Nabil expected to find him here, at the back. When he wasn't there either Nabil became a bit concerned; he hoped that nothing bad had happened to him.

"Finally," Kirsten said to Daniel as the call connected. "I was getting a bit worried."

"Sorry, no signal in the wood. Margaret isn't too well. I'm thinking I might have to stay with her for a day or two."

"Oh." The news was a shock. A host of objections flooded into Kirsten in response, all of which, she knew, were totally unreasonable, but she felt as disappointed as a child whose birthday party was cancelled. "What about the chucks – and the bread?"

"Tricky, I know. I'll have to think. I'll go and see how she is, then come back and discuss it with you. Okay?"

"Okay."

Kirsten sat for a while, staring at the space in front of her. It was a warm and sunny afternoon; the sun was strong enough to cause her to squint against it. As it shone through the window it illuminated the vase on the table, which was empty and wore a thin layer of dust. It was like a scene from a typically English painting, Kirsten thought.

It had been her plan, before the phone call, to cook the meal in time for Daniel's return. His revelation left her feeling unmotivated, but then she told herself, *You're being selfish. Margaret is an old woman. Daniel's a good man for wanting to help her, you should be proud of him.* This roused her to action. The spring air was invigorating, she turned on the radio, chopping, slicing, frying, and singing along to the songs it played.

I'll wait to put the oven on, she decided, *he might have bread to make.* The thought led her to the storage bins, which she hovered over, thinking, *I wonder how he'd feel if I made some?* But she dared not, deciding it was too much intrusion into his domain, so instead she wandered into the garden to enjoy the late afternoon sunshine.

She was squatting, cooing to the chickens, when Daniel pulled up in his van. As he climbed down from it, Kirsten approached him and made to kiss him, but he turned his cheek towards her. Kirsten felt like she'd been punched in the stomach, her throat constricted. She backed away from him. He seemed oblivious to her hurt and was now heading into the house. Kirsten was unable to move; in her mind's eye she collected her things together and left. In reality, she waited ten minutes then went into the house. Daniel was sitting on the sofa with a cup of coffee beside him and his tablet on his knee.

"Thanks for the tea," Kirsten said.

"Bag's in the cup, didn't know what you were up to. Dinner smells good, by the way."

"Hope so. Just got to finish it off in the oven. I was waiting to see if you need to make bread."

"I'm going to do exactly that as soon as I finish the coffee. Once I've done that and had dinner, I'll grab some overnight things and go to Margaret's."

"I thought we were going to discuss it."

"Oh, sorry. She was a bit worse. I have to keep an eye on her, and if I do that, I have to keep my distance from you."

"Because?"

The thought of staying in Daniel's house without him was alarming. After Greg's death it had taken her months to learn to sleep alone. The empty space in the bed was contrasted by a fullness in the night-time atmosphere; his absence more present without the daytime distractions to occupy her mind.

"In case it is *the* virus, of course."

"I thought you didn't believe in it."

"I've never said that. I said I don't believe it's as dangerous as they claim. I said I don't endorse the lockdowns, or believe that's why they're doing them."

Kirsten nodded, feeling disgruntled, but knowing that she was being unreasonable, "So why can't you stay here?"

"Don't want you getting ill, whatever it is. And Margaret might need me."

"Fair enough." She paused before saying, "I don't really like the idea of being here alone."

"It won't be for long. And I'll be on the end of the phone."

"What about the chucks?"

"Will you be okay to see to them?"

"I guess. And the bread?"

"I'm not sure. I've been wondering about that. I could make it at Margaret's. Maybe they won't want it under the circumstances."

"If they don't want you to make it, perhaps I could."

"You think?"

"I've done it before. Not for a while but…"

"Maybe, then. If you have enough time."

Kirsten put the oven on for the dinner, then sat down beside Daniel, whose attention was on his tablet once more.

"Why didn't you want to kiss me earlier?" The words sounded more accusatory than she intended.

"What?"

"I went to kiss you and you offered me your cheek."

"Did I?"

"Yes. And it hurt."

"Sorry." Daniel put his arm around her shoulder, pulled her face towards him and kissed her on the forehead.

Kirsten put her head on his shoulder and cried.

"Oh!" Daniel said, feeling shocked and rubbing her arm.

After a few minutes silence Daniel said, "Right, better get on with the baking."

"Shall I make some?"

"Why not? Better not be as good as mine, though."

Daniel put two large mixing bowls side-by-side on the table, dragged the sack of flour closer and put the kettle on for warm water. Kirsten stood in front of her bowl feeling like she was back in the school cookery class.

"No chance. You can do everything better than me," she said, playfully.

"Not quite," Daniel said. Then, in a more sombre tone, and looking Kirsten directly in the eyes, "I'm not very good at letting people know I care about them."

Kirsten brushed the flour from her hands and touched him on the shoulder. "You are, you do. Your actions do. I'm just silly, wanting to hear the words, actions speak louder."

"You'd like to hear it though. You want to hear me say, I love you."

Her stomach somersaulted. "Only if you do."

"Of course I do."

The silence that followed was full of expectation, Daniel bridged it by leaning across and kissing Kirsten on the mouth.

"Thank you," she said.

They touched hands fleetingly then both dipped them into the sack of flour at the same time.

"The proof of the bread is in the kneading." Daniel said, pressing his forearms into the dough.

"Agreed," Kirsten was pushing the tops of her palms into hers.

Twenty minutes later seven loaves and two dozen rolls were proving, and Kirsten was serving dinner, now feeling completely different. Daniel's words had elevated her to the status of partner as surely as a marriage proposal.

"Um, food is great – thank you." Daniel lifted his glass of water and Kirsten clinked hers against it. "It's weird not having wine."

"You could have one, couldn't you?" Kirsten suggested.

"No, you know I can't. One is never enough. You can, though."

"I'm not that mean. After you've gone, perhaps."

When the meal was over Kirsten put the dishes in to soak, then they checked the bread together.

"Wow! I think mine's risen the best," Kirsten teased.

"Nah! It's good, but mine's definitely the best."

"Wanna put that to the test with a tape measure?"

"The proof is in the taste, but I reckon they're gonna be on a par."

"You said it was in the proving, we won't get to taste it, I reckon you know I've won."

Daniel laughed, as he filled the oven and the Aga with loaves.

While it was baking Daniel gathered the things he would need for an overnight stay. Kirsten went to put the chickens to bed, but discovered they'd already done it themselves. She checked for eggs – there were only two – then locked the door to keep them safe from foxes.

Back in the house the atmosphere was contradictory. The smell of the baking bread was homely and comforting, but Daniel's actions promised loneliness. Kirsten felt it like a hole in her solar plexus. *Don't go,* she wanted to say.

"Phone when you get there, please."

"Of course," he sighed. "I've just been thinking about the logistics of it all."

"I could make the bread."

"It's too much when you've been working all day."
"You can't keep coming here, or there's no point you staying away."

"I might have to take the stuff to Margaret's. Let's see how she goes, she might be okay tomorrow."

"Hope so."

"Well, I can't tell which are mine and which are yours," Daniel said, taking the bread from the oven. "I'll give them ten minutes to cool a bit then I'm off."

"You taking them now? Leaving them in the van overnight? Okay."

"You going to be alright?"

I'll have to be. "Yes, of course."

"Keep your phone on in case, but no one ever comes out here. Give me a call before you settle down."

"It's not people I'm afraid of, it's what happens in my imagination."

"I'll leave the tablet, you can watch something in bed."

"I'll be okay, I'll read."

"Sure?

"Sure."

But as soon as he'd gone Kirsten felt afraid. Her spine tingled, as if she was being watched. The television hid noises from her, so she turned it down, but then the silence offered up ghostly whispers, so she turned it back up. There was nothing that grabbed her attention enough to coax her into watching; not on any channel, so she turned it off.

Checking twice that all the windows were shut, and both the doors locked, Kirsten poured herself a large glass of wine and took it and her book to the bedroom. In the en-suite she washed and moisturised her face without fully closing her eyes and was climbing into bed when she remembered her phone was downstairs. She descended them with her back to the wall. The kitchen light was on the other side of the room, so she turned on the one in the hallway, ran to the table and then back upstairs in the same manner, then climbed gratefully into bed, where it felt safe, deciding she'd phone Daniel after reading a chapter or two.

Margaret was grateful to herself for her habit of cooking extra portions to keep her freezer stocked up, because she didn't feel like cooking fresh today.

She took a lentil cottage pie and put it in the microwave to defrost, then in the oven to warm. Usually, she'd have a side vegetable with it, but today, she felt neither energetic enough to cook it, or hungry enough to eat it.

While the dinner was warming, Margaret sat down to watch the television, pulling the blanket that she used as a throw, from under the cushion and wrapping it around herself. The news, as always, was about the virus, the latest death statistics scrolled across the bottom of the screen. Margaret turned it off, almost acknowledging to herself her fear that she was about to increase the numbers by one.

She turned the radio on to the jazz channel, but it was too hectic for her to listen to, so she turned it off and stayed with the silence. Not that it was silent, there were children's voices close by and the neighbour's television could be heard through the wall. They were sounds that provoked memories and filled her with nostalgia.

When the meal was warm enough Margaret sat down to eat it, but it had no taste. *Loss of taste, that's a symptom.* With the realisation, the seed of fear germinated. *I'll be alright, where can I have picked it up from? Nowhere, I can't have, I'm imagining it.* Margaret continued eating, but still the food had no taste and without it her appetite decreased further. A headache was starting to develop too.

She washed her plate and cutlery because she didn't want Daniel to come and find it undone, she was determined that he would see she was fine and go back home, she didn't want anyone fussing over her, and yet… She sat back down in the armchair, thinking she would put the television on when there was something worth watching. *What time will that be?* She thought, *I can't quite think what day it is. I'll look online in a bit, just close my eyes for a minute or two.*

"Hello, it's me, Mrs. P." Daniel opened the door and peered around it. The sight of Margaret sitting in the chair, her head on one side and her mouth open, sent his stomach to the floor. He was across the room in a second, he didn't stop to shut the door or remove his shoes.

"Mrs. P?" He crouched down beside her and put his hand on her cheek. It was warm and she opened her eyes in response to her name.

Daniel sighed with relief, "Mrs. P, you're…"

"I'm still alive, yes, you don't get rid of me so easily." She squinted at her watch, and then the clock on the wall. "Gosh, I must've fallen asleep."

"I guess that answers the question about how you're feeling." Daniel was back on his feet and crossing the room to close the door. "Have you eaten anything?"

"Yes, eaten, washed, dried, put away. You'll have to take my word for it." Margaret understood by his actions that Daniel was looking for evidence.

"That's a good sign."

"I've only ever been too ill to eat twice in my life."

"Let's hope this isn't the third time."

"I'm sure I'll be fine in the morning. What're you doing? You look like you're fixing to stay."

"I am."

"It's really not necessary," although she had to admit, even if only to herself, that she felt grateful.

"I'm not staying for your sake." Daniel's tone was teasing. "Oh no, I'm saving myself a sleepless night. And I promised Joe I'd keep an eye on you, if you recall."

"On the subject of him, let's not tell him until I'm well."

"Why?"

"He'll make a fuss, probably insist on my seeking medical help."

"You might need it."

"There's no way I'm leaving this house. Promise, please, that you won't involve any doctors."

"I can't promise you that."

Margaret felt like a fence had been put around her; at the moment it was far away and allowing plenty of space, but she could imagine how easily it would shrink.

"Let me tell you this then, I would rather die than end up in hospital. I mean it, Daniel. Old people don't get better in hospital; it's a slippery slope from there."

"Let's hope it doesn't become necessary, then. I'm not going to stand by and do nothing if you get really ill. I'll at least have to consult with your children."

"They'll all condemn me to the doctors."

Daniel sighed, squatting on his haunches in front of Margaret.

"I'll do my best to keep you out of hospital and away from a doctor, that's the most I can promise."

Two hours later Daniel was getting into bed, having settled Margaret – who actually seemed fine – for the night. The strangeness of sleeping somewhere other than home seeped into his bones as he settled down under the duvet. It wasn't an experience he enjoyed, and it provided him some insight into how Kirsten felt. He picked up his phone to call her, but wasn't sure. If she was sleeping, he didn't want to wake her, especially given what she'd said; but he did want to make sure she was okay. He put the phone down on the bedside table, then picked it up again and clicked on the last call, which was from Kirsten – as it almost always was because he had few callers. After three rings he hung up, feeling he'd made the wrong decision.

Kirsten was grateful for the missed call; it was what she needed; like him she had been wondering whether or not to phone. His contact gave her the confidence to return the call. The few words they exchanged, before bidding each other good-night, were all Kirsten needed to settle into a good sleep.

Daniel cuddled into the spare pillow, missing the weight of another human beside him. Strange how quickly he'd become accustomed to that.

During the night Margaret's dreams became feverish. In the corner of the room a person sat in shadow. Despite the lack of visible clues Margaret knew it was her former Head Teacher. *Where are you now?* Margaret asked. *Why are you here?*

Wouldn't you like to know? The reply was accompanied by a mocking laugh.

The blood pounded in Margaret's ears, and she was thirsty. She turned on the lamp to find the water Daniel had put beside the bed, and to banish the nightmare. In the second after the light came on, she saw her parents, her sister, John – and knew they had come for her. She felt comforted by the sight of them, but also afraid – it was more about the uncertainty of where she was going, than of unwillingness to leave where she was.

Her eyes wouldn't stay open. She fell into another restless sleep, taking her relatives with her. "Not yet, love," she heard John say.

There were only a few more days of sick-leave left for Mandeep now, the rest of the time was holiday. The thought made her sad; they should all have been in India. And yet she didn't really want to be anywhere but here and, with the whole family at home, it felt like a holiday anyway.

The thought of returning to work was far from comfortable. She'd have to go back to behaving as if she were in control and she'd have to face an increased threat of infection, one which she felt sure she'd increased by her lie. She wondered how the staff who were particularly afraid of the virus, coped with going into work. They had little choice of course, she knew, but she wished there was a way to help them avoid it.

As for herself, the reassurance that had come from her personal research was short lived. It was like being on a rocking horse, backwards with the bad news; like the death of a nurse in her thirties, forwards with the good news; like the Prime Minister's release from intensive care. And nothing could counteract the fear induced by the daily sermons from the podium, or the death figures scrolling the television screen. Backwards and forwards she rocked, on the rocking horse of worry.

"You okay?" Dev said, coming into the kitchen.

"Just thinking."

"Shouldn't bother if it makes you feel like you look." He put his hands on her shoulders and massaged them. "What were you thinking about?"

"Does anyone think of anything else these days?"

"I'll bring you some accounts to look at, that'll take your mind off it."

Mandeep laughed. "You want to work lots of overtime putting them right, do you?"

"At least I cheered you up. You're getting obsessed."

Mandeep felt criticised. "I'm just so scared of losing any of you. I'm so lucky to have you all, sometimes I don't know what I've done to deserve it."

"Come here," Dev held her close. "Don't talk like that. We're the lucky ones, having you."

"Why aren't you worried?"

"How'll it help? You're doing enough for the whole family. We're young, we're healthy. Anyway, it's in God's hands, who are we to question His wisdom?"

"It's not like you to be so fatalistic."

"I see it as realistic. Do what you need to stay well, take reasonable precautions, but fear and worry definitely don't help."

"I know. Just don't know how to stop."

Dev moved her to arm's length and began looking her over. "Nope, I can't see an off switch. It'll have to be accounts then, that's all there is for it."

In common with Christmas, Emerson's favourite thing about Easter was spending the time with his grandparents. Although he saw them most weekends, the festival times were special. He couldn't even really say why. It wasn't the Christmas stocking packed full of gifts, or the over-sized Easter egg, it was more that the sense of his being special was emphasised at those times. No visit or egg this year, the best he could hope for would be a FaceTime chat.

"I know what you think about what's going on," his grand-dad had said, "but we think we should stick by the rules, just in case."

Emerson felt irritated, but he had no choice, he would have to stay away until they felt safe.

It was almost time to get ready for work, so he turned off the computer. He shook his pillow, put it back on the bed then did the same with the duvet. In the bathroom he checked his appearance in the mirror, reinforcing the decision not to have a shave by running his hand over his chin. He lifted his arms one at a time and sniffed his arm pits. *Better have a shower, I'll ask mother to make me sandwiches.* He opened the bathroom door and called down the stairs:

"Ma. Ma. Mother dear" his voice getting progressively louder and more insistent.

His mother turned the radio down and came to the bottom of the stairs. "Yeah? What?"

"Will you make me sarnies, please? I'm running a bit late."

"Sure." She didn't need to ask what filling, it was always the same. "You had any breakfast?"

"Haven't had time."

"I'll make an extra one for you to eat on the way, then."

"Cheers." *It's so much better without that wanker here,* Emerson thought, climbing into the shower.

"Your *friend* coming this weekend or not," he asked, as he was just about to leave for work.

"No. He's got his kids. And he does have a handle to his name you know."

"Um," Emerson grunted. "See you later, then." That was one piece of good news at least.

It was going to be a strange Easter weekend. Kirsten rather wished she were working it after all. Spending Saturday evening in Daniel's house, without him, felt like being on holiday alone. Everything was provided, nothing was satisfactory.

Usually, she spent Easter morning on the egg hunt with her grandchildren; this year she'd have to be content with joining them on Zoom.

"Not great," Daniel had replied in answer to her question concerning Margaret's health, earlier that day.

"Good job you're there, then."

"I guess."

"You sound doubtful."

"Feel pretty useless that's all. She isn't eating, only sleeping. Doesn't want the doctor contacted under any circumstances she says."

"How d'you feel about that?"

"I'm hoping it doesn't become necessary. She said if she's going to die, she wants to do it here, especially as there'll be no one with her in hospital."

"I get that."

"Me too, but…

"It won't come to that."

"Hopefully not."

"It's a helluva a responsibility for you, that's for sure."

If she didn't hear from him soon, she decided now, she'd call and see how things were. On Saturday evenings Kirsten always ate too late, as it was Daniel's habit she followed. This Saturday she could choose the time, and yet, here it was, gone seven and she was only just preparing it.

She had the television on for company, another habit she'd inherited with her man. She diced, sliced, fried, and stirred to the accompaniment of a wildlife programme. The film crew followed a cheetah round South Africa's Kruger National Park, *that'd be somewhere to go,* she thought. Now the cheetah was creeping through the undergrowth towards its prey, a pretty little impala, Kirsten paused in her activities, holding her breath as she watched. It twitched its ears and looked nervously around, fully on alert. The cheetah pounced, but the impala had been ready and ran off into the bush. Relief surged through Kirsten. Quickly it was followed by something else. It was the sense that the impala was more alive than she had ever been. With vigilance came an acute awareness of life. Kirsten guessed it was the sensation adrenaline junkies sought; one that most modern humans so rarely experienced. *Staying safe is killing us,* she thought.

"Come on Mrs. P," Daniel encouraged, holding the glass to Margaret's lips.

She took it in her own shaking hand and had a few sips. Daniel stopped it from spilling, as she returned it, on a slant, to the bedside table.

"You're going to have to do better than that Mrs. P. If you don't drink, you'll get dehydrated."

The telephone rang. "That'll be one of your children."

"I'm coming," Margaret sat up, spun around to the side of the bed and started to stand up. But the effort caused her legs to give way. She fell back onto the bed, short of the pillow. Daniel knelt on it, put his arms under hers and pulled her gently up to the bed.

The phone stopped ringing.

"Didn't hurt you, did I?"

"No." Now she began to cough, it wrenched at her and made her eyes water. "Sorry," she said. "You should go home and leave me, don't want you catching anything." Then, "I need a fag to sort me out."

"That's more like it, but I hope you're kidding."

"Yes," Margaret barked out between the coughing.

"I'm concerned about you, I think you need taking a look at."

"No!"

The telephone was ringing again.

"I'll have to go and answer that."

It was Joe, "How is she?"

"Not well."

"How not well?"

"Feverish, coughing."

"You need to call the doctor."

"She doesn't want me to."

Joe sighed. "Maybe she shouldn't have the choice."

Daniel sighed too. "She's still trying to control things."

"That's good, but – do you think it's…"

"No way to know."

"Jesus. I don't like this. Call a doctor, will you?"

"It's difficult. I understand your concern."

"You're supposed to be taking care of her. If I was there, I'd be calling someone, that's for sure. Do you know who her doctor is?"

"No."

There was a pause. "I think you should find out who the doctor is, just in case."

"I will. If I deem it necessary, I'll phone the emergency services. I have informed her of that."

"What will have to happen before you 'deem it *necessary?*'"

"At the moment she's still alert and making decisions."

"So, you going to wait for her to lose consciousness? Don't you think that's a bit late?"

"I'm hoping it doesn't come to that."

"Hoping?"

"I'm trying to do my best for her. I'm trying to take into account what you want, but at the end of the day I feel I have to respect her wishes."

"You're not making me feel any better. I don't know what you consider necessary, I don't even know you. I wish I could come and deal with it myself."

Daniel thought for a minute before saying, "Maybe that would be for the best."

A long pause followed. Joe's breathing sounded fraught. "It's not that easy. I'll just have to trust you." Joe said, and then the line went dead.

Daniel sat for a moment, with the silence ringing in his ears.

She had never explicitly said so, but what Daniel imagined was that Margaret feared other things more than she feared death. He thought of his own mother, the resuscitation he'd insisted upon after the stroke that left her speechless. Her tears every time he left the care home, which eventually cut his visits from once a day to twice a week. The thought sent him hurrying upstairs to check on Margaret.

She looked peaceful. From the doorway he couldn't hear any breathing, which only an hour ago had been raspy and loud. Daniel swallowed hard as he went over to the bed, he could see her chest rising and falling but, just to be sure, he put the back of his hand on her forehead.

"Not dead yet," she said, making him jump like a frightened kitten.

"Death wouldn't dare come after you."

She opened her eyes, now, "It'll get me one of these days. Who phoned?"

"Joe."

Margaret nodded. "What did he say?"

"That I should call a doctor. Where will I find the number, if I do decide I need it?"

"Could I have some water, please?"

Daniel lifted Margaret's head from the pillow and put the glass to her lips. She took only a couple of sips. He lay her head back down, stood looking at her for a moment. "If I can't speak to your doctor, I'll have to call an ambulance."

"You're bullying me. It's in the address book, in the drawer under the phone."

"Thank you."

Daniel was on his way from the room when Margaret called him back.

"I don't want to die alone."

"You aren't dying on my watch."

When her phone rang Kirsten was watching Gerald Celente. She was grateful for his company and his Trends Journal, which not only kept her informed of some of the other things going on in the world, but also offered a different view of the only subject that dominated all other channels. He was new to her, courtesy of Daniel. *Like so many things,* she thought, patting Daniel's copy of Thomas Sowell's Basic Economics, which she'd just started to read.

Before she met Daniel, Kirsten had considered herself reasonably well informed. She hadn't taken for granted what she heard in the news, but often gone online to check sources and search out alternative views, but it was nothing when compared to now. It took up so much time, though. *Too much for most people,* she thought.

She paused the YouTube video and her musings to answer Daniel's call.

"How is she?"

"Not too good."

"Oh no, that's not what I wanted to hear. You're worried, aren't you?"

Daniel sighed.

"Obviously. Anyway, better go. I'll phone in the morning. 'Night."

The call was too short and ended too abruptly. Kirsten returned to Gerald Celente, but it didn't satisfy her anymore, her mind kept drifting back to Daniel, and anyway, it was something they watched together. When it finished, she allowed whatever came up to play, without paying any attention to it, but she needed some noise because the silence in this house was profound, and unsettling. Thoughts traversed her mind without really connecting; she struggled to put them in some order. From conversations, both those in which she'd been involved and those she'd overheard, Kirsten knew she wasn't alone in feeling as if she were living in an alternative reality. Didn't matter to which narrative you subscribed, the resulting sense that something was seriously amiss, was the same. It was like waking up to a clock that was running slow, and knowing it, without the need to check. Now she flicked through YouTube, clicking on and off what had become established favourites; but she couldn't settle to any.

"I've got to stop," she told herself, "or else I'm going to lose my mind. I need to find something else to do." The thought led her to Thomas Sowell, which she picked up now and continued to read, but she hadn't got far when she realised she couldn't recall what had come before, so she flicked back a few pages and reread them. She carried on reading without taking any of it in, then put it down and picked up a novel instead. It had been three days since the last time, so the thread was lost and, along with it, the necessary concentration.

Kirsten picked up a pen and paper and started to write down what she was thinking and feeling. It was a technique she'd learned from the time she had counselling; one that always worked for clearing her mind. Then she wrote down some goals, things she'd always intended to do, but never got around to. Suddenly, before she fully realised what she was doing, she had the basic outline for a short story.

Daniel was struggling to stay awake, then, when sleep claimed him, struggling to stay asleep. He'd taken a chair into Margaret's room, deciding it was the best way to keep an eye on her. With him was his tablet and his book. He veered between the two, the one made him sleepy; the other wakeful.

Every snuffle and groan robbed his attention, but their absence, the more so. Sometimes, they were too long in coming and Daniel found himself watching for the rise and fall of her chest, or touching her cheek to check for warmth. This time, it felt a little too warm he feared, but in the absence of a thermometer, couldn't check for a high temperature. *It would have been scary being a father,* he thought.

Daniel settled himself back in the chair and picked up his book to read. It fell on the floor as he slept.

"Daniel?"

He sprang awake, "Yes, I'm here Mrs. P. You okay?"

"Just making sure it's you and not the grim reaper."

"I've been mistaken for worse."

As long as Margaret's wit persisted, Daniel was happy, but he couldn't stop his mind from imagining a court room drama involving him and her faceless children.

Bird song and sunshine were the first things to hit his consciousness, and then the sense of silence and stillness in the room. Daniel held his own breath, listening. Silence. Fear gripped his insides. Hesitantly he reached out and touched Margaret's face. She coughed, he jumped, relief flooded through him.

"I want to sit up a bit." Margaret's weak voice contradicted the words.

Daniel assisted her to sitting, plumped up the pillows and then helped her rest back on to them.

"I'll make you some tea. What would you like to eat?"

"Nothing. No tea, either."

"Water then." Daniel held the glass to her lips. "You must drink Mrs. P."

"I know." But it was such an effort, and she didn't want it.

"Afternoon, sleepyhead."

It was said with affection, Emerson knew, so he accepted that his grumpy reply was uncalled for and saw the tears well up in her eyes.

His mother checked them, rather than him. "Look what was on the doorstep." She called his attention to the large chocolate egg on the table.

"Nan and Pops?"

"Or the Easter Bunny." She resisted the impulse to run her fingers through his hair.

I'm not a fucking five-year-old. "'s not right that I can't go and see them."

"It won't be for long. You wouldn't want to be responsible for making them ill, would you?"

Emerson sighed and shook his head.

"What?"

"You don't wanna know, believe me."

"You are going to phone and say thank you?"

For fuck's sake. "Of course." His tone was curt.

"There might be another somewhere if you care to look."

He didn't, actually, but did it anyway. He knew it would be in the garden, like every other year, but went through the pretence of looking in the house first.

"Freezing," his mother said, then, "warmer," as he opened the back door. He found it in the middle of the Buddleia bush. It too was large; it was as if his mother and his grandparents were competing.

"Thanks, Mum," he tore into the box and broke the egg in half, inside were some chocolate buttons.

"Don't you want some breakfast first?"

"This is it." Finally, he laughed and offered his mother a piece of the egg.

'*I'm having a problem getting on,*' Kirsten texted to Rosie. Zoom was taking her round in circles, launch meeting, she clicked on it again, the screen went blank, then took her back to the same message. Kirsten kicked the side of the sofa. "I'm sick of living in a virtual world," she shouted. Then, suddenly, there was a picture, her living room and her family milling around in the background, but no one was near the screen.

Her text alert sounded, '*Let's do WhatsApp*'.

Kirsten clicked on and tuned to a video call, just as she was doing so an excited voice came from the computer screen. "Nanny, Nanny."

Ryan was jumping up and down, holding a chocolate egg in each hand.

"Oh, the Easter Bunny found you, I'm so pleased."

"We can't hear you, Mum," Rosie said. "Turn on the video."

"I thought I had," Kirsten said, putting her glasses back on and scanning the screen until she found the symbol she needed.

"Finally," Rosie said.

Half an hour later, Kirsten left the meeting. She felt exhausted and frustrated by the whole process. It's better than nothing, she had heard people say, well, she wasn't sure that she agreed. It just felt so alienating.

She poured herself another coffee while she waited for the time to pass. She was going to take a cycle ride and meet Daniel for a few minutes on the doorstep of Margaret's house, because Kirsten craved some face-to-face contact.

The minutes passed slowly, but eventually it was time. Kirsten rolled the bike out and tucked her skirt into the leggings she was wearing, she put a light jacket and a bottle of water in the backpack, locked the door and put the key in the tool cabinet in the shed.

"I'm off to meet your master," she said to the chickens, who paid her no heed. "See you in a little while."

She pushed the bicycle to the end of the track because it was too bumpy to ride. It was warm and sunny, and, with the road devoid of cars, the perfect day for a cycle. Kirsten tried to convince herself that she was enjoying it, although in truth she enjoyed very little at the moment.

The part of town in which Margaret lived was unknown to her. She had only ever been there once at the most. It wasn't so many years since it was a village in its own right, but now it had grown into the town; or the town into it. She felt nostalgic for a time she'd never known, when the village was definitely that. Kirsten thought that the walk across the fields would be quite pleasant, but it was unsuitable by bike, so she stuck to the road.

She cycled past the turning for Margaret's road before realising where she should be going, and so had to turn around. She dismounted and walked along the pavement checking the numbers; when she came to the right house, she put her bike on the lawn and telephoned Daniel. It rang out. While she waited, she took notice of the garden, which was very well kept, but had a slightly wild look to it. Kirsten approved, because she didn't like gardens that looked too formal. She wondered if Margaret had any help to keep it that way.

She rang Daniel again; it rang out again. *Strange,* she thought, *hope everything is okay.* Watching the minutes tick by, time seemed to slow. This time when she rang, he answered.

"Hi, I'll be down in a second."

First, he went to the bedroom to check on Margaret. He stood close to the bed watching, she looked like she was sleeping, but when he moved away, she said,

"I'm thirsty."

He sat down beside her, filled the glass with fresh water from the jug and lifted her head from the pillow. "Here you go, then."

She drank only a few sips.

"Can you manage some more?"

Margaret shook her head.

"You need to drink, Mrs. P."

"I know," she said in a raspy voice.

"I'm just going to the garden. We'll try another sip when I get back. Kirsten is here."

"Checking up on you?"

"Yeah. Told you she was the jealous type."

Margaret didn't reply, she looked as if she'd already fallen asleep again.

Daniel stayed in the doorway with Kirsten standing in the garden. She wanted to embrace him, this time it was more than just his reserve that stopped her.

"You looked exhausted."

"I am rather tired, yeah."

The phone rang.

Daniel sighed, "I'll bet that's Joe again. He's rung three times today." He went into the house to answer it, Kirsten didn't feel she could follow, and, despite the effort, she couldn't hear what was being said. When he returned Daniel looked very strained.

"He says if I don't phone the doctor, he'll phone an ambulance."

"Let him."

"I don't know what'll happen if they come."

"It won't be your responsibility."

He was silent for a while, obviously mulling it over, finally he said, "I think I will call the doctor." He went into the house, leaving Kirsten waiting again.

A few minutes later he was back.

"Well?" Kirsten asked.

"Answerphone message, telling people to stay away if they have symptoms, or call an ambulance if you think it's a life-threatening emergency. Big help."

"So, what if you wanted to see the doctor about something else?"

Daniel shrugged.

"Well, you can tell Joe you tried."

"I'll try again in a bit," Daniel said, as if to himself, then, "That's not the best way to treat your bicycle."

"I didn't know where else to put it. I know it's a quiet neighbourhood, but I didn't want to leave it outside the gate, and I could hardly prop it against the hedge." *I'm okay, thank you for asking. Yes, I do miss you. I don't suppose you miss me.*

Daniel sighed a very heavy sigh. "Anyway, how was the bike ride?"

"It's getting easier."

"Good. Chucks okay? Plenty of eggs? Good."

He looked back through the open door towards the stairs, then back at Kirsten; his eyes showed his mind had already climbed them.

"I think I'll go."

"What? Oh, yeah, okay, yeah. I need to phone the doctor again, not much point in you hanging around."

"You'll let me know how it goes?"
"Course I will."

Kirsten prepared to leave, she approached Daniel. "Hug?"

He grabbed her and wrapped himself around her in the most intimate embrace they'd ever shared. He buried his head in the back of her neck. Was he crying? So unaccustomed was she to tight hugs from Daniel, that Kirsten was beginning to find it uncomfortable. He finally let go. She stood in the silence that followed for several seconds, then turned, picked the bicycle up said a final farewell. Daniel was already on his way back into the house.

This time, after a wait of some minutes, Daniel was told to stay on the line and wait for a doctor. While he did there were two calls to his mobile; one from Joe the other from Alison. He explained what he was doing to both via text, and also suggested they might go on to WhatsApp and take a look at their mother for themselves, just as soon as he'd spoken with the doctor.

Finally, there was a human being on the end of the phone, who told him, "We're not doing home visits at the moment. If you're worried you need to call an ambulance."

"Could you speak to her?"

"The advice is to call an ambulance if you're at all concerned."

Daniel hung up. "We've locked down to save the NHS, correct?" he said to the space around him. "What a wonderful service they're providing!"

He went back to Margaret.

"Feeling up to having a little wash Mrs. P? Nothing too intimate, just your face, yeah? Maybe brush your hair and clean your teeth?"

"Queen coming, is she?"

"Didn't realise you'd make so much effort on her behalf. Joe's going to call on WhatsApp."

"Oh, why?" Margaret sighed and pulled herself to sitting with great effort.

"So he can see for himself how you are."

"What did the doctor say?"

"Call an ambulance if I'm worried."

"I'm not going to hospital."

"Mrs. P, maybe…"

"Run me a bath, will you?"

"Are you sure?"

"Positive."

"You okay getting in?" Daniel asked, after helping her into the bathroom.

"If I'm not you'll soon know."

Daniel sat by the closed door and waited and listened.

"I'm done." Margaret's voice was weak.

From around the door Daniel handed her a clean nightdress. "I'm decent, now."

Daniel opened the door and saw that Margaret was sitting on the dining chair he'd brought into the bathroom cleaning her teeth. Then she brushed her hair, but as she stood up she wobbled. Daniel took hold of her and helped her back to bed.

"I can still take care of myself," she said, sitting down on the bed and allowing him to lift her legs in. "I could try a cup of tea."

"Great."

Daniel put the clothes she had just taken off into the washing machine as he made the tea, but when he took it to Margaret she was sleeping again. He was tidying the bathroom when his phone rang. He came back into the bedroom and put it on video.

"How is she, now?" Joe asked.

"She's alright," Margaret answered.

Daniel shrugged his shoulders and smiled in response.

"Hello, Mum."

"Daniel is taking good care of me."

"Glad to hear that. It's scary for me when I can't see you."

Daniel nodded in agreement. He went downstairs, thinking it best to leave them to it.

Although she disliked being alone so much, Kirsten had to admit she would never have started the short story under any other circumstances and the writing process was so engrossing she lost her sense of loneliness. She wrote:

> As soon as Ursula woke, she remembered, a silent sob left her. She put her hand to her growing belly, there was a movement against it, confirming what she was beginning to suspect. But it was like some kind of dream; nothing made sense anymore.
>
> There was another movement, rage boiled inside her in response; there was no room for loving this new life; not until her daughter was back. Where was she? Where was Norman? Where were all of the others? Rising to sitting, she crouched in the corner, holding her head in her knees.
>
> Suddenly grief was exchanged for fear. What the hell was going on? Where was she? She screamed and bit her arm. She charged at the wall of her cell and shook the

bars of the door, screaming and crying for release, until, exhausted, she cowered once more in the corner.

There were the other voices again, shouting, as she had. She called out, but the noises they were making deafened them to her cries. Ursula was sure she recognised some of them, Norman's, at least. He sounded so lost, afraid. If he was, then what hope for her? Ursula was forced to assume that he too was imprisoned somewhere, otherwise he would have come for her. She hoped their daughter was with him.

Suppose she's not. Then where? What's happened, is she okay? Suppose she's dead. Suppose I'm wrong, that isn't Norman's voice, he's dead too. Suppose I never see them again. Suppose I never find out where they are? The thoughts left her as screeches. It brought the monster, from which she ran to cower once more in the corner.

The last thing she definitely remembered before all of this, they were sitting relaxing, the whole group. It was early in the day, the sun was warm, but not yet hot enough to require sheltering from it. A face appeared, then another, smooth and alien. Ursula stood, picking up Sadie. Norman rose too, she could see he was ready for action. The fear spread, the group members took flight, running in confusion every which way. Norman ran deeper into the undergrowth, shouting at Ursula to follow him. And she did, running as fast as she could, speed impeded by carrying Sadie, but she was just keeping up. Then, a sharp pain in her back. Then. Nothing.

Nothing until… The light she opened her eyes upon was too bright, too white. Everything white. The walls, the light, the thing. The monstrous thing that brought the food, but also the pain. Everything so white; except for the black eyes of the monster and the black bars of the cell.

Perhaps she was wrong. It wasn't Norman's voice. There was no one here that she knew after all.

Finally, Kirsten's attention was brought back to her surroundings by the clock on the computer, it was time to start cooking.

&s

"You too busy to talk?" Mandeep had stuck her head around the door of the study.

"Never too busy for you. What's up?" Dev asked.

"All this stuff on Facebook, people saying the virus isn't deadly, some saying it's not even real. That there's some other agenda."

"There are always conspiracy theories in difficult times."

"I want to believe there isn't a deadly virus."

"Well, they haven't said it is for everyone, only some. Be careful what you look at on Facebook. Some of the things that are being suggested you might like even less."

"Have you looked?"

"A bit."

That she might like it less was true. In fact, Mandeep's stomach had hit the floor as she read about a New World Order that including microchipping everyone. Logic told her it was crazy, but it was plausible.

"Something feels really wrong. I keep thinking it's more dangerous than they're telling us."

"Nothing feels right at the moment. These are strange and trying times. Come here." Dev pulled her close, then onto his lap. "I'll tell you what didn't feel right, being away from you and the girls. You'll never know how glad I am to be home."

"You'll never know how relieved I am to have you here."

They exchanged a kiss, Dev tapped Mandeep on the bottom, as she stood up. "How you feel about going back to work?"

"Mixed. It's irrelevant, anyway, I have to do it."

Mandeep had to force herself into her chores and away from the computer.

From habit she turned on the television that was in the kitchen and always accompanied her cooking. The daily death statistics were scrolling the television screen. The Secretary of

State was on his podium saying that the lockdown was likely to be extended for at least another three weeks. Her throat and stomach constricted in response. They wouldn't do this for no reason. Tears rolled from her face into the cooking.

Dev came up behind her, put his hands on her shoulders and rubbed them, "Turn it off, love," he said.

*

"Margaret," Daniel called gently.

Margaret opened her eyes, but they wouldn't focus.

"John?"

"What was that, Mrs. P?"

"She looks a whole lot worse to me," Joe's voice came from WhatsApp.

"Yes." To disagree would be a lie.

"You need to call the paramedics."

Daniel sighed. *Had she told Joe she was afraid of dying alone?* "Whatever I do won't feel right." Honesty was the best policy, Daniel decided. "She has been adamant about not going to hospital whatever happens, but I don't feel right not calling."

"I'll call them, then."

Joe's tone was decisive, but not angry. For a second Daniel thought he'd tell Joe about his mother's fear of dying alone, but then decided against it, realising if the worst did happen, all it could do for Joe was cause him guilt and to doubt the decision.

"It's okay, I'll do it," Daniel said.

He went downstairs and made the call from the landline, then texted Joe to say he'd done it before turning his attention to Margaret.

"Mrs. P? Margaret?"

She opened her eyes, but it didn't look as if she was there.

"I've called the paramedics. Sorry, but I think you need more help than I can give you."

"No hospital. I need sleep."

Flashing lights were soon visible at the window.

"They're here."

Daniel's heart was heavy as he went to answer the door. The two ambulance drivers wore masks, gloves, plastic aprons, not the hazmat suits that were pictured on the internet.

"Here she is. She's being saying she doesn't want to go to hospital. Mrs. P?"

Margaret opened her eyes a little wider.

"What's the lady's name?" One of the paramedics was already sitting on the bed. "Could you fetch me her medications, please? Hello, love, we've come to take a look at you."

"She doesn't take any," Daniel answered, feeling angered that they ask her name only to address her as 'love'.

"Really? No meds?" Then to Margaret, "Just going to take your blood pressure, temperature, and check your oxygen levels, my love."

Margaret's lips were moving but her voice was quieter than a whisper; then, as the blood pressure monitor was applied, "Get away," waving her arms in the air.

"It's okay, we're here to help."

"Then go away."

One of the paramedics addressed Daniel now. "Does she have any confusion?"

"No, she does not." Margaret's voice was still a little weak, but her temper was not.

"Temperature and blood pressure are a bit elevated, not surprising after that outburst. Oxygen is a little low, on the margins."

"I'm not leaving this house."

"Can't make you, love." Then to Daniel, "No real reason for taking her in, her stats are okay, and she seems clear she doesn't want to go."

"That's good. Yeah, we'll be fine. Thank you."

As he closed the door on the paramedics, Daniel breathed a sigh of relief.

❧

The conversation wasn't intended for Mandeep's ears, but it drew her in.

"You know I don't subscribe to the official narrative," Emerson was on his phone, "but even if I did, I'd have to give these guys a hearing, they're both doctors, think one of them is a microbiologist. Anyway, they say we shouldn't be locking down, it's actually detrimental to the immune system."

Emerson noticed Mandeep now, he smiled, put a thumb up, mouthed, "Good to see you," then picked up his cup of coffee and made his way to the sofa.

"I don't get how you think that," he continued. "I thought you were a fu…," remembering Mandeep was there. "…I thought you were a socialist, how come suddenly you believe what this lot tell us?"

He took a sip from the cup, his body language told Mandeep the conversation wasn't going to his liking. Even if the person on the other end didn't want to hear these doctors' names she did, so Mandeep took her time with making her own drink.

"Misinformation? Well, you could give them a listen before you make up your mind to that."

Emerson was nodding his head up and down and twisting his mouth. "Okay, let's leave it, then. I'll be in touch." He hung up, shook his head at the phone, then threw it down next to him. He sighed, then looked up at Mandeep and smiled. "Good to have you back, Mand, how are you?"

"I'm fine thanks. I couldn't help overhearing, I…"

"It's so disappointing, man. This is a good friend of mine, calling me a conspiracy theorist, just for suggesting she listen to an alternative view."

"I'd be inter…"

"Won't be long before she loses the chance, if she changes her mind."

"What d'you mean?"

"People are being de-platformed all the time."

"We want to be sure we get the right information, don't we?"

"Exactly! So, shouldn't we hear what everyone has to say? Who decides what's right information? They've told so many lies, how're we supposed to believe a word they say? I can think for myself, let me have it all, 'misinformation'…," he clawed the air, "…included."

"You're right, of course."

"We're headed towards global Fascism."

The words drummed their way into Mandeep's psyche, like the roll before an execution. She laughed, although not finding it funny.

"Yeah, I'll bet plenty of Jews did that, just before they got rounded up and put on the train to Auschwitz."

Mandeep baulked, feeling affronted, she wanted to explain herself but instead said, "I couldn't help overhearing, I'd like to hear what the doctors have to say."

"Really?"

"Where will I find them?"

"YouTube."

"Ah!"

"You mean 'Ah', like because it's YouTube it must be misinformation?"

"No!"

"What then?"

"I don't know what I meant." Mandeep would normally have challenged a member of staff for speaking in a tone that was rude, but she knew Emerson could be like that without meaning any offence. "Could you write down some details for me, please?"

She handed him the pen from her top pocket and took a piece of paper from the waste bin.

It was gone nine before she had the chance to look them up. What they had to say both cheered her and frightened her. She went to find Dev.

"You're not still working?"

"Kind of, I keep dipping out to look at more interesting stuff."

"Like?"

He held his hand out and called her closer. "This."

It was a wildlife documentary. Normally Mandeep loved these herself, but today she felt annoyed with Dev for frivolous viewing.

"I could find it on the tablet and cast it," he suggested.

"Don't feel like watching. I've been on YouTube myself."

"Yeah!" Dev said, distractedly, eyes still on the screen.

"Two doctors, saying we're making the situation worse by locking down, they said people need to mix to build immunity."

"Makes sense," his eyes remained fixed on the computer.

"D'you think?"

"Uh huh."

"It scared me."

"Why?" Still, he only partly paid attention.

"You're not listening." Mandeep's tone was angry, she pulled away from Dev and headed towards the door, but he grabbed her wrist and clicked off the screen.

"I am now. Why did it scare you?"

"I don't know what to do for the best. If they're right, we should be doing the opposite of what we're being advised. But I don't want to mix with anyone, unless I have to."

"That's why the government don't want people looking at this stuff."

"I guess, but – Emerson said they have told so many lies they can't be trusted and well, he has a point."

Dev sighed. "Really, I think we have to stick with the guidelines. Don't look for other information, it keeps upsetting you. I can't bear seeing you afraid all the time."

"I'm afraid whatever I do, or do not do."

"I know."

"And I'm responsible for keeping you, the girls and my staff safe."

"The best place to start is by keeping calm."

"And how'm I supposed to do that?"

Daniel woke with a start. What time was it? He had been asleep too long. In it he was dreaming, a faceless Joe, a huge accusing finger, a pallid-faced, lifeless Margaret.

The rasping breath told him the worst hadn't happened, and yet, caused him fear, sounding so much like the last few his own mother had breathed. He approached the bed and put a hand on Margaret's forehead. It felt clammy and she made no response. "Come on Mrs. P." The words were whispered and somewhere between a plea and an instruction.

He went downstairs and made himself a cup of coffee, feeling the need to stay awake.

Strange it should be silence that made staying asleep so difficult, Kirsten considered, as she woke up to it and the darkness for a third time. *But it's noisy in my head, that's the problem.*

She turned from her side to her back and concentrated on slow and rhythmic breathing; trying to cast out the troubling thoughts.

It was no longer fear of being alone in this house that disturbed her. Currently she felt afraid for Daniel: that Margaret would die and, despite his knowing he'd done what she wanted, he would feel terrible. But the biggest fear was one she hardly dared to consider, that he would catch whatever was ailing Margaret. And he would die.

Emerson checked the time on the screen, it read one fifty-two, he knew he should close it down and go to sleep, but he felt that his investigation into 5G was really going somewhere for the first time. He clicked onto another site and found a short video by some Canadian doctors; he could watch it and still be asleep by two-thirty.

Afterwards, with the computer and lights off, he lay in his bed thinking over what he'd heard and read. Headache, fatigue and lowered immune response, one doctor had given as the most common symptoms. No mention of respiratory symptoms, but a lowered immune system would make for an increased risk of catching diseases.

Maybe the virus is real and the 5G is making it more dangerous, he thought. *Maybe it's normal flu and the 5G is making that worse. But they haven't rolled it out everywhere yet, and this – whatever it is – is everywhere. I can't see them releasing something that would put them at risk, though. Maybe the 5G is a part of it.*

His thoughts went around and around, like a hamster on a wheel. *I'll look up some protective measures tomorrow.*

He got up again, rolled and smoked a spliff, then went back to bed.

Just before dawn Margaret's breathing began to sound laboured. She was hot, her eyes, which from time to time flickered open, looked wild and far away. Daniel was beside her, holding her hand. He watched the bedside clock slowly inching its way towards dawn.

Suddenly, Margaret pushed his hand away and sat up as if by reflex, like a newly dead cadaver.

"What d'you want Mrs. P?"

"To get out of here."

"You're at home, Mrs. P."

Margaret offered Daniel a quizzical look. "I need the toilet," she said it as if in response to a preposterous question.

When she returned Daniel said, "You need to drink some water." But all she had was a few sips.

"Could you manage a bite of fruit?"

"Just let me sleep."

She was back in bed for only a second or two before she did exactly that.

Daniel went to the bathroom for a quick freshen up. He felt too worried to be gone for long. He prepared himself some breakfast, but ate it at Margaret's bedside. She looked different this morning, her cheeks hollowed and her lips dry. And something else was worrying him; he didn't feel too good himself. He put his breakfast aside without finishing it. The main concern was staying well enough to look after Margaret.

Daniel was sleeping in the chair when Kirsten rang. *Damn,* he thought, answering it and checking on Margaret at the same time. "I'm fine, how are you? Good. She's not great, actually. Not eating and more worryingly, not drinking. Yes, I might have to," Daniel said in response to Kirsten asking should he call the medics back. "Joe'll be phoning soon, I think I know what he'll say."

"Are you sure you're okay?" Kirsten asked, for a second time.

"Fine, why?"

"Your voice sounds – different – weak."

"I am rather tired. You have a good day, and we'll speak later."

Margaret moaned and opened her eyes.

"Mrs. P?"

The response was whispered and unintelligible. Daniel stood over her with the glass of water. "Few sips for me, Mrs. P. Please."

"Not thirsty."

"If you don't drink, I might have to call the paramedics back."

No response.

Daniel was too tired to think, but an idea occurred to him anyway. He went to the kitchen and then to the freezer. No ice cube tray, they, like so many things, were part of the past. He filled four teaspoons with water and put them in the freezer, thinking they should be solid enough in a couple of hours.

Back in the bedroom he fetched the duvet from his bed and curled under it in the chair with his book. He kept losing the narrative, so had to reread several times, and had to battle against sleep.

His phone rang. It was Joe, "How's things?"

Daniel told him how Margaret was, but not how he, himself, was feeling. Then he turned WhatsApp on, on Margaret's phone.

"She needs medical attention." Joe's tone was unequivocal.

Daniel thought about it for only a second, "I agree. She won't like it, though."

"Mum, we're calling the paramedics back."

The lack of a response underlined the decision. Joe stayed on the phone while Daniel telephoned from the landline. It wasn't long before the paramedics arrived.

One of them was the same as the last time. "She has deteriorated, hasn't she?"

"She isn't drinking."

He put the blood pressure cuff around her arm and the oxygen monitor on her finger. "Blood pressure still a bit high, oxygen a bit low, still marginal, but I don't like the look of her. She looks a bit dehydrated. Best we take her in."

Daniel nodded. Joe verbalised his agreement from the other end of the phone. "Margaret, we're going to take you in, okay?"

No response.

"Mrs. P, you're going to have to go to hospital."

"No."

"Just a couple of days, Mrs. P."

"People die in hospital." Although her voice was very weak it was a relief to Daniel to hear her object.

Daniel took hold of her hand, "That isn't going to happen."

"Pack my day clothes, in case I need to escape."

"That's better, more like the Margaret I know."

"She'll be fine in a day or two, I'm sure," the female paramedic reassured.

Daniel nodded.

When they left, he went to bed. He felt so cold.

Bleeping machines and tap-dance-like footfalls were on the periphery of consciousness, so was the drip in her hand. The tempo of Margaret's dreams was fevered. Whispered voices, both in and outside of them, were meaningless and menacing. But then one came booming in, '*intubate.*'

Did they mean her? She struggled for consciousness. Knowing she must shout to stop them invading her, but every time she tried her voice remained silent. She sensed someone nearby, large and authoritative. She didn't know him, or whether he was from this world or the next. She struggled for the voice she needed, to cry out for help. The figure was standing right over her now, reaching out to do – to do what? Suddenly Margaret was awake. The first thing of which she became aware was the nasal cannula. She raised her hand to it, her instinct was to pull it out. She stopped herself, becoming aware of the room. The voices were coming from behind curtains at the bed beside hers; there was much activity then the bed was wheeled away. She lifted her hand to check on the drip. On the other there was an oxygen monitor. Fear coursed through her veins, then anger – how had she allowed it to come to this? She cried out.

A nurse appeared above her. She disappeared, then reappeared with another, who said, "We'll give her something to calm her down."

Don't talk about me as if I'm not here. Margaret wanted to say, but a tearful, "No," was all that came out and she shook her head. The tears produced mucus, inhibiting her breathing.

"It's okay, love, this'll relax you."

She watched as if she were starring in a film, as a syringe full of something was fed into her line. She wished they'd stop calling her love. *No.* Then she drifted into sleep.

John was there. *You've got to fight, love. It's not your time yet.* But when he left, Margaret felt such a sense of loss that she wanted to go with him.

Next time she awoke it was light. Her head felt heavy, as if she'd been drinking alcohol the night before. Yet, despite this, there was a connection with herself, and an awareness of her surroundings that was grounding

"Nurse, nurse," she called, pulling at the cannula. *Get these bloody things out of me, now.* She had more sense than to try to remove the needle from her hand. She struggled to sitting and then with getting her legs over the side of the bed; she tried to stand, but the effort made her dizzy and she fell back onto the bed.

Now a nurse came running. "What are you doing?"

Margaret's eyes were wild, they gave her the look of character from a horror film, inducing alarm in the nurse.

"I want these things out of me." The words rasped from her, lending the horror impression more weight.

"They're keeping you oxygenated and hydrated."

"I want rid of these bloody things," she waved her hand in emphasis.

"Try to stay calm."

Another nurse arrived, her seniority of rank apparent in more than just her uniform, "I'll get her some more sedative."

Panic gripped Margaret, but she knew she mustn't let it show. "No, please. I feel better. I don't need sedation, I need these things removed. Please."

The nurse hesitated and turned back to her colleague, "Check her stats will you, please." Then to Margaret, "You need to get back into bed while we check you over." She picked up Margaret's hand and looked at the oxygen monitor. "Okay, we'll try you without the cannula." The removal was unpleasant, but a relief.

"Thank you. I'm thirsty. Could I have a drink, please?" Actually she wasn't, but knew it was what the nurses needed to hear. "And I'd like this taking out." Margaret lifted the hand that had the drip attached.

The nurse's demeanour changed. "We'll need the doctor to see you first," then to her colleague, "Fetch her a jug of water, will you?"

Margaret felt like she'd been given a stay of execution, but feared it being reinstated. She looked around the ward and noticed that the occupant of the bed next to her, in common with everyone else it seemed, was wearing an oxygen mask. This had a calming effect on her.

The nurse who'd been sent for water arrived. "Let's get you properly back into bed, shall we?" she said, putting the jug on the locker.

"Thank you," knew the staff were doing their best for her, but also she understood how 'awkward', at her age, could be construed as a sign of deteriorating mental health.

"I want this line out. I want to go home. Please."

"I can't do that without the doctor's say so. And she's busy at the moment, but I'll make her aware of how much better you're feeling. Here, drink some of this."

Margaret did as instructed. The nurse nodded her head in approval then went away.

Alone again, Margaret shuffled to the edge of the bed and scrutinised the ward once more. In the absence of anything else to do she sat watching the time tick away. Occasionally someone emerged from behind a curtained bed, carrying the signs of medical intervention, the bleeping of monitors provided a percussive accompaniment. Other than that, the ward seemed as quiet as a graveyard. *I can't see anyone who looks busy. It wouldn't take long to get demented in this place.*

It was well into the afternoon and Margaret had drifted back to sleep, when the doctor arrived at her bedside. "I understand you feel you're well enough to go home," she said.

"Yes. Please."

"I'm very pleased you're so much better, would you like to try sitting out in a chair?"

Margaret sighed, "I'll do a headstand if it'll get me out of here."

The doctor laughed, "That won't be necessary. It isn't likely to happen for a couple of days, though, my love."

I'm not your love. "Why so long?"

"We need to make sure you're properly ready."

Margaret was shocked at how weak she felt and wobbly on her legs as she tried them out for the first time in… "How long have I been here?"

"You don't remember coming in?"

"A bit.." Now it seemed there was some memory. Changes in the light, the sounds and the faces, that told of the passing of time. Clunks of the double doors as beds were rolled in or out. How many days it all added up to, however, remained unclear.

"You were quite poorly when you arrived, although you did protest somewhat when the drip went in."

"Hum! S'pose I should say sorry." Only she wasn't. "So, it's just for hydration? No drugs?"

"Some steroids. And we gave you a sedative last night because you were so distressed."

Being here is causing me distress. "I don't use medication."

"You seem to be making a good recovery; probably thanks to the meds."

"Hump!"

Momentarily Margaret's attention was drawn to a bed being wheeled from the ward. There seemed to be a lot of that going on. Was the occupant better, worse, dead?

Alone Margaret reluctantly acknowledged how tired she felt. The clock grabbed her attention once again. When she was sleepy, the hands looked as fine as a second hand, when wide awake they appeared sharp and in focus. Five-thirty-seven. When was dinner time, she wondered. Did such a time exist on this ward? There didn't appear to be anyone else who'd be thinking about eating. *Don't suppose hospital food has improved. Not that I'm hungry.* The only times Margaret had been in hospital herself were for giving birth, but the food that had been on offer to John during his several stays, showed no sign of having improved on those times. For the next couple of hours, she drifted in and out of sleep. Then her attention was grabbed by a lot of activity around one bed and she straightened up to take notice. Gloved people in plastic aprons and masks were milling around the patient, then the doors opened, and the bed and its occupant were wheeled out.

She and John had joked about being moved closer to the door the closer death was. They never had the chance to test the theory on him, he'd been at home when he died. There was a second of panic at the thought, she needed to get home she didn't feel like she was dying anymore but couldn't stay here just in case. *I need to stay awake and in control,* she told herself. But, despite struggling to avoid it, sleep reclaimed her. John was there, waving and smiling, but as she moved closer, he held up a hand and shook his head, mouthing something – not yet – was that what he'd said? *You're always telling me that.* The dreaming Margaret felt annoyed with him, but waking again she thought, *no definitely not yet.*

"Don't keep thinking about death, love," her mother ordered from the bottom of the bed.

Margaret jumped to full wakefulness in response. What was she doing here? Alive. Not like John, not from the other side, but here, an escapee from Margaret's memory. This was more terrifying than death. She had to get out.

Feverish dreams and aching limbs inhibited sleep; it was a long night, the end of which arrived too soon and was signalled by the ringing alarm. Daniel silenced it. He sat up, intending to start the day, but a light head and ringing ears prevented him from doing more. He lay back down and returned to fitful sleep. It was interrupted by the phone ringing. Daniel grabbed it, pulled it under the duvet and answered it. It was Kirsten asking how he was.

"Not too bad. A bit tired and achy."

"You'd better rest then. Good job you haven't got Margaret to worry about. Have you heard anything?"

"No."

"I think I should come around."

"That's the last thing you should do."

"I won't stay, I'll bring some food, anything you fancy?"

"I'm not hungry."

"Make sure you drink plenty of water, then."

"I will."

"Promise?"

"Yes."

"Say it."

Daniel sighed, "I promise."

The call ended, he dragged himself from the bed to the kitchen, where he filled a jug with water and took it, and a glass, to the bedroom.

It seemed like only minutes later that he was receiving another call, but as he answered, he noticed the time was one-thirty.

"The same," he told Kirsten in reply to the question on how he was feeling.

"Are you drinking?"

"Yes," Daniel took a swig of the water, it tasted metallic and warm.

"I don't want to hassle you, but I do need to know you're okay." When there was no reply, she continued, "I'll phone again around dinner time and before bedtime. Are you in bed? Still not hungry? Okay, speak later."

The phone fell from Daniel's hand to the floor as he slipped back into sleep.

Fear clenched Kirsten's stomach. *What if it's the virus?* She thought, feeling sick; then, *he's strong and fit, he'll be fine.* Into her head drifted death statistics scrolling the screen and news headlines of the deaths of young fit people. *Please,* she prayed to a god she didn't believe in, *please don't let him die.*

The staff were changing from day to night shift. Someone eventually came to Margaret. "You been sitting there long?"

"Most of the afternoon,"

"Goodness, let's get you back in bed, then."

"I haven't had any offer of food."

"That's appalling, I'm sorry. I'll get you some now. How hungry are you?"

"Quite, but it's late, a couple of pieces of toast'll do." Margaret was lying about her hunger, but she needed to get home.

It arrived with a cup of tea. The tea tasted good, but the food she had to force down. "Will I be able to go home tomorrow?"

"Maybe, but more likely the day after. Who's at home, anyone?"

"Why not tomorrow?"

"You've been very poorly. We'll see what the doctor says. You might still be infectious."

"There's no one to infect at home."

"You live alone?"

"I can take care of myself, I'm not a child," Margaret regretted the harsh tone as soon as the words left her mouth.

"Of course, but from our perspective we need to be absolutely sure you're fit enough. It's a safeguarding issue."

Margaret felt as if an iron cage had been dropped over her. *Safeguarding who? You against litigation. I'm going home, no one is going to stop me.*

There was a new patient in the bed next to Margaret. The curtains had been opened and the staff had gone from her bed. She didn't seem too ill, oxygen was being delivered via a nasal cannula rather than a mask, there were, however, cot sides on the bed. It soon became clear why.

"Hello," Margaret offered.

"Hello, dearie, how unexpected seeing you here. Where's Mummy?"

Margaret felt disappointed, she didn't think answering the question honestly was likely to be helpful and was considering how to reply when she realised there was no need as the woman started chatting to what appeared to be a host of other people unseen to anyone else, and then to sing. Once more Margaret worried about her own hallucinations. *Pray to God they let me out tomorrow before I lose the plot.*

Margaret reached into her locker for her mobile phone, which she now switched on. Her second disappointment in a few minutes came in response to the fact there were no messages on it. It was a relief however, to finally have a date and learn that she had been in the hospital for four days. She sent a text to both Daniel and Joe, then to her daughters. All replied except Daniel. And that was her third disappointment.

This, she realised, was the time when visitors would be asked to leave, but since none had arrived there was no need. The lack of them hadn't mattered until now, but the principle remained the same. *Dreadful, truly dreadful. How was anyone supposed to get through an illness without the love and support of their families?*

It wasn't long before reverie became dreams. And not long before they were interrupted by shouting from the accompanying bed. The confused woman was screaming that there was a rat in the room. Margaret's sympathy was tempered, not only by annoyance at the disturbance to her sleep, but also by fear for her own future.

Through the haze of half-sleep Margaret became aware of activity around her neighbour's bed. Shouting became whimpering, then silence. Margaret fell gratefully into it.

In the morning she awoke to find the confused lady not only quiet, but masked and attached to a line.

Kirsten stood staring out of the window, the phone clutched tight, as if she was afraid that putting it down would end more than a voice connection with Daniel. She stood this way for several minutes. Empty headed and full hearted. The one telling her she needed to be afraid. The other offering nothing to contradict.

It was her day off. It stretched before her like a deserted road. Aware that she needed to fill it, Kirsten decided later she'd go for a walk, but first she'd do some more writing – these being useful ways to lose herself.

The pain was starting again, small to begin with, but then the crescendo took it to a level just within her tolerance. Although she tried not to allow it, a cry escaped her. Instinctively Ursula stood up and paced her cell. The next pain sent her squatting to the floor with another cry. It brought the monster.

Ursula was growing accustomed to it now, its black snout and empty eyes no longer made her fearful, but rather filled her full of hate. This creature was responsible for the loss of her family, she felt sure. It was speaking now, in its hissy alien tongue.

"Oh no Christabell, it's too early."

Ursula didn't understand the words, but the intonation suggested concern. It wasn't the first time it had shown such inclination. Once it had even stroked her face, but Ursula didn't need sympathy, she only wanted her freedom and her family. Right now, she cared only that this pain would stop.

Suddenly she was overwhelmed with the desire to push the pain and the baby from her body. She felt it slip from inside her. She didn't need to look at it to know.

There were two monsters now. Hands scooped up the infant. Although she knew there was no life in it, Ursula grabbed at the baby and screamed. More hands. They held her head and body, a sharpness in her leg. Then. Nothing.

ॐ

"Oh, Margaret, good to see you dressed," the nurse said.

"I'm ready to go home."

"Let's hope the doctor agrees, then." The nurse's words were light and her eyes smiling, although the mask obscured a full-face view.

As far as Margaret was concerned, she was going home. No doctor was going to stop her. Should she wait and hope to be discharged? That was the question. Or just leave without its being sanctioned. She wasn't sure what would happen if she upped and left without it, but she was feeling cross, having done everything they asked, only to be still here.

The day after tomorrow that had been promised, had been and gone. There'd been questions on her home circumstances, and she'd caught a snippet of conversation on her way back from the bathroom that had worried her. She'd hovered around the nurses' station trying not to make it obvious what she was doing, but they soon noticed and their voices dropped to an inaudible level, but not before Margaret had heard the words discharge and care package within a few words of each other. Of course, they may not have been referring to her, but there didn't seem to be anyone else on the ward looking close to leaving alive.

I'll give it until early afternoon, Margaret decided now, having no idea when she would be visited by the doctor. *Please miss can I go now?* That's how it felt.

Twelve-forty, Margaret was becoming impatient. No one had offered her so much as a cup of tea, never mind a meal. Only yesterday the doctor had been objecting to her discharge on the grounds she had to make sure Margaret took care of herself. *I'd do a damn sight better job of it than you do of looking after me,* she thought now. *When's this fucking doctor coming?*

She walked towards the nurses' station, wanting to hurry the process up. No one was there. There were several beds with curtains around that she didn't like to disturb, perhaps all the staff were behind them. She walked out to the corridor and looked up and down it, there was no one in sight, and this filled her with a sense of dread; she felt like she was starring in an apocalyptic film where everyone except her had succumbed to some unknown fate. She went back to her bed, half expecting to find zombies infesting the ward.

Why don't you just go? While there's no one around. But she felt wary of walking out with her bag, frightened it would attract attention to her. *There isn't anyone around,* she thought, so opened the cupboard next to her bed and riffled through the contents. Was there anything there she really couldn't do without? The phone and the charger; she put them into her toilet bag, which she took with her, along with the towel, draped over her arm.

She felt conspicuous in the still deserted corridor, and it made her want to run, but her elderly legs wouldn't allow it. Instinctively she curled in on herself as she passed the security cameras. There was a desk near the main entrance that was normally manned, but currently no one was at that, either. Margaret hurried past it and through the next double doors. As she neared the exit, she finally encountered two nursing staff. The dark blue uniform of one advertised her superior rank. Margaret kept on walking, with a purposeful step.

"Are you okay?" The senior nurse asked.

Margaret's instinct was to pretend to be a visitor, but she remembered just in time that there was no such thing at the moment. "I was looking for…" she almost said, looking for a toilet, but an imaginary conversation played out in which she was labelled as confused and soon a whole series of events robbed her of independence and made her exactly that.

"I was looking for a place to get a good signal on my phone. I thought outside should do it."

"Have you come from one of the wards?" Margaret noticed the nurse notice her washbag.

"I'm going to the bathroom on the way back. I'm going home today. I need to phone for a lift."

"Oh, you don't need to worry about that, they'll sort it on the ward. Which one are you on? I'll escort you back there."

As they walked along the corridor together Margaret felt like a naughty child whose parent was giving the unwanted behaviour minimal attention.

"Thank you, that's very kind," she said, as they arrived. "Actually, one reason I was using my phone is because I couldn't find anyone on the ward. They're all busy I suppose."

"Go back to your bed and I'll find someone for you."

"I've had no morsel of food at all today." Margaret deliberately adopted an annoyed tone. It seemed a good way to deflect the awkward situation and turn it in her favour.

"What? I'm so sorry. I'll see to it right away."

As the nurse walked away Margaret called after her, "I'm vegetarian." And then, "I'm still waiting for the doctor too."

A hand was raised to acknowledge she had heard.

It was clear from the nurse's resolute stride that someone was going to be in trouble. Margaret sat watching as the nurse approached a curtained bedside, then exited and went into another. The seconds ticked by on the clock, until they had marked away several minutes. And that was all it took for a cup of tea and a plate of watery, Quorn cottage pie, to arrive.

It was hardly any longer before the doctor came. "I'm told you want to go home."

"Yes, please."

"And I see your appetite is okay."

"Yes." *I've been a good little girl and done as I'm told.*

"Our only concern is there's no one at home."

"There is. I have a friend staying with me. Here's his number." Margaret fumbled through her phone and presented it to the doctor.

"Okay. I'll get your discharge notes written up, then," she said and headed off towards the nurses' station.

At last, Margaret breathed a sigh of relief.

It took a while for the ringing phone to break through the fevered dream and wake Daniel. He stretched out to retrieve it from the bedside table without lifting his head from the pillow, then, holding it arm's length, he squinted at the number. Ordinarily, he would have ignored an unknown caller, but in case it was the hospital, he answered it.

"Yes, speaking. Coming home today, that's great news. Yes, I… someone can pick her up. Okay, I'll phone her and arrange it. Thank you, Bye."

As he hung up, Daniel checked the time on the phone. "Oh, so late." He sat up, but it felt like he'd left his head behind. Steadying himself, he made for the bathroom. Every part of his body ached, even the roots of his hair and teeth. He surveyed himself in the mirror, yes, he looked every bit as bad as he felt. *How can I fetch Mrs. P. when I'm feeling like this? Maybe a shower will help.* He turned it on and climbed into it with some effort. The water felt like pellets as it hit his body and fell off, but it was warming and refreshing and for a while he did feel better. He cleaned his teeth, decided not to bother with a shave, then went to the kitchen to make himself tea and phone Kirsten.

When her phone rang, she was writing.

The raw, red patches were so itchy, Ursula had made them bleed with scratching. The losses hurt her heart. When would this hell end? Would it ever end? It felt like an eternity since she woke up in this place. Like forever since the baby died. Longer than either, since she, Norman and Sadie were together. There was no point to her life without them.

Waking or sleeping, she sat in a foetal pose, leaning against the wall of her cell. Her captors came to clean and offer food. At other times they came with the sharp pain. There were two of them now.

"She looks depressed."

"They don't feel emotions, like us."

"Really? You sure? They're enough like us to warrant what we're doing to them. Ready? Check the batch number."

The first alien held up the tube with the serum in as it read off the number, the second one agreed and took hold of Ursula. Once she would have fought back, but now she didn't care.

The phone call was annoying because Kirsten was absorbed in the writing, but she was relieved to see it was Daniel.

"Hi, how're you feeling?"

"A bit better, I think."

"Are you up and about?"

"Sort of. Listen I have a bit of a problem."

"What?" Kirsten's tone reflected the anxiety his words provoked.

"Margaret's coming home…"

"That's good – isn't it?"

"Yes, but I'm not sure I'm up to fetching her and certainly not to looking after her and I probably should stay away from her anyway."

"Oh, so you need me to go?"

"'s that okay?"

"Sure, as long as I can get a cab. How soon?"

"I said four. Give you time to get there and me time to clear up and get out. You going to be able to stay with her?"

"What d'you mean?"

"I think it was part of the deal of letting her out. Will it interfere with work?"

"Not if it's only today and tomorrow. Does she know it'll be me? You'd better text me her number. Speak later."

As soon as the call ended Kirsten phoned to book a taxi, expecting it to be difficult, forgetting the times they were in – lack of regular business had the opposite effect.

She was worried about Daniel, his voice sounded weak. It felt wrong to be getting ready to look after Margaret rather than him. She didn't like sudden changes of plan. These two things made it difficult for her to focus and to decide what to put in her overnight bag. She put one set of clothes in, then took them out to replace with another, then took them out and put the original set back in. She also took a pre-cooked meal from the freezer and some breakfast cereal and what was left of the bread. *Hopefully they'll be some kind of spread, the shop's not far anyway,* she thought.

The taxi was ten minutes early. Kirsten felt annoyed, even though she was ready. As she was getting into it, she realised no decision had been made about the chickens.

"Just give me a minute please." She checked for eggs, and that they had ample food, then chased them into the coop. They went in reluctantly and noisily. "I know it's early, girls, I'm sorry."

"Where's your mask?" The taxi driver asked.

"I don't have any."

"You don't have any? We're in the middle of a pandemic."

"I don't really need one out here."

The taxi driver threw a whole box of them into the back and Kirsten took one and put it on, feeling annoyed with herself and the driver: The latter for his aggressive insistence; herself because she complied as passively as a child. She wanted to enter into a discussion to defend her point of view on masks; that being, that they were not merely useless, but bad for the health, especially for people with respiratory symptoms, but at the same time she recognised that the driver was acting from fear and the last thing she wanted was to make him more so. And, if she was honest with herself, she wondered how she would react if a coughing, sneezing individual was forced into a small space with her. She was finding it increasingly difficult to know how to behave like a good human being.

When they arrived at the hospital Margaret was at the door with a nurse. Kirsten got out of the taxi, pulled the mask down and introduced herself to Margaret.

"Thank you so much for coming to get me," Margaret replied, and in the taxi, she too pulled the mask down and said, "Thank God for that. How's Daniel."

"Put your mask back on," the taxi driver ordered.

"I don't wear them."

"What's that round your neck then?"

"The hospital made me wear it."

"You could show me the same respect. What's wrong with you people?"

The words made Kirsten feel guilty and she pulled hers back over her nose and mouth. Margaret did so too, wishing to avoid the conflict. She'd had enough of that, of late.

When they reached her house Daniel's van wasn't outside.

"I guess he's gone home so he doesn't infect either of us," Kirsten said. Although it was what she had expected, she still felt disappointed not to see him.

"He probably caught it from me. Looks like you're fixing to stay."

"Tonight, I thought, just to settle you in. I've brought us some dinner." Kirsten took the lasagne from the cool bag. "It is vegetarian. I hope that's okay. We're not, but Quorn mince is so much healthier."

"Lovely. I am. Thank you."

"That worked out well, then. What time d'you want it?"

"About six, if it's okay for you – you really don't have to stay."

"I think everyone would prefer me to. Just tonight, we'll review in the morning."

"Okay. I am fine, though, rather tired that's all. It was a nasty bug, whatever it was. I hope Daniel's okay."

"I'm sure he'll be fine in a couple of days." Kirsten was trying to convince herself as much as Margaret.

"He can't be too bad, he's cleaned up. It looks tidier than when I left." Margaret patted Kirsten's hand. "I'm very pleased to meet you by the way, and *so* glad to be rid of that place. I think I'm very lucky to have got out."

"It can feel that way in hospital."

"No, I mean really." Margaret shuddered at her vulnerability, inflicted by her body, but also by the system. "I was hallucinating. I didn't know if it was the illness, the sedative they gave me, or if I was losing it."

"Sounds like you were scared. Fever often does that. Some meds too, of course. Anyway, you're okay now."

"Yes, I am. I had to be really insistent to stop them giving me more."I need a fag. I'll go outside."

"No, you won't, this is your house. I'll tell you what, I'll go outside, I need to phone Daniel, make sure he's okay."

He took a long time to answer and in Kirsten's head a melodrama was playing out, one which had her preparing to move between the two homes on her bike administering care, like a district nurse.

"There you are, I was getting worried, how are you?"

"A bit better, I think."

"Good." It was more than that, it was a huge relief.

"Just a bit achy and tired. I'll have an early night, tomorrow I'll be fine."

"If Margaret goes on okay, I'll be back tomorrow."

"Stay a few days, it's best for her and you. You might catch whatever it is otherwise."

"I want to come home." It sounded odd, saying home.

"We'll discuss it tomorrow."

"Okay. 'Night, then."

Margaret was on the phone herself when Kirsten came back into the house. "Joe, my son," she said, hanging up. "He's happy that you're here."

"There, I said people would prefer it. I'll get the dinner on now."

After the meal Kirsten and Margaret chatted. About the current situation, their previous lives, their shared widowhood – and Daniel. "He's a deep one, but a good one," Margaret concluded unequivocally. And Kirsten was bound to agree.

"I wonder what the medication was they gave me. I felt so peculiar, I wasn't sure if it was the meds or me, especially given my age. I thought I was losing it."

"Nothing wrong with your mind, Margaret."

"No," it was said as if something had just occurred to her.

In the end Kirsten stayed one more day, by which time Daniel was almost well, and Margaret entirely so.

MAY

It was always a couple of weeks into Ramadan when Nabil found it hardest to stick with the fasting. The morning had passed quickly enough, a walk followed by work on his journal, but now, at a little before three in the afternoon, boredom and hunger were competing for attention.

Nabil picked up his pen and notepad, he read over the last part of his writing:

> *'Wake-up! Nabil, you must wake-up, now!' Abida was shaking me awake. I opened my eyes, she put her forefinger to her mouth and then mine. We crept from Layla's house without waking anyone else, I needed no telling that everyone was safer that way. My trust in Abida was such that I questioned neither her decisions, nor the things she asked me to do.*
>
> *It hadn't always been that way. I'd always trusted her, of course, but when we were children I protested vehemently at the orders she issued. Now though, now I knew both*

our lives depended upon her, because she was brave and clever, while I was weak with fear.

Reading over these words Nabil began to cry. How was he ever to feel happiness or love in his life again? Sometimes he ached so for both, that he welcomed the idea of death. But God told him He was the one who would decide his fate. And Abida and his parents would want him to carry on. He was the one who got away, he owed it to them to stay alive.

"But sometimes that is such a burden," he said out loud.

He returned to the journal. Although, the memories were painful they brought him closer to the loved ones he'd lost, and absorption in the process kept his mind from the present concerns.

The darkness was pervasive, in it I felt awakened; senses on full alert no sound escaped my hearing, or movement went unnoticed. In fear of death, I felt fully alive.

Nabil paused, thinking back, trying to recapture that sensation. Overwhelmingly, since the arrival of the virus, he'd felt afraid, but not of it, and not of dying, he wasn't so much in love with life. It wasn't like the fear he experienced those nights on the run; that fear was sharp, and, although terrible, it was wonderful too. This fear was dulling. On the run he'd felt his physical existence threatened; this fear endangered his soul. The first kind was born of desire to live, the second of being afraid to live.

With this thought came renewed hunger. It gnawed at his belly, robbing him of concentration.

Abdul had said they were only permitted to go out once a day for an hour and Nabil had already done that today. He sighed as he stood up, then started to pace the room. On his third passing of the mirror, he turned to look at himself. He'd lost weight even before the fasting began, because the illness had robbed him of the desire to eat for several days and stolen his sense of taste even when his appetite returned. And, now that both had, he was having to fast. The mirror image was gaunt, with black circles under his eyes, and pallid skin. *Can this be good for me?* He thought.

Now he lay down and closed his eyes, but two things kept him from falling asleep. The first, hunger, the second, the worry that he would sleep so long he'd miss the chance for eating.

Nabil tuned to YouTube on his phone and the Arabic news. It took only minutes for him to turn it off, as it was dominated by two things: the virus and violence. *I wish I could understand your plan,* he said to God in his mind. *Why didn't you stop all those murders? My parents, my sister: so many parents and sisters, why must I fast when you won't stop the killings?* His head ached, his heart ached. He looked at the food and juices that were waiting for consumption and his mouth watered. He checked his watch and saw that there were still hours to go.

Nabil's parents were inside his head now, rebuking him for his weakness, his lack of faith. In the past, with the whole community to offer support, it was hard sometimes, but there had been a sense of shared purpose. It seemed so much harder now.

Unsure of his will power, but sure of forgiveness from both God for his doubt, and the British Prime Minister for his breach of the rules, Nabil took his notepad, pen and phone and walked to the park.

※

The sun had moved, so now it was obscuring the screen. Kirsten tutted. She looked up and around, searching out a spot that looked as if it would be both warm and shady, it was then she noticed Nabil. He was sitting on the adjacent bench, his head bent over a notebook in which he was writing. He looked so engrossed Kirsten hardly dared to disturb him, and yet she felt such pleasure at seeing him she couldn't help herself.

She closed the lid on her notebook and approached him; as she did Nabil looked up and noticed her. He closed the page on his notebook and stood up to greet her. Without thinking about what he was doing he offered his hand. Kirsten accepted it and shook it vigorously.

"Good to see you, how are you?"

"I am very well, thank you," Nabil replied, mostly from politeness, but also because he knew no other reply.

"We were both writing, I think. It's too sunny on my screen," Kirsten pointed at the computer. "I'm not complaining about it being sunny you understand, just that it stops me being able to work."

"Yes, it is too hot for working, much nicer outside," Nabil replied, in Arabic, taking a guess from the three words he'd understood.

"Don't suppose you're getting any support at the moment."

"I don't understand."

"Of course you don't, sorry. Still, we've had quite a conversation."

Nabil shrugged and smiled.

The situation had become a bit awkward now. It felt neither right to stay or to go. Nabil had no wish to be rude, but he wanted to carry on with his writing. Kirsten felt the same. They were saved by a familiar face.

"Hey there, Kirst." Emerson screeched to a halt on his bike. "Hello."

He dismounted, threw his bike down and his arms around her. Surprised, Kirsten tensed, but then she relaxed and pulled him in closer and patted his back.

She turned to Nabil, who felt confused by the hug they'd shared.

"I expect you recognise each other from the shop." She inclined her head towards one man, then the other.

Nabil nodded, "Hello."

"Good to see you man." Emerson offered his hand, Nabil accepted.

Just to their left stood two women, some distance apart from each other. "Did you see that?" said one, the volume of her voice making it plain for whom the words were intended.

"Yes, and never mind two metres, that's hardly even two inches between them," came the reply.

Kirsten stepped back automatically.

"Listen to the news, d'ya?" Emerson said, directly to the two women. "Certain 'scientific advisor', he clawed the air with his forefingers, "must've been at least as close to his lover."

Kirsten suppressed a laugh; she could always rely on Emerson to put people in their place.

The women looked shocked, but didn't reply, instead they moved away.

Nabil sensed that something had passed between them that wasn't entirely polite, he wondered if it was anything to do with him.

"God, the way people judge makes me so fucking angry."

The only word Nabil understood was the universal expletive.

"People are scared," Kirsten pointed out.

Now Emerson sighed. "Yeah, you're right. I'll try to control my tongue in future."

All three stood silently for a while, looking to and from each other, smiling, nodding, no one quite sure whose move it was. Finally, Emerson said, "I have to go, actually." Then to Kirsten, "You staying?"

"I'll walk with you. Bye, Nabil." She raised a hand to him.

"See you, mate." Emerson tapped him on the shoulder. Nabil flinched. Emerson raised both of his hands, in submission and reassurance.

As he watched them walk away Nabil felt regret. He was ashamed by his automatic response, which had caused offence. He regretted his inability to speak English. And, now that he was, he felt sorry for himself for being alone again.

While he had been standing, the bench had been taken by someone else. Even before the current situation he wouldn't have made any attempt to share with this stranger. English people didn't like it.

The thought took him back home. To the men sitting outside cafés, playing cards, backgammon, talking politics. The women, strolling home slowly from market, making the most of each other's company. Children playing with skipping ropes, drawing chalk games on the floor. Here, people walked alone plugged into earphones. Children parted at the end of the school day and never seemed to be on the streets afterwards.

There didn't seem to be any spare benches now, those that were taken were mostly by single occupants, the rest were dressed in prohibitive black and yellow tape. With nowhere to sit, Nabil headed home to his bedsit.

Kirsten and Emerson talked as they walked.

"How's the old lady?"

"Margaret? She's recovered and is home."

"That's good. Whatever it was didn't kill her then."

"Daniel caught it. Yeah, fine, of course, thanks for asking. Me? No. But I wasn't really in contact. Maybe isolation is a good idea."

"Pah. Remember how people used to go to work when they were so ill they were nearly falling over. Now you have to stay home even when you're well. Madness. Wish coronavirus had been around when I was in school, all the excuses I had to dream up."

"Didn't you like school?"

"Nah. There was stuff I wanted to be learning, but not what they taught us. I guess I was always a bit cynical, knew something was wrong, even then."

"Me too. And I've learnt so much since being with Daniel."

"Yeah! I have the impression he's a smart guy. Anything in particular you've learnt?"

"How politics is informed by economic forces, I see why they say follow the money now. How much of the so-called news is propaganda. Quite a lot of history and how that has been manipulated, too. It looks to me like there's at least as much misinformation and disinformation from the establishment as from the sources they tell us to be suspicious of. It's not been a total shock to me, but last few years I've been preoccupied. Like most, I suppose."

"That's how they keep us down. One way, anyhow. So, why the notebook, you been studying in the park?"

"No, I'm writing a short story."

"Oh yeah, I forgot. You still haven't told me what it's about."

Kirsten sighed. "It not so easy to answer. I could tell you the story line, but that's not what it's really about. It's about – um – I guess the main theme is – who has the right to make decisions for us? Should one group be allowed to force things on another?"

"That's easy, no," Emerson interrupted.

"No, even if it's for the greater good?"

"Who decides that, then?"

"Well, exactly. I guess usually, if not always, it's the group with the greatest power."

"Don't mean they should. Only that they can. Actually, I think it's us, the people, if only we knew it.Sounds interesting anyway, can I read it sometime?"

"It's not exactly Shakespeare. Hopefully, at the least it's an entertaining story. It's the kind of thing I've thought about from time to time, but the current situation has really brought it home. I'm amazed by people's level of obedience."

"Why? People are blind and stupid."

"You sure? Not socially responsible, or scared?"

"Nah! Well, some might be, but most want to be told what to do and have everything provided for them. Like I said, they keep us dumb and dependent to control things. In this situation they're waiting for the great god 'science', to come and rescue them. The knight in shining armour is now a scientist, and his charger is a syringe full of magic formula. Looks more like a wicked witch with a poison apple to me."

Kirsten smiled as Emerson lived up to her expectation again.

"I'll have to leave you in a minute, I'm meeting my daughter and the children. You in tomorrow? Me too, see you then." She walked off in the direction of the rendezvous point. It was only a few minutes before Rosie, Ryan and Sally arrived.

Kirsten squatted down to six-year-old height and opened her arms for them to run into.

"Hello, Mum," Rosie said. "Lovely day."

"Indeed." The children ran off ahead to the swings. "Okay if I get them an ice cream?"

"Course."

"Mandeep's back now, I'll speak with her about the possibility of a job tomorrow."

"Think I'm going to go for care work. They are more flexible with the hours."

"I thought you were worried about working with vulnerable people. How's Andy getting on?"

"I am a bit, but I'm sure they take all precautions. He's okay, ta."

❧

There was still the collection of the foodbank to oversee, then Mandeep could finally go home. Two young men came over to make a deposit, they were lost in conversation with each other so didn't notice a third man staggering towards them. He fell, into them, into the foodbank boxes, then over.

Mandeep's position, both geographically and professionally, deemed it necessary she be the one to help him up.

"You okay?" She squatted down next to him, feeling grateful for the gloves she was wearing and wishing for full PPE in response to the smell of alcohol exuding from him. "Not hurt?"

"I'm a bit drunk, love."

Mandeep nodded in acknowledgement.

"Don't think you can help me. Give us a hand, lads, please." He held both of his hands up to them.

"Sorry mate, coronavirus," from one.

"Nah," from the other, at the same time.

"Thanks a million."

For a minute Mandeep was worried by his aggressive tone, but now he turned over onto all fours and started to push himself up, then, as he fell again, started to laugh.

"Bloody fool, I am."

A spray of saliva rained over Mandeep. Her instinct was to pull away, but just as strong was the inclination to help this man to his feet.

"Grab a chair from somewhere will you, please?" Mandeep asked of the staff member who was coming to help.

Now the drunken man was in the dog pose. Mandeep put one hand on his back and held out the other as an offer to steady him. The staff member and chair arrived.

"Thanks, love, but I don't need that." The drunken man waved the chair away.

"I'd prefer you sit for a minute, please. I just want to make sure you're okay."

"Only thing wrong with me is I'm a bloody pisshead, whoops, sorry, 'scuse me language."

Mandeep didn't reply, but helped the man sit down.

"This situation don't help. Half the time worried I'm gonna catch the bloody bug and die, other half wishing I could, 'cos I miss me family."

The words cut into Mandeep. "Difficult times. Did you finish your shopping? Is that it there?"

"Yeah." He started to stand up.

Mandeep discouraged him. She hailed the security guard, "Call this gentleman a taxi, please."

"No, love, no, I don't need no taxi."

"Don't worry, we'll pay. What's the address?" Truth was, as long as he remained in the store Mandeep felt responsible for him.

She ushered him out of the store and into the waiting taxi. Feeling relieved, she headed towards her office, desperate to wash her face, even though she knew any germs he'd passed on had had more than ample time to infect her. But then he was back again calling out, "Love, hey, love."

Mandeep turned around to see him waving a bag of pasta in the air. "This was for the food bank."

Just before leaving work, Mandeep called her parents. "Anything you need?"

She wrote a list, added her own goods to it, put on clean gloves before she shopped, and again when the purchase was complete.

Her father waved from the window as she pulled up. Mandeep left the shopping on the doorstep, feeling unusually unlike seeing them in person. It felt more important to get home and cleaned up, after her earlier encounter.

What she really wanted was a shower, but she knew Dev would unpack the shopping and put it away without using the disinfectant spray. By the time she was finally able to cleanse herself, more than two hours had passed since she'd been exposed to the saliva. She rubbed her hair and scrubbed her body, but there was no rejoicing in the experience because it all felt too late, and she was sure she'd be ill soon.

When she told Dev about it later, she was surprised to realise how many emotions and opinions she had experienced within the short encounter. Disapproval, in response to the alcohol on his breath, especially since it was daytime. Disgust at the saliva spray; drunken people are dirty. Pity at his words; understand the drinking now. Humility, when he returned with the food bank contribution; shouldn't be so quick to judge. Fear, of the germs she perceived he'd be carrying. Always there was the fear of that. Only some of these feelings did she admit to Dev.

The next few days were spent in apprehension. While she waited for the onset of illness, Mandeep obsessively checked the symptoms and incubation time online. After seven days she began to feel safer and the incident all but passed from her mind.

Kirsten knocked on the office door. "There's a man downstairs asking for you. Well, I think it's you, from the description. He said you helped him out last week and he wants to say thank you."

"Really? Don't know what that's about. Okay, I'll be there in a second, just finish this off."

A few minutes later Mandeep came to the shop floor. The man was definitely sober this time. In his hand was a bunch of flowers.

❧

Margaret was online as soon as she was up, so, when Daniel arrived, she was in her dressing gown.

"Not well again, Mrs. P?"

"I'm perfectly fine, despite their attempts to prevent it." "They being?"

"The hospital. My doctor's been on the phone, checking up on me."

"Seems reasonable." Daniel had never had any concerns regarding Margaret's mental health, but currently her attire and the maniacal look in her eyes generated some concern.

"It is, but what isn't is one of the drugs they gave me. I asked the doctor what it was so I could look it up, wish I hadn't, but glad I did. Put the kettle on, I'll make the tea in just a minute."

"Okay." Daniel's curiosity was roused.

"Thank God I got out of there with only one or two doses. Here, you look while I make the tea."

Daniel did as instructed, with Margaret hovering over him and pointing out the things she most wanted him to see. She had been relieved to see hallucinations listed in possible side effects, it probably accounted for the sightings of her mother. She'd been troubled to see there could be respiratory failure and pointed it out to Daniel. "Don't you think it's odd to have given it to someone who is experiencing difficulty breathing?"

"Well, yes, on the face of it, but I'm not a doctor."

"And look – can cause hallucinations and stop the development of new memories, yet they use it for the elderly and confused."

"Um! Well, I need no convincing on the medication issues, Mrs. P. Seems to me one symptom is relieved and another produced."

"Exactly! My point is, though, are people confused before or after they go on it? Is it given to demented people, or are they demented because it's given to them? And look…" she scrolled down the screen and then back up until she found what she wanted. "Used in end-of-life care. I'm so glad I escaped from there."

"You felt vulnerable, didn't you?"

"Very."

"Well, I'm glad you made a full recovery."

"Yes, no more so than I am. I want to be sure it's God who has called timeout on me. You know, sometimes I think all the medication hurried John on his way." She sighed. "Dreadful to be in pain, though, and if it comes to that, I'll no doubt give in and get drugged. These'll probably see to it, eventually." She waved the cigarette that she just rolled, in the air, then lit it.

With little to do in the woods Daniel was soon on his way home, where there was much to do. His arrival coincided with Kirsten's.

"How nice, we have a whole afternoon together," she said.

"I wish. I have a cabinet to finish."

"Shame, it's such a lovely day. Tea first?"

"Sure. Margaret was in a strange mood this morning." Daniel told Kirsten about the conversation.

"Doesn't sound that strange. In keeping with her philosophy, I'd have thought."

"It was more her manner than her words. She looked half crazy."

Meaning it as reassurance, Kirsten stroked Daniel's face.

"Oh, tickly," he said.

Kirsten laughed. "You're so romantic. You're still worried about Margaret?"

"Not really, just – she was a bit strange today."

"She was probably unnerved by being in hospital. Can't blame her, especially for someone her age, even at the best of times, which these are not. D'you remember that article in the Guardian about taking people off ventilators if they were old."

"I don't think it quite said that."

"I think it said exactly that. It spoke about those with a bad prognosis being taken off ventilators for them to be given to younger, healthier people, as I recall. And there were supposedly 'do not resuscitate' orders being over-issued. And people with learning disabilities being refused treatment."

Reading it had distressed Kirsten so much that she all but changed her mind on assisted dying, of which she'd always been an advocate. Although she understood the arguments against, Kirsten had always believed that, as long as there were proper checks in place, it was the humane option. And Greg's drawn-out death had underlined and bold typed the conviction. But now, along with several other once firmly held opinions, Kirsten was changing her mind.

"Just about everyone's being refused treatment," Daniel interrupted her reverie "unless they're a Covid patient."

"I'm talking about Covid patients. I'd hate to be old at the moment," Kirsten said, almost to herself. "Mind you, being young wouldn't be that great either, with the disruption to education and social life."

"It's an *interesting* time to be alive. As Margaret remarked some time ago, 'may you live in interesting times' is a Chinese curse."

"I know she's feisty and independent, but d'you think she is scared?"

"Of the virus?"

"Generally; being alone and old."

"She doesn't give that impression."

"She wouldn't though, would she? Shall we invite her for dinner? We could maybe even do it once a week."

"That's a nice idea, I'll ask her tomorrow."

When he did Margaret said, "Well, I've considered myself it might be nice to have a shared meal, but I think you two should come here."

"Don't trust meat eaters to cook a decent vegetarian, eh?"

"You're both busy, I'm not."

"It's against the rules, of course. You can come to us because you're just one person, but we'll be two coming to you."

"Which underlines how utterly ridiculous the whole thing is. Anyway, I can't think of a better reason. Shall we say Saturday?"

Margaret was on a high all day. For the first time in ages, she felt a real sense of purpose. She walked into town, enjoying the fine weather. Ever since being told to stay home, Margaret had felt an increasing desire to be outside. The roads were still quiet enough to make the journey a pleasant one.

Outside the supermarket sat the familiar homeless man.

"Hello," Margaret greeted, handing him two pound coins.

"Thank you, ma'am."

She smiled at the rather royal title bestowed upon her.

In the supermarket she met Bill from her literature group. His masked face initially made recognition difficult.

After the formal greetings he asked, "You heard about Alice?"

"No, what?" Margaret felt alarmed, expecting to be informed of her death, which, given Alice's mature years wouldn't be such a shock, but every death reminded her of how close her own was.

"Been taken into hospital with Covid."

"Oh dear, sorry to hear that." She decided not to tell him about her own admission.

"Yeah, we oldies can't be too careful. That's why I have this," he pointed to his mask, "and these," he waved his gloved hands in the air.

Margaret just nodded, rather than offer any explanation for her lack of them herself, which she imagined was what Bill was looking for. She hurriedly completed the shopping and caught the bus home. Once there Margaret acknowledged her tiredness.

Just ten minutes, she thought, as she lay down on the sofa. *Better not go to bed, I'll sleep too long.*

Drifting towards sleep she was forced to admit to herself that the tiredness had occurred since her illness, so, she couldn't really claim to be fully over it yet. Her thoughts turned towards Alice. Even though she didn't especially like her, Margaret felt worried for her. It was always the same, any situation had more significance when brought to a personal level. It wasn't that she didn't feel for the unknown, unnamed people who were generating the daily statistics, it was just hard to care too much about people you didn't know.

The next thing Margaret knew it was five-thirty. Despite taking her nap on the sofa she'd slept too long, so now she only had two hours to prepare for her guests. But she was happy, as she loved cooking for people and rarely had the chance these days.

The two hours passed by in what felt like minutes and soon Daniel and Kirsten were at the door.

"Something smells good," Kirsten said.

"Let's hope so, otherwise it's a trip to the takeaway," Margaret said, with a girlish giggle.

"I'm pleased you're well now, Margaret. Daniel was so worried about you for a while."

"I know he was."

"Not only me, your children too."

Margaret sighed, "I don't want people worrying about me, of course, but I have to admit I'm blessed to have so many who do." Margaret sighed again, "Unlike some, like that young man that sits outside your shop, Kirsten, for one. He's always so polite, too."

"Yes, he is, isn't he? Kirsten agreed. "His name's Roy. We've become quite chatty over the years. I haven't ever asked him his story, though."

"We don't, do we? I mean generally. It occurs to me how little I actually know about you for example, Daniel."

"Aw!"

Kirsten laughed, "That goes for both of us, Margaret." Then to Daniel, "We did discuss you a bit in your absence I'm afraid."

"Aw."

Over dinner the conversation moved to the pandemic, with each of them acknowledging their surprise that it had taken so long for the subject to come up.

"Yes, it's virtually the only topic these days," Margaret said. "I wonder when we'll talk about other things again. I wonder when this'll all be over, and what the world will look like when it is. I hope we're not headed for another war."

"What makes you say that?" Daniel asked.

"History. The Spanish flu and the Wall Street crash, followed by the rise of fascism. The way world leaders are behaving, the inevitable economic crash that's coming, they always take us to war to get themselves out of trouble."

"They might not need to this time."

"Uh?"

"CBDCs – central bank digital currencies. They can control what we spend, where we spend it, what we spend it on and even how soon we spend it. They will never lose control of the financial system again."

"It feels like we're practising for it now." Margaret had in mind automated check-outs in the supermarket, voice and facial recognition.

"Yeah. We're moving rapidly towards a technocracy."

In her imagination Kirsten saw her grandchildren working alongside holographic friends, walking in virtual parks, eating protein packs instead of meals. The word technocratic brought with it no sense of oneness with nature or breathing mountain air.

"I think I'd prefer a war, at least the winners end up free," Margaret said.

"D'you think it's just our age?" Kirsten asked, distractedly.

"*Our* age? I'm considerably older than either of you. But if you mean it's just inevitable progress and we're trying to hold it back, then, no, I don't agree. Progress would make people more free and more economically equal; this is anti-progress."

"Exactly," Daniel interjected.

"How true," Kirsten echoed.

"I hope I'm like Margaret when I'm that age," Kirsten enthused, as they were walking home. "She's as sharp as a razor still. I don't think there's any cause for concern about her mental capacity."

"No. It was only that once."

"And so fearless. My observation is that older people are often on the anxious side. It's like she loves life more than she fears the loss of it. How freeing that must be."

Margaret sat at the empty table. It had been cleared, the washing and drying up done, everything put away. *It was good of them to do it,* she thought. *They seem good together.* She felt jealous that they enjoyed what she had now lost; sad, deeply sad, for her loss, yet grateful at the same time, for these emotions that were an acknowledgement of what she and John had once shared.

It was weeks since Mandeep had been jogging. Just when she knew she needed it most she seemed to have lost her motivation, but the bright and sunny start to the day had given her the push required. And, as she finished the three-mile run, she felt elated for the first time in several weeks, back in control of herself and her life, and it hadn't been anywhere near as hard as she'd expected.

An hour later she was in the car on her way to work. The radio came on with the engine and with it two pieces of news that reminded her of the limits of her control. The first, the row over the Chief Advisor's trip to Durham: the second, the teachers' unions expressing their reluctance to have children return to school.

The confusion she felt regarding the severity of the virus was underlined by both of these, because the first suggested it was mild, while the second that it was to be feared. Confusion was becoming a familiar feeling, and with it a growing loss of confidence in the government's advice. It wasn't that she had blind faith in them, no, she recognised as well as most, there was a level of corruption, but she still believed that there was a general intention to do what was best for the majority. She couldn't go along with Emerson's cynical view of the world.

Kirsten was waiting on the doorstep. "Morning, you look like you've found a pound and lost a fiver."

"Morning. I went for a jog, was feeling great. Then I heard the news on the way here."

"What's happened?"

"Nothing! Just the usual contradictory stuff."

"Yes, isn't it?"

"I'm hoping the track-and-trace rolls out soon."

"That'll make you feel better?"

"Well, yes, at least we'll know for definite who's infected."

Margaret had found the same news broadcast upsetting on the one hand: *Poor kids, even according to the official statistics and narrative they're at no risk. I wonder what's going on in the heads of these people. Is it really about keeping the children safe? Or themselves? Fear of being sued?* And annoying on the other: *One rule for them and another for us. Why can't people see that? First one with his lover, now another on a trip. They don't look scared to me.*

It was time for her Zoom meeting with the reading group. She'd set it up in advance, having learnt this was best when faced, last time, with some technical issues.

"Anyone got any news on Alice?" she asked, as soon as they were all there.

"Ah, I was coming to that," the organiser said, and Margaret's stomach dropped in expectation of news of her death.

"Her daughter phoned to let me know that she's been discharged to a nursing home."

"What? Why not home?"

"Apparently she's become confused."

"She was as sharp as a razor."

"Um, she was, it's very sad."

This news clung onto Margaret's consciousness like gossamer to skin. She couldn't free her mind of it, it interrupted every attempt at keeping up with the discussion. *I wonder what drugs they gave her? I'm so lucky it didn't turn out that way for me.*

JUNE

“Seen this?” Daniel called Kirsten over.

On the screen she saw an elderly, bald headed man. Kirsten found the downward turn of his set mouth and the empty look in his eyes alarming. And when he spoke, the words were almost hissed out in his heavily accented tone. “The coronavirus presents a rare, but narrow opportunity to reflect, reimagine and reset our world.”

“Who's he?”

“Klaus Schwab, founder of the World Economic Forum.”

“Oh!”

“So, there you have it, straight from the horse's mouth, told you this was about the Great Reset.”

“Yes, you did.” It didn't help her mood, which was low and dipping lower. Daniel hadn't noticed, he even seemed a bit excited. Kirsten resented having to draw his attention to her ill humour.

“Just been speaking with Rosie.”

"What's that mean? No one will own anything, and you'll all be happy. Is that a face that you would trust to make us all happy?"

"What's it even mean? How does he know what'll make us happy? Most of us don't know that for ourselves."

"Great Reset suggests something big, wonderful and different; don't think it'll be any of those."

"Exactly." Kirsten sighed again. "Just got off the phone to Rosie. She sounds like she's really struggling."

"Uh huh!" Daniel didn't take his eyes from the screen.

"With the kids – and financially too, I think."

"No news on Andy's job?"

So, he is listening. "They won't take him on during the lockdown."

"You'd think they would, wouldn't you? Surely, he's an essential worker. A dispensing optician must be indispensable."

Daniel laughed, pleased with his own joke.

"Funny phrase that, 'essential worker'." Kirsten ignored Daniel's attempt at humour. "How do you define essential? I mean obviously we need food supplied, and carers to look after the sick and disabled. But what if you live miles from a shop, or your job, and your car breaks down? Isn't a mechanic 'essential'? What if you're disabled and can't clean your house yourself? What if your mental health depends upon swimming every day, or working out at the gym? What if your hair is hanging in your face and getting in your food?" Kirsten was laughing now. "You get my point, though?"

"Course I do."

"Rosie's thinking of getting a job in a care home. I might need to help her out with the kids from time to time."

"Aw."

"Before the kids were born, she started nurse training, but she didn't really like it."

Kirsten expected Daniel to ask why; when he didn't, she offered an explanation anyway. "The hours didn't suit, and it wasn't the job she expected it to be, too much paperwork, not enough patient work, she said. At least that won't be an issue in a care home."

"She has good credentials, then."

"They're glad of pretty much anyone. It's not the best of jobs, hard work, low status."

"Aw."

"I know that it's being blown out of proportion, but I still worry a bit about her putting herself in a vulnerable position regarding the virus. Yes, I know, she's young and she'll be okay, but there's still so many unknowns."

"Aw."

"So, what d'you think?"

"About what?"

Fleetingly Kirsten wanted to hit him. She turned away until the feeling passed. "What are we talking about?"

"If Rosie should get a job in a nursing home? It's up to her."

"She can't unless I help out with the kids. How do you feel about that?"

"It's up to you."

"Yes, I know. I'm just asking your opinion."

"Aw." Daniel looked genuinely puzzled.

Kirsten was grateful that he accepted everything she did, but at the same time she wanted some feedback. She started clearing away the lunch things; by the time she'd finished she was calmer.

"What I'm asking, Daniel, is will it be alright for the children to come here sometimes?"

"Of course."

Emerson, who had just agreed to swap any shifts with Kirsten as she required, had seen Klaus Schwab's post and was telling Kirsten what she already knew, when Mandeep came into the break room.

Sometimes Emerson's rants were entertaining, at others irritating. Today, Mandeep felt positively angry in response. If there were really any such thing as The Great Reset, why hadn't she heard about it? She was sick of these conspiracy theorists trying to deny what was clear to anyone. The virus was demonstrably real, where did he think those death figures were coming from then? And today she felt especially scared, due to hearing that a neighbour, only fifty years old, was in hospital on life support. She kept her feelings internalised, for the sake of professionalism, but the only way she could do so was by blanking his cheerful, 'Hello'.

Kirsten read body language better than Emerson, who continued talking loudly, obviously trying to include his manager in the conversation. The atmosphere grew frostier; still Emerson carried on.

Kirsten offered a gentle shake of her head as a warning, but he missed that too. She looked from him to Mandeep and back again, as she searched for the right words and the right moment to silence him.

"If there is no virus, how come my neighbour has been taken into ICU with it?" The words burst from Mandeep like a firework igniting.

Emerson's flow was arrested for only a second. "Don't know, but no one's isolated this so-called virus yet, to the best of my knowledge. Flu? 5G?"

"Tush!" Mandeep was stirring her coffee as if she was trying to make a hole in the bottom of the cup.

Emerson looked to Kirsten for support, but finding none, continued, "Symptoms are exactly the same."

"So, you been out setting fire to masts?"

"No."

He sounded like a wounded child. Kirsten felt for him, she felt for Mandeep, too.

"Maybe we'll carry on this conversation another time, Emerson," she said, then to Mandeep, "You know your neighbour well? Like them?"

Emerson turned the tap on full, as he washed his cup, splashing the draining board with water. Then he slammed the cup down and left without saying anything.

"It's not about him, I hardly know him, although obviously I wouldn't want any harm to come to him, but it's more about the thing being so close. And clearly, it's real. People trying to pretend it isn't, piss me off."

Kirsten waited.

"D'you believe that stuff he's saying?" Mandeep continued.

"Some of it. Some not. Some I'm not sure."

Mandeep put her head in her hands. "I just want this to be over. I can't see where it's going to end."

Me neither; whatever the truth is. "Hopefully not too much longer."

"Well, it's not looking that way, haven't you seen the news?"

"Not today, no."

"All non-essential shops, pubs and schools are being closed down again and hairdressers reopening has been postponed."

"Oh."

Kirsten understood that this lent weight to Mandeep's fears. Rosie would definitely need her help, then. Most likely Sally wouldn't return to school for the rest of the year. It hardly seemed to be the right time to ask about shift changes, which was a shame because she wanted to let Rosie know.

Later, Mandeep reflected on her behaviour and her feelings. Now she regretted her outburst. She remembered something she'd read in the monthly astrological forecast that said: *A very confusing time. Lots of indecision. Challenge how one asserts oneself, make sure to get what you want without impinging on the liberty of others.*

She took the notebook from her drawer in which she'd written it down and checked. Yes, there it was, attributable to Mars and Neptune conjunct. Mars, clear cut, Neptune dissolving boundaries. The conjunction meaning the struggle between the two. She certainly felt like that much of the time recently and she knew she wasn't the only one. Kirsten had admitted frequently changing her mind about what was really going on.

It's a difficult time for us all. We all have our fears, even if they aren't the same in nature, Mandeep decided. *I'm going to apologise to Emerson tomorrow.*

Then there was Jupiter conjunct Pluto. Both inclined to exaggeration. Pluto, secretive, working behind the scenes, Jupiter exposing and magnifying. It read: *In twenty, twenty, Jupiter is asking Pluto to do what he most dreads – reveal his hidden agenda.* Emerson would no doubt say that proved his point.

Ursula observed a conversation taking place. The whispered tones indicated the content was not for all ears. One of them came over, this time revealing its face, which wasn't so unlike her own. Eyes and nose were more

prominent, and the skin was smoother, but in those eyes Ursula saw the reflection of her own inner world. Perhaps, in other circumstances, they would be kindred spirits.

"Christabell, Christabell, come here." The thing didn't look so monstrous without its snout. The use of that word, in that way, suggested a name, but that wasn't her name and Ursula refused to lose the one that was.

The other one came over. "Don't think it recognises its name."

"You don't give them much credit, do you? Even a dog knows its name."

"So, it's being defiant?"

"Wouldn't you, after what we've done to her?" A pause. "Or maybe she has her own name."

"You give them too much credit." This was said with incredulity and more than a little mocking.

"Christabell, I don't know why you're not responding, but I don't blame you and I'm sorry. I really am. I'm sorry for what we've done, and even more sorry for what we're going to do."

"I'm amazed you can do any of this, the way you feel about them."

A heavy sigh. "So am I, sometimes, but I know it's for the greater good."

"So, you see they are less than human?"

"Well, I see they aren't human. Less than, more than, equal to, is a value judgement, I try not to make those. If I did, I couldn't do it." A pause. "Anyway, if it was to save my mother or my daughter, I can't be sure I wouldn't do the same to another human."

"That's heavy. You heard they're approving this one."

"Yes, apparently so. Although, not for pregnant women at the moment, until the premature births have been investigated some more."

"I heard there was no statistical significance."

"I heard that too."

They were both quiet for a while, watching Ursula watching them.

"At least it's still alive."

"Which is consolation for whom? For her?"

"For us, looks like this one is safe. Well, safer."

"It's not killing them within weeks, no, for the longer term, who knows. Normally we would adopt her out and watch her for her natural life, to determine that, but I think she's not going to be so lucky. Mind you, she doesn't look as if she cares much."

"Actually, I could almost go along with you, seeing how it looks now. It does look kind of sad. Maybe it won't mind being euthanized."

Ursula felt warmth come towards her. Not just from the usual one, but the other one too. Maybe, if they could understand her loneliness and longing, they would return Norman and Sadie to her. She approached the bars, put her hand through. "Please bring my family," she said, turning her head on its side and making her tone pleading to help them understand.

The friendly one put a hand through and stroked her face. The other one backed away, its voice boomed out, frightening Ursula, so she ran back to her usual corner.

"Oh God, man, that's spooky, she just looked too human."

Kirsten sat back, feeling a sense of achievement and catharsis, she'd let Daniel read it first and then she'd try it out on Emerson.

She checked the time on the computer screen, then, deciding she could at least watch the first few minutes, tuned into UK Column. It was her antidote to the mainstream news, which struck her as increasingly propagandist. The words of Frank Zappa's song, The Slime, crept into her head with this thought, and it made her smile.

When it was time to go to Rosie's, Kirsten got her bicycle out. The cycling was a good way to stay fit and she was becoming increasingly better at it. She was also becoming ever more uncomfortable with sitting on the bus unmasked when everyone else was wearing one. Her objection to masks wasn't only political, it was also that it took only a few minutes of wearing to make her feel panicky.

As she locked up her bike, she looked at the window of her maisonette and considered how quickly she'd come to think of it as Rosie and Andy's home, rather than her own. A warm glow flowed through her with the realisation of how far the relationship with Daniel had come in the past few weeks. For them, at least, the lockdown was proving to be positive.

On her way up the stairs she heard her neighbour's voice raised in anger, and a child crying in response. It saddened her and reminded her of how difficult some were finding the lockdowns.

Rosie was on the doorstep.

"Am I late?" Kirsten asked.

"Bang on time. I was thinking I might see if Sandy's okay," she inclined her head in the direction of the shouting, "but not much I can do anyway. I've got to go."

"I don't mind having her lad too, we can go to the park and then to the school. I wonder why he's not in school."

"That's good of you, Mum. I'll suggest it. It's only years one and six that are back, he's year two."

※

The black and yellow tape sealing off the swings almost reduced Kirsten to tears. "Never mind, Ryan, you'll just have to take turns in this one. Who's going first?"

"Me," all three children called out together.

"I'll tell you what, the first one to run and touch that fence gets to go first."

※

Nabil's phone rang. He picked it up without moving his gaze from the wall. The vibration in his hand struck him as interesting, but not enough to provoke him to answer it. He waited for it to stop then dropped it down beside him on the bed, again, without taking his eyes from the wall.

He noted the sun beaming across the floor, and how it spot lit the vacant chair, reminding him of a waiting torture cell. But the thought was abstracted, and it struck him now how easily a person might slip into acceptance of himself as persecuted, or even as persecutor. All that was necessary for either role, was to dissociate.

His phone rang again. This time, when he picked it up, he checked who was calling. It was Mahdi. With the same level of interest, he checked the time, almost one. He put the phone down until the ringing ceased, then picked it up again and watched it until it reached one o'clock, precisely. This was lunchtime. He took a sigh, heaved himself from the bed to his feet and took the necessary items for making his meal. On the landing, outside his room, Nabil listened – hearing no sound from downstairs he crept to the kitchen, quickly prepared the food then hurried back to his room to eat.

Without hunger this was difficult. In a different frame of mind it might have struck him as ironic, that only a couple of weeks ago he struggled with not being permitted to do the thing he now had to force himself into.

He was just preparing to go to the kitchen and wash up when his phone rang for a third time – Mahdi again – this time he answered it.

"Where you been, man?" Mahdi asked.

"Nowhere."

"What were you doing?"

"Nothing."

"Fancy another drive out to the woods?"

"Not today."

As soon as he hung up Nabil regretted it. He hadn't seen Mahdi since Eid, when they'd shared lunch on a park bench. Now he had no other option than to take his daily walk there alone once more.

JULY

"What're you looking at?" Dev grabbed his wife's shoulders and massaged them.

"Wondering how many cases we have in our area. Leicester have gone back into lockdown because they're so high. I was wondering about us."

"And?"

"Going up again."

"They're talking about cases now, have you noticed? Not deaths. My point is, rising cases doesn't mean rising deaths."

"That's true, actually. But still, if cases are rising we stand a better chance of…"

"This is ridiculous. You're going to make yourself get it at this rate. Or give yourself a heart attack or cancer from the worry."

Mandeep hated Dev being angry with her. It made her feel like a child, because when she had been she'd had to wait for either her father or her older brother to forgive her, even if neither of them was the offended party. Her mother's dismissiveness in the meantime, was enough to convince her no such forgiveness would ever come.

Dev pulled her close. "Come on, it's fine."

She didn't know if he was talking about their relationship or the pandemic.

He rested his chin on Mandeep's head and watched their daughters playing tennis in the garden. Manjit's blossoming womanhood was something he found disturbing, not only because it was a prelude to his old age, but also because of the new responsibilities it brought with it.

"Let's go out for dinner," he suddenly said.

Mandeep's stomach and spirits fell. There was an unmarried paternal uncle who, during her teenage years, had taken many opportunities to leave the room during family gatherings at the same time as Mandeep She'd delay her exit to and from the toilet, or the kitchen on an errand, because he'd be waiting for her with his disgusting comments and demands for a kiss. And upon his arrival at the parties, she'd felt dread. She experienced that same feeling now.

"Don't we have to book?"

"I'll phone to check, but I don't think so, not at our usual place."

Dev made the call and stuck his thumb up to Mandeep as he carried on his conversation with the restaurateur.

She called the girls in and told them the plans. They responded with excitement. It seemed only Mandeep was concerned.

"We just need to leave a phone number for track-and-trace," Dev assured her, coming into the bedroom to change his clothes.

"We could sit outside," Mandeep suggested as they arrived at the restaurant. "It's such a nice evening," she added, hoping to hide the true reason.

There were direction markers, one way in and one way out, and hand sanitizers at the door; these helped her feel safer.

In front of them in the queue a couple were making a fuss about the track-and-trace. "You know this is about gathering information for genomic sequencing, don't you?" the woman was saying to the person on the door.

"I don't make the rules, I just follow them and if you want to come in, you'll have to do the same."

"That's what the Nazis said," the man replied, but provided his name and phone number and sanitized his hands just the same.

It amused Mandeep and reminded her of Emerson. Except he probably would have chosen not to enter. His current gripe was with the mandatory masks.

"Have you ever heard anything so ridiculous," he'd said to Mandeep. "There's a virus out there that's so deadly we all have to mask up for everyone's safety; only not for another two weeks. If that doesn't tell you something, I don't know what does."

And she had to admit that he had a point.

Margaret turned off the computer, she could handle no more; she was going to go for a walk. With this thought she put on her shoes and sought out a light jacket; never quite able to get out of the habit in case the weather turned. Her head was stuffed full of uses, side-effects, and contraindications of the drug she'd been given in hospital; no one had even asked her about allergies, or medical conditions. "They'd have checked your doctor's notes, or asked him directly," Joe assured her, when she pointed that out to him. "You're getting obsessed with this."

"I'm just trying to get someone to listen. Alice was perfectly okay before she went into hospital."

"It's an environment that can do that to older people, Mum, that's why you didn't want to go, isn't it?"

"True."

"I know you're worried about the side-effects of that drug, but at the end of the day, even if it is the cause, what can you do? If you keep going on about it, you'll sound like you're losing the plot."

And now that Alison had started phoning every day Margaret couldn't help but feel that a watchful, if distant, eye was being kept on her. She'd sooner die than end up in a care home, like Alice.

Poor Alice. It wasn't as if they'd been particularly fond of each other, but they did have good conversations and it was difficult to believe she'd lost her marbles so quickly. Margaret was so distracted she almost left without her keys, which she slipped now into her side pocket.

She walked across the playing fields reflecting on the need to be careful what she said. *But then, if real conversations can't be had,* she decided, *then neither can real relationships. All I'm doing is seeking the truth, people are quite at liberty to prove me wrong, in fact, I hope they do; but they are not at liberty to suggest I'm mad or senile.* Then a sobering thought followed, *suppose I am, though, I'll be the last to know.* She climbed over the stile that led to the river with little effort.

The route to the river took her through a field of cows, which always unnerved her, especially in her advancing years. The herd were standing in a cluster, close together, swishing their tails. Knowing the passivity of their nature helped only a little, as they turned and looked at her.

"Afternoon, ladies." She hoped the cheerful tone would convince them, and her, that there was no cause for alarm. She remembered using the same technique in years gone by as she walked all three children and the dog through similarly inhabited fields.

On the other side she felt relief, but also a little sadness, as she reflected upon the fact that it was, in large part, due to their ignorance. It wasn't as if they couldn't harm her, neither was it as if, as a representative of her species, she wouldn't deserve it if they did, it was simply that they had no idea of their potential power.

Margaret crossed the bridge that separated her from the cows and joined the path that followed the river. The sun was still hot, but losing its sharpness to the maturing day. The air tasted warm and smelt of ripe things. In this setting there was no time for analytical thoughts, only for being. The path was uneven, so Margaret had to concentrate on each step. This, too, helped stop her mind from straying. By the time she reached the road that would lead her back home, Margaret had successfully shelved her worries and was overcome by a sense of well-being.

A walk through a children's playground was all it took to resurrect her previous state of mind, due to a large portion of it being closed off by black and yellow tape. The colours of danger. As if the play equipment posed the children some threat.

She walked along the pavement, feeling a little tired now. The roads remained quiet, people still adhering to the essential-journeys-only rule, she supposed. As she went to cross the road, she had to wait for a cattle truck to pass. Its living cargo, seemed to offer pleading glances, as if they knew where they were headed, and she was reminded of the image of human arms protruded from a train.

ᴥ

"You going anywhere on your time off?" Emerson laughed at his own joke.

"Thought I might do a tour of Europe," Kirsten replied, in the same vein. "Seriously though, it'll be nice doing my own thing for a day or two. Daniel will be busy for most of it, but we might manage a couple of walks. It's just nice not having to work."

"Yeah, sure is! First school and now work. I was always trying to find excuses to skive off school."

"Did you make a habit of it? I only ever did it once. Went to the cinema with my friend. Got caught. Not surprising really, since we were hitching home at school kicking-out time. How stupid can you get?"

"Iused to make out I was sick. My mum was a soft touch. You were a naughty girl!"

"Yes, I was." Kirsten put the barrier across to let the customers know she was closing.

"You might get five hundred pounds in vouchers to spend in the shops." Emerson continued.

"I won't hold my breath. Anyway, I probably won't want to spend them where they want me to. And it's the taxpayer's money at the end of the day, so like paying myself." Kirsten was standing up ready to leave now.

"Here's what I think about the vouchers," Emerson said. "They're a precursor of what's to come, help introduce us to the idea of government providing us with currency that can only be spent how and where prescribed."

Kirsten laughed. "Could be. I think we're getting plenty of priming for that, with people paying by phone and the portable scanners for shopping. I don't like the idea, but maybe I'm just getting old."

"You are," Emerson laughed, "but you're still right. Ever seen the Black Mirror episode on social credit."

"Oh yes. Scary. I'll be way down the social credit score. I'm one of the 'nutters', she clawed the air with her forefingers as she quoted the Prime Minister, "who won't be getting a vaccine when they come up with one."

"And you think I will?"

Kirsten knew it was a rhetorical question; just as well, as a customer arriving at the till prohibited any answer.

"They're throwing money at us at the moment," Emerson continued, when the customer had gone, as if there had been no interruption.

"Yes. My daughter is hoping to be able to take advantage of the stamp duty holiday."

"You'll be moving back home, then?"

"They've got to find somewhere to buy first." The idea of moving back to her maisonette was both welcome and the opposite.

A few minutes later Kirsten was on her way home on her bike. By now she was coming to enjoy the cycle ride. The absence of cars was something she both enjoyed and abhorred. She liked the quietness of it, it felt calmer, more natural somehow, as if the town had stepped back half a century or more. Yet, on the other hand those same qualities made her fearful that things would never be the same again. It wasn't that there weren't things that needed to change, it was just that she had no choice or control over the direction. And she didn't trust in the integrity of those who had.

❧

Nabil thought that with the opening-up of the country would come the opening of the library. The locked doors, and the notice he couldn't read, disappointed him to the point of anger. It seemed years since he'd just been able go about his business without a lock or a regulation to prevent free movement. Turning away he exchanged a glance with the sad-eyed dog that was tied to the railings. He found an empty bench in the park to sit on.

The day was still, and warm enough to allow for an extended stay outside. Although Nabil was grateful that he was no longer restricted to one hour outside, and for the company of the other people in the park, it didn't provide the same sense of solace as the library. In the open space he felt conspicuous, and concentrating on his writing was made difficult by this. The library walls felt womb-like, and the other users were lost in their own worlds.

Today the words wouldn't come. Nabil closed his eyes, seeking memories that more often came seeking him. To be true to Abida, to keep her alive, Nabil knew he should write it all, even the events that it hurt the most to recall.

Behind his eyes he saw the men grab her, heard her voice as if she were right there with him now, ordering him to run, in a tone too unequivocal to argue with. Instinct made her commands easy to follow, love and loyalty impossible to do so. They were only a few metres from the border, just on the other side of it the car was waiting, engine revving, door ajar. Abida and her captors were one heaving beast, feet kicking, fists punching, teeth biting; contrary orders leaving its lips. 'Go, my brother, go.' 'Stop or we'll kill her.' Fight, flight and freeze seized Nabil in the same instant. The car door closed, and the car started to move away. Nabil turned and ran towards it. It slowed, the door opened, and a hand pulled him inside.

A gun shot.

"No." Nabil pushed at the locked door and kicked at the passenger seat in front of him. A slap silenced him. Strong arms restrained him. Nothing quieted his shame – a shame that had grown deeper with time. Reason argued its case in his mind, they would have killed me too. She would be happy I'm still alive. There was nothing I could do to stop them. And sometimes he considered that she wasn't dead at all, but there was no comfort in these thoughts because when he imagined where she was instead, it was always somewhere worse.

Nabil took the notebook and put it in his backpack, which he now cradled in his arms and rested his forehead upon.

Humiliation curled him around it. He felt himself the most disgusting coward alive. He'd told himself a nice little tale of how he was keeping her alive with his pen, and how the world should hear about the sacrifice she had made for the sake of saving him. Abida the brave. Abida the righteous. Nabil the coward. Nabil the blameworthy. Nabil the liar. This story was for him. An apology. A pathetic attempt at resurrection. He wasn't staying alive for her, for his parents, for all those who weren't lucky enough to escape. He was still alive because his fear for himself had been greater than his love for her.

Feeling disgusted with himself Nabil took the notebook from his bag, walked over to the nearest bin, and threw it in.

AUGUST

"D'you think they say this stuff just to annoy us? Is there any real substance to it?" Kirsten was responding to the announcement that the Prime Minister was considering the locking down of everyone over fifty.

Daniel laughed. "Wouldn't you like being forbidden to go to work?"

"I don't like being forbidden to do anything. I'd like to be so wealthy I don't need to work, but that's different. I'm sick of being treated like a child. Grown-ups make up their own minds."

"There are plenty of adults who behave like children."

"True, but they'll only stay that way by having decisions made for them. Anyway, I won't be forbidden to work, I'm essential, remember, I'll only be forbidden to do the things I enjoy."

"Fun has been outlawed for ages. It's either bad for the individual, the environment, or the pocket."

Kirsten laughed.

Daniel said, "I don't know why you keep listening to the news."

"I need to know what's being said. Where most people are coming from. It's easy to forget that most people don't access the 'alternative' media."

"The predicted redundancies have started I see. British Airways, Smiths and William Hill won't be reopening over a hundred of its shops."

"And we've got them telling us the effects of the lockdowns won't be as bad as expected. I wonder what it takes to make people aware they're being lied to. Weapons of mass destruction, or rather the lack of them, seem to have been forgotten, along with all the other lies. Fear is a good way to control, I'll concede that, it overrides reason. Viruses are even more effective than war. Increasingly it looks like the 'conspiracy theorists', are right."

"About some of it, for sure. The central bank digital currency for one. The Chancellor has already talked about it."

"I keep stubbornly trying to hang on to cash."

"Let's hope it remains an option," Daniel picked his wallet up from the table, as if responding to some unconscious prompt. "They've lost control of the financial system, CBDCs are their attempt at making sure it never happens again."

I think it is. It's a consequence of market forces. Empires rise and then they fall, and another takes its place. And there's always chaos in the transition." perfect example." Kirsten sighed, "Would it be so bad to have everything provided? Own nothing, but be happy? As a certain someone Schwaby says. I've never owned much anyway, and it hasn't made me unhappy. Other things have done that. Lack of fulfilment in my life. Relationships and the lack of them, but never not owning anything."

"The point is 'they', will own us."

"When have they not?" Kirsten sighed.

"True, but we've enjoyed times of relative freedom and if you are the owner of something you have the freedom to use it as you wish. If someone else is the owner, you are beholden to them and their whims. You'll have to do as 'they' say or you'll be locked out of the system. They'll be no more complaining about government. CBDCs aren't like bank cards. They can be programmed and turned on and off."

"That's me screwed then," she laughed. "God help Emerson. I always rejected money. Saw it as a bad thing, a corrupt thing, even, though I get how the lack of it would certainly make someone miserable. Latterly, I begin to see that it's not the thing itself, like most things in themselves, there is no essential quality of good or bad, it's the way it's procured and used that matters. I could be in a much better position now. Could buy some land and a house and be self-sufficient."

"That's what's needed." . dDifferent, yeah?"VeryAbsolutely. It leads to a completely very different place."As for happiness, I think that's complicated. We're pretty comfortable in the West for the most part, and the incidence of mental ill health has never been higher."

Kirsten sighed. "Maybe if all our needs are met we'll be free to self-actualise."

"If you can afford it. And if they approve. I get the sense The World Economic Forum'sidea of equity, though, is they're equally rich, and we're equally poor."

"I feel for those with something to lose. Luckily, that isn't me," Kirsten said. "Anyway, I'd better get going."

Daniel pulled away quickly from the kiss goodbye. It never failed to hurt a bit, even though Kirsten knew it was just his way. She felt this behaviour was unlikely to ever change. Both of them had adapted some of their entrenched behaviours in compromise, while others they stubbornly held onto. Why was that? She wondered now. Was it in the nature of the behaviour, or the level of complaint made against it? Was it that one person found compromise easier than did the other? Often friends had complained that they were always the ones to give, and she had wondered if their partners would have agreed. It was always easier to be the instigator of change than to be the one upon whom it was forced.

She rolled her bicycle out from the shed. There was only just enough room for it with Rosie and Andy's furniture in storage. Kirsten reflected on the likelihood that soon a new house would be purchased, and the shed cleared. Perhaps not as soon as she thought; only last week Rosie had said, "Of course we want to take advantage of the stamp duty holiday, but so does everyone else. And they all want to move to the country, now, too."It made Kirsten sad because she could tell that Andy's move into lodgings for his job was hard on Rosie.

When they did move, what would happen with her maison-ette vacant? There would no longer be a need for her to stay with Daniel, but would she? Would he ask her to? Or just expect her to go home? Did she want to? Home? Where was that now?

Automatically she felt the tyres, even though they had only been inflated a few days before. She mounted the bike with only a little trepidation. It was lessening with each ride. The hill was the part she dreaded most, both going and returning, as the speed of the downhill frightened her and the effort of the uphill was a challenge. This time she reached the summit only a little out of breath, her fitness was clearly improving. *One more thing to add to the list of positives that the lockdown has forced on me.*

As she considered this, Kirsten acknowledged the rarity of hearing such reports in the media, the focus was on the damage being done. *Maybe being forced into things isn't always such a bad thing,* she thought, remembering all the times she'd had to coax Rosie into things that, once tried, she had wanted to do again.

She was cycling on the flat again and speeding along – as fast as she dared to go – so she reached her destination in good time. She climbed the stairs with her bike, not wanting to leave it untended, despite the lock.

Rosie answered the door with, "Gotta fly." So Kirsten was thrown instantly into her role.

The late afternoon sun was warm enough for the park, they called on their neighbour and invited her to join them; she said she would come a little later, but didn't.

In what seemed like no time at all the children were in bed and Rosie returned from work. She always looked a little strained upon her return, but today she looked decidedly anxious.

"Tough day?" Kirsten asked.

"They're not the best of places to work at the best of times, and these definitely aren't. You get this impression from the media about the staff being all self-sacrificing, well, some are, and some think they're saints themselves, but mostly they are freaked out and busy and bad tempered; happily, not usually with the residents, but certainly with each other. The residents' phone is permanently ringing. I'll bet the relatives are getting very frustrated trying to get through." She paused, then said, "There's been a bit of an incident today, too."

"Want to tell me about it?"

"One of the residents died from respiratory distress."

"Oh, sorry to hear that. Someone you were fond of?"

"Yes, a bit, but that's not it. I'm pretty sure he was given too much medication." She paused and brushed her hair back from her face and bit her lip. It was a gesture that dated back to her childhood. "I'm not allowed to do any of the meds, although I can't help taking an interest because of my past training. The gentleman needed to be sat up a bit more to take them, so the nurse put the pot down while we moved him. I glanced at it, it didn't register at the time, but now…" Rosie continued, as if she were speaking more to herself, "…I know what he usually has."

"Would one overdose kill him?" Kirsten felt alarmed herself now, empathising with Rosie's position.

"Potentially. But maybe more than one mistake was made."

"Have you reason to suspect that? Have you said anything?"

"No. D'you think I should?"

"Knowing how these things work it probably wouldn't go down well."

"That's why I haven't, but I feel terrible."

"Would you be feeling like this if he hadn't died?"

"I'd probably have forgotten about it, but he did, didn't he?"

"What're you going to do?"

"Nothing. I don't suppose. Really I should take it up with the person concerned, but I probably won't. I'm a coward and I hate myself."

"Don't do that. It was probably an accident and the person who did it has to live with it."

"God. It never occurred to me it was anything else. It can't have been deliberate."

"It wasn't. Of course, it wasn't. I don't know why I said that. Come here," Kirsten put her arms around her daughter; her stiffness rivalled Daniel's.

Once home, Kirsten shared the incident with Daniel. He'd said nothing, but his face expressed a level of distress that suggested many questions had crossed his mind.

The television had been left playing to an empty room again. Nabil was always annoyed by this, not least because often he was greeted by images he didn't wish to see. What appeared before his eyes today looked like the aftermath of an explosion and it led him to the internet on his phone for explanation.

His initial feeling was one of relief, not because he lacked sympathy for the Lebanese victims but because it appeared the fire was the result of an accident, rather than a bomb.

The images from Beirut left Nabil feeling ill at ease and he contemplated on how fragile was his sense of security. He felt himself to be like an infant, whose moods change in an instant in response to the whims of the caregivers. He wished he had a special adult on whom he could vent his feelings in the knowledge that their love would mean he'd be forgiven.

In the absence of any such person in reality, he turned to the paper one. It had taken only minutes and a short, brisk walk from the park, for Nabil to forgive himself enough to return and retrieve his notebook from the bin. All of the things he'd thought and told himself were true, but in the end, he conceded to his need for Abida.

He sat on his bed and prepared to write, but reading over the last section he was transported back in his mind so vividly that he began to cry and shake. Howling sobs came to his ears, as if from someone else. When they subsided enough, he washed his face, put on his shoes and left the house.

"I don't see your exemption badge," Emerson overheard his colleague tell her customer. *I bet she'd be reporting the Jews who didn't wear yellow stars. She thinks she's so fucking superior, , that one,* he thought.

"Well, I am exempt."

"You look healthier than me." It was said in a tone that suggested jest, but *many a true word spoken in…,* Emerson thought.

And the apparent shock in the customer's answer suggested she felt the same.

"Excuse me?"

"Masks are mandatory."

"I'm exempt."

"You need to wear your badge, then. You could give us all Covid."

The customer sighed. "Oh, I didn't realise the exemption badge stopped it spreading."

The next customer in line joined in, "I think the point the lady's making is that if you had a badge, we'd know you're not one of those people who just won't wear a mask, so clearly doesn't care about others."

"You know nothing about me. Anyway, we're distanced, and you," she turned her attention back to the check-out operative, "have a perspex screen to protect you." She sighed again; her hand hovered over the bag with the last item. "Look, I don't mean to cause any offence. I respect your decision to wear a mask, please respect mine not to."

"You're putting others at risk, I'm not."

"Well, we could debate both of those viewpoints for hours, but you've got other customers and I've got better things to do. I hope you enjoy the rest of your day."

As the next customer went through, he and the check-out operative joined each other in mutual condemnation of the non-mask wearer. Emerson tried to concentrate on his own customer, but his blood was boiling at the overheard conversation. He thought it rather unprofessional too, embarrassing for the lady in question. He might report it to Mandeep later.

Mandeep was busy with the rota for the following week. It was becoming a nightmare to manage, between Covid absences and holidays. *Who can I ask to do extra shifts?* She thought, looking at the overtime list from the preceding two weeks: Emerson, Lisa, Kelly. Perhaps Kirsten wouldn't mind doing one or two, she couldn't keep asking the same few people and Sam had made his position more than clear. He always used to want overtime. Mandeep surmised his current lack of interest was probably due to fear of the virus, especially since his wife had only just given birth. Couldn't blame him for that.

It was then that there was knock on the door. "Hi Emerson, what can I do for you?" Professionalism stopped the words that formed in her mind from leaving her lips, *Please don't ask me for time off, not this week.*

"I feel a bit awkward, I don't like doing this, but I have to tell you something about another member of staff."

Mandeep listened with a degree of disbelief, both towards Abby's behaviour, which was normally exemplary, and in Emerson's inability to recognise how he sometimes conducted himself. Although, she had to admit, she'd only ever observed this with staff members.

"I mean there's no evidence masks work, for a start," Emerson continued. "Some studies suggest they're actually bad for you."

Mandeep had little interest in this opinion, she felt safer with their use, most of her staff did too, she was sure, and anyway, it was the law. She assured Emerson she would do a memo to all staff on protocol, so as not to make it obvious Abby had been reported. Reprimanding staff was the worst part of the job, as far as Mandeep was concerned.

"Cheers," Emerson, said, although he didn't really care if Abby knew what he'd done. He was on his way out of the door, but turned back to say, "If the virus is so bad we need to mask-up against it, why haven't we got bio-hazard bins for disposing of them? Have you thought about that?" He nodded emphatically, then left.

Mandeep hadn't actually considered that, and conceded he had a point. She had, however, remarked to Dev on the potential health risks of masks that were ditched on pavements.

Today would have been her mother's birthday, Margaret realised, as she scribed the date of the next Zoom reading group meeting on her calendar. She'd suggested they do the next one over a picnic in the park but, when general reluctance ruled it out, decided to make one for herself for today and go alone.

Make hay while the sun shines. Tomorrow it might rain, she decided.

This was how Margaret had tried to live her life. Tomorrow it might rain. There was much talk recently about people doing things they'd previously put off, because of a sudden realisation that tomorrow might never come. Somehow Margaret had always been acutely aware of it. There had been no life-shattering incident to provoke it, no single defining event, she had just always known that life was for living and took every opportunity that came her way. Many times, she had wondered at the procrastination she observed all around her.

Her picnic comprised two Quorn sausages, a hard-boiled egg, a packet of mixed fruit and nuts, and an apple. She put it her backpack, along with a bottle of water, the latest book-group read and grabbed her MP3 player, which she put on shuffle.

Momentarily she considered taking her bike, but then decided against it. Although she could go further in the time, it would only encumber her if she decided to walk by the river. As if the mere thought dictated it that was exactly what Margaret did.

By the river she always felt at peace. Living by the sea was the ideal choice for many, but Margaret had no such hankering. Indeed, it was years since her last visit to the seaside. She remembered the nightmare of ensuring the safety of her children during such visits and had always wondered how anyone could relax under the circumstances. And, on the rare occasions she'd gone alone, or with John, she still hadn't found it so. Even the calmest of seas was a little frightening. The act of the waves, whether lashing or lapping, suggested they would grab her and take her away, and the sound they made seemed to coax her in, like a siren calling.

Not so the river. She, and it, ambled along at a mutually agreeable pace, in near silence, grounded by the banks, on which, today, the grass had grown long and yellowed in the sun. But other walkers had left plenty of footfall indentations to make her journey easier.

She breathed in the air, feeling grateful that she remained able to do so, and was reminded of the time she couldn't, and her hospital stay, and consequently, of Alice. Immediately, Margaret began to feel anxiety rising. *There was no sign of any dementia, she wasn't even slightly confused. She was a pain in the arse with some of her opinions, but…*

"Stop it," Margaret said out loud to herself.

After only a few more paces Margaret began to feel tired. She had noticed how quickly this happened of late. Whether it was attributable to her age, or recent illness she couldn't decide.

In August, there was a sense of the summer retreating. The energy and light were beginning to contract. And, although there was often still heat in the sun, it was losing its sharpness. In just a few more weeks it would be time for reflecting on how the summer had been and what the winter would have in store. *The rhetoric as it is, I wouldn't be surprised if there were more bloody lockdowns,* she thought.

Feeling really weary now, Margaret leaned against a tree. The trunk branched into two almost forming a natural chair, but it wasn't quite wide enough, and was rather too high, for it to be useful for Margaret. She imagined picking up a child and sitting them there and was suddenly overcome by nostalgia. All of that was behind her now, but this realisation didn't sadden her, rather she felt grateful for the life she had had, and that it had taken the whole of it to bring her to a sense of completion.

She contemplated the tree. The formation of the trunk moved her, as she considered whether one tree had spilt away to form a twin, or two had joined together. In either case it struck her that nature tended towards pairing and sharing, as opposed to solitude.

When she had eaten some nuts and had a drink of water, Margaret felt much better and returned to walking, but resolved to sit and eat her picnic as soon as she found a suitable place for sitting. It was hardly more than a few minutes before this happened. There was a spot where the river widened, and the bank became shallower. She slipped off her jacket, put it on the ground and sat down in a place where there was enough of a slope to assist with standing again when needed, but not steep enough to cause danger of slipping into the river.

She took her MP3 player off shuffle, intending to select something classical to eat to, and then to accompany a chapter of her book, but, as she did so, she glanced to her left and spotted the young man squatting a few feet away, abstractedly casting stones into the river. Something about his manner disturbed her, and she felt compelled to keep returning her gaze to him.

The town was becoming busier, but still lacked pre-lock-down vibrancy, and in the air there remained a sense of ill ease. The now familiar streets, and even the park, had begun to bore Nabil, but today this wasn't the dominant emotion. He felt humbled by the past. His future was marred by hopelessness, and he was helpless to influence the outcome.

A couple walked towards him. They were late middle-aged, hand in hand, looking content. They reminded Nabil of his parents, of his loss. He wished he could be more certain of their continuing togetherness in the afterlife. He thought of Abida, of all she would never have, of what he might not; of all the things he could no longer take for granted. Sometimes he wondered why he'd fought so hard for safety. He had swapped certain death for uncertain life outcomes. At least in the former state there was nothing left to fear. Or to regret.

Distracted by his thoughts and overcome by his feelings, Nabil walked. As he did so he looked at the ground. Watching his feet helped him focus on what he was doing, although not on where he was going, so, when he returned his gaze to street level he didn't know where he was. In any other mood this would have frightened him, but today he was ready for whatever fate had to offer. At a fork in the road, he was forced to choose between left, or right. He decided on right, but turned left, wishing to tempt providence. Soon he found himself in a rural area, where large houses could be glimpsed at the end of even larger driveways. This place looked more like the England of his imagination than the one he had found himself in.

Beside one of the dwellings there was a path. Nabil wandered up it, more with an attitude of inevitability, than one of curiosity. If it had been a spiritual path he would have cared little if it led him to death or to salvation. It actually led him to a river.

The passivity of water was still and calming, leaving him awed by the thought that simply by flowing it had etched its mark on the earth and altered the lay of the land in its wake. Nabil was reminded of the vastness of time. The majesty of God.

The futility of trying to discover God's plan for him, but equally he was reminded such a plan did indeed exist.

He walked a while, then squatted down beside the river, gathered up a handful of stones and began throwing them into it. He tried to count the number of ripples each made. He soon realised there was no correlation between the size of the stone and the number of ripples. He wished he had the courage to slide into the river to test God's love for him. But, even as he thought this, he knew two things: God didn't like to be tested and he, Nabil, wouldn't be able to resist swimming.

He sighed and looked around. It was then that he noticed the elderly lady, and immediately he jumped up and ran over, seeing that she was struggling and losing her grip on the bank. He quickly grabbed a mask from his pocket, then reached out to the woman, took hold of her gently, but firmly, and helped her to her feet.

Margaret clung to the hand offered and, as soon as she had recovered her breath said, "Oh, thank you, thank you so much."

"Welcome."

Nabil led her away from the edge of the river before he let go of her hand. He was struck by the irony that the river he'd wished to give himself up to had almost claimed an unwilling victim.

Margaret brushed herself down, she felt near to tears. "I'm such a stupid old woman."

She misconstrued Nabil's blank expression as attributable to politely declining to comment.

"You probably think I'm dafter still for saying so, but I was seriously considering I might have to rescue you." Was it the mask that made him hard to read? "Are you wearing that thing for my sake, I wonder."

"Sorry, I don't understand."

Margaret pointed at the mask. "If you're wearing that for my sake, I'd rather you didn't. I'd like to see the face of my saviour properly."

"Uh? This?" Nabil said, shaking his head and pulling the offending article down to his chin. "I don't understand."

Finally, Margaret did. "You don't understand English?"

"Very little," Nabil demonstrated by holding his thumb and forefinger an inch apart.

"See I really am a stupid old woman. Where are you from?" When that didn't work, "Your country."

"Syria."

"Ah!"

Nabil hated the way people said Ah! every time he answered that question, as if it explained everything and they knew all there was to know about him.

Margaret wished he could speak more English so that she could have a first-hand Syrian opinion on Assad, and the West's involvement. Of course, she knew that no single opinion was representative of an homogenous one, but she had never heard anything but the Western perspective on this. And she was very sure that any involvement by them was certainly not for the good of the Syrians.

They stood like two off-duty soldiers whose commanding officer had just shown up. Nabil felt an unwanted obligation to this woman. Margaret sensed this. She wanted him to leave but couldn't think of way to say so that didn't risk sounding rude.

"Where were you going?" she tried.

"I am walking."

Nowhere in particular? "Shall we walk together?" Margaret pointed up the path and started to walk that way, although she really wanted to sit and think for a little longer.

Nabil felt worried because he wanted to return home now and this would take him further in the wrong direction. And it was difficult being in someone's company without being able to speak to them. He looked inside his head for the words, but when they came out, they sounded muddled. "Where your home is?" But the lady seemed to understand.

"This way," Margaret pointed. "Yours? "Where is your home?"

Nabil stopped, turned around and pointed as he said, "This way."

"Then let's walk that way," Margaret turned, feeling grateful.

"No, is okay." Nabil made to continue walking in the wrong direction, but, when the lady persisted, he too was grateful.

When they reached the gap in the hedge that led to the path Nabil had come down, he hesitated. It didn't go unnoticed by his companion.

"Ah, you came this way in, well, that's fine I'll carry on walking, and you go."

The meaning of her words was clear by the way the lady indicated the path and gesticulated as if she were shooing him away like a dog that had followed her and become a nuisance. Margaret was just thinking she would have to go with him when he smiled and said, "Okay, I go now."

"Thank you again for rescuing me," she said, offering her hand. "I'm Margaret, by the way." She pointed at herself, "Margaret."

"Nabil." He shook her hand and offered her a smile, which entirely altered the look of his face. Margaret saw that in other circumstances he had the capacity for dangerous charm.

After they had parted company Margaret strolled homewards, having now lost the inclination for anything else. Once there, she put the kettle on; she sat down to wait for it to boil and finished her picnic as she did so, the food and the walk soon sent her to sleep.

✿

"What's this?" Kirsten was looking over Daniel's shoulder at the screen.

"Yeah, says there were thirty-five thousand there."

"What were they protesting about?"

"Covid restrictions and mask wearing." It was said as if it was so obvious Kirsten should have known.

"Did you know about it? Before I mean? Then why didn't you tell me, I might have gone."

"Aw!"

"Where was it advertised?"

"Twitter. Telegram maybe."

"What's Telegram?

"A social media platform. Yes, I think it's new. Supposed to be more secure."

"Why d'you think it was so poorly promoted?"

"Have to be careful where you advertise things these days. You can still rely on defiance from some, though." Daniel indicated the other piece of news he was looking at, the police attempt to break up a rave.

"I don't suppose I would've gone," Kirsten said more to herself than Daniel. "Last time I did anything like that was two-thousand and three, against the Iraq war. For all the good it did. Made us feel like we could change things at least, I don't even feel that now."

"I was on that march."

"Oh." This fact gave her a greater sense of connection with him.

After a sigh Daniel said, "We couldn't stop that. I doubt we can stop this. It's the Great Reset. All we can do is get ready."

"But I don't want to get ready. I don't want it."

The distress in Kirsten's tone provoked Daniel into taking hold of her hand. "Even wars can be survived if you are ready for them. No point in trying to pretend it's not happening."

"Why did you go on the anti-Iraq war march, then?"

"I didn't say you shouldn't try. And you can be ready for what's coming."

"I'm not even sure what to get ready for. Are you?"

"I'm keeping an eye and thinking. But gold and silver for the financial crash."

SEPTEMBER

Kirsten and Emerson were on adjacent tills, "There was an anti-restrictions demo last week, I didn't even know about it," Kirsten said.

"Didn't ya? I did."

"Did you go?"

"Nah. Might in the future, though. Notice it didn't hit the news? Extinction Rebellion did, of course."

"Yes, interesting."

"It's obvious why."

"Which is?"

"Extinction Rebellion've been infiltrated by the establishment. The climate-change narrative suits their overall plan. They don't want anyone to know how many people are against the restrictions, so they keep it out of the media."

"I'd be interested to hear your climate-change thesis sometime."

"Not much of a thesis. There ain't no climate change. They just want to implement policies that'll keep the developing world from doing that and drag us down to it."

A customer approached the tills, hovered between the two then, chose Kirsten's. She waited until the customer had gone before continuing.

"I get why you would say that 'cos it's hard to believe any policies are made to benefit anyone but the one percenters, but…"

Another customer came to the till. When she'd gone, Emerson's till was busy. Without anyone at hers, Kirsten reflected on what had been said. In the past she'd been on climate marches, and delivered Emerson-style lectures on global warming, to friends. The trouble with her burgeoning conspiracy theorist persona, was that it kept calling into question all her preconceived ideas. How terrible it would be to realise that in fighting for something you believed in, it turned out you were collaborating with the enemy.

"Yeah, you can bet your life they won't stop driving their gas-guzzling Ferraris, or flying their private jets." It was Emerson's habit to carry on conversations where they had left off, sometimes days after they'd started. "I reckon we've got more lockdowns coming, too."

"I hope not, but I think you could be right. We have only just reopened the centre. The centre manager, like all managers, I guess, is in a difficult position, he has to keep everyone 'safe', "and some of the staff and volunteers are absolutely terrified."

"Stupid."

Mandeep was busy on the shop floor and overheard the conversation. She was impatient with Emerson's dismissal of the facts, and was about to say so, but the conversation between him and Kirsten continued.

"Not everyone has the advantage of the counter narrative, don't forget. Without it I'd probably be scared." Kirsten said.

"What counter narrative?" Mandeep interrupted.

"I could give you a list of things to watch and read, if you like, you might not thank for it, though." Kirsten said.

"What d'you mean?" Mandeep asked.

"It's no less scary than a virus."

"I'm surprised you're into conspiracy theories, Kirsten."

"I'm surprised at myself."

Emerson joined in the conversation saying, "Conspiracy theory! That pisses me off. You know where the term originated don't you?"

No, but I've got a feeling I soon will, Mandeep thought.

"From the C I fucking…whoops, sorry…A. They invented it to call people who were questioning their propaganda."

This was news to Kirsten too.

"Well, I don't think it's something we can discuss now," Mandeep said, inclining her head towards approaching customers and making a hasty retreat to her office. But she felt unsettled, and the feeling persisted for the rest of the shift. She was on the verge of seeking out Kirsten to ask for the list to which she'd referred, when she caught sight of the official coronavirus figures on the internet. Deaths were rising, the R rate was up above one again, Birmingham and Oldham were tightening their restrictions.

I wish this bloody thing would just go away.

Later, at home, she said to Dev, "I wish they would hurry up and find a vaccine."

"Oh love, that's not going to happen. Vaccines take years to produce."

"No, they're nearly there with one for this."

"I heard the trials have been halted because someone had a severe reaction, which illustrates my point."

The fear she felt in response to his words induced nausea. "I don't know how we can stay safe without one."

"Same way we're doing now, same way we always have. Good diet, supplements, exercise. If we get ill, we'll deal with it. What else can we do? Come here." He opened his arms to receive her in a hug.

It seemed that ever since their encounter on the riverside Margaret and Nabil kept bumping into each other. This was their second encounter of the day. Margaret was pushing her bicycle because she didn't like the streets now that they were busier again. The other person with him was a surprise.

"Hello," Kirsten said, warmly. "You're brave, on your bike."

Nabil's wide smile made it clear to Kirsten that this wasn't the first time he and Margaret had met. "Hello," he offered.

"Hello to you both. I'm not that brave, otherwise I would be on it. I didn't realise you two knew each other."

"I volunteer at the centre," Kirsten nodded her head backwards in the direction of the building in question. "Nabil comes along as a visitor. We were both surprised to find it closed. A note on the door says it's due to staff shortages."

"Covid tests? This pandemic is being run by them."

"Indeed. Oh, 'bye, Nabil."

Nabil pointed at the time on his phone to indicate his need to hurry. He didn't want to be late for the Zoom English class. He'd gone along to the centre on Abdul's insistence that face to face was good for him, only to be greeted by the note on the door.

Nabil didn't want to see anyone. Although he was sick of his own company, he felt comfortable in it. He felt angry with Abdul, how dare he be so insistent? Yet, alongside this he knew he was right. His bedroom felt like a cell, the walk in the park like his allotted space in a zoo. He understood why, when the cage door was left open, the animal didn't even stick its head out. Nabil talked to himself in reprimanding tones. Abida was kinder and coaxed him. The note on the door had provided both disappointment and rescue.

Margaret was explaining to Kirsten about how she and Nabil had met.

"Have you been okay since?" Kirsten's concern came from a place of caring, Margaret knew, but it made her feel old and vulnerable and she rejected the feeling with vehemence.

"Fine."

Kirsten understood the feeling that generated the sharp tone, she almost apologised but instead said, "I guess you wouldn't be on your bike if you weren't. How long will it take you to cycle home?"

"Twenty to thirty minutes. Not bad for an old'un."

"Very good. I doubt I'd do it any quicker."

"Tell that to my children. They don't approve. One has even offered to pay for an Uber a couple of times a week."

"I'm sure Daniel would give you a lift, but I don't suppose you're cycling because you can't afford a taxi."

"I'm sure he would, and no, I'm not. If I act like I'm too old, I will be."

"I love your attitude, Margaret."

"My kids don't even want me to go on a bus, you know. They think there are too many people and it's too risky in terms of catching Covid."

"They obviously love you a lot."

"Funny thing, that. How does one treat someone they love? There's a fine line between being protective and controlling. And there's a fine line between letting someone do what they like and neglecting them."

"How very true."

And Kirsten thought about this all the way home. How she'd struggled with feeling wanted and loved by Daniel. And how rejecting his emotional remoteness had felt. Now that she knew him better it rarely felt like that. She appreciated his acceptance of her independence and felt safe in his self-containment. There was nothing unpredictable about Daniel and no chance of his over-reacting to any situation. Although, she did wonder sometimes if she could have been with him at any other time in her life. Had it been necessary for her to lose Greg and learn self-reliance before she was able to accept Daniel as he was? Kirsten had felt sorry for the only other woman with whom he'd been, when Daniel had spoken, with obvious confusion, about her tears and tantrums. Kirsten had had to bite her tongue, make sure she stayed with his emotions and didn't impose upon him the feelings that she guessed this woman had experienced.

She was near to her flat now and considered going there instead of home, but decided against it as there was nothing for her to do there. Then her phone rang, it was Rosie. "Hello love, I was just thinking about you, everything okay?"

"I've not gone in to work. Had a positive test. I should probably have rung sooner, but I feel quite rough." Kirsten's stomach sank at the words, she had to remind herself not to be afraid.

"Oh, you should've phoned me to take the children into school. Good job I'm fetching them. I'll take them to Daniel's.

I could come and get their bedclothes, I might be able to keep them all night, but I need to check…"

"I don't want you to do any of that. They might be carrying it. I was going to say just let them in and I'll stay in my room."

Kirsten was rocked by a mix of contradictory emotions: anger, that children should be being blamed for driving the pandemic and asked to protect the adults, sorrow, on behalf of her daughter, both because she was ill and because she was afraid for Kirsten. And even though her rational brain rejected it, Kirsten felt fear, on Rosie's behalf, and her own. "How're you going to take care of them when you're ill?" she asked.

"I don't want you to catch it."

"I come into contact with loads of people at work, I'm at risk all the time." Even as she was saying this, fear gripped her stomach.

"But I'd feel awful if you caught it from us."

"I'm not arguing. I'll come and get their things now. I'll be there in ten minutes." On the way she phoned Daniel.

"Sure," he said in reply to her request regarding the children.

Despite everything she thought, Kirsten worried that her daughter was going to be desperately ill. *Stop it,* she told herself, as into her imagination came a picture of Rosie prostrate and gasping for breath and then an ambulance, blue lights flashing. With pounding heart and shaking knees she turned the key in the lock and entered her flat. Rosie was sitting on the sofa with a hot drink in her hands.

Immediately relief surged through Kirsten. "Oh, you don't look too bad. D'you have a temperature?"

"I don't know."

"There was a thermometer in the first aid kit in the bathroom, d'you think it's still there?"
What Kirsten really sought was permission to look. As soon as she got it, she went and found the thermometer, which then she put gently into Rosie's ear. "No, it's fine." Another relief.

"What are your symptoms?"

"Tired, headache, in fact aching full stop, a bit like flu."

Kirsten remembered her one experience of that illness, she certainly wouldn't have been having a conversation, and definitely not drinking coffee.

"I wish you hadn't come, Mum."

"Nonsense. You need help with the kids while you're ill. Anyway, I needed to see for myself how you are."

Rosie started to cough. She continued to do so for what seemed to Kirsten like several minutes, her eyes ran, and her face turned red. On impulse, Kirsten pulled back from her daughter. She hated herself for it.

"That cough sounds quite bad."

"I'll live."

"I certainly hope so. Shall I make you something to eat, while I'm here?"

"No need. I have stuff prepared. Not very hungry anyway."

These words were unwelcome to Kirsten.

"Maybe I should come here. I don't like the thought of you being ill on your own."

"I'm not that bad, Mum. Too ill for work, yes, but not so ill I can't cope by myself. Besides, I've had the positive test and that means I have to stay home, and you should stay away."

"I'll keep the kids for tonight, we'll review it tomorrow."

"Thanks, Mum. I'm sure I'll be fine after a whole day of rest. Got to start getting organised for the move, so I had better be."

"Any more news?"

"No, still waiting for them to move out. Could still fall through."

"Let's hope not, fingers crossed. At least all of the main sorting out has been done. Shouldn't take long. I'll help, of course." *I'll miss you all,* formed in her mind, but she kept it there.

Kirsten had never liked the school pick-ups, not when Rosie was a child, and certainly not now. She followed the chalked-out footprints, spaced at two metres distance, and waited until the person in front had vacated theirs before moving forward to the next one.

The nursery-school teacher on duty saw her as she took her place. "Ryan," she called out to whomever was responsible for sending the children through the door. He ran out, grabbing his grandmother's legs when he reached her. She picked him up, squeezed him and planted a kiss on his forehead.

"Let's go and fetch your sister."

At the main school gates, they followed the same routine. Sally's subdued mood, however, was unusual and some cause for concern. Kirsten picked her granddaughter up, but Sally pulled back, so hard and so far, Kirsten thought she would drop her.

"Careful, Sally, one of us will get hurt." Sally screeched and squirmed, Kirsten put her down. "Mummy's not well. We'll get the bus to Daniel's house, that'll be fun, won't it?"

"What's the matter with her?" Sally asked, sounding very adult in her concern.

"Just a bit of a cough and cold, she'll be fine tomorrow, I'm sure. We'll leave her to have a good sleep, today."

"Has she got Covid?"

Kirsten hated to lie, but the very fact the question had been asked made Sally's fear apparent.

"You don't need to worry, Mummy will be fine, and we're going to have fun tonight." This last was almost sung to them and Kirsten made a grab for Sally.

Sally shrugged her off, kicked at some stones and pouted.

"Everything okay, Sally?"

She screeched and jumped up and down by way of a reply.

I wonder if something has upset her. I'll try talking to her later.

On the bus Kirsten was the only adult passenger without a face mask. Several people offered her accusatory glances, but no one challenged it. She wondered if it would be the same without the children. Then Sally said, "Where's your mask, Nanny?"

"I don't have one. Oh, look." She wanted to change the subject, so was happy for the distraction.

Both children laughed as they spied the two dogs, a Great Dane and a Chihuahua walking side by side, accompanied by two people of similarly differing proportions.

"Silly," Ryan said.

Kirsten was relieved to get off the bus. Daniel was there when they arrived at the house. He had all the stuff ready for making bread.

"Helloo," he said to the children, then to Kirsten, "Hi," which he qualified with a kiss on the cheek. He returned his attention to the visitors. "In this house you have to make your own supper."

"They might like a drink and a biscuit first." Kirsten protested.

"There's an ogre lives in the cellar, we have to make his too." Daniel said.

"Show me, show me," Ryan said.

"There's no such thing," Sally said, at the same time.

"Oh, no? Wait and see what happens to me when I'm hungry, then. Argh!" Daniel raised his hands in the air, imitating claws.

Kirsten was wrong about the drinks, both children were stripping off their jackets, rolling-up their sleeves and climbing onto the chairs provided for additional height.

"What's the first thing we do?" Daniel asked.

Ryan scrutinised the waiting ingredients. Sally said, "We don't know, you've got to teach us."

"Wash our hands."

Now there was a fight to get to the sink that had to be broken up for fear of a child falling from the chair.

"We'll have a competition, see whose bread rises the most, shall we?" Daniel suggested. "I bet it'll be mine."

Each of them carefully obeyed the instructions and little input was required from either adult.

"Now you need to knead it. It's probably the most important part." Kirsten showed them how.

"Need to knead," Ryan laughed.

"Why did the baker have brown hands?" Daniel asked. "Don't know? None of you? Because he kneaded a poo."

"Ugh!" Sally said.

Ryan responded with an exaggerated laugh, which made it clear he didn't understand.

"Disgusting!" Kirsten had never liked toilet humour and was pleased when Rosie passed the stage where she did. "You're doing well there, that's right, fold and squash."

While they waited for the first proving she and the children went collecting eggs.

"Look at that," she said to Daniel upon their return to the house. "Five. We can have eggs and rolls for tea."

"I only like dippy eggs," Sally said.

"Then you can have your roll cut into soldiers."

"I want that too," Ryan said.

"That's fine," Daniel said, patting Ryan on the head. "Come on then, back to cooking."

"I don't want to."

"You can't have any tea if you don't," Sally warned. "And the ogre might eat you."

"I think you've done enough to earn some food," Daniel said, "but I am very hangry."

"That's not a real word."

"Yes, it is, it means I'm so hungry, I'm angry, so Sally's right, I might want to eat you," he made his hands into claws again.

Ryan screeched, laughed, and ran away, then said, "I want to watch Cbeebies."

Daniel was on his way towards the television to turn it on.

"Good. My rolls will be the biggest, then." Sally's words had the desired effect. Ryan climbed up on the chair next to her and pulled her bowl away from her.

Kirsten brushed her hands down ready to deal with it, but Daniel was ahead of her. "Here's yours, mate. Hands washed first, remember? Right, now we've got to knead it again. Just like last time. Imagine being an angry ogre and it's the bread's fault. Urgh!"

Kirsten watched Sally, her face screwed into a ball, a tight frown upon it.

"Something's made you really cross by the look of it, Sally."

"Yep."

"What would that be, then?"

Kirsten expected the name of a fellow pupil and some particular sin. "Stupid Covid," was the answer she received.

Kirsten exchanged a taken-aback glance with Daniel, before saying to Sally, "Why is that?"

Sally shrugged. Kirsten waited, dreading having to lie about what was ailing Rosie, but Sally said no more, she just continued with the kneading.

"I think that's enough now," Kirsten finally said.

"Next we roll them into balls like this." Daniel demonstrated and the children followed suit.

Kirsten put two potatoes in the Aga to bake, and chicken nuggets and chips in the electric oven. Then she bathed the children one at a time.

Their bread rolls were cooked by the end of the second bath, so were the chips. When the rolls had cooled enough the children had one between them.

"D'you want an egg with it? No? Fresh from our chickens. Specially laid for you. No?"

After the meal the children curled up on the sofa watching television. Kirsten checked the potatoes; they were at the stage where she needed to put the cauliflower cheese in to heat up.

"Almost bedtime, you two."

"I haven't got monkey."

"Of course you have, he's in your bed."

"There's a surprise in the other one," Daniel said.

That did the trick, both children ran to see. It was a teddy bear that looked a lot like Winnie the Pooh, Daniel's childhood comforter.

"He's cute," Sally cradled him.

"I want him."

"Oh, Ryan, you've got monkey." Kirsten said.

Monkey was soon on the floor and Ryan was trying to snatch the bear from his sister.

"No, Ryan. Poor monkey, he'll be jealous."

Ryan stamped his feet and pulled at the bear.

"Careful, he's old," Kirsten said.

"Is he as old as you?" Sally asked.

"Yes, almost the same age as me."

"We've got to be careful of old things, haven't we, Nan?"

"Kirsten laughed, "Yes, you might break me if you pull me like that."

"That's why we can't cuddle you anymore, isn't it?"

"What?"

"'Cos we might make you die from Covid. We gotta stay away."

Now the significance of 'stupid Covid' was clear. Kirsten felt sad and angry by turns.

"Oh, Sally, nothing would ever stop me cuddling you. Come here." This time her granddaughter more than accepted the hug, she threw her own arms around Kirsten and accompanied the hug with a snuggly noise. Ryan joined in. Kirsten cried.

"Why're you crying, Nan?" Ryan asked.

"They are happy tears, because I love you both so much." They all savoured the moment. Finally, Kirsten said, "Better phone Mummy now and then we'll have a story, then you two have to go to sleep, because I want my dinner. And I'm getting hungry enough to eat you both."

The children squealed with delight.

Margaret was preparing for bed. Her head was pounding with all that was going through it. She wondered if there would come a stage when she stopped feeling angry with the broadcasts.

The Russian baddies have poisoned one of their own, have they? Well, maybe so, or maybe not, in any case such hypocrisy, forgotten David Kelly, have they?

She turned the lights off and made her way upstairs.

Another cold war in the making?

She pulled back the duvet.

You'd think with all the information out there now, available at a click, that we'd be better informed. Can't believe we're still falling for the same lies. Easier to control I suppose. De-platform. There one minute, gone the next. Not as obvious as burning books.

She cleaned her teeth, first with the manual and then the electric brush, shaking her head and hating the two gaps from those that were missing.

It's like a conjuring trick. All the bullshit, right before our eyes, hidden in plain sight, as they say. All so much easier thanks to technology. More information, less knowledge. Her thoughts reminded her of a quote she'd read by Arthur C. Clarke. Margaret searched her memory to find it, which was getting increasingly full and harder to access, like an old computer, but then she remembered: *"Any sufficiently advanced technology is indistinguishable from magic."*

Her thoughts kept her awake. *Should probably make the most of every bit of consciousness left to me, but I'll feel like crap in the morning if I stay awake much longer.*

She turned on the light and picked up her book. It did the trick; in minutes she was asleep.

❧

While the children were eating breakfast, Kirsten phoned Rosie. Sleep had been interrupted by imaginings of ambulances and ventilators and a future without her daughter.

Rosie sounded groggy but said, "I've felt much worse with the flu. The worst bit is feeling so tired."

Kirsten didn't feel that reassured, "I'll keep the children a couple more days."

"That would be great, Mum, thanks. I'm sure I'll be fine in a couple of days."

And it was almost exactly that long before she was.

OCTOBER

The rain was relentless. It made the room seem smaller and colder, but Nabil had no desire to leave it. He turned his attention back to his phone. There, images of streets engulfed with water left Nabil with the impression that the chances of death by drowning were equal to those from the virus. In his case, even greater were the chances of dying from boredom and loneliness.

The smell of mould met his nose, the sound of rain met his ears and the sight of both, on the wall, met his eyes. In his memory he heard the sound of his family's laughter. Heard it replaced by the ringing silence after the bombing. He curled into a foetal posture and sought out the comfort of the rubble, that he might fill his nose and mouth with the dust and die. Die one big, hot death, instead of a thousand small, cold ones.

৯১

Kirsten met Emerson as she was arriving for her break, and he was returning from his.

"Glad I saw you; I keep meaning to ask if you're going to the next demo." She asked him.

"Not sure. Why?"

"I think if I went on one, I might feel better. At least feel like I'm doing something. Would be good to have some company."

"Okay, could go, I guess. Hi, Mand. See you later, Kirst."

"You okay?" Kirsten asked of her manager.

"What? Sorry, what?"

"You look like you found a pound and lost a fiver."

"Staff shortages. Trying to keep the place going without wearing out the staff who are here; you being one of them. And Emerson, of course."

"More people called in?"

"Yes. Supposedly sick."

"Supposedly?"

"There are a couple of people who, at any other time, I would be getting in and discussing their 'sickness' with, but at the moment – well, Covid has changed all that. I can hardly ask for proof of a positive test – it'd be rather Draconian."

"They're not accurate anyway, I gather."

"I heard that too, but some say prone to false positives and others say to false negatives – so, who knows?" Mandeep sighed.

"Certainly not me. I'm not sure about any of it."

"You spend too much time with Emerson."

"There's one big difference between he and I, he *is* certain."

"Yes. And he can be very convincing."

"Well, there are a lot of very clever and well-informed people saying the same ashe does. People, at the top of their fields, with nothing to gain and everything to lose."

Mandeep sighed again as she filled the kettle; she looked thoughtful. "Yes. Maybe I'll take a look at this Reset stuff, where do I find it?"

"That's not hard, just go onto the website of the World Economic Forum. I'll text you some links for critiques."

❧

Emerson was just getting his bike out when his text alert sounded. He was feeling grateful for the end of the stormy weather and looking forward to the ride. So nearly ready to leave was he, he was tempted to wait until he arrived at his grandparents', but then decided against it.

Better not come, love, it read. *Granddad's poorly.*

"Great! What'm I supposed to do now?" He let the bicycle slide to the floor, before clicking onto the phone icon to connect with his grandmother.

"Hello. Yeah, only just, was about to leave. I could come anyways."

"No, love, he's not up to it. Besides, don't want you catching anything, especially if it turns out to be…" her voice trailed off into poorly subdued sobs.

"Ain't no such thing, Nan."

"I know your opinion, dear, but we've sent off for a test, in case."

Emerson sighed, heavily. He wished people would just see sense.

"When'm I gonna see you now, then?"

"I'll let you know."

There was a silence, into which Emerson brooded.

"You know we want to see you, don't you, Emerson? And no one could love you more than we do."

"Yeah."

He stomped into the house. His mother was sitting at the kitchen work surface, wearing her dressing gown and a worried expression.

"You've heard from Nan, then." She took a cigarette from the packet, tapped it on the unfiltered end, put it to her mouth, picked up the box of matches, shook them, put them down; removed the cigarette. "It'll probably turn out to be nothing to worry about."

"Course."

His mother stood up and put water in the kettle and turned it on.

"Want one?"

"Nah. Thanks."

The cigarette ritual was performed again, but this time she lit it. "Anyway, nothing we can do. Just wait."

"You sound like he's waiting for a cancer diagnosis, for fuck's sake."

"Covid would hardly be much better, with his heart issues and his high blood pressure."

"Can't have Covid when it don't exist. Anyway, if there is such a thing can't be that bad. Trump's okay and so was Bo Jo."

"They both ended up in hospital."

"Yeah, and one of 'em at least got treated with drugs, when supposedly there ain't any that'll cure it. What is the matter with Granddad, anyway?" Emerson's tone had softened.

"Nan didn't really say. She just said not well, and they'd ordered a test."

"I wish people'd stop with these fucking tests."

Emerson tossed his phone onto the table.

"Emerson."

"What?"

Into their silence came the voice of the radio presenter.

"Why'd you keep listening to this shite?" asked Emerson.

"I like to hear people's opinions on what's going on."

"No wonder you ain't got a fucking clue what really is, then."

His mother tutted.

Emerson turned the radio off.

Now the silence was complete.

I'm forgetting his Asperger's. "You're worried, aren't you?"

"No, I'm fucking annoyed."

"Will you stop with the swearing? Please. Why are you annoyed? Who with?"

"You, Nan, Granddad, brainwashed media fu… presenters, everyone who keeps this Covid lark alive."

He stormed out of the house.

"Where are you going?" his mother called after him.

"Anywhere, but here."

❧

"It's lovely, actually. Bigger than the last place, nineteen-fortyish?" Kirsten looked at Daniel, who concurred with that. "So, well built, good solid walls, a biggish garden, and, near the sea."

"Sounds ideal," Margaret said, putting the ratatouille in front of them and indicating they help themselves. "Nice to be able to hide away. The garden'll be a godsend with the children."

"Yeah, neither of them are gardeners, but both are talking about taking it up."

"Good idea. We need to grow our own."

Daniel nodded in agreement, "Yeah, what with Brexit and rewilding."

"Rewilding. Sounds great doesn't it? At first I thought that was a good idea, but I hadn't stopped to consider the possibility that it might contribute to a significant lack of food in the not-too-distant future." Margret said.

Food security was one of the things Kirsten had latterly become worried about. She put her cutlery down and took a deep breath because she felt overwhelmed, "There's so much to be concerned about these days. I wonder if people will ever start challenging what's going on."

"Oh, they will, don't you worry," Margaret said. "Just hope it will be before it's too late to make a positive change."

Kirsten wanted to cry. The thought of rioters and revolutions was terrifying too, although almost impossible to imagine.

"Unless, of course, they take us to war. An external enemy always keeps them safe," Margaret said.

It was Daniel's turn to take a pause from eating. "There's plenty of historical precedence for that, I'm afraid to say."

"Thank you so much for inviting us tonight, Margaret." Kirsten was keen to put a close on this particular line of conversation, as images of Andy in combat gear jumped into her mind.

"Thank you for your very pleasant company. Not to mention the wine, of course. You wouldn't have wanted to go home and cook after helping with the move and driving all that way." After a pause, Margaret continued with, "I keep meaning to ask, how's that young man doing? Nabil?"

"Centre still not back to normal, so I don't see him except occasionally in the supermarket."

"Hard to imagine how he and those like him feel. Circumstances so dire you have to leave everything and everyone that's familiar. I'm wary of making assumptions and stereotyping, though. It would be interesting to hear his story from his own lips."

"He's from Syria, right?" Daniel asked.

"Yes."

"So much propaganda around that war."

Margaret nodded her head, "Exactly, but that's a conversation for another time."

Kirsten opened the curtains on to a bright morning, there wouldn't be too many more with only a week until the clocks went back. And not so many more until the countdown to Christmas began. As she headed for the bathroom and the morning ablutions, Kirsten thought back on the last one, spent with Rosie and family and, without Daniel, she had only partly enjoyed it. This one promised to be different if Daniel kept his word and went with her to the new house.

She took her time in the shower and getting dressed in the bedroom afterwards, trying to get used to the feeling of being home and alone once more. Right up until the last moment she had hoped, if not expected, to hear Daniel say, "Why don't you stay?" Disappointment manifest as anger, as he helped her get her bags into the van. She silently hung onto it until her home was reached and, as she clambered down from the passenger seat, said, "I can manage my own bags, thank you." Then, "So, see you around."

Daniel lent over to kiss her, she turned her cheek to him.

"Saturday then," he said.

And suddenly Kirsten felt very foolish. "What're we going to have?"

"Lord knows, it's days away."

He would be going back to adhoc meals now, not each one planned and ingredients bought well in advance. Her anger melted and she lent in and kissed him on the mouth. He smiled in response, hopped down from the van and carried her bags up the steps to her front door.

"It'll be weird without you."

Now, preparing breakfast she thought, *I wonder what he'd have said if I'd asked to stay?*

"There were arrests on that march," Emerson said to Kirsten.

"I heard. One of them was an eminent German doctor, I gather. It's all over Twitter. I still wish we'd gone. I'll go next time."

"I'll go too. I'll request the time off as soon as the date's confirmed."

"That would be great. I'd prefer not to have to go alone. How's your granddad?"

"In hospital."

"Oh no, I'm sorry to hear that."

"Yeah, it's a bummer, 'specially 'cos they won't let us visit. Fucking Fascists."

"I'm so sorry, Emerson. Is it…?"

"No such fucking thing."

"I know, but…"

"Yeah, that's what they're claiming. Wouldn't make any difference whatever it was, we couldn't go to see him."

"I know. That's bad. Margaret had it and she is fine now."

Emerson grunted by reply.

Kirsten's opinion on this was that there certainly was Covid, but that the dangers of it had been exaggerated. Margaret's case had convinced her of that even more, but Emerson was adamant and, under the circumstances she didn't feel inclined to challenge him.

"The more I think about it the more I'm convinced it's 5G," Emerson continued. "Course it could be a real thing, they might've released it on purpose. In which case, thank God it was only Covid. Anyway, whatever it was, the agenda's definitely the Great Reset."

"I've no argument with that."

"Whatever way you look at it we're screwed. If everyone doesn't wake up and act up, we've had it."

Kirsten hoped he was wrong, but feared he was right. "People are getting fed up with the lockdowns now. Look at the Liverpool case."

"Not enough of us. People still believe the bullshit they're fed. Look how they treated Jeremy. All that crap about Anti-Semitism, the establishment is full of them for sure, but he's not one of them. And who's protesting about his suspension from the party?"

"Some are."

"Most aren't, just like this whole fucking business. We're screwed."

Emerson did seem particularly angry, Kirsten thought. "Hope your granddad goes on okay."

"Yeah. Cheers. Me too."

NOVEMBER

Mandeep's energy drained away with the announcement of the second national lockdown. It sent her to her bed, where she pulled the duvet over her head and tried to force sleep to come.

There was ticking in her head and ringing in her ears, they combined to make her angry. She heaved herself from her right side to her left. In her mind's eye she saw her parents' graves with this year's dates on the head stones. And then she saw Indrani wired up to bleeping machines, and she and Dev arguing over what treatment should be administered. *Oh, stop it,* she told herself, pushing the duvet away and sliding to the edge of the bed. She draped her legs over the side and went to stand up, but exhaustion pushed her back down.

She turned onto her back and tried to bring to mind memories of happier days – smaller children and involved grandparents – but recollections only emphasised the changes and underlined the feeling that they were permanent. Spiral thoughts spun in her head, she felt trapped in them, like a hamster on a wheel. Finally, she cried. She tried to subdue the tears by pulling a pillow over her face, but some sobs erupted loudly, and they summoned Dev.

He lay down beside her and pulled her in close, cradling her head. His arms felt paternal and safe, but failed to change her emotions or eradicate the thoughts that generated them. It was like waking to parental reassurance but finding yourself remaining in the midst of the nightmare.

As usual, the television was on in the background, the volume too low to be audible, but the expression on Trump's face spoke a thousand words.

"How typical of him not admitting defeat," Emerson's mother observed to him, it being the first thing she had said all morning.

"Don't know why everyone's getting so excited, it won't make any difference."

The reply that came was preceded by a deep sigh. "There's no pleasing you, is there?"

"I'll be pleased when there's reason to be."

They returned to silence. Both of them knew the subject that was out of bounds was the only one either of them was really interested in, but neither knew how to approach it.

Emerson took the coffee he'd come down for, back to his room and continued browsing the internet. His mother returned to sitting staring out of the window, silencing every thought of her father's death that crept into her head. But it was a battle often lost. The memory of the phone call ran around her head like an irritating tune on a loop. "The hospital have rung." A catch in her mother's voice conveyed what was coming before the words did, and in fact, they were never more than implied. "They said it was peaceful and a nurse was holding his hand."

She hadn't asked any questions, not because there were none, rather because there were so many. And the answer to the one she really wanted to ask was already known. They wouldn't be able to see him.

Emerson's reaction had been predictable, her mother's less so, and it hurt more.

"Really I just want to be alone." She'd said.

The problem with them being alone, was that it forced solitude upon her. Barry wasn't much use, he just seemed to want her to get over it and back to normal. And isolation had a tendency to fill itself with bittersweet memories. It was too hard to believe that one of the people responsible for her being in the world was gone forever. What she needed was to be able to believe that wasn't true, that somewhere, in whatever form, there was a version of her father that continued, and most important of all, one day they would be together again.

Emerson's feelings on the subject were clear but her mother's, not so. For the first time in her life, it occurred to her that she had no idea of what either of her parents felt about such things.

Her thoughts were interrupted by Emerson coming back to the kitchen.

"Hello, love," she said very gently.

"I'm going for a bike ride."

"In this weather?"

"Yes, in this weather."

"Please be careful," the thought of losing him was even more terrible than the current loss.

"Um." *I'm not a fucking kid.* "See you later."

"You'll be here for dinner, right?"

Emerson tutted. "Of course."

As he was leaving, he said, "It's so not right – we couldn't go to see him – can't see him now – that's so fucking wrong. They could have done anything to him. These rules are a licence to commit murder."

"Emerson, please. I know you're suffering, but so am I, and frankly comments like that don't help."

"Well, you've never liked the truth."

"What d'you mean by that, exactly? No, actually, don't tell me, not unless it's going to help, which it isn't, is it?"

Emerson shrugged in a self-satisfied manner and screwed his mouth into a sidewise grin, then slammed the door closed behind him.

The day was crisp and bright. Nabil's mood a little less dark as a result. It motivated him enough to go for a walk, but not enough to take him any further than the park, where he hoped he might bump into Abdul as he had before, or Kirsten just so that he could exchange a few words with someone.

It took less than an hour, even at a slow pace, to walk the entire perimeter twice. By the time he'd done so, his mood was dipping down. He looked at his phone, as if willing it to ring, then checked the credit, as if the very act of doing so would put some on it. Then he went home.

Home. Time was when he'd seen this current one as temporary; as a necessary step towards the more comfortable one of the future. Now it seemed that he would be forever in this place. Hope. That was something he'd once possessed. Now he no longer knew what to hope for.

The threats in this country were different to those from his own, and objectively looked to be the lesser, but being forced into communion with himself was actually no less terrifying. The demons there, no more easily escaped; or appeased.

He picked up his notebook and pen. Read over his last entry. Put them both down. Picked up his phone and stared at the news headlines. He understood that there was a new president in the USA. He wondered why the people of the United Kingdom should care. He knew he didn't. What had it to do with – or for – him?

The news of Emerson's loss filled Mandeep with terror. It caused a tremble that wouldn't stay invisible no matter how hard she tried to keep it inside.

"You okay?" Emerson asked.

"I'm just so sorry to hear that. Why are you here?"

"What's the point in my not being?"

"What about your mum?" Then, realising it could sound accusatory, "How is she?"

"She's alright."

Really? This time Mandeep managed to keep the question from her lips and instead said, "Sometimes it takes a while to sink in."

"What's to sink in? He's dead. End of."

Mandeep had to remind herself that Emerson was in shock.

"Well, if you feel you need time off in the future…"

"For the funeral, I will. Never been to one before," he continued after a pause.

"I guess it's been challenging for you in more ways than one."

"Meaning?"

"Well, you know, having to rethink all the Covid stuff."

"I'm not rethinking anything."

"No?"

"He was old, had a bad heart, flu kills frail people."

Mandeep bit her lip, thinking he was behaving like a naughty, and frankly rather stupid, little boy.

There were lots of things she wanted to ask, but propriety prevented it. It wasn't morbid curiosity; it was to uphold the superstition that if she had the right information she was prepared and was less likely to need it. Forearmed, forewarned, never to need – was the philosophy.

"What would you like to do about letting people know? I mean, would you like me to tell people, or would you prefer to do it yourself?"

Emerson shrugged, "Haven't thought about it."

"Well, get back to me when you have."

"No need to be like that."

Mandeep was so close to reprimanding him that she felt like her mind and body had separated. She took a deep breath, "I want to honour your wishes on this Emerson, that's what I meant."

"Oh! Well, sorry, then."

Mandeep nodded.

"Can I go now?"

"Of course." As soon as she was alone Mandeep was overcome with grief. It was as if Emerson had transferred all his onto her. *I didn't even know the man,* she reasoned *Poor Emerson,* but even as she attributed the feelings of sympathy for him, she recognised that fear for her own family was the real driver of her emotions.

Just before the end of her shift Kirsten approached Emerson, who was stacking shelves. "Got five minutes? Come to the break room."

"Coffee?" she asked, once there, closing the door behind them.

"You said five minutes."

"Okay, I just wanted to say how sorry I am about your granddad and if you need to talk."

"Thanks. Can I go now?"

Kirsten's exhale of breath sounded almost like a laugh.

"I wasn't joking."

"Neither was I. I know about loss, if you…"

Emerson took a couple of paces towards Kirsten, into her personal space, "D'you know what? I wish people'd just leave me the fuck alone."

He turned to go, then noticed there were two empty cups left on the table.

"And another thing I wish, is that people'd clear up after themselves." He picked the cups up and threw them into the sink – breaking them both. Then slammed the door as he left the room.

The television was on with no audience when Mandeep returned from her morning run. It was the first for more than a week, because she'd given in to the exhaustion she'd been battling for so long. Feeling annoyed she tutted and picked up the remote control, but in the second before turning off, Mandeep was greeted with the headline: 'First 'Milestone' vaccine offers ninety percent protection against Covid-19', which suspended her action and her irritation.

With this news came the first free breath she'd breathed in months, close behind were tears, as if they were released with her exhalation.

Indrani came into the room. "I was just coming to turn… what's up, Mum?" She asked in a tone that was somewhere between concern and fear.

"Nothing," Mandeep wiped her eyes with the back of her left hand, beckoned Indrani closer with her right, then wrapped her arm around her daughter's shoulders. "Quite the opposite, look, see what they're saying?" Mandeep squeezed Indrani, "I think we're going to be okay."

❧

The news reached Kirsten's ears with the radio alarm. She heard it like being greeted with the offer of bail instead of a prison sentence. Even this level of relief was a feeling she hardly dared admit to.

Usually, the silencing of the alarm and the turning on of the bedside lamp were more or less synchronised, but today she left the radio playing as she climbed from the bed and sat for a few minutes, listening to the bulletin. The last time she did this was the day the Brexit vote results were announced.

She sighed. *It will be interesting to see how this pans out. It's happened rather too fast in my opinion, but I guess I'm going to be in a minority on that one. Let's hope it at least gives people back some freedom.*

Later, at work, she disclosed these thoughts to Emerson, in response to him saying, "My stupid mother's all tearful about this so-called vaccination 'cos 'it's too late for poor Granddad'," he quoted her in a sarcastic tone.

Kirsten felt so sorry for Emerson's mother, but at the same time understood Emerson's sentiments and that he wasn't being cruel, just being himself.

"I imagine lots of people will feel really relieved."

"Not for long, they won't."

"What d'you mean?"

"Not when it starts killing all of their friends."

"I don't trust it and I won't be rushing to get it, that's for sure, but somehow I doubt people will be dropping dead at our feet."

"We'll see. Let's hope you get the choice about having it."

"Uh!" The idea that they would be made compulsory hadn't occurred to Kirsten. "They'll probably make plenty of money without mandates, 'cos most people will be very eager to get one."

"Ain't just money, though. There's the whole control thing. Vaccine passports. And worse."

"What could be worse? Are you someone who believes they have chips in?"

"Not necessarily, but then, why not? They can monitor and control us completely that way. We do it to dogs."

"God!" The thought was terrifying. "They already do it through our phones."

"You can leave a phone at home. It's not just monitoring, they could inflict pain, make you piss yourself, stop you from moving."

"It sounds rather far-fetched." Even so there was a spiking in her spine and a churning in her belly.

"Possible though. Linked to 5G. They want to turn us all into the Borg."

"Stop, please. The Reset is scary enough with the prospect of a social credit system. But transhumanism is something else."

"Just a matter of degrees. In one scenario, if you resist, you're in pain, in the other you're in prison. There's some as say that nice new prison in Northampton is for vaccine refusers."

"I don't know what you're talking about."

"Oh yeah! They built it, then left it empty. Suspicious, don't you think?"

Now Kirsten felt sick and had a ticking in her head. She was aware of her creased brow. "I concede it's all possible, Emerson, pray to God you're wrong."

"No good praying to Him, the Devil is in charge on this planet."

Now, that was a statement it was difficult to disagree with.

When Kirsten returned to the shop floor, the sense of foreboding went with her. Social distancing signs and people queuing right down the one aisle designated for it, reinforced the feeling. She jumped, as if being threatened with violence, when a customer came to the till from the wrong end. "'scuse me, love, I need another bag, mine's broke."

The customer who was unloading, tutted and rolled her eyes, but said, "Go ahead," in answer to Kirsten questioning if it would be okay to deal with the request.

When the shift finished, Kirsten hurried home. She switched on every light in the house and put the radio on full volume.

Later, when she told Daniel about the conversation he said, "Rumours always abound in difficult times."

Immediately she was grounded.

"It does sound pretty unlikely, doesn't it?"

"Sounds like Emerson watches too much science fiction."

Nabil watched his breath cloud the air. He picked up his phone and scrolled through, looking for text messages he knew weren't there. He noticed there were crumbs on the bed, he brushed them onto the floor. Feeling thirsty, he reached for the glass of water that was on the chest of drawers, he emptied it in one. As he went to return the empty glass it fell from his hand. He watched without interest as it hit the floor, cracking, but not breaking.

In the corner of the room stood Abida, her arms crossed, her mouth set in disapproval. He slid under the duvet to hide from her criticism. With his head immersed in the covers, his mother's voice was muffled, but the scornful tone was clear. Behind his eyes he saw his father wearing a sorrowful look. Everyone, it seemed, had an opinion on how he should behave. Everyone chastised him. The only voice that remained silent was his own.

The alarm rang at six-thirty. Mandeep groaned, waking from a light sleep from which she had drifted in and out all night. As a child, excitement had prevented proper sleep the night before Diwali; as an adult, it was anticipation for all there was to do. Dev stretched out and touched her and, rubbing her upper arm, he said, "Happy Diwali. I'll be with you soon."

Mandeep dragged herself from bed and into the bathroom, where she took the briefest of showers since a bath in oils would follow later in the day.

While she drank tea she started on the food preparations, although much had been done the day before with Dev and the girls to help her.

"Is there any need to make all that food and decorate the house this year?"Dev had asked, in view of the fact that the girls were nearly grown-up, and Mandeep's parents were staying home.

But she felt there was, and reminded herself of that before she could suffer resentment that she was the only person up and busy.

She started with the decorations in the living room, wanting it to look and smell nice as the rest of the household got up. She put candles on every available space, the windowsill, the fireplace, the bookcase. In the fireplace she put the photos of Ganesh and the Goddess Lakshmi and sprinkled rose petals all around.

By the time everyone else was up, all the snacks were prepared and on the table.

"Morning, Happy Diwali," she said as Manjit arrived in the kitchen.

"Happy Diwali." Manjit lifted the cloth that covered the food. "Looks nice, I'll have some in a bit, she said, taking a bowl from the cupboard and pouring cereal into it.

Dev did the same with muesli. "You had some?" he said to his wife.

"I never feel hungry when I'm doing all this cooking."

He too looked under the cloth and nodded his head in approval. "What's the plan, Batman?"

"I'll drop some of this stuff off at my parents' house around eleven, come back and we'll eat together."

"Fine." Dev kissed her on the forehead. "I'll do the fireworks after dinner, and pujas this evening, then. See, hardly any different to usual."

"I guess not. But it won't feel the same without Mum and Dad."

"At least we won't have to listen to Granddad snoring," Manjit said.

Although it was light-hearted and true, Mandeep felt more than a little offended on her parents' behalf. Maybe it was simply because she hadn't seen them properly for so long.

"You look nice, dear," Emerson's grandmother told him.

"Scrubs up well, doesn't he?" his mother agreed.

Emerson grunted.

His grandmother continued. "It's not what he would've wanted. He would have wanted his friends there. And a big wake afterwards."

That's what should've been done, then, Emerson thought.

The funeral car arrived. Both occupants were wearing masks. "Emerson's exempt," his mother explained, putting on her own and throwing him a warning look to ensure his silence.

The concrete crematorium was surrounded by woodland. To Emerson it seemed like it belonged in a scene from a horror movie, and the masked mourners, four in all, would hardly have been out of place.

The two other mourners were his mother's siblings, neither of whom Emerson had seen in years. They stood the obligatory six feet apart, observing the social distancing rules.

The service was shorter than he had expected, and streamed for those who weren't permitted to be there. To Emerson his own presence felt like a virtual experience.

As the curtain closed on the coffin, all three siblings and the widow cried. Emerson watched without emotional involvement.

Outside there was a brief conversation between the mourners.

"It was nice, very personal, well done," Emerson's aunt said to her sister and mother. "You both look like you could do with a hug, but better not, eh!"

Emerson shook his head. His mother shook hers at him, half warning, half chastising.

"I thought it better the kids didn't come. I mean even without the Covid stuff, they're still a bit young for this kind of thing. Sorry, Mum, I know you would have liked to see them. Let's hope this terrible pandemic is over soon and we can all get back to normal."

It'll never be that; it's the 'new normal' from now on. Emerson thought.

"Good to see so many there," Emerson's uncle chipped in.

They weren't fucking there.

"Yes, he had lots of friends. Frank was the closest, nearly asked him, but thought it would be fairer on the others to keep it family only."

"He was very popular, and a great dad," Emerson's uncle said, reaching out and patting his mother on the shoulder. "It'll leave a big hole in your life."

When she started to cry, her children shuffled awkwardly towards her, but none of them hugged her.

"I'm going for a fag," Emerson said.

❧

The following day Kirsten asked, "How was the funeral?"

"Strange. Everyone masked up and formal."

"How're you feeling now, Emerson?"

"Annoyed."

"Annoyed?" Yes, Kirsten was aware that anger was a common emotion in the grieving process.

"Yeah. The bastards aren't returning the whip to Jeremy."

❧

It was a while since Margaret had thought about Alice, but the news on the radio had rekindled her interest. It was that the high court had given a woman permission to sue those who were returning elderly infected patients to nursing homes. The reading group numbers had dwindled so much that the meetings only took place every six weeks now, and Margaret was ashamed to admit, along with them her questions on Alice's state of health.

I suppose we'd have been told if she was dead. I'd sooner be dead than live in a place like that. Poor Alice. It's hard in this world when you get old, no more use to anyone and nothing to look forward to. That was why living every day to the fullest extent possible had become so important to her.

The thought threatened to send Margaret's mood spiralling down, especially as she began to recall her own experience of hospital. She would remember to ask after Alice next time.

"Another vaccination," Mandeep said, to the television, as if in conversation with the newscaster. "We're spoilt for choice now."

"This one sounds a little less volatile," Dev said, coming up behind her. "Still wouldn't trust it myself."

Mandeep felt annoyance rising in her like a hot tide; why was he so negative about it? "Well, most people are celebrating the fact, Dev."

"Hey, no need to snap. If it makes you feel better getting vaccinated, go ahead."

"The main thing is, it'll allow us to get back to normal."

"We'll see."

Mandeep sighed. "It's obvious, if everyone is protected the rate will drop."

"Like I said, we'll see."

"You been listening to people at the gym again?"

Dev straightened his posture against the attack and launched his counter move. "You been listening to the mainstream news, again?" Then, after a pause, during which they stared hard at each other, "I do have a mind of my own, you know."

The television had moved on to the local events and a human-interest story that competed with the real life one taking place between Mandeep and Dev. It sparked a different kind of emotion in Mandeep.

"Sorry, she said. "I'm just so desperate for this dreadful pandemic to end."

"I know. Come here," Dev held his arms open, and she fell into them.

❧

It was only a few days later that it was announced three households could mix for Christmas. Mandeep felt annoyed that the same had not been true of Diwali.

❧

In response to the same news, Margaret said out loud, "I'd better stay home, then. That way all the kids can see each other.

❧

Kirsten felt relief upon hearing the same, because the plan for her and Daniel was to go to spend it with Rosie, Andy, and the children.

❧

"I guess it'll be you, me and Baz for Christmas dinner, then," Emerson's mother told him. "Nan will go and spend it down south. I hope that's okay for you."

"Tough if it isn't."

"Well yes, but…"

Emerson strutted out of the kitchen to his bedroom. It most certainly wasn't okay. Not on three counts, no Nan, no Pops, but the twat instead.

❧

Rain ran down the window and through the gap in the frame, forming a puddle on the sill. From his bed Nabil watched, without interest, but pulled the duvet up to his chin. He heard its rhythm, but didn't listen. Really, he should hate the rain for what it had done, but he felt nothing. And in any case, it was drowned out by the sounds from his own body, every part of which played a different and disturbing tune. The noises from his stomach suggested hunger, but there was no sensation to confirm it. The only thing of which there was a growing awareness was the demand for his bladder to be emptied. For the moment it was equal to the need to remain where he was.

Nabil had been alone for several days now. The other occupants of the house were still there, of course, but he only knew that because he heard their movements and saw the leftovers of their activities. But his dead phone ensured no calls from Abdul. And his family had finally given up on haunting him. Could be it was because of the final injury he'd inflicted on Abida?

Finally, the urging of his bladder became insistent enough to cause him to move from the bed. In the bathroom hung the reminder of the damage done. Three-day-old washing; no longer dripping, but still wet. He knew from experience that without a source of heat they would take so long to dry that the smell of damp would be embedded in them as surely as the dye that coloured them.

Back in his room, before he climbed back into bed, he took another look at the notepad, but the pages remained fixed together, the ink blurred. The words forever obscured. Her story had become like his now, condensed into a single, meaningless blob. If only he'd put it in a plastic bag, to protect it from the rain.

✤

Emerson was disappointed with the turnout, a few thousand at the most were gathered in Trafalgar Square. He wasn't interested in listening to the speeches, in fact, he wondered about the need for any. *Preaching to the converted,* he thought, but Kirsten didn't agree, and he felt obliged to stay with her, since they'd come together. He had been grateful for her company on the train journey. Although there were few other travellers, it was comforting not being the only person without a mask.

His attention was drawn away by the conversation of his neighbours, whose voices were raised in competition with those coming from the stage.

"Sheffield, that's a long way to come," the late middle-aged woman observed to her younger male companion.

"It's important."

"Sure is. You done this kind of thing before?"

"No, never. Never been political. You?"

"Yeah, anti-nuke, anti-vivisection, anti-Iraq war. Been on them all. For all the difference it made."

"Blimey, you're a veteran, then."

"It took a while with this, but finally I saw through it."

"What made the difference?"

"When I heard that they changed the way the way deaths are certified. You don't know about that? Oh. It was made more robust after Harold Shipman, with two doctors needed, but through the pandemic it could be done by one, without the deceased even being seen in person. Yeah, that's right – remotely. Then there was all that 'died within twenty-eight days of a positive test'. And you?"

"Saw something about the 'Great Reset', on the internet, well, it was referred to by a financial dude I watch, so I looked it up. At first, I thought that sounds good, all that rhetoric about a more equitable society, but then I thought about it. Who was saying it? A one percenter, billionaire. No-one will own anything? Someone will, though, for the rest of us to rent from. And I started to think about 'equitable.' I doubt it will mean equally rich, quite the opposite. So, then I figured there's not really anything new about it, the corporations will still call the tune. And, I thought, if this is such a Great Reset, why are they bringing it in through the back door? So, then I started researching. They're clever though, got to grant them that."

"Like I said, had me fooled to start with, along with most of my good 'socialist' friends. In fact, I was appalled by the 'anti-maskers', thought they were all selfish, Covid deniers, not socially responsible like me. But, as soon as I started to question, I became aware of other stuff. Like eminently qualified people suggesting alternative treatments, questioning the measures and not being allowed a voice. Well, if this is really a public health issue, shouldn't we listen to everyone's point of view? If not, we might miss something important. Then someone drew my attention to The Great Barrington Declaration…"

"Ah, yeah. Nearly nine thousand signatories, I heard."

Emerson could resist the conversation no longer. "They want to keep us all in the dark, want to get us all vaccinated with their killer drugs. They come from a long line of eugenicists."

"Who do?" The man asked.

"That's going a bit far for me." the woman said at the same time.

"The one percent who control everything. I can refer you to some info if you like."

"Not sure I'm ready for that. I just want to get our society and economy opened up. I can go with the Reset, but eugenics…?" *That's the problem,* the man thought, *lots of these anti-lockdown dudes are bonkers.*

Their conversation was drowned out by the return of the drums and whistles, as well as by cheering and clapping as the speaker left the platform. Kirsten turned her attention toward Emerson just in time to hear him say.

"It's pretty obvious. Just about everything they tell us to do is bad for our health – physical, mental and spiritual."

"Well, I don't disagree with that. But why would they want to kill us? They need us to work for them."

"Increasingly not, automation and AI is taking over. Stephen Hawking said the biggest threat to mankind is AI."

"Did he, indeed?" The woman re-joined the conversation, sounding unsettled.

"Yeah, and we're so convinced by the over-population argument that we're taking it on board big time. I'm always hearing people say there's too many of us, or we're a cancer on the planet. They won't need to kill us, we'll give ourselves up for slaughter."

"You don't think there are too many of us?"

"No, I don't, but suppose there are. What's the cure? Who's going to be killed or forcibly sterilised? There's plenty of everything to go around, it's just too few have access to it, like everything else."

"Can't disagree with that," the woman said, and the man nodded in agreement.

Kirsten joined in now. "The richer nations have fewer children, if we allowed the developing countries to do just that, they might too."

"Good point, Kirst."

The drumming and whistling subsided again, instead there was whooping as the next speaker took the stage.

The whole experience was exciting for Kirsten, it was years since she'd done anything like this, and she felt like a teenager again.

"I think things will be back to normal in the New Year." Abdul sat across the room from Nabil; it had been necessary to clear clothes in order for him to sit down. He'd started by trying to determine which were clean, and which were dirty, but after looking a couple of articles over doubtfully, had put them all in a tidy heap on the chest of drawers.

"You really should keep your phone topped up," he continued, his words muffled by the mask. "What're you spending it all on?" When Nabil still said nothing, Abdul continued with, "Looks like you could do with a shave."

Nabil rubbed his chin in response.

Abdul scanned the room. There was a plate of leftovers on the floor; a cup with a rim of brown around the inside; an almost empty bottle of milk, the cream starting to float. *I shouldn't have left it so long,* Abdul thought, remembering how isolation felt. He risked moving closer to Nabil, who was sitting on the edge of his bed with his duvet wrapped around him.

"Why don't we go for a walk?"

"It's cold."

"More so if you sit around, I think."

Nabil sighed.

"I know it's an effort, but you will feel better for it."

Nabil sighed again, but acquiesced, pushing down with his hands on the bed to aid in the effort of standing. As the duvet fell away, he shivered.

"I always feel warmer after being outside." Abdul grabbed Nabil's coat from the back of the door, but just as he was about to help him into it said, "How about a shave first?"

Nabil sighed, but did as he was told, like an obedient child. He brushed his teeth for the first time in several days.

"You look loads better," Abdul observed. And Nabil had to admit to feeling that way.

Now he needed no help with his coat, and he managed a half smile.

"That's better," Abdul said. "I'm sorry. I should've come before, when your phone was always off. I should've come."

They walked around town, then the park. For England, the day was bright and not as cold as Nabil had expected. He made a pact with himself. *I'll make sure I do this every day.*

They parted company with Abdul promising to phone and Nabil promising to answer.

"We'll do this again, yeah?" Abdul patted Nabil on the shoulder and then they shook hands.

DECEMBER

The day was cold, but bright. A shaft of light shone onto the computer screen, obscuring the words and illuminating the dust. The sun beckoned her away from the screen, the information fixed her to it. The YouTube video on the killing nurses of the Third Reich was terrifyingly compulsive; Margaret was captivated equally by the horror of it and the fascination at how ordinary people could behave in such a way. Most of them were even smiling. She wondered if they had believed it was for the best, or whether they just blindly followed instructions.

Either was dreadful, but the latter more so, she thought, acknowledging having felt the former herself when watching John take so long to die. The irony of it struck her now; he was forced to live out every last second of his life despite it being agony for them both. These children were never allowed to begin theirs. Terrifying to realise this had happened in recent history, in a European country.

Margaret had always been a proponent of euthanasia, but just at this moment the idea frightened her. She remained sure she would want to die rather than live like Alice. Poor Alice. Yet, suppose, when she herself was in the hospital, someone had decided not to offer lifesaving treatment on account of her age. *Oh, don't be so daft, I didn't need any such treatment*, she told herself, *but suppose I had.* The thought sent a shiver through her. *Maybe we should leave it to God after all. But then, left to Him entirely, people would still be dying of appendicitis.*

She turned off from YouTube. The internet headlines that greeted her gave the news that Margaret Keenan was the first person to receive the Covid vaccination.

Rather her than me, Margaret decided of her namesake. *In Coventry of all places.* She remembered that one thing for which Coventry was famed had been named after it and added to dictionaries, coventrate, to devastate by heavy bombing. *What might they call this in the future covaccinate? To vaccinate people with a Covid vaccine, whether they co-operate or not.* She laughed at her own wittiness, but worried that the concept held some weight. . *I suppose I can expect an invite for mine soon.*

The screen now offered an explanation of the tier system. Margaret wasn't sufficiently interested to click on and find out. She'd decided to go into town and start her Christmas shopping.

Saturday evening; a bittersweet time for Kirsten. On the one hand she loved being alone with Daniel and looked forward to staying all night, on the other, as soon as it was over, she was looking in the face of another week of missing him.

Right now, she was snuggled under a blanket while he was choosing a Netflix film. In the meantime, on the television was a round-up of the week's news. Kirsten summed it up in her head: *the number of Covid cases rising, no-deal Brexit likely.* She sighed, "Hurry-up with the film will you, please?"

"No one's even mentioned Brexit for ages, with all this Covid stuff going on. How about this?" Daniel passed her the tablet. *Drama. In a dystopian future, a totalitarian regime maintains peace by subduing the populace with a drug, and displays of emotion are punishable by death* she read.

"Sounds too much like reality. Why are dramas about the future always dystopian? If we can't even imagine a good future, we stand no chance of having one."

"You choose one."

"A future or a film?" She laughed. "You didn't like my last choice. Let's just watch this one. Christian Bale is usually good."

"Sure?"

"I'm sure. Do you agree with me, though? About dystopias?"

"You're always very keen to watch the political documentaries and dramas."

"It's different, though."

"How so?" Daniel was uncorking the wine. He brought it and two glasses over to the coffee table.

Kirsten clicked her tongue as she thought. "Fair question. I suppose because I want to know what's going on now, but I hope for a better future."

"You just asked me to turn the news off."

"Stop picking on me," she laughed, again. "Do you think you'd have voted differently on the Brexit issue if you'd known how it would turn out?"

"I don't think it makes much difference. Europe or America, pick which nation you want to be ruled by."

"I think we'd better try to stay off politics when we're at Rosie and Andy's. They're not quite ready for this yet."

"What do they do at Christmas?"

"What d'you mean?"

"Are they into parlour games and that kind of thing?"

"A bit, why?"

"Could be fun, that's all. We always used to play them when we were kids."

"You do surprise me, I wouldn't have thought it was your thing at all." She was amazed and pleased to be still getting to know him.

ൠ

Christmas lights, glitzy shop fronts, over-full shopping trolleys, but at the same time Nabil observed the strained looking countenances. It was puzzling for him. People preparing for Eid never wore such a look. He wondered if it was the case that people were conflicted, wanting to be with their families and friends, yet afraid of the virus.

He thought back to Eid, and the annoyance Abdul had expressed at not being allowed to celebrate the occasion in the expected manner. He wondered whether the reports he'd seen online around the time had given an accurate account of the Eid celebrations in his own country. Thinking of home increased his loneliness.

Abdul had finally helped him to understand that he needed to book a time to visit the library, and had talked him through the process. Time was when half an hour would not have been enough, but today, without Abida's story to write, it seemed rather too long. After the rain had ruined his notebook, Nabil had bought another, but it stayed in his bag unopened.

He sat at the computer, watching YouTube clips he could just as easily have watched in his room on his phone. He was out of the house in honour of his vow to himself and because Abdul had made him promise to do so for at least an hour every day.

The time-up message scrolled the bottom of the screen. On the news feed behind was the face of the British Prime Minister and a computer image of the virus. Nabil could only make out a few words, but had the impression there was a warning of some kind. He felt a shiver in his spine. *All of my family are on the other side, so why should I care?* But his body didn't agree.

"Well, all I can say is good job it was only ever the three of us. Imagine all those people who've gone out and bought food for a big family gathering," Emerson's mother complained to him. "How dare they do this now?"

"D'you think Nan will be coming after all?"

"Well, she won't be going down south, that's for sure. But I don't know how she'll feel about it. Especially if Baz is here."

"We can't leave Nan on her own."

"It's up to her. We're allowed to have three households mixing for Christmas Day. She'll just have to go home afterwards."

"What about the other one going home," Emerson muttered under his breath.

"What was that?"

"Nothing. Nan was okay with going to Auntie Sarah's."

"That was before the new rules."

"Just listen to the stupidity of it, Mother. You can 'form a temporary bubble for one day only'. There's going to be a virus truce for Christmas. But that's only England; Scotland, Wales and Ireland have different rules. This virus is dead smart, don't you think? And obedient."

"I know what you think, Emerson. I even agree, but will Nan? I get that you're disappointed to think she won't come. I hope she will agree to even though Baz is here, but if not, well, we'll…I'll have to think of something else."

"Maybe I could go there?"

"It's an option. I could plate up two dinners. We'll have to see what Nan says."

In his room Emerson paced the floor, stepping over games that needed returning to their boxes and clothes destined for drawers, or the washing basket. As he paced, he tapped his forehead with his forefinger, as if the action would aid understanding.

He sat on the bed and pulled from underneath it the pile of presents. One each for his mother and Barry; see, he did know how to behave appropriately. One for his grandmother, and the one he'd ordered ages ago that was intended for his grandfather – a book of facts about his football team that was embossed with his name. He turned it over, resisting the urge to deface the book. *What will I do with it now?*

The Christmas tree and one gift each for the girls were Mandeep and Dev's concession to the festive season, mainly on Dev's insistence. "We do live in a Christian country," he'd said.

Largely Mandeep agreed, and now it was a taken-for-granted habit, but every year her parents vocalised their displeasure, despite conceding to a shared family meal. This year her mother's illness put an end to that.

Currently Mandeep was scrutinising the information on the computer screen. The negative test hadn't reassured her because her mother had almost all of the listed symptoms. She was reading them for a third time that day, looking for reassurance, finding only confirmation.

"What're you doing now?" Dev asked, coming up behind her, putting his hands on her shoulders and looking over her head to answer his own question. "Has the information changed since the last time you looked? Well then, why not come away?"

"I just wish they'd had the vaccines already."

"They both tested negative."

Mandeep knew he meant it to be reassuring; it wasn't. "My mother has practically the full list of symptoms and some say the tests are unreliable, given to false negatives."

"Some say they're given to false positives." He paused before continuing. "There's someone at the gym watches a lot of alternative stuff, he says he's seen a doctor online, an American, who reckons he's identified a drug, one in common use, that prevents serious illness developing."

"That can't be true, surely? Why wouldn't everyone be using it?"

Dev shrugged. "Who knows? Shall I find out more, or not?"

"Well, yes, no harm in it."

Dev left the room to make the phone call.

In his absence Mandeep scrolled the astrology charts. This year, with all that had gone on and with the concern over what was yet to come, she felt even more than usual the portentousness of the change of year. She looked for hope in the stars.

Mars in retrograde had been a problem for much of the year according to the article she read. It said:

> *This aspect has been in play for a good chunk of the year thanks to* Mars retrograde, *and this is the last time we'll feel it. We've broken down what isn't serving us well, we've faced fears, and we've taken control, and now we can assess and move on.*

She couldn't help feeling that it wasn't only 'what isn't serving us well,' that had been broken down. And it was true that people had faced their fears, but back in control? It didn't feel to her as if she was.

A few minutes later Dev returned, "What're you looking at now?" Again, he peered over her head and answered the question for himself. "I hope we can bloody move on."

"Here." He handed her the piece of paper on which he'd written the name of the doctor, and medicine. "I've looked it up, you can buy it online. But the guy at the gym got a supply when he went to India, says they're using it over there."

"Really? I find it hard to believe there's something so readily available."

"Just telling you what he said. Look it up and decide what to do." He kissed the back of her head then left the room.

Mandeep typed in the name of the doctor. She'd never even heard of Bitchute, which was the recommended channel, but she'd failed to find him on YouTube. He was presenting evidence to the US Senate on the drug and asking, almost begging it seemed to Mandeep, for proper clinical trials to be carried out. She watched it in its entirety. At the end of it she felt two contradictory feelings: the first, and most straightforward, there was hope in his findings. The second, total bemusement at the reluctance of the Senate to take on board what the doctor was saying. She asked herself *if it's already tried and tested, been around for years, proven to be safe, why are they so reluctant to grant the trials? There must be suspicions about its safety or efficacy. But it's been around for years. Doesn't mean it's effective for treating Covid, though. But he's an ICU doctor, he should know, in any case what's to lose if there's nothing else and you're dying?* The thought and feeling she was left with scared her hardly any less than the pandemic.

She went to find Dev.

"What d'you think then?" he asked.

"I don't know. I can't make up my mind. He seems pretty convinced it works, but there's so much I don't understand in that case."

She relayed to Dev what she'd been thinking.

"Now you sound like a conspiracy theorist. As bad as my mate at the gym. Shall I watch it, give you a second opinion?"

"That would be good. Thank you."

While he did so Mandeep carried out mundane tasks, but her mind kept wandering back to the interview and she felt sick.

She could stay away from Dev no longer and so went to watch the last few minutes with him. "What d'you think?"

"I could be tempted to become a conspiracy theorist."

"Doesn't sound like it can do any harm, anyway. How soon can you get some?"

"I'll phone my mate now."

❧

It was a few days later that Kirsten asked, "How's your mum, Mandeep?" They were crossing paths in the break room.

"They've both tested positive this morning, after days of negative tests."

Kirsten recalled a time when a positive test had entirely different connotations."Sorry, that must be a worry for you. You've had a rough year."

"We all have. But, yes, although I knew from the symptoms, as soon as the word Co…". Mandeep choked on it and started to cry.

Kirsten pulled her into the break room and her arms, pushing the door shut with her foot and saying, "Should you be here?"

The tears ran freely for a few minutes, then Mandeep said, "I've had too much time off already; besides, it helps to have stuff to concentrate on." She straightened herself, blew her nose, and wiped her eyes. "Let's hope it's the new strain, which apparently isn't as dangerous."

"Do you know how they're feeling?" Every time Kirsten heard of a Covid diagnosis she had the sinking feeling in her stomach and felt fear tingle in her spine, while her rational head went through a reassuring dialogue.

"That's the thing, I don't even think they're that bad. My mum was in bed for a couple of days, but she's up now, although she can't do much. It was like flu, she said, cold symptoms and aching, she said the aching was the worst. My dad has only just gone down with it, we'll have to see." After a pause she said, "We got them some medicine that's being used in India. I don't know if it was that that helped."

That piqued Kirsten's interest, she wanted to ask more about it, but didn't consider it would be polite. "Does it matter, as long as they're getting better?"

"No, well, yes, actually, I think it does, because if it was the medicine, it should be out there available for everyone. I watched something online. There seems to be resistance to it. It doesn't make sense. Well, not unless you're into conspiracy theories."

"Don't tell Emerson, then."

They both laughed.

"Seriously though," Mandeep concluded.

When Mandeep next phoned her parents she was delighted to hear that both were feeling better. Immediately her mood was lifted. "Did you take the stuff I sent over?"

"No, the doctor advised against it."

Mandeep felt disappointed and relieved; the latter because, if there had been any chance that her parents' recovery was down to the medicine, she would have to seriously consider the implications.

As she was clearing up after the meal and getting settled for the evening, she remembered there was a rare planetary conjunction coming up, Saturn and Jupiter, the two largest planets. Some were saying it heralded the start of a new astrological age. She went online to look it up, and read:

The great conjunction occurs at 0 degrees. In astrology a zero-degree point symbolizes new beginnings.

The conjunction of Saturn and Jupiter hasn't occurred in Aquarius since 1623.

Saturn represents rules, regulations, government and the traditional ways of doing this. Saturn constricts and contracts. Jupiter represents blessings, spiritual insights, and new ways of seeing things. It's expansive and open. There will be a battle between these two planets over the next year as they travel through Aquarius.

Saturn is called "The Lord of Karma" in Vedic astrology. Saturn asks you to be disciplined and take authority

*over your life. Saturn transits such as this one can give
mixed results.*

*Saturn wants us to grow, evolve and become the owner of
our lives. To step up and be responsible for ourselves. If we
haven't done the work, Saturn can come along and test
us by breaking everything apart. If we've done the work
Jupiter can come along and bless us.*

*This is a big year to focus on our spiritual pursuits, to let
go of old rigid ways and to welcome in new insights, new
ideas and revolution.*

*This next year will be a time of huge blessings but not
without hard work. We will experience immense expansion
and contraction at the same time. Both are needed, both
are valuable.*

As she sat waiting for Joe to come and fetch her, Margaret
thought back to last Christmas. *I hope they don't go on about me
moving again this year.* Yet, even as she thought this, she acknowledged that sometimes she felt the seed of the things her children
worried about, not least among them dying alone. And yet only a
couple of days ago she had thought she was and hadn't felt afraid
at all.

She'd woken suddenly in the early hours. Her heart sounded
loud, she could hear the blood rushing around her body. *This
is it,* coursed through her mind. She waited, anticipating pain,
praying it would be neither unbearable nor prolonged. Thinking
of her children made her sad, she would never see them again;
but the dominant emotion was anticipation, rather than fear.
What was on the other side? Would she know where she was and
what to do? She'd wondered if she would see John, she hoped
so. If not, then she hoped there was nothing there at all. She'd
slowed her breathing and told herself to remain calm. Then the
feeling passed, sleep returned, and shortly afterwards came the
morning and another day.

*At least since Daniel has come into my life, I don't need to
worry about lying here dead for days unnoticed,* she thought. *Still,*

all in all it would be better to have some warning, get the kids to be here, less of a shock for everyone. Needs to be here, though. I need John's stuff around me, it's more likely to attract his spirit. If there is such a thing. I'm certainly not going to hospital. Never going there again.

Her reflections were interrupted by Joe arriving.

"Hello," he called out as he came to the door.

"Hello, son."

"You okay? Where's your bag?"

"It's here." She indicated the small backpack. "I thought I'd come home day after tomorrow, if that's okay."

"Alison and the girls are coming."

"After I've spent a bit of time with them, of course."

"Is this about the virus?"

"God, no."

"Didn't think so. Then?"

"An old horse likes its own stable, that's all."

"Well, I hope I can change your mind, but if not…then, okay. Shame we can't get together with Lily, like we usually do. Let's hope all this nonsense is over with next year."

"I certainly hope so. Yes, shame about Lily. I wish she would reconsider but can't make her."

"It's you she's concerned about."

"If she was that concerned, she'd come, I might not be here next year."

"Don't say that."

"Well, it's true. Anyway, I've had the bloody virus, haven't I?"

"We don't know that for sure. And doesn't mean you won't get it again."

"You were sure enough to send me off to hospital. I'll have natural immunity now."

"Well, Lily feels she doesn't want to risk it. Next year we'll all have been vaccinated."

"You can go ahead. Although, I wish you wouldn't."

"Don't tell me you're considering not having it?"

"Alright, I won't then."

"Mum you…"

"I'm not discussing it, let's go," Margaret stood and picked up her backpack.

Joe took it from her. "Why do you always have to challenge things, Mum? Why can't you just do what everyone else does?"

"Why do you have to try to change my mind about the decisions I've made?

"Because frankly…"

"Let's leave it shall we, Joe? Let's just have a nice Christmas together."

❦

The van was loaded up with Christmas presents. Kirsten was waiting for Daniel to check everything was switched off, tied down or whatever the hell else it was he needed to check on. This being the first time Kirsten had encountered Daniel's going away routine, she was rapidly losing patience.

It's two days, for fuck sake. They couldn't stay longer because of the chickens. *Finally,* she breathed easy, thinking he was ready at last.

He picked up his bag, put it down, tugged at the throw on the sofa, then sat down beside her, but on the edge of the seat.

Kirsten chewed her lip, biting down the tide of irritation. "I thought…"

"Here, you'd better have this," Daniel interrupted, handing her a small, beautifully wrapped package, then pulling it back to his chest. "You can have it now, or when we get back."

"Oh, thank you." Her mood changed instantly. "Why not tomorrow?"

"Thing is, it's a…well, I thought maybe you might want to move in. It was nice when you were here. I thought… I wondered… well, we could get married. It makes sense financially. If you want, that is."

Kirsten felt like she'd turned a corner and narrowly avoided running into a wall, she burst into tears, then into laughter. "That must be the worst proposal ever."

"Oh!"

"It makes financial sense?" Kirsten laughed. "Hopefully it's not only that, because yes, yes, thank you, I would like."

"You would? Oh good."

"Of course I would. Did you think I wouldn't?" She opened her arms for a hug, which Daniel performed in his usual manner. Then he handed her the package.

"Are you sure you don't want me to open it tomorrow?"

"Not when there's other people around."

Kirsten smiled at him, picked up his hand and kissed it, recognising how embarrassing the whole situation was for him. She undid the ribbon, then the wrapping paper, then the box. Inside was a sapphire and diamond ring. "Oh, it's beautiful," Kirsten put her hand to her mouth and patted back tears, then took the ring and was about to put it on when Daniel said,

"Shouldn't I do that?"

Kirsten handed him the ring without saying a word.

"I hope it fits okay," Daniel said.

And it did.

"Almost perfectly. Was that just by chance?"

"Not really. I took your wedding ring into the jewellers."

"How did you manage that?" Kirsten had stopped routinely wearing it when she moved in over the lockdown, because it didn't feel right to do so since she and Daniel had made more of a commitment to each other.

"Wasn't hard, I saw where you were keeping it."

"You never cease to surprise me."

"You do like it?"

"I love it. And I love you," she kissed him. He smiled. "Am I allowed to wear it? To tell people we're engaged?"

"Course." Daniel kept his gaze on the wrapping paper and ribbon as he folded them up and put them on the coffee table, then he put the lid back on the box and handed it to Kirsten. "Right, we'd better get going, it's a long drive. You ready?"

"Only for the past half an hour."

Christmas Day

The midnight church bells chiming woke Nabil from a restless sleep. He felt confused, and for a moment, couldn't think where he was. The dream he was having clung to him. He remembered no details, but he sensed that something terrible had been about to happen, from which the bells had rescued him.

His phone was on the bed beside him; when he picked it up the dark screen became illuminated with the reminder of what he'd been watching as he fell asleep. *Better go to bed properly,* he decided, getting up to brush his teeth and use the toilet, then removing his jeans and socks and climbing under the duvet. He knew that his actions guaranteed wakefulness.

In the hours that followed he lay on his back, then his left side, then his right, in the recovery position, in the foetal posture. He listened to his thoughts, argued with them, tried to ignore them. Several times sleep came to claim him, but was snatched away at the very last second.

Sometimes the light comforted him, at others it annoyed him. Night-time was always the same. Nabil feared it would be like this forever now.

His family had finally left him properly. He could no longer recall his mother's voice, his father's face. Even Abida had gone. Their absence from his mind hurt less than the memory of them.

The next time the bells woke him it was light. It was only as it left him that Nabil realised he had been asleep. He had no idea for how long. The bells reminded him it was Christmas Day, it was something about which he knew little. *I'll see what I can find out,* he thought, feeling a sudden rush of enthusiasm, at the thought of his day having some purpose. *There's always something new to learn,* but even as he thought this, he felt the eagerness of a few minutes ago ebb away and he lay down again, pulling the duvet over his head.

‮ﻌ‬

Emerson was lying under the covers with a torch reading the anime comic, when he heard the click of the door handle. He turned it off and pretended to be sleeping. He could hear his mother's breathing, as she checked that he was, before putting the stocking on the end of his bed.

As soon as the door clicked closed, he turned the torch back on and returned to reading, but he couldn't focus on it any-more, so he sat up, turned his lamp on and his attention to the stocking. He tossed the after shave and the pair of the socks onto the floor, but the English-Japanese dictionary was cool, he'd give her that, and without a second's hesitation he started on the bar of Toblerone.

When he lay back down, he reflected on last Christmas. Everything was normal then. Normal certainly would be new from now on, without Pops. Emerson reached over the side of the bed and pulled from under it his grandfather's gift. Perhaps he could find someone on eBay or Facebook with his grandfather's name who supported the same team. Emerson felt like crying, as he settled down in an attempt to sleep.

It was strange waking up in a hotel room at almost eight o'clock. Every other year, since Sally's birth, Kirsten had been woken early by one or both children. Last year at five, she recalled. This year's restrictions resulted in Andy's parents winning the privilege of staying in the house. And, though she agreed it made sense, *they haven't even seen the house yet and Daniel has said he can afford the hotel,* Rosie had reasoned. Still, if Kirsten were honest with herself, she felt more than a little jealous.

"Morning, Happy Christmas," she said to the stirring Daniel, who answered her with the same words.

At least they would all be together for dinner, and she could watch the children open the presents she'd bought them. She wondered how everyone, especially Rosie, would react to Daniel's Christmas proposal, and thinking this she picked the ring up and put it on, turning her hand from side to side and looking at it from each angle, and getting used to the weight of it.

I'll go and tell Greg as soon as I get home, she thought. *I know he won't mind. I hope Rosie doesn't.*

"What time is it?" Daniel asked.

"Time to get up."

"Very nice," Dev said, in response to Mandeep's enquiry as to how her new jewellery looked. "A good choice if I say so myself."

"Agreed, thank you. Well, I'd better go and give Mum and Dad a call, see how they are. If there's anything they want."

Bored by the television, and banned by his family from working, Dev turned on the computer, intending to find something suitable to cast, a wildlife programme perhaps. He was surprised to find the Rumble channel as the latest listing in the search bar.

"You *are* turning into a conspiracy theorist," he teased when Mandeep returned, then, seeing the look on her face, "What's wrong?"

"They still don't want me going round. I know they're better, but I would like to see for myself, it's been ages. Wish the vaccine roll-out would hurry up."

"Not a conspiracy theorist, then."

"What're you talking about?"

"Just noticed you've been on Rumble."

"There's lots of interesting stuff on there. Doesn't mean I agree with it all, or even any of it."

"Sorry, touched a raw nerve there."

Mandeep sighed, "It's this virus. I keep telling you, I'm sick of it, want it gone. It's causing so much fear and disruption. I can't take much more."

"Sure you can, but hopefully you won't have to. Come on." Dev tapped her on the shoulder. "Let's go for a walk. I need to try out my new boots and we could all do with some fresh air."

❧

Margaret was trying to be sociable, but really, she just wanted to go home. *Christmas is for children and there aren't many of those in the family now.*

As if the thought was a magic spell Alison arrived with Leanne and the not-so-new baby. Both of the adults were wearing masks.

"My, you've grown," Margaret said to her great-granddaughter, holding out her hands in invitation to the baby, who responded by lurching towards Margaret and grabbing hold of her extended arm. But Leanne held onto her daughter and pulled her back.

"Granny needs to put a mask on first." She handed her one. Margaret took it, but not without first scowling at both it and Leanne.

"I can't help thinking it must be rather alarming for children to be looking at masked faces. How are they going to learn to socialise and speak?"

"Don't be silly, Gran. It's to protect you, as well as her."

Margaret grunted by reply, donned the mask, took the baby, and started to bounce her on her knee.

Outside Nabil felt calmer, but no less lonely in the empty streets. Empty and dark, a complete contrast to home, with only the artificial Christmas lights offering any illumination. He walked without paying too much attention, passing en-route the town hall, outside of which stood a decorated fir tree. Then he reached the church. Nabil walked up to it and peered through the open door, wanting to go inside, but fear of unknown customs and expectations, and loyalty to his own religion, prevented him from doing so. Yet even this partial entry gave him a glimpse of the nativity: plastic cattle, plastic sheep and an imitation baby lying in a mock bed of straw. Nabil felt puzzled and sombre as he turned and walked away.

Now he passed the supermarket, which he had never seen closed before. He wondered how Kirsten was spending her day. He carried on walking, intending to turn into the park, stroll around and then return home, but it too was closed, entry barred by an iron gate. Just beside it, however, was a large van with a drop-down hatch from which food and drinks were being dispensed. He felt himself drawn towards it, not from hunger in his stomach, but from the same in his heart.

"Welcome," the mature lady said, leaning forwards on her elbows.

"Hello," Nabil responded.

He was handed a plate of vegetables. "What else would you like? Turkey? Beef perhaps, or the nut roast?" The woman pointed at each as she made the offer, which helped Nabil with his understanding.

"No money," he said.

"Oh, you don't need money, it's free." The plate was pushed towards him.

Nabil took the coins from his pocket and counted them, then opened his hand to show it was all he had.

The woman took his hand and closed it. "It's free. Now, turkey, beef or nut roast?" She indicated his choices once more.

Nabil chose the turkey, thinking it was chicken.

"Hey mate!" Suddenly Nabil was receiving a slap on the shoulder. He almost dropped the plate of food, and his body had already prepared to run, when he realised it was his street-sleeper acquaintance. Nabil was very pleased to see him.

"Where have you been?" he said in Arabic, offering his hand, balancing the plate on the other to make it possible. "I have been wondering about you."

"Don't know what the fuck you're saying mate, but it's good to see you anyway, and to hear your voice. He's from Syria," the homeless man informed the woman who was serving the food. Then he went to sit on the only bench there was outside the park, ripping off the black and yellow tape to do so. "Come and sit here," he tapped the seat next to him.

Nabil looked from the bench to the woman in the van, then back to the bench.

"Come on." The words sounded like an order.

Since no one was reprimanding his friend for sitting there, Nabil joined him. They ate in silence. The food was good. Nabil's first hot meal for a couple of days because he hadn't been bothered to cook. Some other people were approaching the van now.

"It's not usually like this," Nabil's companion told him. "Usually, we have a hall to go to, and we have carols and crackers. Corona-fucking-virus has ruined that, innit."

All Nabil understood was corona-fucking-virus, but it didn't matter. He had some company. Two of the newcomers came over. Nabil, who had finished eating, stood up allowing someone else to have his seat.

They had a crate of beer from which they offered bottles all round. Having never tried alcohol, Nabil felt tempted, but a voice in the back of his head forbade it, so he declined with a wave of his hand and a quiet, 'no, thank you.'

"Come on, it's Christmas," one of the men said, jiggling the bottle in front of him.

"Leave it out, he probably don't celebrate it. Probably don't drink either," said another of them. "'spect he's a Muslim, innit and they don't, do they? That right, you a Muslim, are you?"

Nabil nodded. "Yes." He understood enough of the conversation to keep up. Not for long however, soon all meaning was lost to him. For a while it didn't matter, because his companions were good humoured and made an effort to include him, but soon it became frustrating, and he decided to leave. When he made his intentions clear there was protest from the group, but Nabil gleaned it was largely from politeness. He was grateful for this.

He wandered slowly back towards his house, because being outside felt more natural and there was nothing to hurry back for. A somewhat familiar face smiled at him from under a woollen hat and over a woollen scarf; both garments initially hindered recognition, but as he drew close, he realised it was the Asian lady from the supermarket. He smiled at her as they passed each other, raised his hand, and said, "Hello."

Back in his room he returned to sitting on his bed and scrolling YouTube, but he felt content, as if the day had at least amounted to something.

ॐ

It was while the men were washing up and tidying the kitchen, and the children, having bored already of their new toys, were watching the television, that Kirsten made the announcement.

"I've been waiting for a quiet time to share what Daniel gave me for Christmas," she said to Rosie and Andy's mother.

Rosie gasped when Kirsten held out her hand to show her.

"Is that from surprise or horror?" Kirsten laughed. "I actually thought you might have noticed it."

"I'm so surprised, and no, I didn't. It's lovely. Congratulations! I presume it is an…"

"Yes, and came with just about the worst proposal you've ever heard." Kirsten recounted it for both women.

"Bless him, he's so easily embarrassed, isn't he?" Rosie said. "It's an endearing quality in my opinion. Shy men are nice, no arrogance."

Kirsten felt happy hearing this.

ॐ

"On the whole, I'm glad it's behind us for another year." Margaret had just finished telling Daniel about her Christmas.

"I used to enjoy it when my own children were little, even when the grandchildren were, but not now. It lost its magic a long time ago." *Like most things now, in actual fact.* "I used to stay with whichever child was unlucky enough to get lumbered with me for the New Year too, but not for the last couple. An old horse likes its own stable."

"Mrs. P, you're depressing me. You're not old."
"What are you talking about? You're not a person who usually talks rubbish."

"Your body might be getting on a bit, but you're not old."

"Well, if you put it like that. This week is such a drag, though. And so much worse when you're not at home. Eating chocolates that you don't even want and playing parlour games you're sick to death of, having to be sociable. God, no, two days of that is more than enough."

"Daniel laughed. "That's more like it. So, you're spending New Year alone?"

"I'm perfectly happy with that arrangement. Although I was thinking of finding the most crowded pub I can, full of germ-in-fested youngsters, and dancing my socks off till the early hours."

Daniel laughed heartily at that.

"Well, you know how I like to defy the Government." She took a sip of her tea, "I suppose the latest so-called figures are to convince us that the vaccines are the only way out of this and get us used to the idea that young people need to get them too. As if they won't make enough money out of the oldies."

"You're not in favour, then?"

"Warp-speed vaccinations – you must be kidding. I won't be joining the queue. What I don't like is the way they're being pushed. There's be no mention of boosting your own natural immunity with good, common sense taking care of yourself. Call me an old cynic, but to me it looks like someone is set to make a killing on this, if you'll pardon the pun."

"Oh, Mrs. P, never change, please." Daniel finished his tea, then stood up, putting on his coat ready to leave. "You could spend New Year's with Kirsten and me if you like. I could cook us something. Doesn't have to be late."

"Well, I'm not coming if it isn't."

"It's a date, then. Talking of dates, sometime in the New Year you'll need to set one aside for a wedding. Don't know when yet."

"Your wedding? Oh, how lovely. Congratulations. I'll be there, as long as the reaper doesn't get to me first. Oh, don't look like that, Daniel, there's no point in trying to hide from the inevitable. And as long as it isn't Covid, everyone will accept it. No, it's true, I've made it to my mid-eighties, if I die of anything else people'll be saying, 'she had a good innings'; if Covid gets me they'll be talking like it's the worst tragedy ever."

"You've got a point, actually." And it was a point Daniel kept coming back to throughout the day. He did wonder, however, if she was really as blasé about death as she made herself out to be.

Margaret, for her part, was thinking how nice it was for Daniel that he'd found someone to love. *There's nothing like loving and being loved in return. Better to have loved and lost, than never to have loved at all. I wonder. Maybe if you've always been alone, you don't mind too much, but if you never have been, it's so hard to adjust.* Margaret picked up the photograph of John that she always kept beside her. "I haven't given in to being alone, but I've never got used to it," she told him.

"There's nothing worse than being bored at work," Emerson's colleague observed.

"Really? I can think of plenty. Being boiled alive, hung upside down for days, stuck in a room with Tony Blair, living through the Great Reset, shall I go on?"

"Nah! I get your point."

"It's always like this on the week between Christmas and New Year."

"Yeah, I know. Still fucking boring, though. Whoops, better watch my language in case we actually get a customer. What's the Great Reset, anyway?"

"It's what this whole last year has been about, that's what."

"Ugh?"

"The World Economic Forum wanna reset society, that's why they locked us down, not 'cos of flu."

"Flu? I don't get you. Covid killed your granddad, and you think that."

A hot tide of anger pulsed through Emerson, rising from his solar plexus to his throat, where it burst out in a verbal rebuke. "Who told you that?"

His colleague realised her mistake. "Well, no one actually said…"

"So, you're just making assumptions?"

"Well, I heard on the grapevine that he was ill, in hospital, I just thought – because – I mean – people haven't really been going to hospital for anything else, have they?"

"Who told you?"

"Don't remember, I mean, no one, I just heard on the grapevine."

A customer arrived, she hovered for a second or two between the two tills before eventually deciding on Emerson's colleague.

"Quiet, isn't it?" the customer observed.

"Yeah, it's always like this between Christmas and New Year."

Emerson fumed and smarted, but was calming down by the time the customer left, "The Reset ain't a conspiracy. You can look it up online. I suggest you do it, today. Schwab said, 'coronavirus is an opportunity for the Great Reset'. Yep, he actually said those exact words. Look it up." After a pause of a second or two, "My granddad was sick anyway, like all of the people who died of 'Covid'." They're not even talking about deaths anymore, have you noticed that? No? Well, they're not, they're talking about cases. Of course, you'll get loads of cases if you test for them. Those tests are set so high you're almost bound to."

Emerson's colleague was sick of the conspiracy theorists and Covid deniers and was one hundred per cent sure that because of them the pandemic would never be over, because for sure they wouldn't get vaccinated. She certainly wasn't going to risk getting her head bitten off again by saying so, though. And she certainly wasn't going to look up the Great Reset either.

❧

In 2021, there's a lesson we'll put into place, and there is a lot to be hopeful for. A rare conjunction between Uranus and Saturn will bring people with opposing viewpoints together to talk things out. Lucky Jupiter camps out in progressive Aquarius for most of the year, pointing to opportunities for change.

A rather vague, but none-the-less optimistic prediction, Mandeep felt, as she read the yearly horoscope.

People with opposing viewpoints will come together and talk things out, will they? I wonder if I'll be able to talk Emerson out of his, or will he convince me he's right? She chuckled to herself, but even as she did, she contemplated with some earnestness, elements of the information she'd seen on Rumble. Checking the time on her phone, Mandeep decided she'd better start cooking, especially since a portion of it was to be taken to her parents. She sighed, feeling frustrated that they still wouldn't be joining them in person. *We'll soon be back to normal,* she reassured herself, *now that there's a vaccine.*

When Manjit came into the kitchen she found her mother singing along to the radio as she chopped vegetables. "Shall I help?"

"That would be nice. I like this song." Mandeep returned to singing along.

"So do I." Her daughter joined in the singing.

❧

"That looks lovely," Margaret told her hosts. "You shouldn't have gone to so much trouble just for me."

"On the contrary," Kirsten replied, "Anyway, it wasn't any bother. And I love nut roast, but I can't remember the last time I had one."

"Cheers," Daniel raised his glass.

The two women said the same, as they clinked their glasses to his.

"I don't suppose anyone will be sorry to see the back of twenty-twenty," Kirsten said.

"I expect most people will expect the coming one to be an improvement," Margaret replied.

"Don't you?"

"No, do you?"

"Not expect, but hope."

"There's always hope. I imagine lots of people are thinking the vaccinations will put an end to all this nonsense."

"At least they might put an end to the restrictions, people'll be pretty pissed-off if they don't. I think they could start a whole new set of problems, but hey, you probably don't want to hear this – and we shouldn't have such serious conversations on New Year's Eve."

"I don't see the point in not. The only thing worth pursuing is the truth. I'm well past needing comfortable lies. And I think you're right about the vaccinations. I don't want to trust my health or life to anyone except God." She sighed then said, "Who would have thought this time last year that twenty-twenty would turn out the way it did."

"It has certainly been a game changer," Daniel said.

A restlessness had overtaken Nabil; it took him from his room to the street, and then towards the town centre. Celebration was suggested in the Christmas illuminations, but was contradicted by black and yellow marking tape barring entry, or banning rest. He felt the familiar thrill of fear spike up his spine in response to the small group of people walking towards him in strange clothes; the women wearing garments that were far too flimsy for the weather. As they passed him, he realised he had mistaken the sex of at least one of them.

Fancy dress and parties were traditions about which Nabil had only recently learned. In his home country, the tradition was to call on neighbouring houses with good wishes and with food. Last year, newly arrived in the town, fear had kept him in his room, where he'd been troubled by the sound of the revellers. This year the same noises disturbed him in a different way. They annoyed him; because the celebrators were defying the law, but more especially because they emphasised his loneliness. *I wonder, will I ever have cause to celebrate anything again?*He asked himself.

He walked fast, head down, until he heard the first strike of midnight, and then he turned and hurried homeward amidst a shower of fireworks, that set his heart pounding and his body shaking.

Back in his room equilibrium soon retuned. Twenty-twenty-one. He'd been here for more than a year now, perhaps this was the one in which his asylum case would be heard. With this thought he picked up the new notebook he had purchased, it was too late to write much, but he would at least make a start:

'This was the morning Abida decided she'd cried enough tears. She told me this over breakfast. "It's just you and me now, Nabil, we're going to take good care of each other."'

The same fireworks and shouts alerted Emerson to the change of the year.

"Happy New Year," he said to Alex, through the microphone on his computer, raising his can of beer to his virtual friend.

"Same to you," Alex replied.

Then they resumed their gaming. It was well into the early hours when they wound up and said goodnight to each other.

As Emerson settled down into bed, he realised he had no idea whether his mother was in or not. *Oh well, she's got twat-face with her, I expect, no need for me to worry.* He snuggled down. *So, we've had one of the four horsemen; got famine, war and pestilence to go. Happy New fucking-Year.* Emerson shifted his position. *I'll go and visit Nan tomorrow.* He turned his lamp out. *I wonder if she'd like Pop's present.* He moved to the edge of the bed, then lent over and pulled it out from its resting place. He put it under his pillow. *Might make her sad, but I bet she would.* Feeling satisfied with this decision Emerson was able to sleep.

"Happy New Year," Mandeep said.
"Let's hope so," Dev replied.
The girls offered the more traditional response.

"Sounds like there are plenty of people in the streets despite the guidelines," Dev observed.

"More than can be said for London." Mandeep indicated the almost empty street, although the fireworks were just as spectacular as they always were.

"So, any resolutions, Manjit?"

"Be kinder to people, especially Mum."

"Oh, you're always kind to me."

"Indrani?"

"Um! Keep my room as tidy as Mum likes it."

"I seem to be featuring in this rather a lot. Yours, Dev?"

"Spend more time with you girls and less at work. If there's one thing this year taught me it's how valuable you all are."

"Ah, thank you."

"And you, Mandeep?"

"To think more rationally and not get myself so upset."

"Well, that's a good one too. Hopefully we've seen the back of the pandemic now, or at least the worst. Here's to a good twenty-twenty-one."

"Happy New Year Ladies," Daniel said, raising his glass. "I hope it's not such an interesting one this year."

ABOUT THE AUTHOR

Pauline grew up in rural Wiltshire, but moved to the midlands in her early thirties, where she has lived ever since. She has had a passion for reading and writing since childhood and has always carved out the time for both, even while working, studying and rearing her five children. In her professional life she has worked as a mentor and counsellor, most recently with refugees.

Pauline enjoys books and films in the genre of social realism, particularly those with a political emphasis. She especially enjoys modern day David beats Goliath tales. Her interest in these is reflected in her own writing. One of her novels was short listed for the Yeovil Writing Competition.

www.ingramcontent.com/pod-product-compliance
Lightning Source LLC
Chambersburg PA
CBHW030930120726
47906CB00002B/557